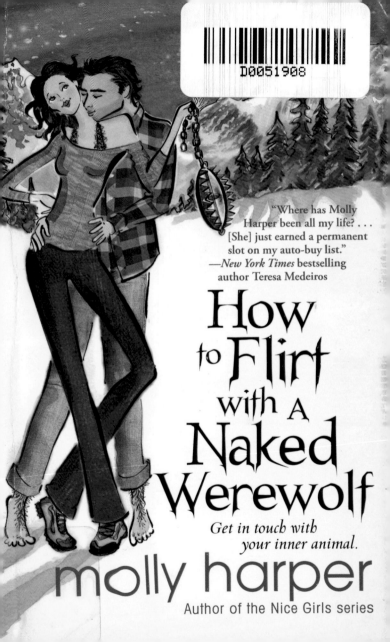

D0051908

How to Flirt with A Naked Werewolf

Get in touch with your inner animal.

molly harper

Author of the Nice Girls series

Can a nice girl really find
a future with a vampire?
Don't miss this sparkling
series by

MOLLY HARPER

Available from Pocket Star Books

How to Flirt with A Naked Werewolf

molly harper

POCKET BOOKS
New York London Toronto Sydney

Pocket Books
A Division of Simon & Schuster, Inc.
1230 Avenue of the Americas
New York, NY 10020

First Pocket Books paperback edition March 2011

POCKET and colophon are registered trademarks of Simon & Schuster, Inc.

For information about special discounts for bulk purchases, please contact Simon & Schuster Special Sales at 1-866-506-1949 or business@simonandschuster.com.

The Simon & Schuster Speakers Bureau can bring authors to your live event. For more information or to book an event, contact the Simon & Schuster Speakers Bureau at 1-866-248-3049 or visit our website at www.simonspeakers.com.

Cover design by John Vairo Jr.; illustration by Robyn Nield
Interior design by Davina Mock-Maniscalco

Manufactured in the United States of America

10 9 8 7 6 5 4 3 2

ISBN 978-1-4391-9586-4
ISBN 978-1-4391-9588-8 (ebook)

For Manda, who is always there.
For Matt, whose kitchen hijinks were inspiring.
-MMM-

Acknowledgments

IN JANUARY 2009, WE had a huge ice storm in Kentucky. We're talking weeks without power, grocery and gas shortages, price gouging on generators . . . male neighbors shaving their heads in their driveways because they were tired of cold shampoos. I spent a week camping out in my in-laws' living room, in front of their fireplace, with two children under the age of five.

These are the times in which family therapy sessions are born.

Fortunately, I used being trapped by frigid weather, in the dark, to get in the right frame of mind to write twenty (longhand) pages of a werewolf romance set in Alaska. That eventually became *How to Flirt with a Naked Werewolf*.

I want to thank my in-laws, Russell and Nancy, for housing us and keeping us going during that time.

Thanks to my husband, David, who always keeps his sense of humor, no matter the situation. And to my mom and dad, who will shake up heaven and earth to make sure their kids are safe. Thanks to my agent, Stephany Evans, and to Jennifer Heddle and Ayelet Gruenspecht at Pocket for their seemingly limitless support and understanding.

And finally, to my siblings, Manda and Matt: I would not know how to write stories about large groups of funny, snarky people without having grown up around the pair of you. You humor me when I boss you around. You keep me on my toes. You call me on my bull. I love you guys.

1
~

When Did My Life
Become a Willie Nelson Song?

WHEN A NAKED MAN shows up on your doorstep with a bear trap clamped around his ankle, it's best just to do what he asks.

This was a lesson I had to learn the hard way. A lesson that I didn't anticipate that crisp June morning as I drove my ailing truck to the town limits of tiny Grundy in the southeast interior of Alaska. As sorry as I felt for my "new to me" four-by-four, I couldn't stop just yet.

"Just a few more minutes, baby," I said, stroking fond fingers over the worn-smooth plastic of the steering wheel. It jittered with every revolution of the axle, like an arthritic lady's complaint, telling me I'd darn well better find a decent mechanic when we got into town. The 1999 Ford, which I'd lovingly dubbed Lucille while driving through Kansas, would need a little pampering to make up for the wear and tear of our first trip together.

I had driven thousands of miles, inhaled endless to-go cups of bad coffee, and endured a three-day ferry ride from Washington to reach the ornately carved "Welcome to Grundy" sign. As it came into view, my heart leaped a little at its declaration that the town was home to 2,053 people. I was about to change that number.

Deciding that Lucille had earned a short break, I pulled over just in front of the sign and put her in park. Her whole body seemed to quiver, then sigh, before she stilled. Stepping out onto the broken asphalt shoulder, I unfolded myself from the driver's seat and stretched my long legs. I ran my fingers along the carved wood, admiring the way the workman had managed to fit motifs from Inuit art into the design without muddying the clarity of the sign. Art and function, all in one.

I stretched my arms over my head, enjoying the crackle of my stiff vertebrae snapping back into place after that last six-hour stretch. Even in the relative warmth of late June, I shivered. Chagrined, I tucked my hands into my crisp new North Face jacket, purchased as a first measure against an unfamiliar climate. I was used to the choking hot humidity of the Mississippi Delta, to air so heavy it seemed to press the sheets down as you slept. I hoped that my body would have time to adjust to my new environment before the temperatures really started to drop.

In the distance, wispy cotton clouds ringed slate-colored mountains. The peaks formed a cupping hand around the valley that held Grundy. Vegetation in my hometown was a relentless green, occasionally broken up by neon splashes of flowers or a gray sweep of Spanish moss. There were so many shades and textures of green, lavender, and gold that I had to squint to protect my eyes.

The sun was already beginning to dip behind the mountains. I wanted to contact Nate Gogan before his office closed. Mr. Gogan, the town's lone attorney, was handling my rental of what he called "the Meyers place." I sincerely hoped that the name was coincidental and had nothing to do with any sort of *Halloween*-inspired massacres at my new home.

I checked that my little U-Haul trailer was securely attached to Lucille—a habit formed over the last few days—and climbed back in. For the twenty-seventh time that day, my cell phone rang. Curse my provider's commitment to omnipresent cross-country cell-tower coverage. I checked the caller ID and stuffed the phone back into my purse. I knew I would spend my first evening in Grundy ruthlessly deleting unheard voice mails from my mother. Because that's how I'd spent the previous evening. And the evening before that.

My cross-country move began as a frustrated lark after a broken engagement. I wanted to be as far away from my hometown as possible, without having to change my citizenship. I'd always been fascinated by the wide, wild spaces of Alaska. And a series of serendipitous mouse clicks led me to the remarkably Spartan home page for Grundy. And by that I mean the town's entire Web site was one page, which described the beautiful hiking trails, the expertly guided hunting and fishing excursions, the "bustling economy" of the handful of locally owned stores. And under a heading of "Rentals Available," it showed the Meyers place. At six hundred square feet, it was much smaller than my current rental, with one bedroom, a living room, a bath, and a kitchenette. But the Realtor's photo showed the view of the forest from the front porch, and I was hooked. I e-mailed Mr. Gogan, resigned from my job at Gulfside Marketing, and gave up my lease within a week.

Grundy came into view as Lucille chugged over the last rise in the highway. Although I'd been prepared for what Mr. Gogan had described as a "charming village," I couldn't tamp down my shock at being able to see the whole town at once. There was a long main drag of shops with a few streets sprouting off to support a few dozen haphazardly arranged one-story houses. Mr. Gogan had told me that most Grundy residents, including myself, lived in isolated homes in the fifty or so square miles that surrounded the town limits.

Main Street looked like something out of the Old West. Big brick buildings that stood the test of time against great Northern winters huddled against the wind. The windows advertised sensible ventures such as a bank, a grocery store, or an out-door outfitter with little flourish. The buildings were buttressed against one another, which I suspected was an effort to save on building materials so as to heat the buildings efficiently. The mountains loomed at the edge of town as if they'd suddenly sprung up at the end of Main Street. Their beauty, the protective curve of the peaks, made me feel small and silly for worrying about things like my truck's gas mileage and appointments with future landlords.

I found a parking space along the main drag, in front of Hannigan's Grocery, and climbed out of the truck. There were few pedestrians on the street, sturdy-looking people of all shapes and colors in light jackets. And they were staring. I felt suddenly self-conscious about the trailer, as if I was advertising, "New arrival!"

I locked Lucille and was grateful for the two-block walk to the attorney's office to stretch my legs. My new hiking boots squeaked lightly against the cracked pavement. The air was cool and clean. I could smell pine, rain, and hamburgers grilling at the saloon down the street. My mouth watered. It had been a long time since that breakfast burrito in Crowley. If I had time, I promised myself I would stop into the saloon, which the ornate wooden sign declared was "The Blue Glacier." This was a time for small, personal celebrations, such as double bacon, lettuce, pickle, and tomato. And maybe some onion rings.

Nate Gogan reminded me of Yosemite Sam, with a fluffy salt-and-pepper mustache and a worn tweed jacket paired with a bolo tie fastened with some sort of horn. He'd been waiting at his office for me, despite the relatively late hour, with the paperwork for my rental. He was a one-man Welcome Wagon, wrapping a grandfatherly arm around my shoulders as he led me back to his office. The room was entirely paneled in warm, sherry-colored wood, with Mr. Gogan's degrees and civil-service awards nailed to every available square inch that wasn't occupied by fishing or hunting trophies. Mr. Gogan, who insisted that I call him Nate, must have kept the local taxidermist very busy.

Apparently very conscious of my thin Southerner's blood, Mr. Gogan plied me with offers of coffee, tea, hot chocolate, even whiskey, to help me warm up while we signed the lease. He seemed extremely pleased with himself as he witnessed my signature, locking me into a one-year commitment to the house.

"I have to tell you, Miss Wenstein, I hope you're happy here in Grundy," he said, smiling beatifically. I didn't bother correcting his mispronouncing my name. Mo Duvall-Wenstein is a bit of a mouthful. And after nearly thirty years as a hyphenate, I was used to people thinking that Duvall was my middle name and not my mother's refusal to conform to "a patriarchal society's campaign to eradicate maternal surnames." Seriously, try explaining that to a college registrar.

"And I'm sure you'll get a warm welcome," he promised. "It's not every day that a pretty, unattached woman moves into town. I know a couple of fellas—nice, good-looking, God-fearing boys—who would be very happy to meet you."

After days surrounded by indifferent fast-food

workers and big-rig drivers prone to obscene gestures, I couldn't help but reciprocate his enthusiasm. I grinned. "Are you a matchmaker as well as an attorney?"

Mr. Gogan's lips twitched under his thick mustache. "I do what I can to help continue the town's population. I found my Gertie when we were in seventh grade at the Grundy Elementary School, been married for forty-three years." He turned a picture frame toward me, showing a smiling, plump-cheeked woman with snow-white hair piled on top of her head. "Not everybody's that lucky. Some people need a little nudge."

"How long have you lived here?" I asked him.

"All my life," Mr. Gogan said proudly. " 'Course, I had to go to the lower forty-eight for law school, but I was only comfortable going as far south as UW. Couldn't bear living so close to the equator as Mississippi. I'd probably melt."

"It's not for everybody," I said, trying to keep my tone neutral. Although I'd griped constantly about Mississippi's climate—and once threatened a coworker with an atomic wedgie if he said "It's not the heat, it's the humidity" one more time—I felt a little twitch of loss, a pang of nostalgia for that bone-softening heat. For the first time since stepping out of the truck, I felt a chill zip down my spine. What if I was making a huge mistake? What if I wasn't strong enough for this? Could I snatch the rental papers from Mr. Gogan's desk and run back to my truck without making a scene?

"Well, we're all set here," Mr. Gogan said, giving

the papers an official-looking stamp and returning them to his files.

That would be a no, then.

Mr. Gogan plopped a worn, brown suede cowboy hat on his head and said, "I'll help you get checked in at the motel."

"Actually, I'd hoped I could just settle right into the house," I told him.

He blanched. "Well, Mo, I'm not sure if it's going to be ready yet. The Meyers had rented the cabin out as a weekend place for hunting groups and the like up until now. We just had a party of fly-fishermen check out yesterday morning. You may want to wait a day or two to let the place, er, air out."

"After such a long drive, I'd really like to avoid another motel, Mr. Gogan. I don't mind if it's a little messy. I just don't want to face another polyester comforter."

Mr. Gogan smiled wanly. "If you say so . . ."

I should have stuck with the polyester comforter.

As charming and picturesque as the cabin was on the outside, the inside was a disaster. My new home looked like a condemned frat house. The first thing I saw was that the tidy little living room I'd been shown online was strewn with empty Doritos bags and dirty clothes. The furniture—sturdy, durable pieces—was tossed around the room, as if there'd been an impromptu wrestling tournament in front of the old slate fireplace. There was a whimsical installation of beer tabs hanging from the light fixture over the kitchen table.

And the whole house smelled like dead fish.

Mr. Gogan seemed embarrassed but not particularly surprised. A faint blush spread over his leathery cheeks as he apologized. "Lynette, the cleaning gal, was supposed to come by and give the place a once-over after she finished her shift at the motel. But I guess she hasn't made it over here yet," he said, flicking a pair of mildewed Fruit of the Looms out through the open front door with his foot. By the steadiness of his gaze I could tell he hoped I wouldn't notice the movement.

"Tell her not to bother," I said, my smile fixed. If I let it falter at all, I was sure my face would crumple. This was not what I had pictured doing that night. Well, maybe in my worst-case scenario I pictured some cleaning. But even in that contingency, I hadn't pictured so much dead salmon. Or the sheer volume of discarded tightie-whities.

Panic flashed in Mr. Gogan's eyes, and I found myself wanting to tamp it down. I could do this. The cabin wasn't a lost cause. Once you looked past the mess—and the smell—it was really very cozy.

"I'll clean it myself," I amended.

Instantly reassured, Mr. Gogan showed me the rest of the house, all four rooms of it. He offered to help me unload a few boxes from the truck, more strings to keep me from bolting from the little cabin. I refused, noting how dark it was getting.

"Mrs. Gogan will get worried," I told him.

"That reminds me," he said as he retrieved Tupperware from the backseat of his Bronco. "My Gertie sent this over. It's her famous pot roast and potatoes. And some berry cobbler. She said a woman shouldn't have to cook for herself after driving so far. She hopes to meet you the next time you come into town."

My reticence, heart, and nerves were instantly balmed by lovingly prepared starches. I smiled at Mr. Gogan. The "scenic view and available men" sales pitch I had expected, but not the neighborly gesture. I was wanted there, and that meant a lot. "Please thank her for me."

Mr. Gogan winked at me as he climbed into his truck. "Welcome home, Mo."

2

Dead Fish and Dying Elk

THE SILENCE WAS DEAFENING.

I thought my little suburban rental home in Leland, Mississippi, had been secluded, but even there I could hear the occasional snatch of conversation, the rumbling bass of my neighbors' car stereos. Here it felt as if my ears were stuffed with cotton. My house was fourteen miles outside town limits and set back a half-mile from the highway by a winding gravel driveway. A bomb could have blown up half of Grundy, and I wouldn't have heard it. I lay in the cabin's little bedroom and listened for some noise. Something to prove that it wasn't some sort of hallucination, that I wasn't still living in my little ranch house, waiting for my life to start.

After Mr. Gogan left, I'd found I had a boatload of manic energy to burn off. Which was a good thing, because I spent my first few hours as a Grundy resident on the Great Dead Fish Hunt. There were dead fish piled in the fridge, dead fish in the bathroom sink, dead fish hanging from a string in my utility room. Fortunately, Mr. Gogan's house-warming gift included all-purpose cleaner and paper towels. The worst part was, as much as I wanted just to chuck the decaying leftovers outside and forget about them, I figured that would be a signal flare to every bear in a hundred-mile radius that I was host-ing an all-you-can-eat buffet on my lawn. So I care-fully double-bagged the remains in heavy-duty trash bags and left them in my utility room. I hoped to be able to run them out to my locking garbage bin at the end my driveway in the light of day.

Honestly, I wasn't terribly afraid of the prospect of bears, wolves, or anything else that Alaska could throw at me. I figured it couldn't be any worse than going out to your carport and finding a six-foot al-ligator sunning himself behind your bumper. Which had happened twice in Mississippi. Not to mention the various snakes, possums, and other vermin that had found their way into my house.

Tired, sore, and stinking like dead salmon, I showered until my hot water ran out and warmed up Mrs. Gogan's offering in my newly descaled micro-wave. While I ate, I gave in to my need to organize, to prepare. I made detailed lists of supplies I would need, furnishings and household items to be re-placed, and the normal little moving chores such as establishing cable and phone service. I felt better for it. Lists and plans made me feel in control.

It was one of the many ways I differed from my

parents, whose only remotely religious credo was "Man plans, the Greater Power says, 'Ha!'"

That was it. That was my entire spiritual education, provided by the son of a deeply Orthodox Jewish family and the daughter of a Baptist deacon.

With my parents in mind, I took some deep, cleansing breaths, crunched my way through two Tums, and listened to my voice mail for the first time in a week.

"*Sweetheart, I'm only calling because I'm so worried about you,*" the messages all started. "*We know that it's important to have your own space. We've tried to respect that, but we didn't expect you to take it this far. You're our baby, our precious baby. We just don't understand how you could do this to us.*" And then a litany of worries, complaints, and recriminations followed, each of which ended with my mother pleading, "*Won't you please at least call us, so we know that you're safe? Even if you have to use your cell phone to do it . . . but you know, I worry about you using that silly phone so much, you're going to get a brain tumor from all those rays being aimed right at your ear. I've told you time and time again just to use your phone at home . . .*"

And on and on it would go until my voice mail ran out of space.

I leaned my forehead against the counter, grateful for the cool, smooth Formica. And despite the fact that any number of studies had proven that my cell phone was perfectly safe to use, I was annoyed to find that I'd placed it on the far side of the counter, where it couldn't zap me with its deadly brain-mushing waves. This was the problem with dealing with my mother. Sometimes she made just enough sense to get to me, and then I was all the way back to square one.

My mother was originally Lynn Duvall, from Brownsville, Texas. She met my father, George Wenstein, at a seminar on recycling in 1975 in Chicago, and they'd been together ever since. Still clinging to the free-lovin', consequence-free Age of Aquarius, the closest thing they'd come to a wedding was their naming ceremony, in which Mom redubbed my father Ash Wenstein. Years later, I was not the only person who found it appropriate that my father had the temerity to name my mother Saffron, a spice that sticks to your skin and clings there for days.

Ash and Saffron had some very definite theories on how to raise a daughter. Those standards didn't include little things such as religion, television, junk food, Western medicine, or pets. (The pet thing wasn't an animal-rights issue. Dad was just allergic.)

There were literally no walls in my childhood home, a barely refurbished old barn that served as the central building of my parents' very own self-sufficient, ecologically responsible commune for forward-thinking, government-hating vegans. Dad dubbed it Sunrises but eventually changed the name because people kept dropping their drugged-out teenagers at the front gate. They seemed to think it was a rehab.

People drifted in and out of the community constantly. And while I loved the laughter, the music, the energy that they brought to my home, I learned not to make friends. Kids would be gone in a few months' time, their parents unable to make the transition into what my parents called "living responsibly." Even those who fit in rarely stuck around longer than a few months, their restless natures keeping them on the road.

Still, my days were filled with adventure and fun, whether it was my dad's sudden decision to spray-paint the family VW van an Easter-egg purple or my mom toting me along to a nuclear-energy protest dressed as a radioactive Statue of Liberty. Every day brought something new, something exciting. And I adored my parents—their love, their generosity, and their attention to me. I loved being the center of their world.

But what's fun for a toddler can prove tiresome to a growing adolescent. I was home-schooled until age thirteen, when I realized that if I didn't get into public school, I would never get into college. My mother was my teacher, keeping complex and detailed lesson plans on hand for when the county education officials inevitably showed up for their surprise inspections. And while her intentions were always good, her lessons rarely went past the planning stage. She'd decide that some cause needed her attention, and suddenly my understanding fractions or knowing the state capitals didn't seem so important anymore. Most of the time, she'd leave me alone to do "independent study." If my father hadn't been a CPA in his pre-Ash life, I probably wouldn't be able to balance my checkbook to this day.

When I rode my bike to the Bowdry County Public Schools office and asked to enroll, I had no proof of my existence beyond my birth certificate and an essay entitled "Why I Need to Be Enrolled in Public School—Right Now."

Fortunately, the superintendent was walking by as I tried to explain my plight to his secretary. After he established that I wasn't being neglected or abused, he told me that every child had the right to attend public school. He even offered to go to my parents' house and explain my wishes to them. But I was so afraid of the idea of him seeing our strange, colorful little world, that he would find me a lost cause—or, worse yet, that he would drink my father's "sun tea"—that I declined.

That afternoon marked the first argument I'd had with my parents—well, with my mother. My father seemed to think that if my parents were going to encourage me to make my own choices, that should include supporting me when those choices included public school. My mother warned of dire consequences, peer pressure, the influence of uncaring and underqualified teachers, a revisionist curriculum that would only prepare me for life as a drone, and, worse yet, refined sugars in the cafeteria food. But she eventually signed the enrollment papers, and I was the newest student in Leland High School's ninth grade.

My mother wept as I dressed for my first day of classes, insisting on packing my lunch with honey-oat cookies, a peace offering. I dropped them into the garbage in the cafeteria and bought my first school lunch with birthday money from my loving, capitalist grandparents.

When I look back, I realize that was the breaking point. I got to school and realized exactly how different I was from other kids my age, how unprepared I was for the outside world. And I was pissed. Every act of rebellion, whether it was wearing leather shoes or voting conservative in a mock election, made me feel more normal. I flourished in high school. I became just like everybody else. I made good grades. I had a best friend, Kara Reynolds, who was happy to school me in the customs and rituals of "regular people."

I even got a job as a car hop at the Tast-E-Grill Drive-In after school. That afternoon, I ate (and promptly threw up) my first bacon cheeseburger. But Bernie Harned, the owner, helped me slowly build my processed-foods and fats tolerance up to Frito Pie as I worked my way from car hop to manning the grill. I used my hard-earned wages to buy new clothes, CDs, makeup, junk food—forbidden little treasures that I kept in an old steamer trunk at the foot of my bed.

My enrolling at the University of Mississippi seemed to fry something in my mother's brain. Well, more so than her concert experiences from 1966 to 1972. Her charming kookiness helped her get a security pass into my dorm and, later, my off-campus apartment building, so that she could, in her words, visit anytime. Mom used this access to "help" me sort through the things I didn't need anymore, such as lunch meat (the fact that I was eating animal flesh was bad enough, but think of the nitrates!), non-organic produce (poisons posing as nourishment), chemical cleaning products (baking soda and diluted vinegar work so much better). When she tossed out a full bulk-sized box of Hostess Sno Balls, I took to keeping my junk food in a locking plastic tub. And then I came home to find that she'd taken the tub to a recycling center.

Mom really thought she was doing what was best for me . . . in her own twisted, self-centered way. After all, how could I tell my own mother she wasn't welcome in my home? How could I be mad at her for throwing away a bunch of junk that was bad for me anyway? She was only thinking of my health. And hadn't she replaced it with nine-grain bread, tofu dogs, carob cookies—all the things I'd loved when I was a kid? Arguing with her was like trying to grab a greased eel; once I thought I had a grip, she'd squirm away and switch tactics.

So I studied hard and dreamed of using my marketing degree to get a job in Illinois, New York, California—as far away from Mississippi as I could get. I dreamed of solitude, of privacy, of owning a home that my parents couldn't just barge into by virtue of the spare key they'd wheedled out of my maintenance man.

My dad embraced pacifism. As in, he didn't want to get between my mother and me when we were fighting. And then, about a month before graduation, Mom and I were arguing over whether she and my dad would be coming to the ceremony. Mom wanted to attend a conference that weekend on pharmacological waste's impact on the water supply. When I objected, she said I shouldn't be participat-

ing in such an overblown, elitist, meaningless ceremony in the first place. I said it was *my* overblown, elitist, meaningless ceremony, and it wouldn't kill her to put her multitude of principles aside for a morning and make me happy for a change.

"This is just so damned typical!" I yelled. "You try to take over every part of my life. You practically follow me around collecting my toenail clippings for posterity, but when something is really important, important to *me*, you couldn't care less. Because I didn't go to an environmentally responsible school. I didn't study the right subjects. You think my teachers brainwashed me. You know, most people would be thrilled that their daughter was graduating from college with good grades. When are the two of you going to act like normal parents?"

And that's when Dad sort of keeled over and had a massive heart attack.

Apparently, there's only so much that oat bran can do for your cardiac system.

With my mother in full-on histrionic mode, I had to step in to take care of the decisions at the hospital and talk to the doctors. I moved back to the commune to help out while my dad recovered. And when he was back on his feet, I found a job at a little company outside Jackson that sold advertising inserts for newspapers. The hour-long drive back and forth to check in on them was exhausting, but it was worth it to be able to go to my own little house at the end of the day.

Mom soon returned to her old ways. Morning, noon, and night, my parents showed up at my doorstep with huge dishes of marinated tofu, herbal teas, some THC-soaked mementos from my childhood. This only grew worse after my engagement to Tim, an insurance adjuster whose offices were next door to mine. My mother often commented that our meeting at a Starbucks every morning for lattes was proof that the relationship was doomed to fail. Nothing associated with the Evil Caffeinated Empire could be good in her eyes.

Tim Galloway was everything my parents loathed. Conservative, Christian, the product of a two-parent, two-income household. He paid his taxes cheerfully. He had a membership with the Steak of the Month Club. Even if he was the opposite of my usual type, I felt safe with him. He was level-headed, funny, and kind. He had a five-year plan, which, after an appropriate number of very conventional dinner-and-a-movie dates, included me. If there was no fiery passion or leg-bowing sexual escapades, that was fine. I knew what to expect.

At least, I thought I did, right until the moment Tim met me for lunch one Wednesday and asked for his ring back. He couldn't even give me a good story to take back to Kara. He wasn't seeing another woman. He brought me flowers to break up with me, for God's sake. He just felt that he'd made a mistake in proposing so soon. He did mention my parents a few dozen times and the fact that I seemed so hell-bent on being "normal" that I didn't care what it cost me.

When I went home to help Tim pack his things and move out of my house, I realized that I felt more guilty than hurt. And it should hurt to lose someone you'd planned to spend the rest of your life with. Tim was right. I'd chosen him because I knew my parents wouldn't like him. For that matter, I'd chosen marketing because it was something they would never do. Dad said my advertising job made me a cog in the corporate machine and went against everything they'd taught me. They told people that I worked with recycled paper.

I'd almost doomed myself to a lifeless marriage and an unfulfilling career because I was rebelling in my own silly way. Even though I'd worked for years for independence, I was still letting them influence every decision I made. I was twenty-nine years old. It was time to stop living my life like a spoiled, scared teenager. I wanted to start fresh, to go somewhere where I was an unknown quantity, where people didn't know me or my parents, where my parents couldn't reach. At the same time, I was scared of starting over. What if I'd been using my parents as an excuse for all these years? What if the reason I was unhappy was that I was just a generally miserable person?

I'd moved to Grundy knowing that I probably wouldn't be able to find a job I was qualified for anywhere near the town. But I had a tidy little nest egg, inherited from Grampy and Nana Duvall. Long before they passed, my mother told them she didn't want the "blood money" from their family-owned butcher shop and barbecue stand. This made me my grandparents' sole heir. I saved and invested the inheritance carefully, and it had helped ease the burden of living on college stipends and my pitiful early sales commissions. And now it would help me establish a life in Grundy.

My plan—because, of course, I had a plan—was to live in Grundy without a purpose, to drift along, for one year. While I enjoyed my job at Gulfside, selling advertising space didn't exactly turn my crank. I didn't go home at the end of the day thinking, *Wow, I really made a difference to someone today.*

I wanted to discover what I wanted to do with my life when I wasn't making choices out of spite. I had enough savings to live comfortably for a year or two while I figured it out. And if I made it past one year, I would put a down payment on the Meyers place, find some gainful employment I was qualified for, and set down roots. If not, there was always Washington or New York. Heck, I'd live in Monkey's Eyebrow, Kentucky, if I could find my place there.

It's a real place. I looked it up.

The only person I regretted leaving behind was Kara, who also happened to be the only person, besides the postal clerk, with whom I'd entrusted my new address. Baffled but not exactly surprised by my move, Kara had made me promise to e-mail her every day—which reminded me that I needed to find out what my Internet options would be in Grundy.

It had probably been cowardly to pack up my house while my parents were out of town at a civil-rights conference. Drastic action had been required and taken, even if it made my stomach pitch with that instinctual squeeze of guilt and irritation that always came with dealing with my parents. But I'd avoided the tearful scene I'd been dreading. And Mom was always telling me I needed to be more un-predictable.

In the dark, with Yaya Wenstein's quilt pulled up to my chin, I made more lists in my head. Things to do, things to buy, things to unpack. I rearranged the cabin's furniture in my head. I thought of the meals I would make as soon as I cleaned the rest of the dead fish out of the kitchen, the long nights of uninterrupted sleep I would get without my parents' constant calls. I hoped I would be happy, or at least content, in Grundy.

I WAS STARTLED awake by a frantic bleating outside my window, followed by the crash of bodies through the brush. I bolted up, dizzy and disoriented in the darkness. I beat the nightstand with flat, numb fingers for my glasses, slipped them on, and stumbled toward the door. Or, at least, where my bedroom door was located in my old place. I smacked head-long into a wall. Cursing vehemently, I felt my way through the living room and found the front door. I opened it, expecting to find an injured sheep caught in the brambles. Where a sheep would come from I had no idea, but I was half-asleep.

My eyes adjusted to the darkness. The moon was full and alive, casting enough silver light to make shadows. Just beyond the tree line, less than twenty feet from my door, lay an injured elk, panting and panicked. A thick stream of blood flowed from a wound on its neck, making an oily black patch on the grass. Hunched over its body stood the largest black wolf I'd ever seen.

I don't think it realized I was there. It was concentrating completely on its dying prey. I gasped, stepping back into the shadows of the house, but somehow unable to close the door. The wolf snarled, its huge jaws poised over the elk's throat.

Without thinking, I screamed, "No!"

The wolf's head snapped up. Its wide eyes, an unearthly shade of blue-green, glowed with angry intelligence.

Whoops.

The elk, sensing the wolf's distraction, stumbled to its feet and crashed back through the brush. The wolf's eyes seemed to narrow at me, silently berating me for disturbing it. I stared back, my fingers finally loose enough to fumble for the doorknob and close it behind me. In my panic, I wondered if closing the door would do any good. Could the huge predator just tear through it?

Through the window, I watched the wolf stare at the door. I held my breath, trying to think of anything in the house that could be used as a weapon. The fireplace poker. The elk antlers hanging over the fireplace, which would seem a sort of karmic justice when used against this thing. Suddenly, the wolf perked its ears toward the sound of the elk lurching through the bushes. It let out what sounded like a frustrated huff and sprang away from the house, loping through the woods after its bleeding meal.

I sank to my knees and crawled toward my bed, knowing I wouldn't sleep another wink that night.

3

Thumb Removal for Dummies

THE BLUE GLACIER SALOON was part general store, part restaurant, part bar. It was my fantasy come true, a Stuckey's that served shots.

After ridding the cabin of the last of the fish and returning the emptied U-Haul trailer to a dealership 220 miles away, I'd finally called my parents. No one picked up. They didn't believe in answering machines. And by that I mean they believe the point of not being home is not answering the phone. They do believe that answering machines exist. So, having dodged that bullet for a few more hours, I was in a fine mood. And I was starving.

As I drove through town, I was struck again by the obvious effort people made to maintain the buildings. Every structure was occupied. Every square foot of indoor space was made useful. Mr. Gogan had told me that even if businesses closed down, the storefronts were used as storage space, an improvised church, extra classrooms for the high school. The weather and the expense of shipping construction materials made it difficult to build there, so wasting precious interior space was not tolerated.

In the South, between the wet, baking heat and passage of time, the decay of buildings was expected. People walked away from their businesses, leaving them frozen like some museum exhibit on bad management. It was common and depressing to drive through a town square and see an abandoned gas station with the self-service signs intact, the rack of Black Jack chewing gum moldering near the register, houses rotted, their splintered gray walls overgrown with kudzu, usually with a newish trailer installed just a few yards away. I found the continuity of my new home, the commitment to preservation, to be comforting, and I marveled at the exquisite old woodwork on the door to the Glacier.

While Hannigan's Grocery provided milk, eggs, and produce, the men of Grundy generally made an afternoon of buying their dry goods at the Blue Glacier, playing pool or watching a game. The dining room was lit by afternoon sun streaming through huge picture windows. On the opposite side of the dining room was a huge black metal woodstove that seemed to be the centerpiece of the room, giving it a homey, lived-in feeling. The wood-paneled walls were decorated with a mix of neon beer signs and hand-painted wildlife scenes. The scent of potatoes fried in peanut oil had my mouth watering.

The saloon's lunch crowd was thick and talkative. Conversations and booming laughter seemed to bounce from every corner. Most of my new neighbors sported thick flannel shirts and worn hiking boots. You could spot the occasional "in-town professional," such as Nate Gogan, or the bank manager, Mr. Riggins, in a suit and tie. But overall, this was a working crowd. A wide range of ethnicities was represented, but across the board, each of them seemed to exude this sturdiness, an air of capability. If the roof caved in or a bear came moseying through the front door, I suspected every person in the dining room would know exactly what to do. I wondered if I would ever seem so confident in my ability to take care of myself up here.

I introduced myself to the proprietor, Evie DuChamp. Evie was quietly beautiful, with wide brown eyes and stick-straight hair as black as a raven's wing flowing down her back in a neat braid. Her skin was nut-brown and impossibly smooth. Her husband, Buzz, was a huge blond mountain of a man. I guessed his nickname came from his severe military haircut. Buzz looked like the example you'd be given in a sketching textbook on "How to Draw an Angular Face"—lantern jaw, square chin, nearly flat head. He was obviously devoted to Evie. Every time he looked at her, a warm, silly grin spread across his face like boiled molasses.

After seeing several rather unremarkable burgers cross the scarred pine lunch counter, I ordered a turkey melt and chatted with Evie. She'd known who I was the moment I walked through the door. Nate

Gogan was a regular lunch customer and had apparently talked about his new client at length, privacy be damned. I might have resented the intrusion, but Evie was the sort of person who made you want to talk about yourself. She had a calming way about her that instantly put you at ease. Before I knew it, I'd told her about my sleepless night and the wolf incident. She told me it was common for local wolves to worry livestock and the occasional garbage can but that they normally ran away when confronted by a human. Particularly when that human was holding a shotgun.

Our conversation was interrupted several times by locals who approached me to introduce themselves. Well, local *men* who approached me to introduce themselves. Big, burly, and in most cases barely shaved, they were polite, even courtly, as they sidled up to my bar stool to offer to buy my lunch, fetch me a beer, or, in the case of Abner Golightly, just flirt shamelessly. Abner Golightly, age eighty-seven, was a self-proclaimed latter-day prospector who reminded me of Blue from that *Old School* movie. Not that I would ever admit to seeing that . . . or owning the complete works of Will Ferrell on DVD. Even *Bewitched*.

Abner told me that if I moved into his cabin on the outskirts of town, my feet would always be warm and the toilet seat would always be down. I thanked him for the tempting offer. He winked at Evie and toddled back to his burger before the very cute Grundy High chemistry teacher asked me to join him for a beer. I declined for now.

Something about the way these men approached me made me think I was being evaluated as breeding stock. I'd inherited my dad's thick coal-black hair, which I'd cut off two years ago after finally conceding my lifelong battle with Mississippi humidity. Kara had said I looked like a shorn angel, in the best possible way, that somehow the spiky pixie crown balanced out the high cheekbones and slightly top-heavy lips passed down from my mother and the large more-gray-than-blue eyes I'd inherited from I don't know where. However, I think my potential suitors were thinking more along the lines of: *Breasts? (Check.) Pulse? (Optional, but check.)*

Vaguely inappropriate old men notwithstanding, I hadn't considered the possibility of starting a relationship in Grundy. For one thing, I didn't know how long I would be there. Second, I hadn't known what the candidate pool would look like. True to Mr. Gogan's word, that pool was deep and well stocked. My history consisted of relationships that could be packed away in neat little boxes once we'd parted. No recriminations. No burning of their stuff. I received Christmas cards from most of them. What would I do if I got stuck there for a whole winter, dodging the hang-dog face of a fling gone terribly awry? Besides, my vast goodie-drawer collection of condoms had been entrusted to Kara during the move, since she was far more likely to need them on her one-woman tear through the male population of Mississippi.

"Is this some sort of screw-with-the-outsider scenario?" I asked Evie after Leonard Tremblay offered to show me "a good time." Evie shook her head, and after Leonard departed with a good-natured grin, she warned me that his idea of a good time was firing up the home-rigged hot tub on his back porch. I was going to ask how one home-rigs a hot tub, but the look on Evie's face told me I was better off not knowing.

She smirked. "Oh, honey, you're reasonably attractive and have all your teeth. You're the hottest thing this town's seen since Herb Thorpe got half-scrambled Cinemax on his satellite."

"I don't see why the 'reasonably' was necessary, but thanks," I muttered, sipping my Coke. "That must be why your waitress is staring daggers at me."

Lynette, the waitress/cleaning gal, was the girl-next-door type, if you happened to live next to a cathouse. She was probably pretty once, but chasing the next good time had aged her quickly. Her hair had been processed into an indeterminate shade of pale something. The too-bright lipstick was already starting to feather into the tiny networks of lines that spider-webbed out from her mouth. Her hip bones jutted sharply from under her fraying jeans. I would learn later that even in subzero temperatures, she wore midriff-baring tops under her parka . . . so she was a smart girl to boot.

"Don't mind Lynette," Evie said, rolling her eyes. "She convinced herself a long time ago that she is always the hottest thing in the room, and she lives to prove it. It actually makes her a pretty great waitress. She knows how to go after the tips. But having every guy in the bar talk to you just to hear your accent must be annoying the hell out of her."

"Is that why they kept asking me to say 'ice'?" I asked, a little irritated. I'd worked for years to downplay my accent, a mix of my mother's faint Texas twang and my classmates' slow Delta drawl. I thought I had it down to where I only "got Southern" when I was upset. I grumbled, "Y'all sound Canadian to me, by the way."

"Just enjoy it. It's a little harmless flirting. You don't have to worry about serious intentions until they start offering you meat."

I arched my eyebrow. "Is that some sort of gross double entendre?"

Evie's dark eyes twinkled. "No, actual meat. It's sort of a tradition in Grundy, a macho provider thing. They want to show you that they can feather your nest, so to speak. It's pretty Neanderthal of them but sweet at the same time. When a Grundy man offers you a rump roast, it's the equivalent of asking you to go steady."

"Wow," I said. "And on that note, please excuse me."

I hopped off the bar stool and was heading for the bathroom when my foot caught on an uneven floorboard and sent me pitching into the wall of man standing behind me. It felt as if my whole body had burst into flame. My cheek tingled where it had brushed against his chest. I could feel the heat from his steadying hands searing through the sleeves of my shirt.

I exclaimed something like "Oof!" and looked

up. It was the eyes that stunned me into silence—
the same electric blue-green that had stared out at
me from the woods the night before. I shook off
the sleep-smeared memory and tried to smile politely.

"Mo, meet Cooper Graham. Cooper, this is my
new friend, Mo," Evie said in a bemused voice.

With a gulp, I swallowed the drool puddling in
my mouth. You noticed the eyes right off the bat,
wide and bottomless blue over sharp cheekbones,
and a slim, long nose that had obviously been broken when he was young. His hair seemed both
dark brown and black, not long enough for a pony-
tail but too long to keep under that faded maroon
baseball cap he was wearing.

Cooper was exactly the type of guy I would
have sex with *before* the first date back home. Dark,
rough, athletic. Here I was faced with my own personal sexual kryptonite, and I'd abandoned my con-
traception.

Cooper offered me a brief view of brilliantly
white teeth as he set me on my feet. He had the
biggest hands I'd ever seen. I wondered how they
would feel on my skin, whether his fingertips would
touch if he had both hands on my hips. Whether he
was that big everywhere—

I was snapped out of my subconscious ogling
when Cooper looked to Evie. "Vacationing?" he
asked in a husky, no-nonsense tone.

Apparently, he wasn't bothering to address me directly.

"New blood," Evie said wryly, shaking her head.

"Mo's renting the Meyers place. With an option to buy."

"I've heard that song before," Cooper rumbled. His smile was sharp and not terribly friendly. He pressed his lips together and exhaled. With lips quirked, he told me, "Try Evie's apple-raisin pie. It's a life changer."

My eyebrows shot up as he turned and walked toward the end of the counter without another word. I noticed that while most of the diners were greeted with slaps on the back and manly jokes about work ethic or penis size, Cooper was left unscathed. It wasn't a cold shoulder, exactly. In fact, several people acknowledged his presence with a nod. But there was a distance, a pointed lack of familiarity with the other Grundians. Except for Lynnette, who scurried over to drape her bone-thin frame beside his stool under the pretense of taking his order.

I turned to Evie. "Did I do something to offend him?"

"Oh, Cooper's just . . . well, he's surly as all hell, but he's family, so I put up with him, even when no one else will. He's a cousin on my mother's side, so we sort of grew up together over in the Crescent Valley," she said, shaking her head. "He's got a thing about outsiders moving up here. Just don't let him hear you say the words 'commune with nature,' or the top of his head will pop right off."

While I'd experienced little of it so far, I'd read about the Alaskan feelings toward outsiders, a general attitude of distrust and exasperation for people who came to their home looking for the peace and fulfillment of living off the land. You could live there for twenty years and still be considered an outsider. I'd been warned by Mr. Gogan that the local postmaster, Susan Quinn, wouldn't bother delivering my mail until I'd made it through my first winter. I'd have to pick it up at the post office myself. Susie Q, as the natives called her, was a bit of a character in a town full of them. Platinum blond by the good grace of Miss Clairol, with a countrified 'do that would put Dolly Parton to shame, she wore tight western shirts on her heavily endowed frame and drew a little beauty mark on her cheek every morning. But when it came to running the post office, she was all business, save for the fact that she kept her beloved dachshund, Oscar, in the mailroom for company.

I eyed Cooper again, trying to discern exactly where the territorial bubble he seemed to have established began. No one got within a foot of him, everyone shying around him to place orders at the counter, reach for ketchup. Again, except for Lynette, who couldn't have communicated her eagerness to burst that bubble any more clearly if she'd been wearing a sandwich board that read, "10 Seconds from Naked!" So far, Cooper hadn't responded to her overtures with more than a few disinterested grunts.

He was a charmer.

"If you stay past the first big snow, Cooper might actually speak to you without rolling his eyes," Evie offered, her voice full of hope.

I muttered, "Well, woo-freaking-hoo. And you know, we had winter in Mississippi."

Evie gave me a pitying shake of her head.

"We actually had to wear long sleeves," I told her, but she seemed unimpressed.

"Shit fire!" I heard Buzz yell from the kitchen.

My eyes went wide, but everyone else seemed too occupied with their food to respond. Evie read my expression, smiled to herself, and rolled her eyes. "My husband, the poet."

But then someone called in a stage whisper, as if not to disturb the customers, "Evie! I need some help back here." A lanky Asian teenager in a stained white apron stepped around the corner, pulling a pale Buzz in his wake. Buzz's hand was wrapped in a white dish cloth already soaked with blood. Evie's expression changed to one of alarm.

"What happened, Pete?" she asked, concern roughening her voice. I quietly stepped around the bar and helped Pete steady Buzz. We took him back into the kitchen and sat him down on a case of canned chili beans. I gently lifted Buzz's arm over his head so Evie could pull the cloth away. I saw enough of the wound that I thought I might have to sit down, too.

"Just a little accident," Buzz mumbled, wincing with pain.

Poor Pete had worked himself up into a fine froth. Whether it was panic from the sight of blood or fear of losing his job, I had no idea. He babbled, "We were waiting for the fries to finish, and we got a little bored. And you know, Buzz just got these new knives, and he was bragging on them and try-ing to tell me that they were sharp enough to cut through a beer bottle, and I said, 'No way.' And he said, 'I'll prove it to you . . .' "

"John Matthew DuChamp, are you trying to tell me that after getting through two tours of duty unscathed, you've maimed yourself trying to cut a beer bottle in half?" Evie demanded.

Buzz was looking rather sheepish at the use of his full name . . . and green.

"It's pretty bad," Pete told her. "We need to get him to the clinic right now."

"I'll take him," Evie said, whipping her apron over her head and reaching for her purse.

"It's the middle of the lunch rush," Buzz protested queasily. "You two can't leave. I'll drive myself."

"You can barely stand," Evie told him. "I'll take you. Pete can handle the counter."

"Alone?" Pete squeaked, sounding panicked. "You know what happens when you leave, Evie. Homer Perkins picks apart his food, yells that I got his order wrong, and throws stuff at me."

"Oh, it was one time," Evie said, patting his arm.

"It was an ax handle!"

Evie kissed Buzz's forehead. "Fine, I'll stay here, but Pete's going to take you to get that looked at."

"Well, if I take Pete with me, who's going to cook?" Buzz asked.

Evie chewed her lip.

"Evie's a disaster in the kitchen," Pete explained to me, a conspiratorial note in his voice. "She started a fire boiling eggs once."

"But Cooper said to try her pie," I whispered.

Evie was too distracted with Buzz to pay either of us any attention. "He said it was a life changer."

"Well, being trapped on the can for a week probably would change your life," Pete conceded. My jaw dropped, and I glared at Cooper. Well, that cinched it. He was an asshole. I was definitely going to end up sleeping with him.

From what I recalled of the menu, it was very basic all-American diner food with little embellishment. Burgers. Fries. Pancakes the size of hubcaps. Bacon. Eggs. Steak, steak, and more steak. I'd done all that and more manning the stove at the Tast-E-Grill.

"I can do it," I told Evie. The words had left my lips before the implications of taking on such a task settled heavily in my chest. I scanned the kitchen and saw hamburger patties already shaped, veggies already chopped. There were several orders close to burning on the grill. "I worked my way through school at a drive-in. It looks like most of your prep work is already done. And I can do short-order stuff."

Evie's face flooded with relief. "Would you?"

Buzz was not so eager to relinquish control of his grill. "Really, Evie, I think I'll be fine in just a—" He stood up, turned two shades paler, and little beads of sweat popped out on his forehead. He leaned heavily on Pete and said, "Yeah, I need to go to the doctor now."

Cooper, who'd had difficulty getting around the determined Lynette to help immediately following the accident, managed to steal around the counter before Buzz slumped to the ground. He caught

Buzz's elbow and held him upright, sort of dangling by his good arm.

"You want me to go along, Evie?" he asked in his gruff baritone. "Pete won't be able to hold Buzz down when they try to stitch him up."

Evie chewed her lip. "Would you, Cooper?"

"Buzz is scared of needles," Pete confided in me. "Just about loses his mind over getting shots. He threw Dr. Gordon halfway across the room when he had to get a tetanus booster."

Cooper ignored Pete, shrugging in Evie's general direction. "Sure. Otherwise, I'd just end up bailing Buzz out of jail later, after he tears up the clinic."

Buzz was packed off to the clinic with another kiss and a stern look from Evie. She returned to her place behind the bar with a fresh apron and a serenity I wouldn't have thought possible just a few minutes before.

Except for the pooled blood, the kitchen was meticulously clean. I got out the rubber gloves and disinfectant and carefully wiped down any area that might have been affected by Buzz's accident. I washed my hands carefully and turned the heat down on the monster griddle, hoping I could save most of what Buzz had been cooking. In keeping with his haircut, Buzz also had a military eye when it came to organization and ordering. In bulk. So it was easy to find my way around the kitchen.

I eyed the waiting tickets and turned out two plates of steak and eggs and a tuna melt. The next few hours were a blur of filled plates and pleasantly popping grease. It was funny how quickly my hands recalled those summers at the grill. The sounds and smells hadn't changed. Only now, there was a murmur of conversation, which had been contained behind car windows at the drive-in. Several customers praised their lunches and asked Evie about "that new girl behind the stove." Occupied by constant orders, I was able to keep my head down and pretend I couldn't hear.

Pete called to report that Buzz had severed a tendon in his finger and would have to go to the nearest hospital, 127 miles away in Dearly, for surgery. Evie took this in stride, considering, and asked me if I wouldn't mind working through the dinner shift. They ran a brisk business for lunch, but Evie said the crowd would lull from two to four before the dinner crowd came in. The grill was scheduled to close around six, when the lunch counter became the bar. The nighttime regulars were far more interested in booze than in burgers.

By the time Ben, the night bartender, arrived to relieve me, my feet ached, my sweater was ruined by splattered grease, and I was up to my elbows in dishwater. Evie sank against the pallet of chili beans, took a bottle of iced tea out of the stock, and sighed. "I love Buzz, but honestly, what the hell do men think when they do things like this?"

I grinned, wiping down the counter. "I don't know if thought is really part of the 'this is going to be so cool' planning process."

Evie smiled and closed her eyes. They popped back open a few seconds later when the phone next to her head rang.

"Buzz?" she said, an edge creeping into her voice, as if she were finally allowing herself to absorb the panic of seeing her husband injured. I turned my back and let her have her moment. I heard the soft rush of conversation, the endearments, the threats against Buzz's most delicate manly parts if he ever did anything like that again. I smiled to myself but focused on washing the dishes. Evie hung up the phone with a sigh.

"They're staying in Dearly for the night. Buzz is good and looped on pain meds. The doctor told Cooper it's going to be months before Buzz has full use of his hand." Relief and worry were stark on her straight, even features. "He's not going to be able to dress himself, much less cook."

"Oh, Evie, I'm so sorry. But I'm sure Pete can handle the kitchen until Buzz is ready."

"Pete's a good general dogsbody. He can crack eggs and chop vegetables, though considering today, I'm thinking about taking all sharp objects away from both of them. But he can't run the kitchen by himself," she said, a faint line creasing between her eyebrows. "He's not consistent. He gets flustered when there's a rush of orders, and he's been known to walk out of the kitchen crying."

I shrugged. "Well, maybe if Buzz is there to direct him . . ."

"Buzz's style of direction is why Pete has been known to walk out of the kitchen crying," Evie told me. "Mo, do you think you might like a job here? Full-time, while Buzz is out? Maybe take over the baking?"

"But you barely know me," I protested. "You just met me this morning."

"And I like what I've seen. You don't faint at the sight of blood. You're willing to help out a near stranger. You're a solid, consistent cook. And you had several opportunities to swipe tips out of the jar and you didn't touch a cent, which is more than I can say for a few of my employees."

I pressed my lips together and considered. Despite my plans for an idle life in Grundy, I'd had a good day. I liked being in the kitchen. I felt like a part of the room, but I wasn't in it. I had privacy. And I liked the saloon. I liked the friendly voices, the chatter. I liked being near Evie. It felt as if I was taking a baby step into the community.

My mother had always told me that everything happens for a reason. Of course, she'd also told me that dyeing my hair and using commercial laundry detergent would mutate my chromosomes. But I'd embraced her resistance to the possibility of co-incidence. Maybe I was supposed to be in Grundy. Maybe I was supposed to be sitting at the lunch counter when Buzz pulled his bone-headed Ginsu demonstration. Maybe this was my place.

I turned to Evie and smiled. "I think I would like that."

4

Drinking the Kool-Aid

I'D FORGOTTEN HOW MUCH my feet hurt after a cooking shift. Or that eventually even your contact lenses feel as if they're filmed in grease. I started keeping my work clothes in the hall closet so I could keep my good clothes smell-free. But I was happy.

I was building a routine. I got up every morning, put on my most comfortable boots, threw whatever leftover baking scraps I had into the backyard for the birds, and drove Lucille into town. Word traveled in Grundy much the way it had traveled back home, in kitchens and school hallways and the town's lone beauty parlor. The saloon was the social hub of the town. When word spread that there was a new girl there, our dining-room crowd almost doubled.

Buzz had hovered over me at the stove the first day or so. He obviously resented being replaced in the kitchen but couldn't do much beyond stirring with his bum hand. I'd only gained his trust on my third day, after one of the customers paid his tab in elk meat, which was his usual monthly custom. I didn't bat an eyelash at the strange-smelling, almost purple cuts of meat. I asked Buzz whether he'd rather I grind it for meat loaf or marinate it in Coca-Cola to eliminate some of the gamey taste in a roast. Buzz stammered that a meat loaf would be a good daily special, then supervised as I prepared two huge pans.

"How do you know so much about cooking wild game?" he asked after he took a test bite of the finished product and declared it "all right." From Buzz, that was practically gushing.

"This is nothing. Call me when you've tried deep-fried gator. Or chitlins. Actually, I don't recommend the chitlins."

Buzz shuddered. "No thanks."

He ambled away to sit at the counter, drink coffee, and talk to Evie. She kissed his forehead, then turned and winked at me.

I had a place here, my own space. After a few days, my Grundy neighbors called me "Mo from the Blue Glacier." I found myself coming out of the kitchen more often, taking orders, pouring coffee, eager for conversation and new faces. I wasn't identified by my parents' needs or beliefs. I wasn't invisible. I was Mo, a contributing member of the community and frequent target of good-natured romantic overtures. There were those who didn't speak to me, because I was still too "new." It wasn't outright rudeness, just an unwillingness to acknowledge my presence until I'd proven my mettle. But most of the unattached men in town had made at least a halfhearted attempt to flirt with me. It was kind of sweet, a sort of inappropriate initiation.

The town's female population seemed divided between women who saw me as competition for prime male stock, such as Lynette, who didn't have much to say to me beyond barking orders, and those who seemed happy to "share the burden" of the attention. In fact, Darby Carmichael, a checker at Hannigan's, responded to Evie's introduction by sighing and saying, "Another one? Thank God!" Darby immediately pledged her undying friendship if I got Leonard Tremblay off her back. She seemed to understand when I declined.

Among my furry, fervent admirers, the most persistent was Alan Dahling, a U.S. Forestry ranger who oversaw the massive Evanston Game Reserve that surrounded the town. If Nate Gogan were to run an ad campaign featuring Alan titled "Move to Alaska, and you will meet men who look like this," there would be a flood of single women into Grundy. Alan was blessed with a headful of sandy, wavy hair, big blue eyes, and sooty lashes most women would kill for. And the crisp green uniform molded to a fit, trim, and very tall body didn't hurt, either.

Nate was sitting with Alan at the counter on my first Friday at the stove. When he saw me coming over to say hello, Nate took off Alan's baseball cap and straightened his uniform tie for him. Absorbed by his patty melt, Alan seemed confused until Nate sent me a pointed look.

"Mo, this is Ranger Alan Dahling," he said, nudging Alan with his elbow. "Alan, this is Mo Duvall-Wenstein, the latest, greatest addition to our little community."

"I've been hearing all about my pretty new neighbor from Nate," Alan said, his dimples winking. He grinned broadly at me. "I see that the stories didn't do you justice. As the closest thing to law and order in this town, let me serve as the official Welcome Wagon." He stretched his tanned, rough hand across the counter and shook mine.

"Watch it," warned Buzz, who served as the part-time constable of Grundy. It was an elected position that meant he got to wear a badge and break up bar fights. Anything more serious was called into the state police post about forty miles away. But since most of the fights took place in Buzz's bar, it was a pretty convenient arrangement.

I didn't know how to respond to that except by blushing. "Nice to meet you, Ranger Dahling."

At the sound of my voice, an awed grin spread across Alan's face. "Would you mind if I sat here and listened to you talk all day?"

I smiled back, pleased with the little butterflies taking flight in my belly. With the exception of my first-meeting hot flash with Cooper, it had been months since the butterflies had seen any airtime. "As much as a captive male audience would fulfill one of my ingrained female fantasies, I think I would burn a lot of lunches that way."

"Well, it's worth it, just to hear you call me darlin'," he said with another broad, beautiful smile.

"I said 'Dahling,' your last name."

"That's not how I chose to hear it. I'm almost tempted not to ask you to call me Alan. But between the accent and your cooking, I'm afraid you've ruined me for all other women," Alan said solemnly. "So we might as well be on a first-name basis."

"Nah, I think I just ruined you for all other hamburgers. You're lucky I don't flutter my eyelashes. I'd own your sorry butt."

"Well, I'm going to have to keep coming back until we know for sure." Alan grinned impishly and winked at me. "I happen to be your closest neighbor. The ranger station is five miles as the crow flies from your place. Anything you need, just let me know."

I couldn't help but return the smile, with more feeling this time. Alan quickly became one of my favorite regular customers, quick with a flirty smile, a compliment, and a generous tip. It was like getting a daily self-esteem booster shot; a conversation with him made me feel good for the rest of the day. Alan generally waited until Evie was too busy with other customers to take his order, meaning I would wait on him. He ordered the same thing every time, a patty melt and a piece of apple-raisin pie, which was a less life-altering experience now that I'd taken over the baking. He sat at the end of the counter, where he could see me in the kitchen. Sometimes, if the dining room was quiet enough, he would talk to me as I worked. They were fluffy, getting-to-know-you conversations about music, movies, hobbies. He seemed to know that I wasn't ready to discuss much beyond that. Unfortunately, some of the other customers figured out that if you sat at the end of the counter, you could get the new girl's attention, so Alan ended up jockeying for his position on most days. But it was sort of entertaining to see him show up at 10:30 for lunch.

I served. I chatted. I earned my living. Every time Mr. Gogan saw me smile at a customer, he seemed so pleased with himself I worried that his face might freeze in an expression of smug exhilaration.

THE GLACIER WASN'T open on Sundays, so I had the day off. I seriously considered driving two hours to stock up at the Sam's Club in Guidry, but I figured the best way to build relationships with my neighbors was to shop local.

Of course, that was before I saw the $3.65 loaf of wheat bread.

I was going to have to start baking my own bread again. And possibly milling my own flour. Maybe there were some advantages to being raised by people who didn't believe in store-bought glutens.

Hannigan's looked just like any locally owned grocery store anywhere in the country, except that the prices were higher and there were a lot more products geared toward cooking wild game. I pushed my cart through the store, grabbing ice cream and Sno Balls along with fruit, whole-wheat bagels, peanut butter. Even though I ate most of my meals at the Glacier as part of the "benefits package," I felt the need to stock up. I had a feeling my first week's paycheck was going to be used in one shopping trip.

I turned the cart around the corner, paying more attention to the display of fresh fish than to my steering, and smacked into another cart.

"You need to do something about your depth perception," Cooper Graham grumbled from several inches above my head.

I glanced up at him. Cooper hadn't been in the Glacier since that fateful day when Buzz experimented with do-it-yourself amputation. Evie said that Cooper was a professional field guide, leading tourist parties of hunters and fishermen through the local hot spots. She said it was normal for him to disappear for days at a time. Still, I deeply resented the way I fruitlessly checked the dining room for him every morning. It didn't stop me from doing it, but I resented it all the same.

He looked tired, with dark circles under his eyes, which were almost hidden by his worn maroon cap. His cheeks were drawn and covered in thick, dark whiskers. I wondered if he'd been sick, if that was what had kept him away from the saloon. But ultimately, I realized it was none of my damn business and it was in my best interest not to care.

"Are you having a party?" he asked, eyeing the contents of my overloaded cart. He seemed to choke on the words, as if it literally hurt him to have to interact with another human being. How did this man make his living leading people around in the wilderness? Didn't they expect some civility for their guide fees? Or had he convinced them that Yukon Yankee rudeness was all part of the experience?

"No." I pursed my lips and peered into his cart, which contained bacon, ham, sausage—meat as far as the eye could see. "Are you on Atkins?"

He rolled his eyes. "No."

And so we stood there staring at each other. Well, Cooper stared holes through my head. I stared at his massive, long-fingered hands and had all sorts of indecent thoughts about proportionality. My eyes flashed up to Cooper's, and I realized that he saw where I was looking. I hated the blush that crept into my cheeks, knowing that it would eventually spread over my chest and down my belly and leave an inconvenient warmth settled there. I blew out a breath and tried to will the rush of blood away.

Another silent moment passed.

Cooper cleared his throat. "Evie said you needed some help out at your place, hauling some stuff in from your garage? She said I should offer to lend you a hand."

I quirked an eyebrow. The only thing in my garage at the moment was my elliptical trainer, which I'd managed to drag out of the U-Haul but not into my house. I'd told Evie about having to work out in the garage until I could get someone to move it in for me. I would have to talk to Evie about the difference between me making idle conversation and dropping hints to match me up with some burly social misfit willing to move heavy objects. Then again, I think it amused her to watch me squirm around Cooper that first morning.

Thank God I hadn't mentioned hauling my "collection" three thousand miles with me. Evie would have had a field day. I was something of a lingerie connoisseur. The previous winter, after saving up for a year, I'd placed a massive order with La Perla, swearing that my mother would never find out that I spent enough on underwear to feed a Third World village and buy the villagers a goat farm. And she didn't. Until she went through my bills under the guise of "helping me organize."

We didn't speak for almost a month over that one.

It was worth it. I loved lingerie. I loved the feel of satin and silk on my skin. I loved the juxtaposition of wearing a pair of two-hundred-dollar lace panties under blue jeans, like the pair I was wearing at the moment. Lingerie was a personal statement that you didn't have to declare to the world. You could be as demure or as naughty as you wanted to be, and no one ever had to know unless you showed them . . . or were injured in a serious car accident. After living with people who wore all emotions and opinions on their sleeves, having a few wearable secrets was the ultimate turn-on.

I had fond memories associated with almost all of my little ensembles. I still had the classic white lace strapless bra I'd worn under my senior prom dress. I kept the red satin bikinis I'd almost lost in a heady tangle with a U. Miss. teaching assistant whose name I couldn't remember. And despite the way my engagement turned out, I'd held on to the black lace corset set I'd worn the night Tim proposed. I couldn't think of the underwear without thinking of the man associated with it, and vice versa.

Hey, I find scrapbooking to be far more disturbing. Knowing my limits in terms of self-denial, I'd hauled the entire collection with me to Grundy. It was kept in sturdy, labeled, individual boxes, carefully arranged on my closet shelf. And if I'd told Evie about it, there was no doubt she would have shared this with Cooper, too. The woman clearly had no scruples when it came to matchmaking.

"It's just some exercise equipment," I told him. "I know it seems like a silly thing to haul all the way up here. But there isn't a gym up here, so no kick-boxing, no racquetball. I didn't want to gain forty pounds my first winter, so . . ."

"Oh, I wouldn't worry about it." Cooper snorted. His tone implied that he didn't expect me to make it through a winter, so weight gain was the least of my worries.

"Well, what do you do for exercise?" I asked, my eyes narrowing.

"Chop and haul wood, hike, you know, work to support myself?" he said pointedly.

"Right, what's that like?" I asked.

Well, that was way more snotty than I intended it to be.

Cooper sighed, almost huffing out in annoyance. "Look, if Evie wants me to help you, I will. Just tell me when you want me to come over."

The command, the irritation in his voice, struck a nerve. Out of everybody in town, why did this one person make me so angry? There were others who had been less than welcoming. Heck, Lynette still called me "Hey, you" when she called out her orders. But somehow, coming from Cooper, it grated on my nerves like steel wool.

I snapped, "I don't. It's fine where it is."

"It won't be fine when it starts to get cold and your engine block freezes because you can't pull your truck into your garage."

I gave my most saccharine smile. "Well, I don't want to trouble you. I'm sure I can get someone else to help. Alan Dahling sort of made a standing offer."

Cooper's nostrils flared at the mention of the ranger. "Well, I guess it's settled, then."

"I guess so. But thank you anyway."

I steered my cart around Cooper's and tried to depart without any undignified flouncing. I changed my route around the shelves, deliberately avoiding Cooper until we somehow managed to hit the checkout lanes at the same time. Darby Carmichael watched me glare at Cooper while another girl checked him out at Register 2.

"Why are you giving Cooper Graham the 'eat musk ox and die' look?" she asked after he sauntered out of the store.

"I don't think that's the expression," I told her.

"Have you ever had musk ox?" she asked.

"I have not," I conceded. "You know how some people just rub you the wrong way? Well, Cooper's my own personal sandpaper."

"He's like that with everybody," Darby assured me. "Don't take it personally. Some people were just born with a pinecone shoved up their butts. In Cooper's case, it's lodged sideways."

"Well, that is an entertaining mental picture, so thanks."

"You know what would really make him mad?" she asked, her eyes a-twinkle. "Dating Leonard Tremblay."

"Nice try, Darby."

"Well, you can't blame a girl."

I TEND TO bake when I'm upset. Or bored . . . or premenstrual . . . or if it's a Tuesday. I'll use any excuse.

When I got home, I unpacked my groceries and baked six dozen chocolate chess squares to take into work the next morning. Chess squares are a Southern delicacy, derived from chess pie, a custard pie that uses cornmeal instead of flour for thickening. And when I used Reba Reynolds's secret recipe, they turned out a sort of combination of brownie and cheesecake. Grown men have wept upon tasting my chess squares.

I'm a little cocky about my kitchen skills.

My plan was to use them as a sort of opening volley to persuade Buzz and Evie to change the Glacier's menu. It wasn't that the Glacier's food was bad, it was just a little bland.

Fine, fine, I was hoping to get them to change the menu because I was bored. But Evie had already let me change a few things, such as adding spices other than salt to the burger mix. While she'd never admit it to Buzz, who sat at the counter every day with a slightly sulky expression, Evie said the customers were happier with my cooking than with his.

My plan was to suggest small alterations, soups, omelets with lots of fillings, an expanded dessert menu. We would serve good, wholesome diner food that wouldn't leave me smelling like Ronald Mc-Donald at the end of the day.

While my last batch of squares was cooling, I turned on my computer and found that I'd finally gotten Internet access through the local phone company. It was surprisingly fast considering the distance the lines had to stretch. I had thirty-two new messages in my Hotmail in-box. Four of them were from Kara.

"Mo, I know you won't have e-mail for a few days, so it's sort of pointless to write, but I miss you already. It's weird. We've lived hundreds of miles apart for years now, but it seems worse now that there's an entire continent between us. I keep thinking, 'I should call Mo and tell her this,' and then I remember that (a) you're not at your house anymore, and (b) not only are you no longer in residence, but you chose to move your sorry behind across the freaking hemisphere.

"So, here's how I've spent the last few days: Terrible first date on Tuesday night with that guy from the gym. Turns out his sweating issues were not related to treadmill time. I thought I was going to have to towel off when he hugged me good night. Book club on Wednesday night, which I failed to read the book for. Let's be honest, I joined the club for the free wine and readily available men. Thurs-

day night, I quit the book club and joined a new gym. So, really, it was a very productive week.

"Dad's birthday is this weekend, and I'm heading home, which will give me a chance to break the news about your move. I'm sure Mom and Dad will be thrilled for you, though.

"Please call or write when you can. Love, Kara."

I snorted. Kara's mother used to call us the Tortoise and the Hare. We moved at different speeds, but we usually arrived at the same place eventually. Kara was the tiny blond dynamo. I was the freakishly tall observer. You would think that sharing most of our classes, working together, and spending all of our spare time together would sow discord, or at least occasional cattiness, between two very different teenage girls. But Kara and I skipped over those friendship growing pains. She never seemed to mind that I basically took up residence in her home, taking up her parents' time and attention. For her part, Kara insisted that I didn't know what I was getting into, that her parents were intrusive and overbearing, too, but on a less obvious scale than mine. Still, I will never forget John and Reba Reynolds's willingness to bring "that hippie girl" into their home, despite dire warnings from gossipy neighbors. I'd spent a lifetime among people who extolled the benefits of sharing and giving, and I was still awed by the Reynoldses' generous souls.

Scrolling through her increasingly manic missives, I clicked on the message she'd sent me that morning.

"Mo, I am assuming from your lack of e-mail ei-

*ther that you have had trouble getting Internet service
or that you have been devoured by a grizzly bear. Come
on, woman, I want all the details. How was your drive?
What's your house like? What's Grundy like? Are you
meeting any nice people? Are there any stores in town?
Do I need to have the National Guard airlift Diet Coke
and Twizzlers to you? I'm dying here. If you don't respond by Friday, I'm going to call you, long-distance
charges be damned. Love, Kara. P.S. Don't make me give
your new address to your mother."*

Giggling, I dialed Kara's number on my cell
phone. My carrier provided nationwide long-
distance in every state but Hawaii and Alaska,
so it was going to be expensive. But at this point,
I didn't think an e-mail would soothe Kara's
wounded pride.

The phone rang maybe half a beat before it was
clattering off the receiver. "Mo?" she demanded.

I felt a mile-wide smile stretch across my face. "I
did explain that I was moving here to get away from
whiny emotional blackmailers, right?"

Kara blurted out, "I'm so sorry, Mo."

Instant alarm zipped down my spine at Kara's
voice. "What's wrong? Are my parents OK?"

"Everybody's fine," she said quickly. "I'm sorry, I
didn't mean to scare you. But . . . I screwed up. I'm
so sorry. I told you I was going to tell my parents
that you were moving? Dad said it was about time
and to consider that your birthday present to him.
And Mom said she was sorry she couldn't help you
pack."

This made perfect sense. From what I remembered of high school graduation, Kara's mother offered to dress in black, paint her face in camouflage, and smuggle me into my college dorm in the dead of night. "And?"

Kara sighed. "Well, my mom ran into your mom at the library yesterday, and she couldn't help but rub it in a little bit that you'd finally escaped. And then Mom made some comment about how difficult it would be for your dad's van to make it all the way to Alaska for a visit. Your mom fell on the information like a lion on a zebra carcass, and the next thing my mom knew, Saffron had dragged the town name out of her, too. I'm so sorry, Mo. Your mom has some sort of evil hypnotic power. And my mom has a big mouth."

I took a deep breath. *Oh, please,* I begged silently, *just let me have this a little while longer before Hurricane Saffron and her destructive wake suck me under.* The breath I was holding hissed out through my teeth as I pried the Tums bottle open. "It was going to happen eventually, Kara. Don't worry about it. And tell your mom not to feel bad. It's not like she gave them GPS coordinates or anything."

Kara let out a relieved sigh. "Thank you. Mom feels terrible."

"Don't worry about it," I said while crunching the antacid tablets.

"Now that we have that out of the way." She squealed. "Oh, my God, tell me everything. Is it beautiful there? Have you seen a moose yet? Is it horribly, horribly remote and desolate? Are the people anything like the cast from *Northern Exposure*?"

"Yes, no, no, and sadly, no. Because every girl could use some John Corbett." I sighed.

"Well, what are they like?"

"They're just people, Kare. I mean, they're a little eccentric and independent. But no weirder than anybody we knew in Mississippi. Some of our classmates' parents were carnies, for God's sake. For the most part, they've been really kind, and I've been welcomed with open arms. Of course, I think it's because they want me to enter some sort of contract marriage and breeding program . . ."

"I knew it." Kara hissed in mock triumph. "You drank the Kool-Aid. Thirty years of resisting your parents' indoctrination, and you fall victim to a breeding mill. I'm just going to have to move up there and scope out the prospects for myself."

I broke down laughing and told Kara about the Glacier and Buzz's accident, about Evie, Alan, Nate, and Abner, about my marketability as a marriage prospect in Grundy, about my little house, which was becoming ever more habitable. I left out descriptions of Cooper's surly hotness. I didn't want Kara to seize on hostile locals as a reason for me to come home.

"So no close encounters with bears yet?" she asked. Kara had a secret phobia of bears, particularly grizzlies, which was sort of ironic, as the only specimens within a thousand miles of her lived in zoos. She was the only person I've ever known who was creeped out by the Snuggle the Fabric Softener Bear.

I sighed, knowing that what I was about to say might keep Kara from ever visiting my new home.

"The closest I've come is a wolf chasing down an elk right outside my door the first night I was here."

"Oh, my God!"

"It was nothing," I assured her. "I haven't seen it since."

"Well, just remember that yeah, the animals are majestic, beautiful, and noble and all that crap, but they're still dangerous. Look at what happened to that grizzly guy. He spent his whole life trying to protect the bears and ended up feeding them. Literally."

"I will not try to live among the wolves," I promised.

"I have to admit I'm just the teensiest bit disappointed. I was sort of hoping you might not like it there. And move, I don't know, back into the same hemisphere as me."

"I think I'm happy here, Kara."

"I know, I can tell by your voice." She sighed. "Damn it."

It took two more Tums, an hour of yoga, and a chocolate chess square before I felt mentally prepared to call my mother. I'd put it off for too long, and now that she had a general search area, I needed to take preemptive action before she did something drastic. I dialed my parents' number and prayed that they were outside in the garden or that maybe my dad would pick up. Ash wasn't exactly the reasonable parent, but he was a rank amateur when it came to lecturing and guilting.

"How could you just run away like this?" my

mother demanded the moment she picked up the phone.

"Mom."

"Do you have any idea what this is doing to your father? Or how we felt when we came to your house and found it empty?"

I'd noticed that my mother did manage to sound a lot like a "normal" parent when she was upset with me. But that sort of observation, or commenting on the fact that they'd gone to my house *unannounced* to find it empty, wouldn't be helpful at this juncture. "Mom."

"You know how important it is for us to be able to visit you. You know we need to spend time with you. How could you *move* in the dead of night without a word?" She sniffled, her voice thickening with tears.

"Mom."

"I don't understand what would make you do this!" she cried. "What did we do to make you hate us this badly? All we ever did was love you too much."

"You're right, Mom. You do love me too much!" I exploded. "You love me so much that you go through my kitchen and throw away half of my food because you've decided it's bad for me. You called my boss to discuss me taking days off for Burning Man, which I never agreed to attend. And I had to explain to my boss what Burning Man was, which was a humiliation all its own. You tried to get the receptionist at my doctor's office to give you the results of my annual gyno exam—"

"I'm just a concerned parent. I never mean to get

information I'm not supposed to have. If they aren't supposed to tell me something, how is it my fault if they tell me anyway?"

"You walked into my apartment unannounced, found me in bed with Ray Ridley, and didn't bother walking back out!"

"Oh, baby, you know I don't care about that sort of thing. I've always told you that sex is the most natural expression of your inner being."

"That's the problem, Mom. You don't care about that sort of thing, but I do. Most men do not want to stay naked in bed with a woman while her mother is sitting on the foot of said bed touting the benefits of tantric sex."

Mom sniffed dismissively on the other end of the line. "Well, any man you date is going to have to understand that loving, involved parents are part of the package. That's why I never saw things working out with Tom."

"It was Tim. And men don't want to date families, Mom. It's hard enough to find someone who likes you for all your flaws. Adding two more people into the mix is just too much. But that's not why I left. I just need to be alone for a while. To find out who I am when I'm away from you. I need some space. I need to *breathe*."

"Oh, you've always been your own person," she huffed. "I don't know where you get the idea that we've had any sort of influence on you. You use plastic grocery bags, for heaven's sake. But your father says that if we want to make our own choices in life, we have to respect yours—even if they go against everything we've tried to teach you."

"This isn't about what you've tried to teach me. This is about me, what I want to do with my life. You and Dad want to fight the system. Fine. Personally, I like the system. The system brings electricity to my home, schools to my neighborhoods, Ben and Jerry's to my local Wal-Mart."

"You shop at *Wal-Mart*?" Mom screeched.

I held the phone away from my ear as my mother launched into a diatribe about the evils of a homogenized, centralized retail empire that treats its employees like chattel. "Yes," I said. "Now you know my secret shame."

"So, you're just going to sit in the middle of nowhere, shop at Wal-Mart, and *breathe* for as long as it suits you?" she asked derisively.

"No, I'm also cooking in a restaurant. I'm meeting new people every day. I'm involved in the community. I like it here."

"What sort of restaurant?" my mother asked, suspicion tinting her voice.

"A normal restaurant with normal food with seminormal people."

I could hear her teeth grinding on the other end of the line. "So, you're charring animal flesh again?"

"Yes, the restaurant serves meat," I told her, waiting for the inevitable clang as Mom struck her "anger gong" to release her negative feelings. The anger gong had to be replaced when Mom found out I'd been cooking at the Tast-E-Grill for six months before telling her. I'd ended up fund-raising for PETA as penance for that one. But the minute I turned eighteen, I went right back to working at the drive-in after school and during the summers while I was in college.

Mom dealt with it by pretending that it wasn't happening. And beating the hell out of a gong.

"I'm not going to get angry," Mom intoned now, although I could hear the faint, reverberating *ping* of the gong in the background. "I am the master of my feelings. My feelings are not the master of me. It's obvious that you don't care about what we think or feel. And that you've totally abandoned the principles we've tried to instill in you. I'm not going to lecture you on the horrors of the slaughterhouse or what the consumption of animal flesh does to the interior of your colon."

"Mom, I am not going to pay roaming fees to talk about my colon."

She exhaled loudly through her nostrils. "I'm just going to ask you, as your mother, the woman who gave you life, who suckled you and nurtured you and loved you, to please give me your new address and phone number so we can contact you when we need to."

I stayed silent, mostly because I really hated it when she said the word "suckled." If I gave her my home phone number, the receiver on my nightstand would be ringing morning, noon, and night. I could turn the cell phone off, at least, or I could send her calls to voice mail. More important, it was a piece of information I could keep in my control, one more boundary I could maintain. I chose my words carefully. "I don't think that's a good idea. I'll call you when I can. And you can always e-mail me if you want to."

This was a dirty trick, and I knew it. My parents had yet to invest in a computer. I was pretty sure they believed that e-mails arrived in envelopes that popped out of the disk drive.

"But how will I get ahold of you?" she cried. "What if there's an emergency? What if your father has another episode?"

"Call my cell phone and leave a message."

"Sweetheart, please, don't do this!" I could hear her beg while I pulled the phone away from my ear and hit "end." I blinked back the hot moisture gathering in my eyes. It was stupid to cry, to feel guilty. I wasn't wrong to want a life on my own terms. Maybe I'd gone to extremes to get it, but there was no taking that back now.

5

When Options A and B Both Suck

THE CHOCOLATE CHESS SQUARES were a big hit during the next day's lunch rush. Gertie Gogan bought a half-dozen, which she said she was going to take to Nate's office. But when I saw him later, he had no idea what I was talking about. Abner Golightly upped his offer to warm feet and a permanently reclined toilet seat, *and* he'd break down and buy a color TV if I moved in with him. I kissed his cheek and politely declined. Even Buzz, who seemed to be resenting his mummified hand less and less, had to admit that they were "pretty damn good" and asked if I would bring another six dozen the next day.

I sensed victory on the horizon. Caught up in my sugar-based triumph, I didn't even mind when Evie left the saloon in my care during the predinner lull. She needed to take Buzz to the clinic for a follow-up visit. But then Ben, the night bartender, got sick halfway through his shift, which left me alone with Lynette. She was, at best, an indifferent helpmate. I ended up pouring drinks, washing glasses, and keeping tabs while she hung out by the pool table and flirted with Leonard Tremblay.

I made a mental note to call Darby and let her know that there might be some hope for her yet.

Most of the thin crowd consisted of regulars, who were patient when it took me longer than usual to fetch their beers. Heck, they were willing to wipe the counters down for me if it meant they could stay to watch the last few minutes of the game while I washed dishes.

"Hey, honey, you in the kitchen."

I looked up from the sink and wiped my hands on my apron. There was a stranger sitting at the counter. He was tall and muscular, with big brown eyes and dimples that winked from the corners of his mouth when he smiled. Given the worn green jacket advertising Harris Transport, I guessed he was a trucker. They frequently stopped in Grundy to catch some sleep at the Evergreen Motel or a hot meal at the Glacier. Most of them were nice, family guys, a little lonely, who came into the Glacier for a side of conversation along with their food. If you asked them to see pictures of their kids, they'd tip you forty percent.

But something about this guy put me off. It wasn't just the three days' worth of growth on his cheeks or the long, appraising look he was giving me while I dried the last of the dishes. I shook off the little shiver of apprehension and pasted on my most polite smile. "Can I get something for you?"

"Beer," he said, flashing those dimples again. "Why don't you have one, too?"

"I don't drink on duty, but thanks."

He dipped his head in an exaggerated hang-dog expression. "That's a disappointment. So how does a pretty girl like you end up behind a bar at this time of night?"

"A trusting boss and the ability to sling beers with laser precision," I said, stacking dried pilsners carefully under the bar. I wanted to keep busy. I didn't want to encourage this guy, to make him feel he had too much of my undivided attention. But Buzz and Evie wouldn't want me ignoring a lonely customer, either. It was a fine line to walk.

Trucker Guy focused those baby browns on me, tilting his head as he asked, "Don't you have someone waiting for you at home, honey? Somebody to keep your feet warm?"

"Yes, a very thick pair of wool socks," I told him solemnly. He laughed, and I couldn't help but smile in return.

"Luckiest damn socks on earth." He snorted. "Wonder how they'd look rolled up on my floor in the morning."

"See, you were doing so well, and then you ruined it by using the tired 'clothes on the floor' thing. Sorry, I have really strict rules about men who use bad pickup lines."

He winked. "Well, you know what they say, rules are made to be broken."

Before I could answer, Walt Gunther, one of the Hockey Night crowd, beckoned me over to his table. I excused myself with a nod and made my way to him.

"That outsider fella bothering you, Mo?" Walt asked.

I offered him a grateful grin. Something about the way Walt said "outsider" made me feel sort of warm inside. I was included. I wasn't an outsider. "Nah, he just can't take a hint."

"Well, honey, if he gives you any trouble, me and Abner know where to hide a body," he said.

"Let's hope it doesn't come to that. Can I get y'all another round?"

Walt rubbed his bulbous belly absentmindedly. "No thanks, Jeanie's already going to skin me over being out this late. Don't want to add half-drunk to her list of complaints."

I poured Walt a Coke and kept Abner in peanuts through the third period. Walt kept a careful eye on me while the trucker finished his beer. Trucker Guy refused another and left me forty-six cents as a tip, which cinched my feelings of ill will toward him. He had long since disappeared by the time I laughingly chased Abner and Walt out the front door and flipped the "Closed" sign over. Walt insisted on walking me to my parking spot in the alley before climbing into his truck. I smiled and waved as he pulled away.

I'd gotten as far as putting the key in the ignition when I realized I'd forgotten to take out that night's garbage. The lunch special had been oyster stew. If I put it off until the next day, the kitchen would stink to high heaven in the morning.

Grumbling to myself all the way, I went back through the kitchen entrance and grabbed the garbage bags. I pulled my jacket closed, noting how thin and insubstantial it felt against the growing evening chill. In just a few short weeks, I would probably need to upgrade to the heavy down parka I'd just ordered over the Internet. I was about to lock up when I heard footsteps crunching on the gravel behind me. I whirled, raising the bag of garbage like a plastic-coated hammer. My hope was that I could gross out whoever it was with day-old garbage, giving me time to run away.

No such luck. It was the outsider, the trucker from before.

"Hey, here we are again," he drawled. His smile was friendly, but it didn't quite reach his eyes. Some instinct had me putting my back against the wall, my keys clutched between the fingers of my right hand. "I think I left something on the bar earlier, a blue knit cap. Did you see it?"

I shook my head, trying to keep my face a blank, pleasant mask, despite the frisson of fear rippling up my spine. "No, I checked the bar over when I was closing up, and I didn't see anything. But maybe if you come back in the morning, you might find it."

He furrowed his brow, his expression one of practiced disappointment. "Well, I'm heading out early, before dawn. I won't have time to stop by. It would only take a minute for us to duck in and check. It's my favorite hat. You don't want me wandering around bare-headed, do you? I could catch cold."

"I really can't," I said as I dropped the garbage bags to the ground. "I can't let anyone in after hours."

"We don't have to tell anyone," he said, winking at me. Something about the way he said "we" had me gritting my teeth. He leaned close. "Come on, it'll just take a minute."

I gauged the distance to my truck, too far for me to make a break for it. "Sorry. Maybe you can pick it up next time you're in town."

"You're being awfully rude, honey. I'm not asking for a big favor here."

For a moment, I felt guilty. He wasn't asking that much. How hard would it be just to let him back into the bar to look for his stupid hat? I was being sort of rude. But some organic alarm deep in my brain was telling me not to go into the darkened bar with him, to get out of the alley and get home as quick as I could.

"Come on, be nice. Just let me in," he said, grinning widely even as I took a step around him.

Not by the hairs on my chinny-freaking-chin, my brain yelled back as his hand clamped around my arm.

My heart thundered in my chest as I realized how trapped I was. Even if I made it to my truck, if I managed to get inside before he stopped me, I would have to run him over to get out. Could I do that? I took in his huge, hulking form, his cold, dry hands, and I shuddered at the thought of either touching me. Yes, yes, I could.

I'd taken a women's self-defense course when I moved out on my own. Somehow my dad's safety advice, "Just try to reason with them," didn't seem adequate walking alone in Jackson's darkened parking structures. I tried to remember what I'd learned, but all I could recall was the instructor's advice for women living alone to put muddy men's boots and a huge dog's dish on the porch so it looked as if the home was well protected. That didn't do me a lot of good at the moment.

"Look, I just want to leave. Leave an address at the motel, and I'll send the hat to you." I tried to jerk my arm out of his grasp, but he was too strong.

He twisted my arm behind me and shoved my face against the rough brick. His voice was still so soft, even friendly, as my face scraped against the wall. "You have a choice to make here, honey. I don't want to hurt you. But I will. You don't want to make me hurt you, do you?"

I winced as he wrapped his fingers around the back of my neck. "Yes or no, honey?" he asked.

I whimpered. "No," I choked out, wincing at the grinding pain in my cheek.

"You're going to hand me your keys, and we're going to go inside and take a look at the register. It was a nice busy day for you, right? Probably lots of cash in there. Is there a safe in the office? Do you know the combination?"

"No, I just started working here," I said, thinking of the full night-deposit bag I'd left under the counter. Evie had said that dropping it off at the bank every morning was easier than messing with the bulky old safe at night. She said the crime rate was so low in Grundy that robbery wasn't a big concern. I hated being the exception to a rule.

"How about I hand my keys over and you open the door yourself?" I asked, hating the tremor of fear that kept my voice reedy and thin. "I don't have to be with you when you do this. Please, just let me go."

"And what? Let you run off to call the police while I'm inside? I don't think so, honey. We're going to spend some time together, you and I. Maybe I'll just toss you into my goody bag and take you with me." He laughed so hard that he had to lean against the wall for support. Carefully, I stepped right, trying to get out of his grasp. His grip on my neck tightened. "You don't make rules here, you got it? You don't tell me what to do. You do what I say. That's how this works."

He pulled me toward the door, loosening his hold on my head for just a moment. Swinging up with my hand, I tried to imagine my arm as a striking snake. With the last flick of my wrist, I scored my keys across his cheek, the metal teeth dragging cruelly through his skin. And while he leaned over, cursing, I turned, grabbed his head, and brought my knee crashing into his face. Biting back the urge to cry or vomit or both, I scrambled across the pavement for my truck. I felt his hand snagging the hair at the base of my neck, hooking it around his fingers, and jerking it back so hard I could see stars exploding behind my eyelids. Tears stung as my scalp screamed. My keys tumbled from my fingers.

"You bitch, you messed up my face!" he yelled, his voice wet with blood. I could feel the warmth gushing down my shoulder, soaking through my light sweater. His hands clawed their way up my torso, scraping at my throat until the fingers locked around my airway.

With everything I had, I fought the instinct to pass out. I had to put up some fight. God knew what he would do to me while I was unconscious. On the other hand, blissful ignorance might help me cope if I lived through this. Pass out and forget, or stay awake and endure?

This was an extremely shitty internal debate.

At the end of the alley, I heard a low, warning growl. In the faint lights, I could see the outline of the wolf, electric blue eyes glinting as he kept his head low on advance.

"Just stay still," the trucker grumbled at me, twisting my hair again. I yelped. The wolf's growl grew louder.

The trucker's grip loosened as the wolf came closer. Panic had the edges of my vision blurring dark. This seemed an even bleaker choice. Mauled by a wolf or featured as a victim on Nancy Grace's next broadcast? Suddenly, my self-defense instructor's voice came back to me, clear as a bell. *Kick.* He'd told us that if someone had us from behind, the best way to get away was to kick back like a donkey, aiming at the knees or groin.

If I was going to die, it would at least be in a manner that I chose. And my choice of kicking my attacker seemed to startle the wolf. I kicked back, just clipping the inseam of the trucker's jeans with my heel, catching him right in the undercarriage. The wolf huffed and darted right. The trucker howled and doubled over. I turned and kicked him in the face, knocking him back onto the pavement.

And suddenly, I realized I had my back turned to the other predator. I turned slowly, expecting the wolf to be crouching, preparing for an attack. But the huge black creature wasn't even looking at me. His focus was on the trucker. He edged around me, the fur of his tail brushing my leg as he crept toward the barely conscious man.

I plucked my keys from the ground as the trucker came to. He screamed at the sight of the wolf and skittered backward across the blacktop like an injured crab. The wolf lunged, snapping his jaws and just missing the trucker's face as he scrambled back against the alley wall. His strangled screams as the wolf snapped into him were almost enough to make me feel pity. But I had my truck backing out of the alley in less than a minute. My last image of the trucker was my headlights sweeping over him as the wolf lunged at him.

I'M NOT SURE how I drove home. The next thing I remembered was running through my front door. I wanted to hide in my shower forever. The smell of the trucker's blood on my clothes had me stumbling to the bathroom to vomit. My stomach empty and my throat raw, I carefully stripped off the coat and sweater. I peeled my tacky, dried-out contacts from my eyes. I looked in the mirror and saw faint purpling bruises, on my throat, dappling my breasts. One of my favorite bras, white eyelet lace with little pink ribbons sewn at the straps, was stained and ruined. There was a large patch of bloody, raw skin on my left cheek where the bastard had scraped my face against the brick. I took a deep breath and, with shaking hands, called Buzz and Evie's number.

It took a couple of stops and starts to explain what happened, but it took Buzz only a few minutes to arrive on my doorstep with his official law enforcement hat in place. He tried to stay calm and professional as he asked me those first few basic questions, then threw his arms around me in a crushing hug. Despite the horrific events of the night, I found myself chuckling into Buzz's polyester uniform coat. I hadn't realized he cared.

A pajama-clad Evie, who was supposed to be waiting in the truck, gently pushed Buzz aside and wrapped her arms around my neck. I blew past the lump in my throat, burying my good cheek against her warm skin, and felt better for it.

"Did you check the alley?" I asked Buzz when I finally came up for air.

"There was a little smear of blood, but you said you popped this guy in the nose pretty good, right?" He paused, and I nodded.

"But the wolf attacked him," I said, my brows furrowing. "There should have been a lot of blood. And maybe some . . . parts."

Buzz looked a little uncomfortable. "Mo, I didn't

see any tracks in the mud, anything to show that a wolf was there. And they don't normally go all the way into town . . ."

"I'm not crazy," I told him. "The wolf was there."

"No one's saying that, Mo. If you say the wolf was there, it was there," Evie said gently, giving Buzz a stern look. "But why were you there all alone? Where was Ben?"

"Ben got sick, so I covered the rest of his shift. And Lynette was there, or at least she was until I looked up around ten and realized that she and Leonard had disappeared," I grumbled. "I didn't want to bother y'all, because I wanted to prove I could handle it. Obviously, I was wrong."

"Next time, you call us," Buzz said. "There's a reason we don't let people close up alone."

I nodded, knowing that this wouldn't be an issue, as I wasn't going to think about closing alone again.

"I stopped by the motel. The clerk said one of the guests, a trucker named John Teague, matched your description. His stuff's still in his room, but his rig's gone," Buzz told me. "He probably just took off. I called the state police, gave them his name and vehicle info. I'm going to need to send them your statement. And I'm going to need to take some pictures of those bruises and your face."

I nodded, silent. Buzz was exceedingly gentle, asking Evie to take me into the bathroom with his Polaroid and get pictures of my face and neck. It was over in a few minutes. Evie quietly handed the pictures to Buzz, who put them in a sealed black plastic bag.

"A trooper might be stopping by tomorrow to talk to you," Buzz said. "I can sit in if you want."

I smiled, grateful.

"I'm going to call Dr. Gordon and have him drive in to the clinic to check you out," Buzz said.

"I'm fine," I protested. "Just a couple of scrapes and bruises. There's no reason to wake him up."

Evie shook her head. "Mo—"

"I said I'm *fine*," I insisted.

Something in my voice must have convinced Evie that I was close to snapping. She sighed and pushed my hair out of my eyes. "I can stay with you tonight if you want."

"No," I told her. "Besides, Buzz needs you at home in case he has to brush his teeth or something."

Laughing now, Buzz made a rude gesture with his bandaged hand.

"Well, take the morning off," she said. "Believe it or not, we can run the place without you."

"No, you can't." I laughed.

"Yeah, you're right, we can't, but take the morning off anyway. We'll manage."

"I just want everything to be as normal as possible," I said. "And that means following my routine and going to work. I can't let this make me afraid of the saloon. I like working there too much."

It took another hour to persuade them to leave. I forced myself to take a long shower, to slip into my fluffiest jammies, to drink some chamomile tea. But I still jumped at every little sound. My hands shook as I tried to find a book to read before bed. Every time I passed a window, I looked out into the trees, expecting to see a hulking male shadow outlined against the moonlight. And some part of me hoped for blue-green canine eyes to wink out at me from the darkness.

6

Kiss My Patois

I<small>T WASN'T NEARLY AS</small> difficult to talk Evie into changing the menu as I thought it would be.

Whether it was residual guilt over my being assaulted on the premises or the power of the almighty chocolate chess square, I was just happy she was open to new ideas. And it gave me something to think about other than the "incident."

Against Evie's protests, Buzz and I had decided not to tell anybody about my near-miss in the alley. The menfolk tended to get a little overvigilant when the delicate flowers of Grundy womanhood were threatened, despite the fact that most of those flowers could wield a chain saw with a surgeon's precision. Still, Buzz didn't want to cause a panic.

If customers asked about the scrape on my cheek, I told them I tripped on a porch step and took a header onto the ground. Abner and Walt offered to come by and fix the step for me, which made me feel loved but slightly guilty.

When Lynette asked me what happened, I told her Leonard Tremblay forgot our safe word.

Buzz and I managed a discreet meeting with Trooper Brent, a short, squatty bulldog of a man, in the saloon's office. Trooper Brent was far more worried about whether we had more applesauce cake than about taking my statement. As far as he was concerned, I was unharmed, so there was no foul. I identified John Teague from a photo lineup. When Buzz tried to hand over the pictures of my injuries, Trooper Brent slid the envelope right back to him.

"There's no need," Brent said gruffly. "Teague's truck was found twenty miles outside town. We think he lost control of his rig and rolled off an embankment into a ravine. Nobody saw the wreck, so it was burning for hours before anybody showed up. We're still waiting for dental records to identify the body, but we're pretty sure it's him. And you can't charge a dead man with assault."

It seemed as if all of the air had been sucked out of the room. I couldn't seem to feel anything but the rush of relief flooding through me. The man was dead, and I was glad. Well, not just glad. I was almost dizzy with savage delight that he was dead and that he had probably suffered quite a bit. What the hell was wrong with me? What kind of person would be filled with glee over another person being pinned in a burning vehicle? Maybe the changes I was going through in Grundy were not *entirely* positive.

What had happened to John Teague? What had happened to the wolf? I found that I cared far more about the wolf's welfare than about Teague's.

"Did Teague have any injuries besides what he might have sustained in the wreck?" I asked.

Brent lifted a bushy brown brow, as if he were surprised I knew such big words. Asshole.

"Well, as you can imagine, since the body was burned to the point that we're relying on dental records to identify him, there wasn't much left of it. Why do you ask?"

Buzz interjected before I could open my mouth. "Mo punched Teague in the nose in the alley. I think she thinks maybe if the body has a broken nose, it might make it easier to identify."

I shot Buzz a puzzled glare. He pressed his lips together and sent a significant look toward Brent, who was brushing the crumbs from his third piece of cake off the front of his uniform. Apparently, Buzz didn't want me to mention anything about the wolf or Teague's potential claw wounds. I guess losing a short-order cook to an involuntary forty-eight-hour mental-health evaluation would be damned inconvenient.

"Well, honey, he had a couple of broken bones," Brent said in a condescending tone as he slid a file folder across the desk. "From the truck turning over and all, it was hard to find any bones that weren't broken. Dental records are a far more reliable way to ID the body. But good for you for giving him a good pop for his troubles."

I'm sorry, did he just say "for his troubles"? Buzz

sensed the growing tension in my arms, the way I was clenching my fists. He patted my hand and shook his head.

"You're a very lucky young lady. This guy's a suspect in robberies at diners and dives up and down the highway. He's put a couple of women in intensive care. He picks a waitress from the pack after closing time, jumps her in a secluded parking lot, and gets her to let him into the safe. And then he . . . Well, you're not the first one to fight back, but you're the first one to get away."

I opened the file folder and lost my grip on it at the sight of a skeletal face, charred black, its teeth bared and open in a never-ending silent scream. My eyelids slammed shut of their own accord. This was so much worse than anything you'd see on the news or TV, because I'd seen the flesh covering those bones, looked into the wasted eyes. Pride was the only thing that kept me glued to my chair, instead of leaning over Buzz's wastebasket and tossing my pancakes into it.

"What the hell is wrong with you?" Buzz yelled, shoving the folder back at Trooper Brent. "Hasn't she been through enough? She doesn't need to see that shit!"

"I thought she'd like to know he's gone for good," Trooper Brent said, shrugging. He looked somewhat chastened, as if it had just occurred to him that Buzz might have more loyalty to me than to his fellow law-enforcement officer and testosterone vessel.

"How in the hell is seeing that going to make her feel better? And why haven't I heard about any of this? I should know if my people are in danger, Scotty. Damn it, I'm the closest thing to law enforcement in town, and I didn't get so much as a heads-up."

"Most bars aren't big on getting all-points updates to protect waitresses," Brent mumbled.

"Well, this one is," Buzz shot back, slapping his palm against his desk.

Brent seemed to sense that he'd stepped directly onto Buzz's bad side now. "Look, he's gone. Your waitress is fine. It all worked out. We'll get back to you when we confirm the ID. And from now on, Miss, maybe you should just be a little more careful when you work late. Be more aware of your surroundings. Don't walk in dark alleyways alone."

My teeth clicked together, grinding so hard my jaw ached. He made it sound as if it was my fault, as if in a nice, safe office job, I wouldn't have been hurt.

"I don't work late anymore," I shot back. "And I just want to forget the whole thing, pretend it didn't happen. Let me know if you identify him, but otherwise, I really don't want to talk about it again. Buzz, thank you for how you've handled this. I appreciate *your* help."

Without waiting to be dismissed, I got up from my seat and walked out of Buzz's office. I hid in the kitchen for the rest of the day, trying to keep the images of Teague out of my head. The way he stood over me, the smirk on his face when I screamed. The stilted, unnatural way he scrambled away from the wolf, cornering himself against the wall. Blood soaking through his shirt in three long slashing lines. Then there were the images I created myself. The truck tumbling into the ravine. Teague's anguished cries as the cab caught fire around him, his mouth falling open into that last gasping scream. His skin splitting and turning black. When Evie caught sight of my pallor, the overbright, feverish glint to my eyes, she sent me home, saying she would close the kitchen a little early that afternoon.

But even with the door dead-bolted behind me, my comfy jammies on, and three cups of Sleepy Time tea in my stomach, I couldn't seem to settle. I forced myself to go outside, to avoid shutting myself up in my little house. I sat on the porch, wrapped in a quilt, watching as a small black-tailed deer crept out of the trees and nibbled at the bread crusts I'd left in the yard. I stayed perfectly still to keep from disturbing it, but eventually, I had to sneeze, and it bolted back into the woods. I sat for almost an hour, scanning the tree line for . . . what, exactly? My furry black savior? The extra-crispy ghost of Teague? Was I afraid that he'd somehow escaped fiery death and was coming back for me?

After baking, yoga, and way too much bad TV, I gave up on resting and used the manic energy to complete my menu proposal. I worked through the night, searching for the right recipes, cost analyses, shopping plans. I crashed somewhere around 3:00 A.M., got up at dawn, baked some more, and beat Evie to work so I could set up my new dishes in the kitchen. I gave her my proposal for reasonably priced comfort foods—chicken noodle soup, beef stew, meat loaf, my aunt Sherry's secret-recipe pot pie, chicken and dumplings, and, of course, all of the burgers and melts. My expanded dessert menu offered the improved apple-raisin pie, chess squares, my killer applesauce cake, banana pudding, and brownie à la mode.

"Just give me time, Evie, and we'll be busier than a one-legged man in an ass-kicking contest in here," I promised.

"Oh, how I love your genteel Southern patois," Evie said, eyeing my overcaffeinated, jittery self with an expression I can only describe as wary concern. "I thought you belles were supposed to be all verandas and mint juleps."

"How about this one? We'll be busier than a one-armed paper hanger."

She pursed her lips. "Why are all your metaphors amputation-based?"

"I honestly don't know," I said, shaking my head.

"Well, lost limbs aside, this is great. I've wanted to revamp the menu for a while," she said as we whispered over the crackle of the fryer. "But when you don't do the cooking, it's pretty difficult to try to change what's cooked. We'll just tell Buzz that Pete dropped all of the menus in the sink and we have to print new ones."

"There's no way Buzz is going to believe that," I said with a laugh.

"Hey, Pete," she called into the dining room. "Could you bring me that stack of menus?"

I watched in shock as Evie went to take the menus from a compliant Pete, bumped his arm, and sent the menus plopping into the dishwater with a loud splash. My mouth popped open. Pete stammered an apology.

"Oh, honey, don't worry about it. It was mostly my fault. Why don't you go serve Abner his coffee, and I'll clean this up, OK?" Clearly rattled, Pete nodded, grabbed the coffeepot, and slunk out of the kitchen. Evie looked very pleased with herself.

"I underestimate you," I told Evie.

She shrugged. "Most people do."

Eager to erase the dirty gray smear Teague had put on the Glacier for me, I threw myself into our plans for the next week. I even solemnly stood by Evie as she fed Buzz her "Pete dropped the menus" story with an alarming lack of guile.

One afternoon, fresh from Larson's Antiques, a glorified secondhand shop that specialized in the leavings of former Grundy residents who wanted to make a fast escape from town, I breezed into the saloon. I had a mile-wide smile on my face as I carefully balanced a box of glass cake plates on my hip. I'd managed to get six plates for fifty dollars and hired Sarah Larson's son, Nick, to come chop a load of firewood for me that weekend. All in all, it had been a very productive afternoon.

"Hey, Mo!" Buzz said in his best impression of Curly from *The Three Stooges*. It had taken him all of a week of knowing me to come up with that inside joke, but now that he considered himself my de facto big brother and protector, he felt free to tease me at will. Quietly pulling me aside a few days before and telling me that Teague's body had been positively identified had been some sort of bonding moment for him. Alaskan men were very strange.

Pete stepped around the bar and helped with the heavy box of leaded glass.

"Look what I found, Evie!" I said, gingerly unwrapping my purchases. "I figured we could use them to display the new desserts. None of them match, but I thought that would be sort of quirky and fun."

"Looks great, Mo." She offered a wide smile as I tied on an apron and looked over the pending orders.

"When's the big launch?" I turned to find Cooper sitting at the counter, glaring at me despite the relative calm of his voice.

"We start the new menu on Monday. What can I get for you?" I asked.

"I'm not hungry, thanks," he said. "I'll stick with coffee."

"Not hungry," Evie scoffed. "I've seen you eat five of Buzz's flapjacks and tell him to hurry up cooking the sixth."

Cooper shot Evie a warning look. She took her coffeepot and circulated among the booths.

I started to carry the stands into the kitchen before Cooper grumbled, "Settling right in, aren't you?" He didn't even look up to speak to me. Just stared down into his coffee as if he could divine my answer there.

"What is your problem?" I asked, taking another pot from the warmer when I saw that his cup was nearing empty. "I'm helping out a friend. I didn't expect to make friends here or get a job that I love, so I'd like to do what I can to pay Evie back for her kindness."

When he looked up, there were dark circles under his eyes as if he hadn't slept well in weeks. "No, you're setting Evie up for a fall. She's already started depending on you. Her business is picking up, because people want to come in and get a look at you. And when you pack up and leave, she'll suffer. But you'll be too far away, 'finding yourself' in some other place, to give a damn."

I felt like growling that if getting attacked in the alley behind my workplace didn't scare me out of town, not much would. But Cooper didn't know about that, and I didn't particularly feel like sharing with him.

My throat tight, I said softly, "Has it occurred to you that this is none of your business, and you should let Evie and me figure it out?"

"Has it occurred to you that you're never going to find whatever you're trying to find up here, contentment or fulfillment or a closer connection to the land or whatever you outsiders come up here looking for?" he growled back. "If you didn't have it in the lower forty-eight, you're not going to find it just by switching locations. You come up here in your Range Rovers and your three-hundred-dollar hiking boots and spend God knows how much setting yourself up in houses you don't need because the first time the temperature dips below zero, you figure out, 'Oh, my God, Alaska is cold!' And you whine and you complain to anyone who will listen because you can't find your favorite brand of toothpaste. Or because you have to drive four hours to get to a Starbucks. And you turn on everybody around you, treating them like shit because they're content to live in 'a little pissant town' and making them miserable until it's thawed enough for you to make tracks for the nearest airport. And you, you're worse, because you're trying so damn hard to pretend that you belong here—"

"Enough." At first, I didn't realize that raw, harsh whisper had come from me. I pursed my lips to hold back the torrent of angry, hurt responses. Because they would have been loud, possibly quite profane responses, and I didn't want to cause a scene.

"Pour your own damn coffee," I said, dropping the pot next to his cup with a clatter. "Evie, I'm going to get some air."

"Sure, sweetie." She patted my back as I ducked through the kitchen. I heard her smack Cooper's head and Cooper's sharp oath. "What did you say to her?"

I shut the staff entrance door behind me with a click and leaned against the cold brick of the alleyway. The tears I expected to come rushing out stayed settled in my chest, a heavy weight against my heart. I doubled over, braced against my knees, and rubbed at my sternum with a shaking hand.

Returning to the scene of the crime didn't really help my frame of mind. The scrape of the pavement under my shoes, the sour smell of the Dumpster, brought images bubbling back to mind. I could feel his breath on my neck, the warmth of his blood soaking my shoulder. Suddenly nauseated, I closed my eyes and took deep breaths. I thought of the sweet, heady scent of honeysuckle, the huge trucks that hauled cotton from fields every summer back home, leaving bits of snowy white in their wake.

"Evie says—"

"Gah!" I screamed, swinging out and clipping someone's jaw with my clenched fist. My eyes flew open.

I hadn't even realized I'd been making a fist, but just the tiniest part of me was happy to share *that* with Cooper.

"Jesus!" he yelped, rubbing a hand over his jaw. "What was that for?"

"You startled me!" I cried, shoving at his chest. "What the hell is wrong with you, sneaking up on someone like that?"

It was galling that I was pushing Cooper at full force and wasn't even moving him. He caught my hands with little effort and held them to his chest. The warmth that radiated from his hands soothed, which seemed to irritate me all the more. I didn't want comfort from this man. I wanted to kick him in the balls. His even warmer breath feathered over my cheeks, drawing my attention to his wide, full mouth, a scant few inches away from my face. I could taste him, the spicy musk that was Cooper, even before his lips closed over my own with a defeated groan.

Everything inside me seemed to still at the same time. I could feel with perfect clarity the soft, insistent pull of Cooper's lips against mine, the mingling of air. The cold brick wall against my back as he leaned against me, slipping his warm, rough hands under my jacket, pulling me tight against him. My hands threaded into his hair, soft and silken against my fingertips. His hands, the very fingers I'd obsessed over, were impossibly gentle as they cupped the curve of my jaw. The tip of his tongue traced the line of my lower lip, then swept tentatively across it. I sighed and wondered how it had taken us so long to get here. Why couldn't I have spent the last few months like this, wrapped in his arms, drinking in the warm, spicy scent of him?

Oh, wait. Cooper was a complete dick to me, that's why. He'd been rude, sarcastic, and hurtful, for no reason. And he didn't like me. He'd made that much clear. He was kissing me now because I was one of few available females within a hundred miles and he caught me at my weakest. He was using me to scratch an itch.

With a snarl, I raised my knee with lightning speed, right into Cooper's now-bulging zipper. I slid out of his embrace and stood panting beside him as he leaned against the wall for support while his crotch recovered.

"What the *hell*?" he grunted.

"You don't get to kiss me," I told him. Embarrassment and confusion had hot tears pricking at my eyes. "I do not mess around with men who don't even like me. Just stop screwing with my head, Cooper. Leave me alone."

Cooper took in my face, the quiver in my lip, the heaving of my chest as I fought to catch my breath.

He leaned closer, running the tip of his nose along my throat as he inhaled deeply.

Forgetting his own pain, his brows furrowed as his warm fingers brushed along the turtleneck I was wearing. He pulled the collar down, revealing the ugly yellow shadows of healing bruises. I slapped at his hands, pushing myself away from him.

"Don't pretend you give a shit," I spat. "You've made it very plain how you feel about me. It's mutual. Stay away from me, and I will sure the hell stay away from you."

"I'm sorry," he said, his face paling to an ashen gray. "I didn't know."

Cooper backed away into a shadow, the blue-green eyes trained on mine, glinting out at me. The same blue-green eyes that had shone through the dark alley, zeroed in on Teague.

Even I am ashamed of how long it took me to connect Cooper with the wolf. My brain just couldn't seem to keep pace with the information. So many little tumblers fell into place. The eyes. Cooper's living so far away from town. His frequent "hunting trips." The ridiculous amount of meat in his grocery cart.

I looked back at him, mouth gaping, breath ragged. His expression shifted moment to moment, from anger to shame to some unreadable mix of fear and relief. I pursed my lips to say something, but he darted out of the alley on soundless feet.

I leaned against the wall, sliding into a sitting position. I ran over every conversation, every exchange I'd had with Cooper. Someone in the alley kept saying, "Cooper is the wolf . . . the wolf is Cooper . . ." It took me a couple of repetitions to realize it was me.

The rational side of my brain had a hard time catching up to my rampant disbelief. I mean, it made sense on a certain level. The man had too much general pissiness to fit into one corporeal form.

I leaned against the wall, grateful for any distraction that drew me out of my panicky remembrances of the alleyway. So if werewolves were real, what was next? Ghosts? Chupacabra? Would I run into Sasquatch if I strayed too far from my cabin?

Teague's death scene took on a new character in my mind's eye. Cooper had bitten Teague, ripped into him, and made him bleed. Teague made it to his truck but was either too seriously injured or too freaked out to drive safely. Cooper had contributed to Teague's crashing into the ravine and dying a horrible death. I searched my soul and couldn't find it within me to be disgusted or frightened by that. John Teague was a bad man who did vile things to defenseless women out of no other motivation than greed. The world was better off without him. If Cooper made that happen, all I could feel was gratitude toward him . . . underneath a healthy crust of annoyance and irritation.

What exactly is the etiquette involved when one finds out that her sworn enemy is a mythical creature of the night? Should I tell someone? Start smelting silver bullets? Call animal control?

I burst out laughing as I pictured Cooper getting

tranqued and thrown into the pound. My laughter bounced around the alley, the bitter, hysterical edge of the sound grating my ears. I clapped a hand over my mouth, but I giggled again. And then again. Once I started laughing, I couldn't seem to stop. It just poured out in hoarse, racking guffaws that bent me over and had me bracing my hands against my knees.

"Werewolf!" I snickered. "I think he's a were-wolf!"

I was going to have to ask Evie where a girl could get a quick no-questions-asked prescription for anti-psychotics.

Wait, no. Knowing Evie, she would ask me what was wrong and my answer would be *I think your cousin morphs into a giant wolf at night, keeping the alleyways of Grundy safe for womankind.* There's a friendship-ending conversation.

I wiped at my eyes, lips trembling a little as one last nervous chuckle escaped. The wolf theory was probably the product of shock, hysteria, and an overdone breakfast burrito. I shook my head. Back to reality. Werewolf hallucinations aside, nothing had changed, really. Cooper didn't like me. I didn't like Cooper. If he could ignore the whole kissing-in-the-alley situation, so could I.

I wiped my sweaty palms on my jeans and walked back into the kitchen with my well-practiced calm, unaffected face on. I joked with Evie, whose brow remained furrowed and confused for the next few hours. I smiled and poured coffee. I ignored Coo-per's half-empty plate, which sat cold at the end of the bar.

7

Thundereggs and
Doughnut Etiquette

BIRTHDAYS HAD ALWAYS BEEN a weird time for me.

When I was a kid, I welcomed every birthday, as it put me one year closer to my moving out on my own. But birthdays also marked another difference for my family. Instead of celebrating with a cake (too full of poisonous refined sugars) and presents (too materialistic), my mother would come into my room at exactly 3:57 A.M. to tell me the story of my miraculous emergence into this world, as if it was some fairy tale. Although I supposed few fairy tales involved the words "vaginal flowering."

When I moved out, Mom would call me, again at 3:57, to give me the early-morning audio version. That helped me make friends with my dorm-mates. Given that I was a water birth, I supposed I should be grateful that she didn't climb in the tub and reenact it every year.

I'd never had what you'd consider a traditional birthday party. As in the case of Christmas, Hanukkah, Easter, and any other tradition celebrated by ninety-nine percent of the population, my parents just didn't see the point in birthdays. In high school, I'd had small annual celebrations with Kara and her parents. But they'd kept it low-key, in an effort not to offend my parents completely. Kara's mother would make a German chocolate cake, and we'd go to the movies. When I turned sixteen, the Reynoldses bought me a little silver charm bracelet, just like Kara's. Every year, they added a charm—a graduation cap for our senior year or a little magnolia to salute our roots. Kara had already sent me this year's charm, a silver moose to mark my move to the Great North.

The morning I turned thirty was the first time I'd missed out on one of Mom's dramatic monologues. I just wanted a nice quiet day at work. But when I walked into the saloon that morning, it was dark, which was unusual. I heard the faint sound of hurried whispering, of scuffling footsteps behind the counter. I backed away, thumping into the door, nearly dropping the morning's baking to the floor as I fumbled for the knob.

No.

No, damn it, this was my home. I was tired of crying, of being afraid. This was my place. I didn't care if I got robbed again, no one was going to send me running out of here. I quietly set my bags on a nearby pool table and picked up a cue. I rounded the corner of the lunch counter, prepared to swing for the fences when the lights flicked on and a deafening roar of "SURPRISE!" filled the room. I screamed and sent the pool cue clattering to the ground. Evie, Buzz, Pete, Walt, Nate, Gertie, Susie Q, and a few of the breakfast regulars popped up from behind the counter blowing on noisemakers.

My eyes blinked against the flood of light. I could see now that the bar was strung with pink and white streamers. Everybody was wearing silly paper hats and wide grins. There was a banner that read, "Happy 30th Birthday, Mo!" in homemade construction-paper letters. And on the counter was an obscenely large stack of doughnuts with candles stuck in them. The rush of relief, of love toward them all, squeezed at my chest.

"How did you know?" I asked, still shaking as Evie wrapped her arms around me.

"I do actually read the employment forms, you know," Evie teased as Buzz moved in for his bear hug. "The question is, why didn't you say anything?"

"I'm not a big birthday person."

"Well, get over it," she told me, holding a powdered sugar doughnut up to my lips.

"No, no, faux pas, Evie," Gertie *tsk*ed, her double chin quivering in mock disapproval. "When a girl turns thirty, she gets the chocolate doughnut. Powdered sugar is for when you turn forty."

Evie laughed and plated a chocolate doughnut with a flourish.

"That's why we keep her around," Susie informed me, strapping a big pink "Birthday Girl" hat on my head. "Her extensive knowledge of etiquette."

I laughed, dabbing at my eyes. I hadn't even realized I was crying until the first tear rolled down my cheek. I wiped at it self-consciously.

"Aw, hell, boys, we made her spring a leak," Abner cursed.

"Thank you, all of you, for this. This is the best birthday party I've ever had."

"Well, that's plain sad, honey," Walt said, shaking his head.

I expected the party to break up when the breakfast crowd started filtering in, but the new customers just joined us for doughnuts. It was a little overwhelming, the hugs and well wishes from people I'd known for such a short time. I expected to bristle at the attention, to want to run into the kitchen for some peace and quiet. But I found that I didn't feel crowded or pressured for a positive reaction. People here just wanted me to be happy, and not on terms carefully prescribed by them.

"Aw, shoot, I missed the surprise." I turned to see Alan walking through the door with a little blue gift bag.

"Sorry, Mo's an early riser," Buzz said. "You have to get out of bed pretty early and all that."

"If only . . ." Alan shot a dazzling smile my way. I rolled my eyes at the obvious joke. He slipped an arm around my waist and gave me an affectionate squeeze. I waited for the butterflies, but mostly, I felt a warm rush of affection, the same love I felt for Nate or Walt or Abner.

"Evie said no presents, but I wanted to give this to you," he said, handing me the gift bag.

"That's very sweet. You really didn't have to—" I pulled out what looked like a tiny fire extinguisher. "Wow. Alan, I don't know what to say."

"It's bear mace," he said, proudly showing me the label. "I worry about you, all alone out there at your place. The bears are coming closer and closer into town every year. I want you to carry that at all times. But don't flip the lid unless you really mean it, because that stuff stings . . . and stains."

I nodded. "That's very thoughtful," I assured him.

"A fella really has to like a girl before he'll give her pepper spray," Nate said, winking at me. He could not have been more pleased.

"Do I get to kiss the birthday girl?" Alan asked, leaning close. I could smell Scope on his breath. Obviously, he'd come prepared for this. "They say it's supposed to be good luck."

"Says who?" I asked, teasing.

"Well, I'm sure someone says it," he said, shrugging good-naturedly.

As Alan leaned in, I gave him a friendly peck on the lips. He laughed and gave me another in return, murmuring, "One to grow on."

My eyes widened as Alan leaned in and brushed his mouth over mine. He definitely knew what he was doing in the kissing department. I felt the warm, soft pulse of his mouth all the way to my toes.

"She's thirty, you know," Nate said. "That's a lot of kissing."

"I've got to get back to work at some point today," I protested in mock horror as I gave Alan a hug. His returning squeeze was warm and strong, and Lord help me, I couldn't help but lean right into it. Alan smelled of fresh minty breath and a good woodsy aftershave. I could hear his steady heartbeat against my ear and feel the warmth of his breath against my hair. I felt completely relaxed for the first time in weeks . . . so, of course, that was the moment that Cooper chose to walk through the door.

Over Alan's shoulder, I saw Cooper take in the streamers, see me straightening out of what looked like a clutch with Alan, and frown. He turned on his heel and walked back out. Despite the quick sting of hurt, I pointedly acted as if I hadn't seen him.

"You know, I was thinking that you shouldn't have to cook for yourself on your own birthday," Alan said, brushing a piece of glitter from my cheek. "I was thinking you should come over to my place tonight after work so I could make you dinner."

"Well, that's mighty neighborly of you, Ranger Dahling."

"Alan makes a mean lasagna," Nate added with a wink.

"Don't oversell it, Nate," Alan warned him. "I'll have to throw away the Stouffer's box before she comes over."

"I'm sure anything you make will be fine," I told him. "Can I bring anything?"

"Nope, just yourself. And maybe wear the hat. It's pretty damn cute."

"I can't just not bring something for my host. It's practically against my religion."

Nate and Alan gave me skeptical looks.

"Southern counts as a religion," I insisted.

The party eventually broke up when some tourists came in looking for steak and eggs. Susie and Gertie tried to get me to wear my birthday hat all day, saying it would help our health-code rating if my hair was covered. I politely declined.

That afternoon, close to the end of my shift, there was a little white gift box on the bar. Inside was a spherical lump of rock about the size of a baseball. I thought it was a practical joke, until Evie, a wide grin on her face, grabbed the tool kit out of the utility room and took me out to the alley. Using an awl and a hammer, she carefully tapped at the top of the rock.

"Evie, what are you—"

"Shh. I'm concentrating," she said, chewing her lip. "I haven't done this in a couple of years."

With one final ringing tap, the rock split open. Even in the dim light of the alley, I could make out the glimmer of milky crystal surrounded by dark slate-colored agate.

"It's a thunderegg," Evie said, her eyes twinkling. "The ancients believed that when the thunder spirits in the mountains were angry, they'd chuck these things at one another. It takes just the right geological conditions to make them, and they're pretty rare, even around here."

Thanks to my hippie parents, I'd seen a lot of crystals and geodes in my day but nothing compared to this. The patterns, the dance of light across even the rough slice, were hypnotic. "But why would someone leave one on the bar? As a tip?"

"It's for you, for your birthday."

I rolled my eyes. "Evie, it could be for anyone. Some tourist could have just left it there by accident."

"Do you see anyone else turning thirty around here?"

"OK, if it's for my birthday, who's it from? Why didn't they leave a card?" I asked.

"Sometimes the gift is message enough," she said in her "wise" tone. "Fine, I saw him drop it off. I think someone feels a little guilty over how he's treated you."

"Cooper? But he—he—"

He howls at the moon and murders defenseless elk.

"He doesn't like me," I finished lamely.

"Aw, honey, he's been nicer to you than he is to most of the locals. Sometimes a man just has to pull your pigtails a few times before he can deign to admit that he likes you. Honestly, I don't know why we put up with any of them. You just wait and see. He's coming around."

"I don't see how not insulting me or openly sneering at me for a few days can be considered being nice to me." I snorted weakly. I looked down at my watch. I was supposed to be at Alan's house in an hour. "Crap. I've got a date."

"Well, that's the right attitude to head into a date with," she said, smirking.

"Alan's fixing me dinner."

Evie sighed. Loudly.

"What?"

"Mo, it's not that I don't like Alan. I love him to death, but he's not right for you. You need a challenge . . . like, say, my idiot cousin, who apparently doesn't know about signing gift cards so he can get credit for what is clearly a romantic gesture. A weak and somewhat backward romantic gesture, but—"

"Evie," I huffed in a warning tone.

"Cooper needs someone who won't put up with his surly crap, someone who will sift through all that and find the great guy he used to be. And you, you need someone who's going to make you work a little bit. And Cooper will make you work like a dog just to get him to ask you out."

"Well, you make it sound so appealing," I muttered. "And what do you mean, the great guy he used to be?"

She preened. "I have you intrigued now, don't I?"

I glared at her.

"Look, I've watched you every day since you moved here. You don't trust anything that comes to you too easily. And Alan is the definition of easygoing. Anything you have with him will be doomed from the start."

"It will be now that you've put your evil date voodoo on it. Jesus, Evie!" I pushed to my feet and shoved the thunderegg back into the gift box.

"OK, 'doomed from the start' was probably going a bit too far," she said, following me to my truck. "I just think you need to be careful how you handle this."

"I will be." I slid into Lucille's driver's seat, rolled my window down, and started the ignition, all the while glaring at her. "If I go into your office and find an Alan doll with pins stuck in its crotch, I will be super-pissed."

I drove at highly illegal speeds to get home. I put the thunderegg on my mantel, rushed into the shower, and spent fifteen minutes scrubbing Eau de Blue Plate Special from my general person. And then another fifteen debating among the few nicer outfits I'd brought with me. I was torn between a sweater and jeans and a low-cut red party dress, which was a little too much for a dinner in.

I settled on jeans and a sky-blue silk blouse that brought out the color of my eyes, a birthday gift from Kara the previous year. With her in mind, I put on my silver charm bracelet as I thumbed through my bathroom drawer searching for my eye-liner, which I hadn't used since I moved. Overall, the effect was quite nice, considering I'd been assembling tuna melts only an hour before.

I managed to slide into Alan's driveway two minutes early, which I figured was polite but not desperate. And because I was physically incapable of not bringing some sort of hospitality offering with me, I presented Alan with a batch of chocolate chess squares when he opened the door.

"I told you, just bring yourself," he said, feigning a stern tone. I fought against the giggle forming in response to the little plaid apron he was wearing over shirt and jeans. He said, "I have dessert covered."

Just then, the loud screeching of a smoke alarm sounded over Alan's shoulder. As he turned, I could see smoke billowing from the kitchen. Alan paled. "Oh, shit."

I chuckled. "Would that be the dessert you have covered?"

Alan dashed into the inferno and came back with what appeared to be a large charcoal briquette. I assumed that at one point, it was a pan of brownies. Alan chewed his lip. "You know, with enough icing, it might not be half bad."

"Alan, take the chess squares, and stop being stubborn."

"Thank God, my hands are freaking burning!" he yowled, ending his manly acceptance of second-degree burns by tossing the burning lump into the bushes.

"Don't you want to salvage the pan or something?" I asked as he ushered me into the house.

"Nah, I'll get it later. The stench will keep the bears away."

"Nice," I said, snickering as he led me into the great room, a combination dining room, living room, and office. In the corner, I could see a radio, several maps on the walls, a huge first-aid kit, all of the equipment you'd expect a forest ranger to need on hand. But the rest of the house was all Alan, exactly how you'd expect a single man living in the woods to decorate his home. We're talking a lot of plaid and hunting trophies. But it was clean and tidy. There was a comfortable little blaze going in the big stone fireplace and a pretty pine rocker next to the hearth. The table was set with dishes that matched and wine glasses that didn't. There was a basketball-sized bunch of blue petals blooming from an old crockery pitcher on the table. And the smell of slightly singed brownie filled the house.

"Forget-me-nots?" I asked, rubbing my fingers against the tiny, velvety blue petals. He nodded. "That's very sweet."

Alan shrugged. "Well, it sounds nicer than eating by a bouquet of wooly lousewart."

I considered that for a moment. "That it does."

"I wasn't kidding about the Stouffer's box. Tonight's menu consists of bagged salad and frozen lasagna. I don't cook for myself much, which is why I come to the saloon for most of my meals. Well, it's not the only reason," he said, winking at me. "The company isn't bad."

"Yes, Abner, Buzz, and Leonard are charming," I conceded. "I appreciate not having to cook. I'm sure anything you serve will be great . . . with the obvious exception of the brownies. Can I help with anything?"

"Nope, you just sit, and I'll get everything on the table." I climbed up onto a bar stool near his kitchen counter, watching as he got dinner on the table with all the agility of a wounded moose. I would have offered to help, but I figured it was a point of pride for him. All I could do was watch, cringe, and try to make polite chitchat. As we ate, we talked about his job, his huge family back in Montana, how he had adjusted to life in Alaska.

"It really wasn't that different from home," he said as he tried to dish a third square of lasagna onto my plate. Stuffed beyond capacity, I waved it off as I poured both of us healthy glasses of red wine. "The same kind of weather. The same kind of rough living. I missed my family a lot at first. I'm the only one of seven kids to have moved off the ranch. Everybody else married and set up house right there with my parents in a sort of complex of those prefab houses. I told my dad if they added too many more, they'd end up on the news like those weird polygamist groups."

I choked on my wine.

"You have to move on and be your own person eventually, you know?" he said, sipping thoughtfully. "It's not that I don't love them all like crazy, but sometimes . . . I don't know, sometimes I wished I was an only child, just so I could finish a sentence, finish a meal without some dramatic announcement, get through a holiday without wanting to throw a turkey leg at someone's head and yell, 'Nobody cares what you think about the next election!' "

"Well, I'm an only child, and I couldn't do any of those things, either, if it makes you feel any better," I told him as we moved over to the big, comfy brown corduroy couch. "Except for the turkey legs. My parents are vegetarian. I had to throw brown rice."

"Hmm. The grass isn't greener. Nope, that doesn't make me feel better at all. You're destroying my childhood fantasies here."

"My childhood fantasies involved vaccinations and parents who didn't see the PTA as some sort of conformist conspiracy. By my calculations, you *lived* my childhood fantasy."

"Hippies, huh?" he asked, his face suddenly sympathetic.

"The hippiest."

"We get a couple of those up here every year, wanting to build a cabin in the preserve and live off the land Thoreau-style. Generally, I end up rescuing them off the top of a bluff because they didn't spend enough time researching or preparing for life up here. They don't plan for the right kind of gear, clothes, food, shelter. They go toddling off half-assed and end up getting hurt."

"Is that what you think I did?" I asked.

"No!" he exclaimed, squeezing my hand. "You've got more common sense than most locals, Mo."

Clearly, Buzz hadn't told him about my tendency to get cornered by wolves and serial waitress robbers.

Alan moved in closer, and I could smell Irish Spring soap, wine, and the homey warmth of pre-packaged tomato sauce. "I think you're fitting in just right."

Alan was a first-rate kisser, right up there with Jeff Moser, my date to the senior formal and claimer of my virginity. Alan covered all the bases. Soft, increasingly insistent brushes of his lips against mine. Cupping my chin in his hand and running his fingers along my jaw. Pulling me close enough to show me how much he wanted me without making me feel as if he was grinding against me.

I could have gone on kissing Alan all night. It was certainly a more pleasant way to spend the evening than my solo birthday plans, which centered around Sno Balls and *Sixteen Candles*. But when Alan's hands moved to the buttons of my shirt, I stopped him, tilting my forehead to rest against his. I just wasn't ready for this yet. Alan was a sweet guy, but there were no guarantees that having sex with him wouldn't turn out to be a huge mistake I would have to cringe over every time he came into the saloon for the next six months. I liked Alan. I wanted more time with him and a lot more kissing. But I couldn't help but feel that we were falling into this just a little too easily.

God damn it, Evie.

I would spend the rest of my evening in a cold shower, contemplating whether it was a worse punishment to give her a kick in the butt or deny her chess squares for the next week.

I groaned and buried my face in the crook of Alan's neck. "I'm sorry. I think I should get going."

"Too fast?" he asked, grimacing.

"I'm not saying never, just not tonight," I told him. "I don't want to rush into anything."

"Neither do I," he assured me, kissing my cheeks. "As long as we get there eventually."

"Maybe we can do this again sometime?" I suggested. "I'll cook."

"I knew it. Dinner was below your culinary standards." He shook his head in mock shame.

"Hey." I kissed him again. "You did your best."

"I bow to the master," he said, pulling me to my feet.

"Don't you forget it."

"I'm sorry it took me so long to ask you out," he said, sliding my coat onto my shoulders. His long fingers tucked the collar under my chin and remained there for a few seconds, warming the skin and making me smile. "You just seem, well, cautious. And you seemed to be getting so much attention straight off when you got to town, I didn't want to spook you."

"I can appreciate that," I told him. "And you don't spook me. In fact, nonspookiness is one of your better qualities."

Considering his biggest competition at the moment was a werewolf, I felt that was a fair statement.

Alan snickered. "Well, something has to balance out the bad cooking."

Alan walked me to my truck, gave me a knee-buckling kiss good night, and asked me to call him when I got home safely. Sweetest. Guy. Ever.

I pulled into my driveway, glad that I'd remembered to turn on my porch lights. The night was clear and bright, but I felt better being able to see whatever or whoever might be lurking near my doorstep. Humming a silly country tune, I hopped out of Lucille and paused to pick my house key out of the jumble of metal on my key ring.

"Why do I have so many keys?" I wondered aloud.

The moment I stopped moving, I felt it, a familiar presence over my shoulder on the east side of the little clearing that surrounded my house. I turned to see the black wolf standing there, just staring at me, his blue-green eyes burning eerily in the reflected light of the waxing moon. I took an instinctual step toward the door, but I dropped my keys. I crouched down to pick them up, keeping an eye on my visitor to see whether he moved when I was a smaller, more vulnerable target. He simply sat on his rear haunches, watching me with his head tilted at a quizzical angle, as if he was saying, *Come on, hurry up, you're the last stop on my security detail, and then I can take off and chase rabbits for the rest of the night.*

I slipped my key into the door and pushed it open, turning toward the wolf to—I don't know, say good night? But he was gone. The branches where he'd been standing weren't even stirring. I scanned the rest of the yard. Nothing.

Had I imagined the whole thing? Was I going through some sort of delayed PTSD reaction? What if the wolf never existed? What if my subconscious just made up my canine companion to protect me from memories of killing Teague, dumping his body, and setting his truck on fire to cover up my crime? I mean, I'd never shown previous signs of multiple-personality disorder, but that sort of thing could develop under extreme duress, right?

These were not the ponderings of an emotionally well-adjusted person.

Oddly enough, though, this didn't even rank on my "top five weirdest ways I've wrapped up my birthday" list.

DESPITE EVIE'S CLAIMS that Cooper would be "coming around," he pointedly avoided coming into the saloon, even though I saw him walking right past the window sometimes. I didn't know how to feel about that. I felt guilty, because Cooper was changing his schedule and missing time with his friends because he wanted to stay away from me. I was annoyed with myself for assuming that his issue was with me, annoyed with myself for caring either way. And then I was back to guilty. It was a vicious cycle.

Fortunately, I was distracted by a whole new kind of annoyance. A week after my birthday, Susie Q came into the saloon with a smug Cheshire cat's grin and told me there was a package waiting for me at the post office.

I told her it couldn't be mine. I'd already received my birthday package from Kara. No one else would send me anything here.

"Well, it's a pretty big box," Susie said slyly. "It took me a while to figure out it was for you. There was no address, just sent to the post office in care of the postmaster, Grundy, Alaska. And then I saw the name on the label. It confused me for a little bit, too, but you are the only Wenstein in town." Finally at her point, Susie grinned. "Mo is a clever nickname. I never would have guessed your full name is Moon—"

"Shh!" I cried, pressing my hand to her mouth before anyone at the counter overheard. Susie snickered against my fingers. My full name has been a thorn in my side since the day I started public school. The stunned gasp following my announcement at my high school graduation stalled the ceremony for a full three minutes.

Sure, I could legally change it, but my parents effectively kept me "off the grid" until my late teens. I'd barely gotten my social security number in time to apply for college. The idea of erasing what little personal history I had because my parents were unapologetic hippies was just irritating. So I carefully guarded all personal information and forms and suffered through. I really didn't want to do that in Grundy.

"Sorry," I said, snatching my hand away from her face.

"Oh, I think it's a lovely name," Susie said, teasing. "Very unique."

"What do you want?" I asked, my eyes narrowed. "How do I buy your silence?"

"A dozen of those chocolate chess squares ought to do it," she said, nodding at the glass-domed dish.

I wrapped them carefully. "On the house," I told her. And by the house, I meant me.

"Pleasure doing business with you, Moon—"

"Shh-shh!" I spluttered, making a "zip it" motion with my hands.

Susie snickered and hopped off her stool. "You can pick up your package anytime before three."

"What was that all about?" Evie asked as I gave a departing Susie the stink eye.

"Nothing," I grumbled.

There was only one person who would address a package to me using my full name. My mother.

I left the package sitting at the post office for three days while I stewed and did some compulsive baking. I finally picked it up out of morbid curiosity and a desire to keep Susie from claiming the package was abandoned, opening it, and finding whatever humiliating thing my mother had sent.

"Are you going to open it?" Susie asked, her curiosity evident as she helped me heft the box to my truck.

"When I get home," I said. "Did you enjoy the chess squares?"

"I took the lot of them down to the Cut and Curl," she said, grinning. "They were a big hit. Gertie Gogan asked what I'd done to merit a full dozen, and I told her I was just helping out a friend." Susie looked mildly embarrassed now. "Of course, some of the ladies down at the beauty shop hadn't been into the Glacier since you and Evie made all those changes. They hadn't heard of you yet. So Gertie and I told them all about you, about you being a transfer and all . . . and then somehow, yourfullnameslippedout."

Honestly, first Kara's mom spills her guts, and now Susie. Didn't I know any discreet people?

I shrieked. "Susie! I thought we had a deal!"

"It just happened!" she squealed. "It was all that chocolate. I wasn't thinking straight."

"Well, you are cut off. No chess-square privileges for a month."

"But Mo!"

"A month!" I repeated, climbing into my truck. I rolled down my window. "I'll sell you the lemon bars, but that's it!"

Her nose wrinkled in distaste. "But I hate the lemon bars!"

"I know!" I called, rolling my eyes as I drove away.

In the safety of my cabin, with the shades drawn, I opened the box from my mother. Inside I found a very long letter, which I didn't read, a copy of *The Jungle* by Upton Sinclair, *Fast Food Nation*, a cookbook called *The Vegan's Journey*, and a lavishly decorated photo album, filled with pictures of me and my parents in happier times. There was four-year-old me having my face painted by Lutha, a "body artist" who lived at the commune for a few months. Six-year-old me sitting on my father's shoulders when we saw Jerry Garcia in concert. Nine-year-old me standing with my mother in front of the Mississippi Supreme Court with signs that read, "Save our future!" The sad thing was, I couldn't tell what we were protesting.

At the bottom of the box, her famous sugar-free honey-oat cookies, a carton of wheat germ, Sun Life Colon Health Fiber Biscuits, and Sun Life Colon Health Fiber supplements with a detailed pamphlet about caring for my digestive tract.

My mother had spent one hundred dollars on shipping to send me cookies, antimeat propaganda, and laxatives.

8

The 100-Yard Naked Dash of Shame

It was Saturday night, and I was content to sit home sifting through the old photo album with a mug of hot chocolate.

I didn't have to spend Saturday night alone. Alan had called, offering to take me to the movies in Dearly. Somehow a four-hour round-trip seemed like an awful lot of effort for the Kevin Costner movie he wanted to see. Or, really, any Kevin Costner movie. But our plans were canceled when Alan was called out to a trail on the preserve where a large black wolf had been spotted by some campers. We made tentative plans for dinner the next weekend, he wished me sweet dreams, and I returned to my childhood pictures.

I'd found myself pulling the album out more and more often lately, even though I knew that's what my mother intended. It made me happy to see that little dark-headed girl and the adoring looks she gave her parents. It gave me some hope for the future.

Of course, this renewed affection for Ash and Saffron was tempered by the fact that my full name was still spreading around town like a virus. But so far, most of the snickers had been covered by polite coughing. Well, Lynette made some snarky comments about Deadheads and pot smoking, but mostly, there was just snickering. Walt even patted my hand as I poured him coffee the other morning and confessed that his first name was Marion. Just like the rest of me, my hippie-dippy birth name had been accepted in Grundy.

Through with reminiscing for the evening, I popped a Duffy CD into the stereo and picked up *Walden*. It seemed an appropriate selection. I'd just read the opening paragraph when I heard a thumping, dragging noise on my porch.

My blood ran cold, an unpleasant watery sensation that made my legs tremble. Yet some stupid, potentially fatal curiosity had me moving toward the door, even as my brain screamed at me to run in the opposite direction. This was the kind of noise that the blond, barely clad starlet heard just before the mask-wearing psychopath burst into her isolated cabin and turned her skin into some sort of household furnishing.

I crept to my window and peeked out. I saw a flash of bare golden skin. Whoever it was seemed to be breaking into my house in the nude.

A low, hoarse voice from outside the door whispered, "Please help."

Whoever was out there was injured. The pain was apparent, even in his voice. Then again, I'd read about Ted Bundy putting a fake cast on his arm to elicit sympathy from his victims . . . *Gwa-thunk*. I looked out again to see that my nighttime visitor had slumped in front of my door. I opened it and was presented with an ass in the air. Even in my shock, I had to admit it was a very nice ass.

I glanced down to see that he had a bear trap clamped around his ankle. The cruel metal teeth were digging into his flesh, oozing blood in a way that made my stomach turn. "Oh, my God. I'll call nine-one-one."

"No doctors," he mumbled, rolling toward me.

"Cooper? What the—" My eyes narrowed. Was this a trick? An elaborate scheme to chase me out of town or lure me out of the house so his werewolf fangs could silence me for good? I didn't think Cooper could fake the greenish pallor to his face or the hideous trap-related wounds. But if the guy was a werewolf, anything was possible. If I was smart, I would tell him to stop bleeding on my porch and hike his injured, unclothed butt into town.

Cooper panted. "Please, you can help. Tools?"

Gah. I couldn't believe it was taking me so long to respond. Yes, he was a jerk, but he was a human being . . . ish. And he had saved me from a violent trucker. I at least owed him basic first aid.

I ran for the Craftsman tool chest I kept in my kitchen. Everything in the kit was brand new. I hoped that was enough to stave off infection, because I didn't think I had time to sterilize. I dragged the heavy plastic box to the living room, where Cooper was curled in front of my fireplace.

"No doctors," he repeated, his face now an icky blue-gray. "I'll be fine by morning. Just let me stay here, OK? And no matter what you see, just don't be afraid."

My eyes locked with his, and I found that I believed him. Even with all of the horrible, dangerous implications, I trusted him.

"Deep breaths," I told him.

My glasses slipped down my nose as I used the pliers to depress a spoon-shaped metal lever of the trap, while I held down a corresponding lever on the other side of the foothold. The jaws slowly relaxed, allowing Cooper's limp leg to slide out. He whimpered as his foot dropped to the floor.

"Thank you," he whispered before letting unconsciousness claim him.

At those words, the trap slipped out of my hands and clanged loudly on the floor. I winced, my eyes flitting to his face, which was still lax and peaceful.

How on earth had he been able to get through the woods with this thing clamped on his leg? Was he a victim of some sort of weird *Saw* copycat? Or did he poach animals in the nude, some weird wolf thing? Was that why he didn't want me to call for an ambulance? He didn't want to answer rangers' questions?

If my mother had been there, she'd have made a tincture of yarrow and applied a poultice to the wounds. She would have sprinkled cayenne over his abrasions and chanted to the western winds. I, on the other hand, put my faith in a higher power: Neosporin. I went to the kitchen for my first-aid kit. I grabbed the peroxide and ran back into the living room. Even when I poured the bubbling mixture over his ravaged skin, he didn't wake up. The wounds didn't seem as bad after I cleaned them. The edges seemed smoother, shinier. I turned my head to reach for bandages and saw that the wounds had shrunk. The surrounding skin was a healthy pink. I packed the punctures with antibiotic ointment and wound gauze around his leg.

I threw a quilt over Cooper and another two logs onto the fire. I sank to the couch and wondered what exactly you did in a situation like this. I was overwhelmed with the compulsion to boil water. For what I had no idea, but in the movies, when someone is injured in the wilderness, they're always boiling water.

I tilted my head, watching the firelight play on Cooper's skin. I don't think I'd ever really grasped how huge he was—long, rangy arms and well-muscled legs that stretched well beyond the limits of the blanket. His feet were long, narrow, and highly arched; the pads were dirty and covered with shallow, healing scrapes.

In all of the injury hubbub, I hadn't had the acuity to look at his . . . lower forty-eight. How wrong would it be for me to lift the quilt? I mean, technically, he did owe me his life. And if he had an incredibly small penis, it might explain why he was such an ass all the time. Watching his face, I lifted the blanket and snuck a peek.

Wow.

"There goes that theory," I muttered.

Cooper shivered and stirred as the cooler air seeped under the blanket. He whimpered, curling his body protectively around his leg. Blushing, I tucked the quilt around his body.

If I were smart, I would call Evie or even Alan right now. But something about this Cooper, the vulnerable, honest Cooper, made me want to protect him. Or at least find out what the hell he was doing. There had to be a compelling reason for him to be running around outside my house naked with a bear trap on his leg. Even with the odd assortment of characters I'd met in Grundy, even when you factored in the werewolf issue, that was the sort of thing that merited attention.

I coiled in the corner of my couch and pulled the quilt up to my chin. I closed my eyes, enjoying the way the lights danced behind my eyelids. I dreamed of running. I was racing through the woods. My feet were bare, slapping against the blanket of pine needles on the ground. A living canopy laced over my head as my legs stretched in front of me. I expected the leaves, the low-hanging pine branches, to slap and sting, but they were caressing fingers, welcoming me to come deeper into the forest. I wasn't afraid. There was something waiting for me deep within the dense gathering of trees. Something I needed.

When I woke, there was a large black wolf curled up on my rug. I shrieked, springing up from the couch. I scrambled over the back and landed with a thump.

Ow.

For the briefest second, I thought I was going insane. Or that my mom had slipped peyote into her honey-oat cookies. Really, either option was possible.

"It's true," I whispered. "Holy shit! It's true?"

The wolf lifted his head and looked up at me. I tensed and wished I had thought to grab the fireplace poker. I wasn't frequently confronted with fairy-tale stock characters. I didn't know what to expect.

Cooper had told me, no matter what I saw, not to be afraid, that he wouldn't hurt me. So I stood slowly. The wolf yawned and lowered his head to rest on his paws. He didn't look vicious. He looked tired. His eyebrows quirked up with interest as I moved toward him. I tentatively held out my hand, fingers tucked in, so if he snapped at me, I could keep them. I stroked my knuckles behind his ears.

He closed his eyes and leaned into my hand. He opened his huge jaws, and a flash of panic zipped along my spine. I had miscalculated. He was going to kill me. I wondered if I would even have time to back away before he lunged for my throat. I waited for the strike. I opened my squinched eyes to find him watching me, as if to say, *And why did you stop the scratching?*

I froze, keeping absolutely still as the wolf leaned forward and ran his nose from just behind my ear to the hollow of my throat. I held my breath. Kara was right. No good can come of living with the wolves. The wolf gave me a sloppy, warm lick across my neck.

"Yech." I shuddered, giggling despite myself. "Cooper spit."

As he was not interested in mauling me, wolf-Cooper yawned again and went back to sleep. I sank to my knees and stared at the animal. How could this be possible? How could people not know about this? How, in this age of video phones and Facebook and blogging about your breakfast habits, could there be people out there in the world who could turn into wolves and not tell anyone about it?

Tentatively, I edged my hand toward his fur. I wasn't familiar with wolves; I couldn't even remember seeing one when my parents protested at the San Diego Zoo. I sank into a corner of the couch and spent the rest of the night just watching him sleep. I figured I wouldn't have another opportunity to baby-sit a werewolf, so I should make the most of it.

Around sunrise, the wolf raised his head and yawned loudly. He shook his way to his feet and stretched. There was a shimmer of golden light along Cooper's fur, a ripple of air, and there sat the surly, taciturn hunting guide I'd come to loathe. I preferred the giant wolf. Sure, canine Cooper might lunge for my throat, but at least he couldn't talk. Cooper draped the quilt over his bare lap, trying and failing to maintain his dignity while surrounded by a pink chintz double-wedding-ring pattern. I used his moment of awkward silence to smirk and admire.

Cooper seemed a little startled when his eyes focused on me, as if he'd forgotten I was in the room. I would have said he looked sheepish, but that seemed like an inappropriate word to apply to a wolf.

I wanted to say something, but seriously, what do you say in a situation like this? *Hey, nice tail?* And even if I found something to say, would he understand me? Was there a wolf-to-human dictionary?

There was a flash of light, a warm golden glow that rippled along the wolf's form. And just like that, the wolf was gone. Cooper was sitting there, wrapping the quilt around his waist, his lips pressed into a mortified line.

"There is no wolf. This was all just a dream," he said in a deep, resonant, Obi-Wan Kenobi voice, and waved his hand in front of my face as if to project his Jedi mind trick. My eyes narrowed at him. He shrugged. "It was worth a shot."

I crossed my arms over my chest and arched an eyebrow at him. "You showed up, seriously wounded, on my doorstep. Naked. I didn't call doctors or the police, even after you turned into a *wolf*. I'd say you owe me an explanation."

"Er, I'm a werewolf."

I nodded, lips pursed. "That I gathered."

"Trust me, I didn't want—that is, I wouldn't have come here if I could have helped it. I was, you know, a wolf, and I stepped in that damn trap, and yours was the closest house. I didn't know what else to do." He cleared his throat again. "So . . . I would appreciate it if you wouldn't tell anybody about this."

"Who would believe me?" I rolled my eyes.

"Good point."

"But I want you to say it," I said, pushing up from

the couch. My limbs were sore from camping there all night. And I was wearing bloodstained flannel pajamas imprinted with little purple daisies. But nothing could have stopped me from crossing the room and poking my finger dangerously near Cooper's bare chest.

"Say what?" he asked, the friendly tone thinning into a more familiar, hostile tenor.

"I want you to admit that I saved your ass. I didn't faint at the sight of blood or run away screaming when you turned into a giant wolf in my living room. I stuck. I did what needed to be done. I. Saved. You." I accentuated each of the last three words with a jab of my finger against Cooper's sternum. I pulled my hand away fast, fingertip tingling from the contact with his warm, smooth skin.

"So?"

"So I think someone owes someone here an apology."

He grimaced. "I thought I owed you an explanation."

"The explanation was just a down payment. Say it. Say, 'Mo, I was wrong. I'm sorry. You're not a weak, pathetic outsider.' "

"You are not a weak, pathetic outsider," he said without any enthusiasm.

That was probably the best I was going to get.

"Thank you."

"This doesn't make us friends, you know," he said, peering up sulkily through the dark hair that had fallen over his brow.

"I don't want to be your friend," I assured him.

"You're still pretty much a jerk as far as I'm concerned. Now I know that you're a jerk who turns into a wolf. Not much has changed."

"Good. I'll just be on my way." Cooper stood, dropping the quilt. He smirked when my eyes wandered south, even when I tried not to look.

Dang it.

Clearly, I had been alone in this cabin for too long. I needed male companionship in the worst way. But not from Cooper, I reminded my racing hormones. I'd done the revenge-sex thing and the strictly-due-to-great-chemistry sex thing with equally satisfying results. But Cooper and his Mighty Morphin Power Penis were absolutely off limits. I did not sleep with people who openly disliked me.

"I have questions for you," I told him. "Lots of them."

"About the wolf thing?"

"No, I was hoping you'd give me your opinions about global warming," I retorted. "Yes, the wolf thing! How is this possible? Were you bitten by a werewolf? Does Evie know about this? What were you doing so close to my house—mmph!"

Cooper was across the room before I could blink. His hands tangled into my hair, yanking my lips toward his. It wasn't so much a kiss as his attempt to stop my mouth from moving. I squealed in protest, shoving at his bare shoulders, but his hands held my face in place as he seemed to steal the air from my lungs. His thumbs ran along my jawline, and his mouth relaxed into a slow, dragging rhythm against mine. The hands that were supposed to be shoving him away slipped around his shoulders and pulled him closer. His teeth nipped at my bottom lip. He took advantage of my soft little gasp by sliding his tongue into my mouth. His hands slid down to my hips and pulled me tighter against him.

I didn't care if he was surly. I didn't care if he was supernaturally gifted. I wanted him. I could deal with the rest. I let loose a happy moan, and something in Cooper seemed to grind to a halt. By degrees, he pulled away, loosened his hold. The man who had just claimed my mouth was replaced by Cooper's hardened, smirking face.

He stepped away. "Kissing shuts you up. I'll have to remember that."

Bastard. Furry werewolf bastard.

I gasped and reached for a handy blunt object to toss his way. Cooper sauntered over to the front door and jerked the handle. I could see that he was about to make one of his patented, oh-so-clever parting remarks, so I beat him to the punch.

"You're still naked!" I called, smiling nastily. "It's cold outside. Expect shrinkage."

"Gah!" He grunted, phased back into his wolf form, and ran out of sight.

2

Bears: Not as Friendly as the Honey Packaging Would Have You Believe

AFTER COOPER DID THE naked dash of shame, I went to work as if nothing had happened. I figured it was my best defense against an appointment in a rubber room.

Well, I didn't pull total nonchalance. Every time the door opened, I looked up, expecting Cooper to walk in, which was stupid, because what on earth would I say to him? Could I possibly behave as if, one, I hadn't seen him naked, and two, I hadn't seen him covered in a black fur coat? I poured two cups' worth of coffee into poor Alan's lap because I was too distracted to aim for his mug. When I knocked a stack of dishes off the counter with a loud, crashing rattle, Evie made me take a break.

I leaned against the wall of the alley, calculating how much I should offer Evie to replace the broken dishes. She popped out of the kitchen entrance and offered me a bottle of water. "You OK, Mo? You seem kind of hyper."

I took a deep breath and tried to compose a believable lie in my head. Hot date, too much caffeine, chain-store shopping withdrawal. But then I saw a flicker of recognition on Evie's even features. Her face wasn't in its natural warm state. It was a polite, detached mask.

Evie was in on it.

"You know, don't you?" I said, my eyes narrowing.

"Know what?" she asked, her tone far too guileless to be genuine.

"You know what Cooper is, about his extracurricular nighttime activities."

Evie started to shake her head, her lips parting to start her denials, but then she sighed. "Yes. How did you find out?"

"Figured it out a while ago. And then last night, there was a thing with a bear trap."

"Bear trap!"

"Cooper's fine now, I promise. Can you . . ." I lifted my brow as I let the question hang in the air between us.

"Wiggle my eyebrows?" she asked. I think at this point, she was still hedging against the possibility that we weren't talking about the same thing.

"No! Can you turn into a wolf?" I asked.

Evie laughed, and her shoulders loosened, as if they had shrugged off some heavy weight. "No one in my branch of the family can. We're what the pack calls a dead line."

"Ouch. Wait. You knew about this, and you still tried to set me up with him?"

"Well, it's not like he's going to huff and puff and blow your house down," Evie said, glaring at me. "Cooper was one of the first kids in his generation to become a wolf. Everybody in his line has been able to change. It's sort of a big deal. Every generation produces a pack. Every pack has a leader. It's the natural order of things. Cooper was supposed to be his generation's alpha, the leader. Everyone could tell the minute he first phased. He was the fastest, the strongest. But he chose to leave the packlands, the valley where my family lives, and move a hundred miles away to Grundy. For a werewolf, that's one of the most difficult things you can do. Even moving this far away was devastating for him."

"Why? Why is leaving so hard?"

Evie took a pull off my bottle of water and shrugged. "Centuries of instinct. A wolf's brain is hard-wired to protect a certain area of land, to hunt there, to live there. And that's the way it's been for the pack for almost a thousand years. Everything in Cooper's body is telling him to return home. Imagine fighting against that kind of draw, every waking moment of every day. You'd be kind of cranky, too."

"But why did he leave?"

Evie pressed her lips together. "That's pack business," she said, shrugging. "My line is dead. I don't change. Anything important that happens while the pack is in wolf form stays within the pack."

"But that's so . . . exclusive. Why would they cut off a whole section of their community just because they aren't part of their special wolf club?"

"It's nothing personal," Evie said, and she seemed shocked that I was so put out about it. "And they are friendly and loving and open. They love us dead-liners just as much as we love them. But they handle some pretty serious stuff for the village. The fewer people who know about it, the better. They don't talk about it with us. When Cooper left, all we were told was that the village had been put in danger and that Cooper defended us all. They said he was hurt, taking some time to recover. But then, a few months later, I saw him here in Grundy, and he was fine—physically, anyway. Before, he was always so lively, funny, a lot like our cousin Samson. He wasn't the same man anymore. He wouldn't talk about going home, the pack, or the family. He went out of his way to avoid making friends. Hell, I was surprised he talked to me. It was months before anyone in the family admitted that he might not be coming back. If you really want to know, you should ask him."

"Oh, yeah, that's likely." I snorted. "Does Buzz know about this whole wolf thing?"

"It wasn't really something I could work into our dating conversations," she said, smiling as she shook her head.

"But if he didn't know, why did he get so wound up over not telling the police about the wolf attacking Teague?"

Evie gave me a sheepish little smile. "He thought maybe you imagined the wolf. He didn't want that to get around. This is a small town. You don't want to become known as Crazy Mo."

"I knew it!" I exclaimed. "I knew he didn't believe me."

Evie shook her head at my incensed tone. "Mo, my family, the pack, we don't tell outsiders our secret. For Cooper to have trusted you with this, it means something."

We pushed our way back through the kitchen entrance. I sighed. "Evie, don't start—"

I stopped short when I saw Buzz, Abner, Walt, Nate, and Gertie gathered around the counter, looking stricken. Nate's arm was around Gertie. Gertie was wiping tears from her face, leaving streaks of mascara on her round china-doll cheeks. Walt looked as if he wanted either to cry or to punch something.

"What's wrong?" I asked Buzz.

Buzz squeezed Evie's hand. "There was an attack, out at Susie Q's place. Gertie found her in her driveway this morning. Susie's pretty messed up. Her throat's practically torn out. If Gertie hadn't come along when she did . . ." He cast a sidelong glance at Gertie, who let loose a little sob. "The ambulance took her to the hospital in Dearly. She's in intensive care."

I pulled Buzz and Evie aside, my voice low. "Did someone beat her up?"

"No," Buzz said, his jaw clenched. "This wasn't a person, Mo. It was an animal. There were tracks everywhere and some fur. It looks like Susie was attacked by a wolf."

My stomach flipped. How could it be a coincidence that the morning after Cooper went on a "wolf run," Susie was found bleeding and bitten in her driveway? Honestly, how many giant wolves could there be running around Grundy?

Wolf-Cooper hadn't so much as snapped at me, even in the painful aftermath of the trap. He'd been gentle, friendly. And he hadn't had a speck of blood on him besides his own. But what if he'd just been too weak to want to eat me? Maybe werewolves knew better than to bite the hand that bandaged them. What if I'd rescued the wolf that had attacked Susie Q?

People came and chewed over Susie's attack with their burgers and fries, and each seemed to have some story about seeing a wolf or chasing one off their property. Walt grumbled that the "damn tree huggers" and their programs that declared wolves a protected species increased the population, and now we were all going to be overrun with predators. Alan gently reminded Walt that the government had instituted bounty programs for hunters who brought in wolf carcasses and allowed hunters to shoot wolves from aircraft as "predator control." Abner retorted that maybe we should start our own bounty program in Grundy. The conversation had me reaching for my Tums and praying for a distraction.

I was grateful when Gertie mentioned that someone needed to go by Susie's place to take care of her dog. I volunteered to go on my lunch break. I loved to scratch behind Oscar's ears whenever I visited

Susie at the post office. The idea of him padding around the house, alone and confused, was a little heartbreaking.

As I pulled up to Susie's neat little A-frame house, two miles outside town, I could hear Oscar frantically scratching at the door. He was used to being out and about all day and seemed indignant about being locked up. I walked to Susie's door, ignoring the obvious bloody patch of grass near the driveway, and used Gertie's key to let Oscar out.

Oscar was a pitiful black-and-tan specimen of dachshund-hood. If you looked in the breeding manuals for dachshunds and saw all of the things professionals try to eliminate from their lines, you'd have a description of Oscar: barrel-chested, with a wide, fat head and flat, chubby paws and a perfectly rounded stomach that refused to arch. He looked like a Rottweiler that had been shrunken and then stretched out horizontally. And to top it off, he'd lost part of his ear in a fight with an unnamed woodland suspect, so it was permanently stuck out, a spade-shaped sail on the side of his head.

At the moment, Oscar was wearing a seafoam-green doggie sweater with a turtleneck. When I opened the utility-room door to look for his food, I saw that this was just one of many sassy ensembles for Oscar. There were little doggie sweaters, a doggie parka, even a little dog-sized bumblebee Halloween costume.

Yikes.

I let Oscar run for a few minutes while I filled his food and water dishes. I walked along the perimeter of Susie's yard, looking for . . . something, some proof that Cooper was innocent of postmaster mauling. Near the edge of the driveway, I found tracks, huge paw prints in the mud. They were big enough to be Cooper's, but for all I knew, they could be bear prints.

"What are you looking for?"

"Shit!" I yelped, turning to find Cooper standing behind me, his hands shoved into his pockets. He looked so upset—scared and upset and pretty pissed off to see me crouching over wolf footprints as if I was some cross between Nancy Drew and Steve freaking Irwin.

"Have we talked about your tendency to sneak up behind me?" I growled.

"What are you doing here?" he demanded.

"I'm checking on Oscar."

"Oscar's over there." He jerked his head toward the driveway. Oscar was on his belly, crouched down near the spot where Susie must have been found. He looked miserable and confused, peering up at me with those brown-black eyes. "What are you looking at?"

I stepped out of his way. "You tell me."

He looked down at the ground and, with a pained expression, said, "It's a wolf print. A big one."

"What do you think of that?"

"What do you think I should think of it?"

"Look, let's just cut through the bullshit, OK?" I cried. "You show up at my house after being caught in a bear trap as a *wolf*, and the next day we find out that one of our neighbors was mauled by a *wolf*. The timing, to me, seems a little weird. So I'm curious, Cooper. What do you make of that?"

"I don't know," he confessed, his face downcast. "I don't remember being here last night. I don't smell my scent here. I just smell . . . blood. Susie's blood. I don't know what to think."

The hollow anguish in his voice let all of the steam out of my good old-fashioned storm cloud of mad. I was deflated and helpless, which seemed to be how he felt as well. I took a deep breath and stepped closer to him. He mirrored my movement, backing away. "For right now—just for right now—I'm going to choose to believe you didn't have anything to do with this. You can be a real jerk sometimes, but I don't think you could hurt a defenseless woman—even knowing what you did to John Teague."

Much to my frustration, Cooper looked away and shoved his hands into his pockets. His mouth was set in a thin, unyielding line to keep any errant words from escaping. I lowered my voice and stepped closer, almost close enough to touch him. I kept my hands at my sides. "You've had plenty of chances to hurt me, in human and in wolf form, and you haven't. So I'm giving you the benefit of the doubt. I'm not going to tell a soul what happened at my house. I'm not going to behave any differently toward you. But so help me, Cooper Graham, if I find out that you're taking advantage of that trust, if you're the one who hurt Susie Q, I'll tranque-dart your ass myself and deliver you to Alan's front porch wrapped up with a little pink bow."

His lips quirked. "You've got a dark streak, Mo Wenstein."

I jabbed my finger into his shoulder. "Don't you forget it."

Oscar let out a long, plaintive howl. I turned to him and called, "Hold on just a second, Oscar." I continued with Cooper, "I have a couple of questions, though, about being a werewolf. Now, what do you mean—" I turned back to where Cooper was standing.

He was gone. He'd managed to disappear into the woods without making a sound.

I grumbled, "And now I'm talking to myself. Damn werewolves."

I ambled toward Oscar, muttering to myself about Cooper's poor social skills and how easily ipecac could be slipped into a certain werewolf's chili special.

"I'm sorry, buddy," I said, scratching behind Oscar's ears. "Susie's not going to be coming back for a while. But we'll take care of you. Come on, let's go get you something to eat."

I tried to coax Oscar into the house. No dice. I tried carrying him in, and he trotted right back outside. I took the doggie dishes out to him, and he rolled onto his back and turned his nose away from the bowl. "Not hungry?" I asked, holding a few pellets up to Oscar's snout. Oscar rolled away.

Stupid cylindrical dog.

"OK, Oscar, I've got to go bye-bye, so if you're not going to eat—"

The moment I said "bye-bye," Oscar hot-footed

it toward Lucille . . . just in time for me to realize that in my haste to get the caterwauling Oscar out of the house, I'd left my driver's-side door open. "No, no! Gah! Oscar, out of the truck!"

Who knew that dachshunds could leap five times their height? Oscar, who had made himself quite comfortable in my passenger seat, woofed as if to say, *Too late. I called shotgun.*

"Crap." I laughed and shook my head at the silly dog. I doubted that Gertie would be in any shape to come back to Susie's house after what she'd seen that morning. So my feeding Oscar was probably going to be a long-term arrangement until Susie got out of the hospital . . . if Susie got out of the hospital. It would probably be easier for me just to take Oscar to my house anyway. I rolled my eyes and ran back into the house for Oscar's bag of food and bed. Oscar's tail was thumping impatiently against the seat when I climbed back into the truck.

"No loud parties. No smoking. And you get no remote-control privileges," I told him. Oscar yapped and turned in a circle, which I took as an OK.

"I'm a cat person," I grumbled, pulling the truck into gear.

SUSIE Q'S PROGNOSIS was good, but she was still in intensive care. She had suffered extensive damage to her trachea and jaw, broken ribs, and internal injuries and had lost two fingers from her right hand trying to fend off the wolf. The doctors didn't know whether she'd ever speak again. The idea of never hearing that bawdy twang again struck me as the saddest part of this ordeal. Between the injuries and the painkillers, Susie hadn't been able to scribble more than a few words for the state police: "big wolf bit me." For days after the attack, Alan hiked in circles around Susie's house, searching for signs of the wolf, but he said the trail dried up a few miles into the woods.

"The tracks just disappeared, like the wolf sprouted wings and flew away," he told me one day at lunch.

"Um, they can't actually do that, right?" I asked him.

"Not that I'm aware of," he said, shaking his head, but the idea seemed to lighten his foul mood a bit. "I called an expert in wolf behavior at ASU. He said it's not unusual for a wolf to attack a lone, defenseless person if they happen to be out at night. But he said an attack like this is usually preceded by signs that the wolves are circling closer to town, problems with livestock being killed, pets going missing."

"I haven't heard anything like that," I said.

Alan shrugged. "He said he'd send me a bunch of articles that should help me try to predict the wolf's behavior patterns, unless, of course, it's sick or wounded, in which case there's no way to predict what it will do. I just want to find it before people go looking for it. This is the sort of thing that can get people crazy."

"What do you mean?" I asked.

"Have you seen *Jaws*? All those crazy fishermen going after a twenty-foot shark with a dinghy and a flare gun? It's like that. People get all fired up about protecting their own. They're far more likely to hurt themselves or each other than catch a monster."

I shuddered at the image of my neighbors forming a torch-toting mob and hunting Cooper.

"Hey," Alan said, seeing my stricken expression and squeezing my hand. "It's OK. Don't worry. I'll catch it before anybody else gets hurt."

I smiled, a little shaky. "I know you will. Is there anything I can do?"

He shook his head. "Just stay inside at night. Don't leave the house after dark, even to take out your garbage. And carry that bear mace I gave you— at all times."

"That doesn't really help you."

"Knowing you're safe will help me considerably," Alan told me. "I hear you're keeping Oscar for a while?"

I nodded. "Gertie asked if I wouldn't mind keeping him until further notice. And I don't. He's the best roommate I've ever had. He doesn't eat my carefully labeled food or run up the phone bill. I don't have to fight for TV or computer access. As long as we keep rent out of the equation, I think we'll be fine."

Alan grinned at me. "I think you might have been getting a little lonely. Oscar will be good for you."

"You're probably right."

I liked coming home to Oscar every night. I'd open the door, and he would be sitting there at the stoop expectantly, tail thumping against the floor.

Oscar liked to watch me cook. He'd sit politely at the kitchen doorway until I dropped something, then helpfully snarf it up before I could reach for it. At night, he slept over my feet, keeping them warm as I read. We made a habit of taking a short walk near my house before sunset. It tired Oscar out and kept my thoughts from constantly circling around Cooper.

My not-quite-friendly neighborhood werewolf had been spending a lot of time at the Glacier lately. I think he was trying to figure out whether I could keep my word or spill the beans about his furry little problem. We kept our conversations short and what could pass for amicable . . . in a Robert Altman movie. Every word had a double meaning. Every exchange left me wondering why Cooper bothered to keep coming in, day after day, when I'd made it clear I had no plans to "out" him. Part of me was just glad we could stop being blatantly hostile toward each other. It took too much energy to keep thinking up all those clever insults.

Even more astounding were Cooper's efforts to have actual conversations with people besides Buzz and Evie—which, again, likely had more to do with keeping tabs on what I was telling people than with a desire to get to know his neighbors. While it made the regulars a little uncomfortable at first, they soon figured out that Cooper told some pretty great stories when he wasn't snarling or growling at people. And good storytellers were always welcome at the Glacier.

For instance, that afternoon, I overheard Cooper telling Walt about taking a group of pharmaceutical reps from Alabama moose hunting and getting them to coat themselves in moose urine and mud to disguise their human scent. He sipped his coffee and guffawed over one of the hunters asking if the urine had been pasteurized.

I slid their orders in front of them and, before I could stop myself, commented, "I don't get how someone who is so hostile to outsiders could make his living off taking them hunting."

Where Cooper would normally scowl or just stop talking, this morning he smirked. "Oh, it's hardly hunting. I'm just trying to keep the tourists from devastating the ecosystem or shooting each other. I stall them until we find something worth their time, and then I put them in a position where it would be impossible for them to kill it. I give them the big talk about being spirit brothers with the animal they missed, so they're responsible for protecting the species. They've got a good story to take home, I get paid, and everybody goes home happy."

"What happens if they manage to actually hit what they're shooting at?" I asked.

He shrugged. "Hasn't happened yet. Hey, I'm not a total fraud. If they go out with me a couple of times and prove that they're not total assholes, I start taking them to better spots, putting them in better positions. If they're decent shots, they have an honest chance of a decent kill. Until then, I see myself as a conservationist, protecting the local wildlife from idiots with firearms."

I rolled my eyes. "You just get a kick out of getting middle-aged men to rub mud on their faces, don't you?"

"And the moose urine. Don't forget that."

I refilled his coffee cup. "You are a sick man." I glanced down at his breakfast, a bloody steak, six links of sausage, six strips of bacon, a slab of ham, and a tiny piece of toast. The toast was for appearance's sake, I guessed. "Can I get you anything else? Maybe something leafy and green? A pamphlet on the nation's worsening heart-disease epidemic?"

"If God didn't want us to eat the animals, he wouldn't have made them so tasty, Mo."

"You know, I got grounded once for wearing a T-shirt that expressed that very sentiment to an animal-rights rally," I said. Cooper flashed a wide, sincere grin at me. It knocked me back on my heels. He'd never smiled at me before, unless he was mocking me in some fashion.

It felt as if someone had dropped a Malatov cocktail at my feet. My whole body became flushed, hot, uncomfortably tight. I muttered some excuse about burning eggs and ducked back into the kitchen. Cheeks aflame, I made a beeline for the walk-in freezer, slammed the door behind me, and braced myself against a rack of frozen beef. Maybe I was coming down with the flu, I told myself. *Please, Lord,* I prayed, *let it be the flu.*

It was not healthy for one man's smile to make my panties spontaneously combust.

I did not want Cooper to have that sort of power over me, especially when I was on such shaky ground with him. I just had to concentrate on other things, other people. Alan, for instance, who, as far as I could tell, had only one corporeal form.

I spent a good five minutes in the freezer, fanning cold air onto my face. I was careful to spend the rest of the afternoon in the kitchen. I cooked with my back to the dining area and worked like a dervish to keep the kitchen clean so I could leave the minute my shift ended, a rarity for me.

Oscar was waiting for me at my door, looking quite dandy in his little red argyle sweater. I gave him a scratch behind his ears before he streaked into the yard. We took a longer-than-usual route around the house that afternoon as I mulled the odd turn my life had taken. Why was Cooper being nice all of a sudden? And why was I responding to it? Hell, I was excited by it.

Maybe it was just an overabundance of hormones, a response to a sexual starvation diet. I'd been without for so long that my body was craving the worst possible thing for me. Cooper was carnal triple chocolate cheesecake, deep-fried on a stick.

Alan, on the other hand, was angel food cake, sweet, wholesome, and nothing you'd regret. He was smart, honest, open, and thoughtful. So why did I keep thinking of him as "my friend Alan" when what I should have been thinking was "sex on legs with a side of fantastically compatible personality"?

I cursed my contrary id and looked up at the sky. It was getting darker much earlier these days. I wondered what it would be like in a few months, having just a few hours of sunlight each day. But I wasn't uneasy now. The verdant jungle surrounding my hometown had always seemed so forbidding, with a constant, threatening undercurrent of man-eating mosquitoes and water moccasins, not to mention the occasional alligator. Here, I felt welcomed by the fragrant green, the cool, deep shadows. But as enchanted as I was, I knew that I didn't need to be this far from my cabin after dark, bear mace or no bear mace.

"Time to go back to the house, Oscar. Come on, buddy," I called. Oscar, who seemed to see leashing as some sort of personal insult, took two steps toward me, then suddenly turned as fast as his chubby little legs would carry him and took off into the trees.

"Oscar, no!" I cried as he began barking frantically.

I chased after him, slowed by thick branches and underbrush.

"Oscar!" I yelled after the echoing barks. I muttered to myself, "This is not a smart thing, Mo, following a tiny canine canapé into the woods when there's a bloodthirsty wolf on the loose. Why not just rub yourself in meat tenderizer and put an apple in your mouth?"

I thought about turning around and letting Oscar find his way home. Clearly, he could get through the brush easier than I could. And he could smell a predator coming, couldn't he? He'd be able to run. But the thought of him alone and defenseless, in his silly little doggie sweater, kept pushing me forward.

I could see a clearing ahead, the branches thinned in the dimming light. Oscar seemed to have stopped, because his growls and yaps were staying in one place. I jogged ahead, trying to remember if there were skunks this far north, because I was not prepared to destink a dachshund. I pushed through the last barrier of branches. "Dang it, Oscar—"

And that's when I heard the roar.

I skidded to a stop and landed on my butt as my legs flew out from under me. The grizzly bear, already agitated by the yapping dog, reared up on its legs, standing a full eight feet tall. That thing was bigger than my first car! The sheer size of it was enough to make my primal brain scurry to a corner of my skull and whimper in the fetal position. In the rational part of my brain, I knew I had Alan's bear mace in my pocket, but I couldn't seem to make my hands reach toward my jacket. My reactions were limited to screaming or wetting my pants.

I went with screaming.

I scrambled back, scraping my hands against the rocks and branches. The forest that had seemed a welcoming fairyland just a few minutes ago was now a living nightmare. How ironic was it that my nature-loving parents were going to be mourning a child who was *eaten* by nature?

The bear lurched back onto all fours. Its breath was hot and rank, sweeping across my face in damp puffs. My mouth went dry and slack as the animal barreled closer. The bear's massive front paw drew back as if prepared to take a swipe at me. My brain seemed frozen, fixating on the obscenely long claws fanning out from the paw and wondering if there was a good place to be hit with them. The answer was a definite no. I flinched, throwing my arms over my head, waiting for the blow, and a lot of things seemed to happen at once.

The blow didn't come. I opened my eyes to see wolf-Cooper, standing between the bear and me, his stance wide, defensive. The hair on his back was as bristled as a wire brush.

I felt a rush of gratitude for the idiosyncrasies of the human brain and its effort to protect me from bear snack-time horrors. In a last-ditch effort to dull the shock of growling, clawed death, my mind had produced a fantasy image of my furry savior. I was sure this last heroic image would be a small comfort to me as I made my way though Not-So-Gentle Ben's digestive tract.

The wolf growled, a low baritone over Oscar's panicked staccato barks. I shook my head, rattling brain cells back into their proper orbit. Wolf-Cooper was real.

Oscar, who apparently didn't want to be outdone in the canine bravado department, lunged at the bear's front leg, sinking his little teeth in. The bear roared and flicked Oscar away with a shake of his paw. Oscar yelped, and his small body landed inches from me. I scooped him up and kept him in my lap as he strained to get back into the fray.

The bear advanced, eliciting a snarl from the wolf. The bear attempted to circle right, pushing the wolf counterclockwise, away from me. But the wolf stood his ground, advancing against the bear's charge. The bear attempted a left-hand strike, which earned it a nip on the nose from the wolf. The wolf backed up, his long tail swishing against my feet as he moved into a defensive crouch and let out a vicious snarl.

The bear reared up again and gave a roar that had my ears ringing. When this display of ursine testosterone failed to chase Cooper away, the bear dropped to all fours and huffed at me, a sort of 'you can eat her, she's not worth it' gesture. Sure that it had made its point as the loudest, meanest, biggest animal in the clearing, the bear sauntered off.

I let out a long, trembling breath, burying my face in Oscar's sweater.

Cooper phased back to human. He was naked, sweaty, and quite angry. *Hmm.*

When I was no longer paralyzed by fear and the blood was circulating properly in my brain again, I was going to evaluate what it said about me as a person that I had some strange kind of relationship with a man I didn't particularly like, in which he was naked at least half of the time we spent together. And I didn't seem to be bothered by it. I really had to have sex sometime soon.

"Are you out of your *mind*?" he shouted as I hesitantly pushed myself to my feet. The relief I felt finally allowed my brain to process what had just happened. A cold chill swept through my body, and I had to brace my hands against my knees to stay upright.

"Give me a minute," I wheezed, holding up one hand.

"Do you realize what could have just happened to you? What is wrong with you? Do you enjoy putting yourself in harm's way?" Cooper's hands clamped around my arms and gave me the slightest shake.

"Which question do you want me to answer first, Cooper?" I asked, my voice uncharacteristically calm. I broke eye contact and looked down, and we both realized exactly how unclothed he was. Cooper stepped away, and his arms dropped to his sides. Now that the angry red had faded from his cheeks, he seemed embarrassed by his outburst.

"I was walking Oscar. He got away from me," I said. "If I'd known there was a bear, I would have run in the opposite direction, trust me. I don't have any death wishes or adrenaline addictions that I'm aware of. Here lately, I seem to find myself in the very wrong place at the very wrong time. What are you doing out here, anyway?"

Cooper flushed again. "I can change anytime I want, but the urge to do it is a little stronger during the full moon." Cooper gestured to the faintly glowing orb rising in the distance. "When the urge to phase is this strong, I usually end up hunting."

"So close to my house?"

"You've been throwing bread crusts and scraps out in your backyard for the birds, right?"

I nodded.

"Well, you might want to stop," he said. "Free food attracts all kinds of animals. Squirrels, foxes, elk. There's a particularly lazy family of rabbits that cuts through your yard every night, scarfs up the buffet, and heads to that stream," he said, nodding through the clearing. Now that the blood was no longer roaring in my ears, I could actually hear the musical splashing of water over rocks. "Smaller animals attract larger predators."

"Such as yourself."

"Or bears, which you seem to think will be chased off by whimpering and screaming."

"Hmph," I snorted, not quite convinced. "Well, do me a favor. Don't snack on your prey on my front lawn. It disturbs my sleep."

Cooper's brow creased. "What do you mean?"

"My first night in town, you brought down an elk right outside my front door. Scared the crap out of me. Of course, at the time, I thought you were a real wolf, not a Cooper wolf. Not that there's a whole lot of difference." Cooper's stare was blank and embarrassed. I asked, "You don't remember any of this?"

He shrugged. "I don't remember everything I do when I'm a wolf. It's sort of like dreaming. You remember bits and pieces but not everything. My grandfather says it's the weak human mind's way of protecting us from remembering the less pleasant aspects of wolf life, like eating raw meat. Some wolves are better at keeping a clear picture, though. It helps if you run with a pack. Some say it's like having a collective memory. My cousin Samson says it's like having a bunch of frat brothers ready and willing to remind you of the stupid things you did when you were blackout drunk."

That explained a lot, particularly his uncertainty about whether he'd attacked Susie. And he didn't remember helping me in the alley, because it hadn't been important enough to remember. Or he did remember and didn't think it was important enough to mention. Somehow I was glad he couldn't guess how much either option hurt me.

"Are you OK?" he asked, his voice soft as he stared at the ground. "You're not hurt or anything?"

"I'm a little shaken up, and I'm never going to be able to hear 'Teddy Bear Picnic' without flashbacks, but physically, I'm fine."

"Good," he said, clearing his throat. "I don't want anything to happen to you, Mo. I—people around here couldn't stand that."

I shrugged it off, as if I hadn't noticed that sentence had started with "I" before he tacked on "people."

"It's my pancakes," I told him solemnly. "They inspire loyalty."

"Stop that. Stop making jokes when I'm talking about you getting hurt," he said, looking me in the eye now as his fingers wrapped around my arm, pulling me closer. The warmth of his hand burned through my clothes and traveled up my arm. "You have to—nothing can happen to you, do you hear me? You have to take care of yourself."

My brow furrowed at his sudden shift in demeanor. "OK, I'm sorry."

"Promise me," he insisted, the timber of his voice lowering to a rumble that vibrated through my chest. "Promise me you won't take risks like this again. That you'll stay inside at night, where it's safe."

His mouth was close, his breath gliding over my cheek like a caress. The heat of it, the intensity, had me dizzy. Everything around me was fluid motion and bleeding color. But Cooper remained still and constant.

"Promise," he whispered huskily.

"I promise, Cooper," I said, reluctantly pulling away from him. The loss of contact seemed to sober him. He straightened, his face smoothing out from the worried lines that creased it. He reached down to pat Oscar. My little sausage-shaped buddy shied away from contact with the recognized top dog.

Cooper sighed. "Let's get you and Oscar home."

He lowered into a crouch. I saw the light of transformation spread this time, starting with the skin over his chest and moving to the long, rangy limbs. I was so caught up in watching that he'd almost completely changed when I spluttered, "W-wait, what are you doing?"

"Phasing," he said, looking annoyed when he had to switch back to human. "That bear could circle back, and it's best if it sees a threat right away if it catches up to us. Besides, I don't like walking through the woods naked. The limbs are dangerous to my . . . parts. And it's awkward being naked in front of you."

I nodded. "Agreed."

Cooper phased fully this time, the light rippling across his skin, leaving black fur and sinew in its wake. He gave a short bark to Oscar. I had a half-second to wonder whether they could understand each other when Oscar fell in line with Cooper and marched through the brush toward home, the two of them sweeping my flanks like some canine military escort.

Cooper led us to the porch. As relieved as I was to see the warm, yellow light pouring out of the windows, the smoke rising from the chimney, I wasn't quite ready to leave the woods yet. I had too many questions for Cooper.

I stood there staring at him. Cooper let out a sharp huff and jerked his head toward my front door. I guessed I was getting the kiss-off version of the werewolf good night.

"Um, good night, Cooper."

Cooper whined and blew out another breath.

"Happy hunting?" I offered. This seemed to pacify him. He let out another sharp, commanding *woof* to Oscar, who answered back with two staccato yaps. Cooper nodded his head and darted away, his black fur melting into the darkness.

I looked down at Oscar, who seemed to be standing at attention. I rolled my eyes. "Did you just get left in charge of me?"

Oscar let out a deep growl that would probably be quite intimidating to squirrels everywhere.

"Great."

10

Remind Me Not to Lick Any Flagpoles

HELL ISN'T HOT. HELL is cold—eye-watering, tooth-chattering, razor-sharp goose bumps cold.

Winter started off small. Wanting to keep my coat on hours after I'd gone into the kitchen. Not being able to put my bare foot down on my bedroom floor without losing my breath. Then, one morning, I walked out the door, bundled into my thick down parka, felt the icy slap of the air against my cheeks, and ran right back into the house.

I was sleeping later and later each morning to avoid waking up in the dark. I was aware that my thin blood made the transition to cold weather worse. My pride was the only thing that kept me from arriving at work wearing a full-body snowsuit. But in the mornings, I would allow myself the luxury of burrowing under four full-size quilts and waiting until the last possible second to get up and get dressed.

And that's exactly what I was doing when Evie came into my room on my next morning off and whipped the covers from over my head.

"I thought we were going shopping today," she said, bouncing the mattress and jostling the pillow from under my head.

"This is a direct violation of the 'tell your friends where your spare key is hidden' trust," I told her, huddled under the blanket.

It was Sunday. Evie needed to drive to Bulk Wonderland in Conover to get some supplies for the saloon. While they relied on suppliers for food and drink, it was cheaper to buy some restaurant paraphernalia in bulk and drive it home themselves. I jumped at the chance to go with her, which was just a sad commentary on the current state of my social life. We decided to make a girls' day of it. The agenda included lunch, manicures, and buying industrial-sized air freshener for the men's room.

"It's so galdamn cold, I think my eyelids have frozen in place," I whimpered. "What made me think I could do this? I need heat. I need to get into a car and wince when my legs touch the seat. I need to have reason to know all of the symptoms of sunstroke, which I had memorized by the time I was twelve."

"You'll feel better this summer," she assured me. "The days will get longer. You'll be able to peel down to two layers of clothes. Come on, Mo, you promised."

I whined and pulled the comforter back over my head.

"If you don't get up, I will mention this episode to Cooper the next time he comes into the bar. Imagine the taunting that will follow."

I gritted my teeth, whipping the covers from over my head. "You're a hard woman, Evie DuChamp."

"Don't you forget it," Evie said, patting my head. "By the way, did you say 'galdamn' back there?"

"There's an inverse relationship between my temper and my ability to control my accent. If you hear me say 'Fiddledeedee,' run for the hills, because I'm getting ready to take out bystanders."

Evie coaxed me into the car with the promise of mocha lattes and shopping malls. I thought it might be a little strange at first, to spend time together away from the Glacier. But on the long car ride there, Evie cranked up the B-52s, and we sang hideous renditions of "Love Shack" and "Rock Lobster." I was grateful for the distraction. It kept me from firing questions about Cooper at her for two hours, and it was nice just to be silly and girly for a little bit.

When you live in a place as rough and Spartan as Grundy, the little feminine things you do for yourself are the first to go, such as pretty, impractical shoes and hairstyles that won't stand up to wind or a knit cap. But by the time we passed the Conover city limits, I wanted to curl my eyelashes and gossip about prom dresses.

Conover would have been considered a midsize, average town in Mississippi, but I was surprised at how crowded and metropolitan it felt now that I'd spent so much time in a one-street village. I felt a little dizzy as we buzzed through heavy traffic, intersection after intersection. The blazing neon signs for McDonald's, Best Buy, and Kmart seemed painfully bright. I realized with a touch of disbelief that I'd adjusted far too willingly to a quiet, weather-centered existence, that I'd probably never be comfortable in a big city again.

Lunch was at a frou-frou café called Anjou that served mostly salads and quiche. Evie had wanted to try it for years, but Buzz refused to go in on principle. We stopped at a brutally pungent strip-mall nail salon and soaked our hands in a mixture the manicurist refused to divulge the ingredients for—though she did confirm that we weren't allergic to shellfish before dunking our hands. That made me nervous, but Evie seemed to take the possibility that we were soaking our fingers in crab goo in stride. Evie had her fingernails painted a deep wine color that would have looked ghoulish with my skin tone but complemented her russet hands. Since cooking and general nervous nail biting kept my nails short, I opted for a deep cuticle massage and a coat of clear polish. No one wants to find flecks of iridescent pink in their chili.

From this feminine haven, we were thrust into the gray, industrial reality of Bulk Wonderland. I helped Evie load boxes of paper napkins, paper towels, aluminum foil, and plastic wrap into the cart. I couldn't seem to stop myself from buying the ridiculously oversized bottle of shampoo and the huge box of tampons. I also purchased a one-hundred-count box of condoms, which I tried and failed to hide from Evie.

"Alan's asked me to dinner again this week," I told her. "You never know what could happen."

Evie had stopped in her tracks but recovered enough to say, "Oh, you know that we're going to spend a lot of time talking about that, maybe even the entire drive home."

As we wandered among the shelves of Bulk Wonderland, I went into hoarding mode. In truth, I was getting more worried about the approaching winter. I found myself constantly checking my cabinets. I worried about keeping enough personal groceries on hand, about keeping the baking supplies I needed for the saloon. Did I have enough eggs, cereal, toilet paper? Should I buy more in case there was some drastic change in the weather? I started throwing weird items into my cart—a three-pound jar of peanut butter, a 120-count box of Sno Balls, enough chocolate chips to sink a battleship. When Evie caught me buying a six-pound block of cheddar cheese, she went into what she called a "first-winter intervention."

"Sweetheart, it's important to keep emergency supplies on hand, but you're venturing into crazy survivalist territory," she said, prying the cheese out of my hand. "Most people keep enough in their homes so they won't have to go out in the really nasty weather, but it's never gotten so bad that your truck *couldn't* get to Hannigan's or that someone couldn't get to you. It's not like you're going to be reenacting scenes from the Donner party."

"I know, I know," I grumbled. "It's just, it's getting colder, and I know the first big freeze of the winter is coming up. I'm a little nervous."

"Don't be. You're going to be fine. Besides, the first freeze is big fun in Grundy. We have a big party at the saloon, lots of food and dancing," she said, grinning as she tossed more sensible supplies into my cart—batteries, a case of bottled water, powdered milk, cans of Sterno. "It's a great time."

"Why would you celebrate the first freeze of the year?"

Evie shrugged. "For a lot of people, it's their last chance to socialize. Afterward, most people don't make it into town to visit."

I cried, "I thought you said it didn't get that bad!"

"I said that people *don't* make it into town, not that they can't. If you had to decide between staying at home, where it's cozy, or trudging through two feet of snow just to run into town for toilet paper, what would you do? The Big Freeze is a tradition passed down generation to generation," Evie said solemnly. In a hokey "resonant Indian folktale" voice, she added, "For many moons, it has provided a way for unattached men and women of Grundy to find the person they plan on shacking up with for the season."

At the look on my face, she burst out laughing, with just enough malice that I wasn't sure if she was kidding or not.

"There's not a lot to do here during the winter." She shrugged. "It's either sex or curling."

I shuddered in horror at the thought of any sport

that involved ice, heavy stones, and brooms. "I'll take the sex."

Evie winked. "That's my girl."

"But not with Cooper."

"Well, now you're just being obstinate," she huffed.

For most of the ride home, Evie and I argued over whether (a) I would attend the Big Freeze party as a guest or hide out in the kitchen where it was safe and (b) what I would be wearing. I insisted that I would enjoy myself much more if I was out of Leonard Tremblay's range of fire. Evie insisted that I suck it up and dance like a big girl, preferably in the low-cut red party dress she'd seen hanging in my closet.

"No way!" I cried as we parked in the alley of the saloon. "I don't even know why I brought it up here."

"Because you look hot in it," she said, climbing out of the SUV. "You know that, which is why you hauled it across a dozen state lines. Admit it, that's your 'going to get some' dress."

"I don't have a 'going to get some' dress," I insisted, cringing when she dragged my bulk box of condoms out with a flourish.

"Exhibit A," she said, looking down her nose at me.

"Fine, it's my 'going to get some' dress."

Note to self: Find Evie a hobby that doesn't involve getting me laid.

11

Red Light, Green Light

Buzz's hand healed, but he hadn't mentioned coming back into the kitchen. He was devoting his attention to inventing new ways to use Jägermeister. *Please, Lord, let me never hear the words "Jäger 'n' eggs" again. Breakfast should not burn on the way down.*

In other medical news, Susie Q had been released from the hospital. Since she lived alone and would need pretty steady care for the next few months, her doctor told her to move down to West Texas to live with her daughter for a while. Susie's grandkids were supposedly allergic to dogs, so I would be playing hostess to Oscar for a little while longer—most likely, permanently, but no one had the heart to tell Susie.

Grundy was already a little less fun without Susie's big hair and sassy Western wear. It seemed bizarre to plan a menu and pick out party decorations when one of our own was leaving town on a gurney. But Evie and Gertie said the Big Freeze was one of the highlights of Susie's year, and she would have wanted us to go on with the dance. We planned to put her picture on the bar, with a little candle and her favorite beer.

Such was life in any small town. Tragedies knocked the population on its collective butt and were chewed over for weeks, and then adjustments were made. We knew we couldn't do more for Susie Q, so we tried to go back to normal. The lunch crowds found something else to talk about. Gertie took over the postmaster position, which meant I was actually getting mail delivered to my house, a new and unexpected luxury. And Gertie seemed to enjoy being a "working gal" for the first time in her life.

Alan spent weeks tracking "Susie Q's wolf" through the area. He found tracks circling through town, but nothing else. No animal remains, scat, tracks, nothing. He never even saw an actual wolf. What astounded him most was the number of times he was led past my house while tracking wolf signs.

"I've never seen anything like it, Mo," Alan told me one afternoon over a cheeseburger platter. "It's like you're living on some sort of wolfy scenic route. I can't believe you haven't seen anything."

I giggled, the hysterical edge giving my laughter an authentic ring. I tried my hardest not to sneak a glance out the window, where I saw Cooper parking his truck near the curb.

"Nah, the only thing I've seen out my way was a bear a little while back."

Alan's eyes widened in alarm, and his hand reached out reflexively for mine. *Oh, crap. I probably shouldn't have said that.* Sure, it was better than blurting out, "Oh, well, I have a werewolf who drops by every once in a while." But now I had to give Alan a heavily edited version of the bear incident and find a way to tip off Cooper so he wouldn't slip up.

I gave Alan a quick and dirty explanation, cautiously omitting exactly how close I'd gotten to Yogi's bastard cousin and how involved Cooper had been in chasing him off. I tried to ignore the way Alan's jaw tightened when he heard that Cooper was at my house. That didn't bode well.

"I'm going to put some more traps out by your place. I'll give you a map and mark them with orange hunter's tape, but be careful of where you and Oscar walk," Alan said. I nodded and turned to pour more coffee for Walt. Alan put his hand on mine again and stopped me.

"I'll be careful, Alan. I promise." I smiled at him and patted his hand. Alan caught it in his fingers and squeezed.

I looked up and saw Cooper coming through the door. I caught his eye dipping toward our joined hands, and he scowled. I moved my hand behind my back. Cooper sat at the far end of the counter and called out to Evie. When I smiled in greeting, he gave me a single curt nod and trained his eyes on his coffee cup.

Apparently, we were back to not being civil. *Great.*

"Good morning, Cooper," I said in a deliberately cheerful tone.

"Morning," he mumbled. He looked tired again and sort of pouty, which was a strange expression on him.

"I was just telling Alan here about the bear we saw out near my place," I told him, sending a significant look toward Alan. "It's a good thing you got me and Oscar into the house before it got too close."

"Why'd you tell him about that?" Cooper grunted.

"He was just telling me how many *wolf tracks* he'd seen near my house, and I told him that was nothing, he should have seen the bear."

Cooper's eyes locked with mine, sweeping my face in search of . . . what? Suspicion? Anger? Alan started asking Cooper questions I wasn't prepared to answer about the bear. I'd been too terrified to notice how tall the bear was, any significant markings, whether the bear was tagged. Cooper's face tensed as he rattled off plausible details, but he kept his eyes trained on mine.

"What exactly were you doing out at Mo's place?" Alan asked.

Cooper's eyes narrowed, his lips curling back ever so slightly, showing his even, white teeth. "Just being neighborly."

Great, that was just vague enough to let Alan assume that we were having torrid monkey sex on my front porch when we were rudely interrupted by the bear.

Alan's own teeth showed. "Well, it's nice to hear

that people are keeping a close eye on Mo for me."
He slid his hand across the counter and laced his fingers through mine.

I was not an expert in animal behavior, but even
I recognized when territory was being marked.
Alan might as well have been peeing a circle
around my feet. He grinned up at me. Cooper
scowled. I arched my eyebrows and pried my fingers gently out of Alan's.

"I am choking on all the testosterone, so I'll back
away into the kitchen," I muttered.

When I was at a safe distance, the tension seemed
to ebb out of Alan's face, while Cooper seemed to
grow more agitated. He slid off his stool and slapped
his baseball cap back onto his head.

"I've got to go," he grumbled.

"What about your order?" Evie called as the front
door jangled closed.

"Feed it to Alan," he huffed.

"What was that about?" Evie asked me, putting
aside the list of supplies we would need for our party
menu of crab cakes, fancy ham biscuits, and "cheese
pies." (We couldn't call them mini-quiches, or the
male guests wouldn't eat them.)

"I don't pretend to understand the male mind,
Evie, that one in particular."

Evie shook her head. "The Amazons had the
right idea. Keep men around for procreation only."

I nodded. "And don't let them speak."

IN THE END, I wore the red dress to the Big Freeze
party, just to get Evie off my back. And because I'd

decided that I wanted to take Alan home with me that night. If anything would get that message across, it was the red dress.

Alan was the right choice, I told my reflection as I painted my mouth a bold poppy color. He was the only choice that made sense. And he couldn't have communicated his interest any more clearly if he'd used a billboard. *Why am I nervous?* I wondered, smoothing my hair one last time before I slipped into my parka. Alan was a slow mover, but he was clearly interested. I wasn't going to be rejected. I'd never been nervous about first-time sexual encounters. I didn't get nervous about sex, period. I tried to shake off the weird aura of apprehension on the drive over, concentrating on the fun of the party, of flirting, of ending a particularly long sexual dry spell.

When I walked into the Glacier, I was apprehensive for a whole new reason. I felt both over- and underdressed. The men were in ties (with jeans) and the ladies in dresses that had probably been mail-ordered from the JCPenney Sunday Best collection. And then there was Abner, who was wearing an old suit made entirely of forest-green corduroy.

I shrugged out of my coat at the door of the saloon, and people stopped talking.

Awkward.

I gave a nervous little smile and ducked into the kitchen, where I found Evie warming the batches of appetizers I'd made that afternoon.

"I'm going to kill you," I told her, pulling the little flared hem over my now-conspicuous knees.

"Why, because I insisted that you be pretty?" She smirked, handing me a tray of crab wontons. "You look gorgeous, and you know it. Pretending to be nervous about it is just annoying."

"I'm the only one showing this much skin!" I hissed. My needle-thin heels clicked impatiently behind her as we put the food on a table set far away from the bustling dance floor that had been set up near an improvised stage.

"Well, I don't think anybody minds." She cast a deliberate glance out to the bar, where Cooper had walked in and was talking with Buzz.

Cooper was wearing a light blue button-up shirt that looked as if he threw it in the dryer for a few minutes rather than iron it. His shaggy hair was slicked back. He was staring intently at his beer and trying to ignore Lynette, who seemed to be pulling on his arm and asking him to dance. Buzz looked up at Evie and elbowed Cooper. Cooper looked at me and nearly lost his grip on his bottle.

That was the kind of reaction a girl is looking for when she straps herself into support garments. It was too bad it came from Cooper.

"Well, I see someone doesn't mind that you dressed up," Evie said.

"I'm putting my coat back on," I told her.

"Now, that would be a shame."

I turned to find Alan standing in front of me. He was wearing a black suit jacket over a pristine white Oxford shirt and jeans. Given the way he swaggered up to me, I think he might have had a couple of beers in him. I smiled, giving him the slightest of eyelash flutters as he held out his hand and pulled me to the dance floor.

Buzz had hired a band from Burnee to come in and play a mix of country-western and classic rock. The current selection, a gruffer version of "Brown Eyed Girl," had Alan spinning me fast toward the center of the crowd.

"Have I mentioned that you're the prettiest girl in the room?" he asked over the peppy guitar riff.

I blushed. I couldn't help it. I was all girled up in my little red dress, and he complimented me. A blushing response was practically coded in my feminine chromosomes. "No."

"Well, I will."

I laughed, dipping my head and bumping it against Alan's shoulder. He chuckled and ran a hand along the bare skin of my arms. I pursed my lips, waiting for a reaction, a shiver, a quiver. Hell, I would have settled for a twitch. But Alan's touch didn't give me any response besides a warm rush of affection. My brows creased. I deliberately splayed my fingers across the back of Alan's neck, stroking the smooth skin there. Alan's eyes warmed, and his head tipped toward mine. I felt nothing beyond that vague impression of approaching disaster. I gritted my teeth. Why weren't my stupid hormones working right?

Over Alan's shoulder, I saw Cooper scowl. Now, that I had a reaction to—a white-hot spear of awareness, of annoyance, that shot right through to my toes. I narrowed my eyes at him, ready to snarl. Fortunately, Alan spun us so that my back was turned to Cooper.

Alan was a good dancer, an excellent lead. He made it easy to fight off my sour mood, although I couldn't seem to manufacture the lustful feelings I wanted for him. We coasted around the dance floor as he grinned and joked with the other couples, including Nate and Gertie. The Gogans moved smoothly in a box step with the ease of two people who'd learned to dance together. Nate was clearly thrilled with my choice of partner. I could see him drawing up the purchase contract for my house in his head.

I formally met a lot of my neighbors who didn't bother coming into town unless it was a special occasion. There was the expected reticence on the part of a few, but the fact that I was dancing with Alan seemed to smooth it over. It was as if he was vouching for me somehow. I felt grateful for it.

"So how do you like the local night life?" he asked, the tip of his nose grazing my cheek.

I peered around the room, watching my boisterous friends trying to squeeze every last drop of fun from the evening before they faced long months of winter seclusion. I tilted my face at an inviting angle, then immediately straightened so that my mouth wasn't quite so close to his. "It's lively."

If Alan was aware of my conflict, he certainly didn't seem fazed by it. He pressed me closer, his mouth almost brushing my ear as he said, "You know, there are still a few days before the cold really sets in. Last chance to get out and see some of the backcountry. I know some really good trails, places nobody else around here could take you. And the weather is supposed to be stable this weekend."

"Wouldn't it be kind of dangerous? What with the attacks and all . . ."

"I'll protect you. I can be your own personal wilderness bodyguard."

I chuckled. He slipped his hand ever so subtly down the small of my back to curve around my left butt cheek. I stiffened, inadvertently pressing my breasts against his chest. He took this as a green light and clutched me even tighter against his waist. The rational part of my brain screamed at me to relax and see where this might go, that Alan was an attractive, uncomplicated specimen and possibly my only chance this winter at halfway decent sex that didn't involve batteries. The more primal part of my brain had me arching back from him, wriggling my hips away from where he had me pinned against his body.

What the hell was wrong with me? This was what I wanted. Why did I feel so off center? Why did it feel so wrong? I willed myself to relax, to move closer, but some magnetic repulsion kept me at a respectable distance.

"Sorry," he said, loosening his grip when he saw my distress. "I just don't want you to slip away."

Before I could cobble together some response, someone tapped on Alan's shoulder. We turned to find Cooper standing behind us. "Mind if I cut in?"

My stupid, traitorous heart fluttered against my

rib cage. I'd only seen people "cut in" on dancers in old movies. Alan didn't seem too pleased by the interruption. His grip on my waist grew just a fraction tighter before Cooper blithely peeled Alan's arms away and twirled me to a corner across the room, leaving Alan scowling in the middle of the dance floor. Lynette sidled up to him and offered him another beer.

"I didn't expect to see you here," I murmured as Cooper's hands slid against the fabric over my back. My breath caught, and a warm, liquid wave of sensation spread from my chest to my belly. *Gah! Stupid sexy werewolves!* This was why I couldn't take Alan home. Because as much as I cared for him, he had never made me, *could* never make me, feel the way Cooper did. I would know it. And considering my responses so far, if I went to bed with Alan, he would know it. And the last thing I wanted was to hurt him.

Fine. Alan wasn't the right choice, but that didn't mean sleeping with Cooper made any more sense. I had to think of nonsexy things. Baseball. Bill O'Reilly naked. The dead, fetid smell of Delta mud on an August day. Leonard Tremblay's hot tub. Wet socks. Muddy, wet, naked Cooper in a hot tub. *Dang it!*

"Well, you are waving the red flag in front of an awful lot of bulls," he said, glancing down at my crimson dress. He smirked, not bothering to hide the fact that he was looking straight into my cleavage. "And you know me, always coming to your rescue."

I gave him a sweetly acidic smile. "Oh, really? Well, maybe if you'd spend less time lurking, you wouldn't feel the need to come to my rescue all the time."

"Lurking?"

"You heard me."

Irritation crept into Cooper's voice. "Well, maybe if *you* had the sense not to walk into dark alleyways alone or go wandering blind into the wilderness, I wouldn't feel the need to stay so close." He lowered his voice so our dance-floor companions wouldn't hear us.

"You know, I know where to get more bear traps. I'll bet if I told Alan I was having a problem with a wolf wandering outside my house at night, he would set up a minefield of them," I hissed back.

"Well, hell, I'll bet you he'd move right in." Cooper scowled back. "Now that you two are—"

"What I may or may not be doing with Alan is none of your business," I said, my cheeks flushing. "And why would you even care?"

He admitted, "I don't like seeing you dancing with him."

"So it's a dog-in-the-manger thing?" I snorted, lowering my voice. "I'm sorry, is that culturally offensive to werewolves?"

His eyes narrowed and his nostrils flared as he demanded, "What do you mean, dog in the manger?"

"You don't want me, but you don't want anybody else to have me."

"I never said I didn't want you," he said, his husky voice so soft I was absolutely sure I was the only person in the room who heard it. He was looking down, his thick black lashes resting on his cheekbones. His hands pulled me closer, pressing me against his chest. My heart thudded erratically. Every face and every voice in the room faded away as I focused on Cooper's mouth, the generous peach-soft curve of his lips. I surrendered to the gravitational pull that had me leaning closer, mingling my breath with the spicy warmth of his.

Alan's voice boomed over my shoulder. "I think you've monopolized Mo's time for long enough, Coop."

We both jumped. The moment, the spell, whatever it was, melted away. I looked back to find Alan giving Cooper a pointed glare. And did Cooper just growl?

Fortunately, Abner Golightly chose this opportunity to pull me into a lively dance he called the "Tennessee Tornado," which was a cross between the jitterbug and the watusi.

"I used to do this one with the girls at the USO," Abner told me with a wink as he spun me under his arm. For a withered little man, he had surprising upper-body strength. Still, I don't know who I was more afraid for when he dipped me.

I managed to catch glimpses of Cooper and Alan while Abner spun me back and forth. Alan had joined Buzz at the bar and was sulkily nursing a beer. Cooper had retreated to a table in the corner. His eyes tracked me back and forth, back and forth, as if he was planning the best course of attack on particularly irritating prey. His focus made me edgy, nervous, so I threw myself into staying as busy as possible. I tried to hide in the kitchen, washing dishes, warming up food, but Evie kept chasing me out. I danced with anyone who asked me, leaving me with extremely tired feet and the added problem of renewed hope on the part of Leonard Tremblay. Alan pulled me over to a secluded table, where our conversation was frequently interrupted by Walt. He was desperate to escape dancing and to discuss sports. As I had no stake in this conversation whatsoever, my only real entertainment was watching Cooper dodge increasingly aggressive overtures from Lynette, including her spilling an ice-cold beer in his lap and then "frantically" trying to mop up his crotch.

I pleaded exhaustion at around eleven. Alan offered to see me home, but he was sidelined by a debate over the Maple Leafs' offensive line. I tried to use his distraction as an opportunity to make a polite escape, go home, and slap my indecisive id silly.

Evie seemed unhappy that I was leaving early, but short of holding on to my leg and dragging me, there wasn't much she could do to stop me. I slid into my parka, said some quiet good-byes, and ducked out to Lucille. As I was opening the driver's-side door, I felt someone behind me. I turned, knowing it would be Cooper standing there.

"What do you want?" I asked.

He glared at me. "I don't like to repeat myself."

"So you want me?" I stated, my lips twitching smugly. "*You* want *me*? Sorry, I just think it bears repeating."

Cooper stayed silent.

"Well, it's nice to know," I told him. I stepped closer. His arms tensed at his sides. I peered up at him, enjoying the way his blue eyes grew dark around the irises as I moved closer. His lips parted as I stopped just short of brushing my mouth against his. "Good night."

I leaned back, a barely concealed smirk lifting my cheeks. Cooper did not have on a happy face. I snickered a little as I climbed into my truck and gunned the engine. That was oddly satisfying, considering I'd barely touched him.

As I drove home, little white tufts of snow started to swirl against my windshield. I'd only seen snow on TV. It was mesmerizing to watch the flakes dance across the dark horizon. I parked my truck in my driveway and climbed out carefully. I didn't want to slip and fall on my first snow-walking experience. I paused, tipping my face up to the sky, enjoying the feather-light kisses of snowflakes falling against my cheeks. I hoped I would still feel this sense of wonder months from now, after seeing a metric ton of this stuff fall from the sky. Sighing, I put my key in the door.

And that's when I heard the howl.

12

Crying Wolf (Screaming Wolf, Yelling Wolf, Moaning Wolf . . .)

BEHIND ME, SOMETHING WAS tearing through the woods. Thinking of the bear, I turned the key and popped the door open. I heard it break through the tree line and immediately recognized Cooper's wolf form.

He phased to human while running, his bare feet slapping at the cold ground as he leaped onto my porch and slammed into me. He latched his mouth onto mine, a hot contrast against the bitter cold. He pushed us through the door, shutting it behind us in one swift motion.

"Hasn't anyone ever warned you not to cry wolf unless you mean it?" he growled, nipping my bottom lip lightly as he pushed my coat from my shoulders and hiked my legs over his hips. He carried me to my living room, to the floor.

My dress disintegrated somewhere between the

couch and the fireplace. He dropped to his knees, stretching our bodies across the worn, soft cotton of the rug. His skin was warmer and his scent stronger than I remembered. His hair brushed over my throat as his lips traced the lines of my collarbone, down the curve of my breast.

Tonight's lingerie selection was one of my favorite sets, lavender silk with lace insets in the shape of tulips. The bra consisted of two tulip-shaped silk cups held together with wisps of silk and a prayer. I didn't have any past encounters associated with this set . . . which was good, because Cooper ripped it to shreds in about five seconds.

As the scraps of my panties floated to the floor, the wide pad of Cooper's tongue lapped at me. He nibbled and kissed in teasing little circles that had me arching my hips off the floor to meet his mouth. I yelped his name as the very tip of his tongue tweaked that sensitive little pearl of flesh, sending me over the edge into a screaming, writhing orgasm. I might have been embarrassed by my hair-trigger response, but I just didn't have the required cognitive ability. The most profound thought my brain could cobble together was *YAY!*

Cooper chuckled against my stomach and rolled me to the floor with a playful growl, pressing me against the rug as he nipped and kissed along the curve of my spine. A little flare of panic shot through my belly. I was about to have sex with a werewolf. I'd never had sex with a supernatural creature before. What if he lost control? What if I ended up getting hurt? What if he could only handle that one position that canines are so well known for?

Determined not to become a horror-movie bad-sex statistic, I rolled, hooking my foot under Cooper's calf and pinning him under me. Cooper grinned wildly, pulling me down to him and claiming my mouth with his own. Just as he was poised under me, his hard length just brushing over my warm, slick skin, my eyes flew open.

Condoms. We were going to need condoms. Lots of them. I scrambled over to where he'd dropped my purse, searching for my "contingency kit"—tampons, backup contact case, and a *long* strip of condoms. I whipped them out of the little cosmetics bag with a grunt of triumph and crawled back to Cooper with my hands full of protection. His eyes were wide now as he took in the wealth of little foil packets.

"What?" I asked, hoping that after all this, he wouldn't balk at safe sex.

"I don't know whether to be intimidated or just really, really happy."

Grinning, I ripped open the first little envelope on the chain. "Let's go for happy." I pushed him to the rug and settled over him. My voice was muffled against his lips as I rolled the condom on. "Really, really happy."

Without further preamble, I straddled Cooper's hips and wrapped my fingers around his warm, smooth length. My breath left my lungs in an exultant *whoosh* as I guided him inside me. The slight discomfort of stretching to fit him gave way to newer, far more pleasant sensations. I froze, eyes closed, reveling in that full, heavy feeling. When I opened them, Cooper was watching me, staying absolutely still.

I growled, a low, aggressive sound that started in my chest, surprising even me. Cooper's eyes widened when I combined it with a deep, quick thrust of my hips. I chuckled. "You're in so much trouble."

Cooper seemed both thrilled and slightly alarmed as I brought my hips down to his again. I arched my back, forming a bridge as I circled my hips over him. Balancing my weight on my knees allowed me to take as much of him as possible, while keeping those low, smooth motions going. Any pretense of control on Cooper's part evaporated. The man whimpered, a sharp, begging note, through parted lips as we rode together.

Cooper sat up suddenly, his fingers twined with one of my hands while the other held me precariously balanced on my knees. He kissed me deeply, matching each of our thrusts with sweeping rasps of his tongue. I braced my hands on my calves. The sensation of him cupping my bare ass in his hands made me gasp. I ground down just as he arched up. I threw my head back, howling as he hit the spot that I could rarely find myself.

I was unable to keep control as every fiber of my being focused into a hot, pulsing star. Cooper grabbed my hips, forcing me to keep time with him as I tightened convulsively around him.

He rolled, settling me on my side, close to the warmth of the fire. I made a weak, protesting groan when he left me. He pressed my back against his chest and held me tight as he slid inside me. He pulled away completely, only to slam his hips against me, teasing my tight, sensitive core, repeating the action again and again. I moaned, loving the way his hand spanned my hip, keeping me pinned to him. The other was cupped gently around my neck, tilting my face toward him as his movements became more feverish. Both arms coiled around me, clutching me to him. He gave a loud, throaty growl and bit down lightly on the nape of my neck as he came.

Cooper stilled, his face buried in my shoulder as his breathing evened out. I closed my eyes, the warmth of the fire and of Cooper's breath on my neck making me dreamily drowsy. He pulled away from me, grabbing a quilt and slipping it over us. He tucked his chin over my shoulder and nuzzled my neck. Our breathing slowed, and I thought he might have fallen asleep, but then he asked, "Um, how do you do that thing, with the balance . . . and the arching?"

I giggled, turning toward him as he sat up. "The one thing I took away from my upbringing was an aptitude for yoga. I was doing sun salutations before I could walk. And now I practice for about an hour whenever I can, usually when I'm waiting for something to come out of the oven. I have very, *very* good balance," I said, nipping at his lip.

He shook his head as if rattling something loose. "Everything you said after yoga is kind of a blur. Can you put your foot behind your head?"

"Yes, yes, I can. And if you're a very good boy, I'll put my foot behind your head."

Cooper swiped a hand across his mouth. "I think I'm drooling."

There was a tiny patch of light purple fabric clinging to Cooper's hand. It took my hormone-flooded brain a few seconds to realize it was a remnant of my underwear. I sat up and looked around the room in horror. There were little shreds of purple silk littering the floor around us. It looked like pastel confetti. Very expensive pastel confetti.

"You destroyed my underwear," I said.

"Well, yeah, it was in my way," Cooper said, as if that justified mutilating La Perla.

"You just destroyed four hundred dollars' worth of underwear," I told him.

Cooper paled. "You pay four hundred dollars for *underwear*?"

"Yes."

Cooper chewed on his lip. "I would say that's ridiculous, but really, it's worth every penny." His grin was, well, wolfish. "You'd better start a tab for me."

"Oh, no," I said, poking him in the chest. "You *will* treat my lingerie with the reverence it deserves. Next time, you will stop and appreciate—hell, you'll marvel at the miracle of my ass clad in silk."

"Next time, huh?"

"Oh, shut up, you know there's going to be a next time," I muttered. I looked down at his lap, and my eyes widened. "Well, it's a little sooner than I thought it would be . . ."

Cooper pulled me under him, pinning me to the floor. "Quick recovery time. One of the perks."

I sighed as he began a long, slow slide inside me. Werewolves could be such horndogs.

IN THE MORNING, I woke in my bed to find Cooper curled around me, his body warming me even with the blankets kicked to the floor.

I yawned and stretched, enjoying the new twinges and aches. My muscles screamed, *We had sex, lots and lots of athletic sex!*

Cooper snuffled in his sleep and threw an arm around me when he felt me move. I chuckled, inhaling the sleepy scent of his skin. He drew my back against his chest and tucked his chin over my shoulder, which was quickly becoming my favorite way to be held. "Morning," he grumbled, his voice just as gruff as you'd expect a werewolf's to be first thing in the morning.

"Hi," I said, enjoying the way his stubble gently scratched at my neck. "Hungry?"

"Always," he said, yawning as I clambered out of bed.

I shrugged into my robe. Cooper wrapped a sheet around his waist, as he'd apparently abandoned his pants somewhere in the woods. We raided my fridge for a breakfast of French toast and bacon. I laid out two full packages of bacon to fry, more than I could eat in weeks. But I'd seen the way Cooper could throw down the pork products at the saloon. I was going to have to spend a lot more on groceries if he hung around often.

I tamped that thought down. Making plans for

Cooper was dangerous. As far as I knew, this was a one-time thing. Still, I was already certain that I wouldn't sleep with another man while I was here. What was the point now? Brad Pitt could be stranded outside my door in a blizzard, begging me to use my body heat to prevent him from getting hypothermia, and any number of tricks he could come up with would not compare to Cooper and the Mighty Morphin Power Penis. Alert the male population of Grundy: I was ruined for all other men.

Of course, the number of orgasms I'd had in the last nine hours would probably keep me for the next year, so I was grateful either way.

So, instead of calculating my sexual schedule or lack thereof over the next few months, I mixed the French toast batter and thought of Evie, of how smug she would be if she knew how completely her Cooper-related predictions had come true. And how absolutely unnerved I was by Cooper's intent interest in my movements around the kitchen, something that didn't go unnoticed by Cooper.

"So I guess I make you a little nervous, huh?" he asked, smirking.

"No," I said, huffing out a laugh. "Why would you say that?"

"Because you're putting garlic in the French toast," he said, nodding toward the bowl, where I was indeed sprinkling garlic salt with beaten eggs, vanilla, and brown sugar. I smiled, rolled my eyes, and dumped the bowl into the sink to start over.

"That was not because of you, that was because

I don't have my glasses on," I told him primly.

"Yeah, yeah, futile denials of my animal magnetism don't put French toast in my belly. Hurry up, woman."

"Nice." I snorted, cracking more eggs. "So, you realize that we can never tell Evie about this, because she will gloat for all time."

"I'm willing to enter the sexual witness-relocation program as long as they place us in the same city."

"Agreed."

"So, what do you want to do today?" he asked, watching as I slid the first slices of battered bread into the frying pan. I tried to hide the trill of happy nerves. He wanted to stay. The proud intellectual portion of my brain made well-organized, thoughtful arguments for us to get to know each other better, while the hornier, dumber cranial lobes screamed, *Sex! More sex! Let's hear more of Cooper's orgasm noises! Naked Cooper, now!*

I tried to be more eloquent than my id.

"Well, pardon me for pointing this out, but you don't have any clothes here," I said, trying to look innocent. "It kind of limits our options."

He grinned. "I was hoping you'd notice."

"You know, you don't have to put up a 'dating guy' front with me. If you want to spend the day having sex, that's all you have to say."

"We may have to call in the National Guard to airlift us more condoms," Cooper said, snickering and pulling me into his lap.

"I bought the economy pack at Bulk Wonderland," I told him. "I think we're covered." Cooper's expression flip-flopped from paralyzed fear to outright joy. I shrugged. "I like to be prepared."

WHEN I WOKE on Monday morning, Cooper was gone. He'd left a note on his pillow saying he had to meet an elk-hunting party at Becker Ridge. The weather was stable, if a bit cold, and as long as it held, he would be gone for three or four days. He promised to come back as soon as possible. "Do me a favor," he wrote. "Don't wash me away. Wash your hair, your face, anything but the scent of me from your body. It's a wolf thing. I'll explain when I get back."

"Ew," I said, wrinkling my nose. Cooper was going to have to deal with my indifference to "wolf things," because I was not taking a three-day bathing break. "Surely, this is some sort of practical joke at my expense," I said to myself.

I stepped into the shower and reached for my body wash. And I found I didn't want to wash him away. Not because he told me not to, but I liked being able to smell him on my skin, that musky woodruff and spice flavor. And I hoped, wherever he was, he hadn't washed me away, either, that I would stay with him.

"I can't believe I'm doing this," I grumbled, shutting off the shower and moving over to the sink. I ran the water hot and shampooed my hair carefully. I took what I considered a conscientious sponge bath and prayed I wouldn't develop noticeable BO over the next few days.

I dressed for work and bundled into one of my

"mid-range" coats for milder winter weather. It was only supposed to get down into the twenties that day. I loved how the locals said "only in the twenties," as if it was no big deal. In Mississippi, a half-inch of snow would close the schools for three days and cause a panic at Wal-Mart. There is some sort of instinct coded into Southern DNA that sends us all running for the bread and milk aisle at the slightest sign of frozen precipitation. Snow days were a rare and precious thing when I was growing up. So it seemed wrong, somehow, to be getting ready for a workday when I could see a blanket of white out of my window. But work would keep my mind off Cooper, which was a much-preferred alternative to mooning and cabin fever.

I stepped out onto the porch. The ground was covered in an increasingly fluffy blanket of white. The air seemed cleaner. The day was quieter, the earth and its sounds slightly muffled. Everything crackled and shone in the bright but somehow shallow light. I stood still for a long minute, taking it all in. I felt blessed to be able to see that sort of beauty, to know that this was home. I was grateful to Tim for breaking off our engagement. Hell, I was grateful to my parents for driving me across the continent, if it meant I could wake up to this. Charmed, I took one step off of my porch and—

FWIP! Splat!

I was laid out on my back like a rag doll. I lay there for a long, silent moment, staring at the foot-long, obscenely shaped icicles that clung to the edge of my porch roof, and flashed back to the scene in *A*

Christmas Story, where Ralphie Parker fakes an ice-related eye injury. Was Mrs. Parker right? Did people really die from icicle injuries? This would be an extremely embarrassing way to meet one's maker—impaled through the head with penis-shaped ice skewers because my legs were too worn out from a sex marathon to keep me upright.

I giggled, trying to imagine how my obituary would read. I just lay there and laughed like an idiot in the snow for a full five minutes before going into the garage to break open my brand-new bag of rock salt.

I was so glad Cooper wasn't around to see this. I would never live it down.

AMONG OTHER THINGS, the first big snow showed me how woefully unprepared I'd been for winter, clothing-wise. I stepped into my first ankle-deep snow drift while climbing into my truck and realized exactly how permeable my three-hundred-dollar hiking boots were. Faced with an entire day of running around the kitchen in soaking-wet, squeaking boots, I knew I had to replace them and fast. And if I was honest, I was going to need two or three pairs, plus a load of sweaters, thermal shirts, snow pants, and winter-weight jeans. I really wanted to do it while Cooper was out of town, so he wouldn't be able to do the "I Told You So" dance.

All Evie had to hear was "shopping" and she planned yet another girly-day extravaganza for the following afternoon, featuring outlet malls and facials. I tried to put her B-52s CD in the stereo as we reached the town limits, but she turned the volume all the way down and gave me a pointed look.

"OK, spill," she said.

"I'm sorry?"

"Something's different about you. Your eyes are bright. You've had a big, stupid smile on your face for days." Evie's eyes narrowed at me. "You've had sex."

I blanched but tried to play off my surprise with a smirk. "Yes, I'm thirty years old. Being a virgin at this point would be rather sad."

"I mean recently," she accused. "You have had sex recently. And you didn't tell me!"

"Evie, I must confess," I said in mock solemnity. Evie's grin was a mile wide and quite smug. "I finally succumbed to the charms of Leonard Tremblay. The dark delights of his hot tub were simply too delicious to resist any longer."

Evie's mouth drooped to one side as she shuddered. "Ew."

"Let that be a lesson to you about asking prying questions," I scolded.

She shook her head in horror, focusing her eyes on the road. "The images you just put in my head will never go away. That's pure evil."

"Is this why you agreed to come with me today, because you want to rip answers from my tongue?"

"No. I really do need some new clothes, and Buzz hates shopping with a passion. This is just a clever use of our driving time." She shrugged, turning back toward the wheel and staring out the windshield. She didn't speak for a long moment.

I glared at her. "So . . . you turned my girls' day out, a rare treat that I've been looking forward to all day, into an ambush interrogation. And you've made me very uncomfortable and spoiled my mood—not that I'm trying to make you feel bad."

"So, I guess I'm paying for the facials, huh?" she muttered.

"And maybe some waxing," I said primly.

"I am not getting a Brazilian," she told me. "Even my guilt has its limits."

Evie managed to protect her nether regions from hot wax, but she did get the technician to "surprise" me with an eyebrow shaping while I was in the facial chair. She laughed more than should be legal in a hair-removal situation.

"I DON'T SEE why you're still bitching," Evie snickered as we hauled a few shopping bags in through the kitchen entrance of the saloon. It was just after closing time, and the bar was empty. Buzz was supposed to be waiting for us so Evie could give him a ride home. "You had a beautiful natural arch to your brow that was just begging to be set free."

"It's all fun and games until I end up looking permanently surprised," I countered.

The saloon was unnaturally still and quiet without customers. All I could hear was the faint echo of the jukebox playing some old Waylon Jennings song.

Evie called, "Buzz, there are two ladies in need of assistance out here!"

Pete popped his head around the corner from the bar. "Hey, Evie, let me take those."

Evie quirked her lips. "What are you doing here, sweetie?"

"Buzz asked me to wait for you. Alan got a call from the state police," he said. "Some hikers went missing on the far northwest edge of the preserve. You remember those kids from ASU who came in the other day, tried to show fake ID for beer? They were planning to go up the mountain and play *Survivor Man* before the big weather hit."

I shook my head. I couldn't remember a specific pair of hikers over the last couple of days. So many tourists filtered through town that I'd stopped paying attention. The guilt of not being able to remember their faces gnawed at me. I'd started to see the world the way most people in town did. People who were from Grundy and people who weren't.

Pete shrugged. "They were supposed to check in with friends today, but the last time anybody heard from them was three days ago. Buzz and a couple of the other guys from town went to help with the search. He asked me to stick around."

"The far northwest side of the preserve," I said, doing some distance calculations in my head. "Near my house?"

"Yeah," Pete said, shrugging.

"We'd better put some coffee on." Evie sighed. "When they wrap up for the night, they'll head back here. Alan's place is too small for a debriefing."

"That's a scary, official-sounding word." I grimaced.

Pete nodded, patting my shoulder. "We take missing people seriously around here. All it takes is a turn in the weather, a minor injury, or a fall, and people can die after just a day's exposure."

"They probably just got off the trail and got a little lost," Evie assured me, though she didn't sound convinced herself.

I stuck around to help prepare for the search party. The temperatures hovered in the twenties, and I worried about Alan, Buzz, and my friends. I wondered what manner of idiot would want to hike in weather like this and whether it was worth the risk of my friends' safety to look for people who'd put themselves in such danger.

I made biscuits because I couldn't think of anything better to do. Folding the dough, rolling it, and punching through the buttered surface with a cup seemed to ease the tension in my head. Long after it turned dark, Buzz led the charge into the saloon, the men coughing and groaning and stomping the icy mud from their boots. Evie and I passed out mugs of coffee as if they were lifelines.

"Are you all right?" I asked as I nudged a mug toward a pale, exhausted Alan. He'd been atypically distant for the last few days. I'd been prepared for him to ramp up his flirting, with Cooper out of town, but he'd hardly spoken to me, keeping his eyes wary and downcast whenever I approached. I worried that he sensed that something had happened between Cooper and me, that he was going to give up any pretense of being friends now. But he seemed happy to see me as I plied him with caffeine and buttery carbs. His tired smile was genuine, if a bit apprehensive.

"I'm better now," he admitted, drinking deeply and wrapping his hands around the warm mug as I poured a cup for Abner.

"Any sign of them?" I asked, giving him a refill.

Alan grimaced. "The kids who reported them missing gave us directions to where the boys planned to camp. We found their site. The tent was torn to hell. Sleeping bags, food, everything they had was thrown around like a tornado had swept through. There were tracks, big tracks."

My stomach dropped, and I had a heavy feeling of déjà vu. I tried to concentrate on breathing deeply, on the musical clanking of spoons and cups and male grunts as my neighbors warmed their bellies.

"Wolf tracks?" I asked, not really wanting the answer. Alan nodded. "Like the wolf that attacked Susie Q?"

Alan nodded again, looking stricken. "There were smears of blood all over that campsite. But no bodies, not even, uh, parts. It's like the kids put up a fight and were dragged out of the site, kicking and screaming. They had rifles with them. There would have to be more than one wolf to surprise and then kill two full-grown boys like that. But you normally don't see packs behaving this way. Even packs of wolves will shy away from humans if given the opportunity to run. Normally, when a human is attacked, it's by one sick or scared animal. This seems . . . organized, like the wolf knew how to get in and get what he wanted without getting hurt." Alan laughed hoarsely, rubbing his eyes. "I'm sorry. I ramble when I'm tired."

"You need one of us to drive you home?" I asked.

Alan beamed at me. Seriously, his lips parted, and it looked as if heaven had opened up. Sweet, simple, strictly platonic heaven. *Please, Lord.* "That's sweet of you. But I have to have my truck at my place. I'm heading out again in the morning. The state Department of Wildlife is sending out reinforcements at first light. We're going to search a little deeper in the forest than I was comfortable going with volunteers."

"Can I get anything else for you?"

"Nah." Alan patted my hand and then seemed to think better of it, pulling away from me. "This has been good, though. Thanks." He cleared his throat and added, "So, I've been meaning to ask . . . We haven't talked much since the party, and uh, I've just wondered, did I do something to offend you?" He lowered his voice. "I know I had a couple of beers the other night, and I might have been a little . . . forward."

"Oh!" I exclaimed, suddenly remembering Alan's mild case of Roman hands. I laughed, which seemed to startle him. "No, no, don't worry about it. You didn't do anything wrong. I've just been a little preoccupied the last few days, that's all."

"So we're OK?" he asked, his brow creasing, as if he still wasn't hearing exactly what he wanted.

Hmm. How to define "OK" between Alan and myself? Were we still friends? Of course. But now that I'd started some semblance of a relationship with Cooper, whatever I'd been heading toward with Alan was completely derailed. It felt unfair, wrong, to make him think otherwise. But he was exhausted, stressed, and sitting in the middle of a gaggle of his closest manly-man friends. Now was not the time to try to explain anything to him.

I gave him a quick nod. "We're going to be fine, Alan."

He seemed to relax, drinking deeply from his mug and sagging against the bar for support. And I felt like an awful, awful person.

AT BREAKFAST THE next morning, the dining room was buzzing about the missing hikers, Craig Ryan and Jacob Bennett, and how they might have met their gruesome end. With the pawprints found at the campsite fueling their paranoia, the locals were getting restless. Walt wanted to organize a "wolf shoot," which I guessed was similar to the turkey shoots my high school used to fill local food pantries—only, you know, much scarier. One more thing to worry about, my boyfriend getting shot by an angry mob of our neighbors.

On the opposite end of the spectrum was calm, cool, and collected Nate. He was worried about the potential loss of tourists to the area. I tried not to think badly of him. Nate was a big-picture kind of guy. And he was right. All it took was a couple of news stories about killer wolves and missing hikers, and Grundy's tourism-based economy would dry up. Tourists brought money into the town without using its tax-funded resources, and losing that would be devastating. As jobs dried up, families would move away, and the town Nate had spent his life preserving would slowly die.

In the middle of this kaleidoscope of worry was yours truly. My brain was caught in an almost constant loop of contradicting explanations. The most cheerful opinion was that the culprit was indeed just a sick, injured wolf that was straying too close to people. A tiny, needling voice in the back of my head reminded me that I'd seen Cooper sink his teeth into John Teague myself and that he would be the most likely suspect. I tried to keep a lid on that voice as much as possible. *Stupid voice.*

I rubbed my eyes and remembered with fondness the days when my biggest worry was my mother sneaking into my apartment to toss my junk food.

I hadn't thought of my parents in weeks. I hadn't heard from them in almost two months. They'd stopped calling, stopped leaving voice mails, and it was . . . fine. In her e-mails, Kara mentioned seeing them, so I knew they were OK. I wasn't wracked with guilt for not calling. I wasn't worried about whether their electricity, phone, or water had been turned off. They were grown-ups. If they didn't pay their bills, that was their problem. I chuckled, just a little bitterly. I wished this level of emotional maturity hadn't come at such a high price.

I didn't help my maternal guilt issues when the day after the search party returned empty-handed, the parents of Craig Ryan and Jacob Bennett arrived at the saloon with stacks of neon-yellow fliers that screamed, "Have You Seen These Boys?" Evie and Buzz readily agreed to display them at the bar, although the fliers were already plastered on every available surface. They were just kids, really, nineteen years old, with braces-perfect teeth and a sprinkling of acne across their cheeks. Their photos smiled out from the flier with the invincible confidence of the young.

"They were here, weren't they?" Mrs. Bennett demanded of Buzz, her voice skating that hysterical edge between shouting and shrieking. She was a thin, fine-boned woman, who was probably very pretty when she wasn't wracked by despair. "You spoke to them? How were they? Did they seem like they were all right?"

Evie shook her head, choosing to gloss over the fake-ID story for obvious reasons. "We didn't get to spend a lot of time with them—"

"Did they seem like they were OK or not?" Mr. Ryan shouted, plunging the already quiet dining room into silence.

"They were fine," Buzz said gently. "Just a couple of kids, glad to be heading out on the trail. Happy to be out of school."

Mrs. Ryan's lip trembled. "So they were happy?"

Faced with their wild-eyed, hopeless grief, I took the coward's way out. I hovered in the kitchen. Knowing that it was possible that I knew something about their sons' death, that I could speak up, and that I wasn't made me feel guilty and useless. Then again, what would I say? "Hi, I think it's possible your children were eaten by werewolves"? How would that help them?

I told myself it was sympathy for the parents that kept me from sleeping, because it felt criminally self-indulgent to think about an absent lover when people were missing their children. Still, I tossed and turned in bed, unable to sleep, tangled in sheets that smelled like Cooper. I stripped the bed, but the clean sheets left me unable to sleep *and* missing his scent. So I ended up putting the Cooper sheets back on.

I was not proud.

Instead of sleeping, I searched the Internet for stories of wolf attacks in our area, but the last proven mauling within one hundred miles was in 1987. And it involved a hunter who tried to chase a hungry wolf off the elk he'd just shot. It didn't exactly fit with our wolf's pattern. It was far more common for campers to be injured by bears or moose. I read about the various species of wolves living in the state but couldn't find anything that looked like Cooper, who seemed to be a cross be-tween a black-furred wolf and a common gray. I read about their diet, scent marking (ew), and body language, hoping to be able to decipher Cooper's moods better when he was in wolf form. For in-stance, I learned that if Cooper folded his ears back and ducked his head, he was scared. And even if he was scared—which would be an indicator of some-thing pretty bad, since he was an apex predator and all—I shouldn't run like hell. If we were facing an-other wolf, running would decrease my chance of survival. I didn't find this to be very helpful infor-mation.

Unable to channel my energy elsewhere, I was eager to get to work every morning, hoping it would help spin out the hours, but everything seemed to be moving in slow motion. I threw myself into cooking, hopping on every ticket the minute it came through the window. I practically launched the plates out of the serving pass for Evie. But I'd look up at the clock and only a few minutes had gone by.

At least, I could count on Abner to keep me entertained. On the fourth and final day of Cooper's trip, Abner smiled broadly as I slid the plate in front of him. He inhaled the fragrance of home cooking, took my hand in his, and pressed it against his bony, flannel-covered chest. "OK, gal, this is my final offer. Come live with me and cook like this every day. You'll get a toilet seat that's always down, warm feet, color TV, and I'll even install central heat."

I giggled. "Abner, I'm holding out for a convertible. I'd only be able to drive it for a month every year, but I think it would be worth it."

He chuckled, forking pot pie into his mouth.

"Abner, has it occurred to you that you're sexually harassing Mo?" Alan teased as I walked back into the kitchen. Alan, who'd made a trip into town to meet with the state police for a status report, was scruffy and trail-worn, with large dark circles under his eyes. He looked as if he could fall asleep facedown in his patty melt.

"The female mind is one of nature's greatest mysteries," Abner informed Alan solemnly. "Every woman is a puzzle waiting to be solved. Mo's just a tougher puzzle than most. But someday, I'll find the answer. And she and her home cookin' will be mine, all mine."

Alan frowned. "Abner, what you know about the female mind wouldn't fit in your sock drawer."

"Doesn't keep me from tryin'," Abner retorted.

I heard the bells over the front door jangle as it swung open. I was still laughing at their good-natured banter when I turned toward the noise. Cooper stepped through the door, his face tired and covered in three days' growth under the worn maroon cap. I felt all of the air leave my body in a happy cry. Alan's brows drew together as his eyes bounced between Cooper's relieved smile and my own jubilant expression. I rounded the counter in a few quick steps.

I paused to kiss the top of Abner's head and ducked around several diners to launch myself at Cooper. It was embarrassing how natural it felt to throw myself into his arms, to wrap my legs around his waist and let him lift me as I pressed kisses to his jaw. The constant drag of confusion from the last few days melted away, and my whole world was centered on Cooper's mouth. Maybe it made me callous or selfish, but at the moment, my need for him just wouldn't let me care.

When Cooper finally released me, I leaned back and grinned goofily down at him. "Hi."

"Hi back," he said.

"I missed you," I told him.

"You smell so good," Cooper murmured into my hair as he rubbed his heavily stubbled cheek against mine.

"I smell like grilled onions," I told him.

"Yeah, to a werewolf, a woman who smells like a

patty melt is all the more tempting," he whispered.

"I'm not sure if that was a compliment." I snorted as he looked past me to the bright yellow flier featuring the missing hikers. His brow furrowed for a moment, but he shook it off, returning his focus to me.

I expected Cooper to put me down on my feet, but he held me where I was, his hands cupping my denim-clad butt to keep me anchored to him as we spoke. And it suddenly occurred to me that I was making a giant spectacle of myself in front of half the town. But when I turned, there were a lot of smiling faces. I'd lived among them long enough to know that the minute we left the room, we'd be chewed over like yesterday's lunch special. And maybe they were grateful for a more cheerful topic of conversation. I shot a look over at Evie, whose smug expression threatened to sprain her cheek muscles.

"Um, Evie, I'm going on my break."

"Just go," Evie said, waving us out the door.

Cooper grinned at Evie, threw me over his shoulder caveman-style, and marched me out the door. I snagged my coat from the rack, catching a glimpse of Alan's deflated, slightly resentful face. I felt a flare of shame blossom in my chest. Alan hadn't deserved to find out about Cooper and me this way. But I pushed it away in favor of finally feeling happy, at peace, for the first time in days.

"Drive fast," I told Cooper as he gunned the engine and sped toward my cabin.

I WAS GOING to have to retrieve our coats and boots from the porch before it started snowing again.

Giving Cooper a sneak preview of today's selection—cobalt-blue lace bikins with a rather stunning demibra—while he was driving proved to be unwise. He almost ran off the road. So, really, I had no one to blame but myself when he pulled me out of the truck, slung me over his shoulder again, and started stripping me before we got to the front door. I was never so glad not to have neighbors.

We managed to navigate through the dark cabin blind, falling into bed. With the blue lingerie now fully in view, Cooper uttered a low moan.

"Now, this is not the underwear of a woman from Grundy," he assured me, reverently running his fingers along the waistline of the little panties. His breath came in a long, labored wheeze.

"Well, pardon me for not knowing about the thermal-only panty rule," I said, smirking as he dipped his head to nuzzle one of the silky bra cups. "I'll rush right out and buy some long johns."

Pausing to look up with perfect sincerity, he promised, "If you do, I will weep. Like a little girl. In public."

My clever retort was cut off when his hot, strong lips closed over my nipple and bit down gently through the delicate material. I made an unintelligible, inhuman noise as my hips arched up. Tracing a steady path down the length of my torso, Cooper's nose bumped at the spreading patch of moisture on my panties, sending a sensation singing through me. He inhaled deeply and pressed a kiss just over the waistline of my panties. He smiled up at me.

I rolled my eyes, shaking my head. "Fine, fine, I did what you asked, OK? Now, explain, please. Give me a plausible reason for adopting less-than-stellar hygiene habits."

"It was knowing that you were mine," he said, smirking up at me, his eyes smoldering little holes right through my defenses. "That if another man came near you, some primal, animal part of his brain would sense that scent on you and know you were taken. That if he tried to take you, he would be incurring the wrath of a very large predator."

I gasped. Was that why Alan was suddenly so shy around me?

"So, it's like an olfactory chastity belt?" I huffed out a shocked laugh, slapping at his shoulders. He snickered, grabbing my arms to ward off further blows. "You have some serious issues to work out," I told him as he pulled me close.

"Well, I played my part, too," he said, his tone teasing. "Of course, I was out in the woods without a shower, but the effect was the same. Every time I moved, shifted the slightest little bit, the scent of you would come wafting up from under my clothes. I was distracted the whole time. The clients complained that I must be recently concussed or recently in love from the way I was mooning around."

I ignored the little trill in my belly at his use of the "L" word. "Concussed?"

"They were doctors." He shrugged.

He pulled me tight against his chest. "And when I slept, I dreamed of you."

"Oh, that line's almost good enough to make the

poor hygiene all worth it." I sighed, climbing out of bed.

"Wait—what—where are you going?" Cooper stammered, waving at the now-empty bed.

"I'm taking a shower," I told him. Cooper's face fell. "I didn't say I was doing it alone. Come on."

I pulled him out of bed, but he ended up beating me to the bathroom. Werewolves can be such cheaters.

SOMETIME AROUND MIDNIGHT, Cooper and I were sitting in my bed, carbo-loading with big plates of pasta, when I worked up the nerve to say, "So, we haven't talked about the werewolf thing yet."

"We haven't?" he asked, feigning ignorance.

"No. I would remember," I assured him. "We've just been otherwise occupied. You have to know that there are about a zillion questions bouncing around in my head right now."

"I was sort of wondering when you were going to get around to asking," he said with a resigned, grim expression. He set his plate aside. "Where do you want me to start?"

I shrugged. "The beginning. How are you able to do this?"

"How are you able to curl your tongue? How did you get that little dimple in your cheek? Why are your eyes such a pretty shade of forget-me-not blue?" He shrugged, pulling me close. "It's just genetics. It's a part of us, the same as that little dimple or the color of your eyes. We're not alone. There are packs all over the world. We're a relatively small group compared with some of the rural Southern clans. We've had more and more dead lines over the years as we've married outside the pack. But my grandfather says that's for the best. Nothing worse than a bunch of inbred werewolves running around."

"Now, there's an image."

"We weren't always wolves. The people who lived in the valley were there for many generations before the first white man crossed the frozen oceans, made his way over the mountains, and married a woman of the valley. My grandfather believes the Northern Man must have come from Russia or Northeast Asia, where there are a lot of packs. Either way, something about the mixing of their bloodlines produced the first wolf-sons. There were two boys, who grew into good, strong men. There was a bitter winter, and the hunters couldn't get enough food for their families. People were starving. The Northern Man's older son wished for the strength of the wolf so that he could provide for his family and neighbors, and that he wished so strongly that he was able to transform. And then his brother, seeing what he could do, joined him. They hunted and gathered enough food for the whole village. They became protectors, leaders. They had many sons and daughters, all of whom could transform, and their children, and their children, and so on. As time went on, the generations went on, and the pack grew."

"What does it feel like, when you turn?" I asked.

He laced his fingers through mine and nibbled on the pads of my fingertips. "The first time, it was like being ripped in two. I knew it was coming. Everyone in my line can change, from my grandfather to my great-aunt Doris. I knew what was happening, and it still scared the hell out of me. As you get older, become more practiced, it doesn't hurt as much. I don't even notice it now."

I ran my free hand along the line of his back. "I expected some gross Stan Winston skin-ripping thing. It just looks like a trick of light, like your human form is some sort of mirage . . . it's a pretty mirage, considering. So, you were the leader for your pack, right? The alpha?"

Cooper's brow furrowed.

"Evie," I explained.

He rolled his eyes. "My cousin has a big mouth. Every generation has an alpha. It's not hereditary. You never know who it's going to be. One day, you're just a bunch of stupid adolescent pups, getting used to your new abilities; and the next, somebody you've known all your life tells you to do something, and you do it without even thinking about it."

"What, like being brainwashed?"

"No, it's nothing that cruel. Think about real wolves. They have to work together to make sure that everybody in the pack is fed, healthy. They're conditioned to work in harmony under a clear social rule: Obey the alpha. Werewolves have all those little human flaws that wolves don't—pride, anger, lust—so our pack instincts have to be that much stronger. So, when the alpha tells you to do something, even if you know that what he's asking is stupid or dangerous, you'll do it. And you're happy to do it, you're compelled to, because it's for the good of the pack. You need that community, the common purpose, because without it, you have nothing."

"Yeah . . . I'm still hearing brainwashing."

"OK, when I say it out loud, it does sound bad," he conceded. "But my grandfather was happy being a foot soldier. He described pack life as being part of something bigger than yourself, serving a greater purpose, sharing the best part of your life with your best friends. That's what I wanted."

"I don't understand. It's a pack of wolves, not an army," I said.

"Well, in a way, it is. The alpha serves as a sort of leader for the village, making important decisions for the pack and its families. The pack also chases off threats like wild animals, criminals, or just plain undesirables. I had a hard time sending people I cared about into a fight. I took a lot onto myself. And I hurt people. I hurt a lot of people."

"I don't believe that," I said, careful to resist my urge to back away from him, to put space between us. It had taken me this long to get close to Cooper; rejecting him now was unacceptable.

He caught my chin and forced me to look him in the eye. "Believe it."

"Fine, I don't believe you could hurt someone unless you had no other choice."

"There's always a choice," he insisted. "And I made a lot of bad ones. I couldn't live with what I'd done, what it did to my family, so I left."

I got the impression that was probably the most

detailed explanation I was going to get at this point, which was maddening. So I switched tactics. "What about your dad?" I asked carefully. "Was he happy being a foot soldier?"

"I never really got to talk to him about it." Cooper stared down at our hands. "My dad died in an accident when I was little. He was running with the pack, and one of my uncles was caught in one of those cage traps. Bunch of scientists were tagging wolves, tracking their movements for research. Pretty harmless, really. We're usually able to avoid them, but my uncle, Samson's dad, wasn't very bright when it came to stuff like that. Dad volunteered to stay behind to try to get my uncle free, when the researchers came back to check the traps. Dad was still a wolf, and he got aggressive. They had a rifle. My uncle got free, but my dad, he was hurt pretty bad—shot in the head. He managed to make it into the woods so my uncle could bring him home. They couldn't do anything for him."

"I'm sorry."

He shrugged. "The humans didn't know what they were doing. It took me a while, a long while, to stop being angry with them. They were being attacked by a huge, angry wolf. You've seen what I can do. Can you blame them?" When I didn't answer, he seemed annoyed by my silence but continued. "Samson's dad took off a while after that. He couldn't stand seeing us every day, feeling like it was his fault that we didn't have my father anymore. Samson's mom died when he was a baby, so he moved in with us. He was always more brother than cousin, anyway."

"Don't you miss that? Would you ever go back, do you think, to be part of the pack again?"

He shook his head. "My mom comes to visit. I see Samson every once in a while. And our cousin Caleb helps me with hunting parties whenever he's in town, which isn't often. My sister . . . it's pretty complicated with her. I haven't been home in a couple of years. Every time I tried to visit, it just ended in an ugly scene."

"Why?"

Cooper looked as if he was on the verge of telling me something important, then switched mental lanes before it could come out of his mouth. "She feels betrayed, like I left just to spite her or something. And she's always been so damn pigheaded. Once she makes up her mind that you've screwed her over, you're on her shit list for life."

"And I assume that she doesn't settle for the time-honored Southern tradition of passive-aggressive comments and insulting your cooking?"

"The last time I was home, I lost part of an ear and three fingertips."

"Jesus!" I exclaimed, tilting his head so I could inspect both of his perfectly normal ears.

He butted his head against my hand playfully, pushing it away. "They grew back. It stung like hell, but they grew back. Maggie's always been pretty hard-core. She had to run the fastest, fight the hardest, kill the biggest game. As much as I loved Samson, she was the one I wanted at my side and covering my back. Being in the pack, that's her whole existence. There aren't a lot of places in the world where a girl like Maggie can feel normal, accepted. I mean, there are lots of women in the pack but no one like her. And instead of feeling like she has to apologize for it, she's admired. She knows how rare that is, so she puts what's best for the pack above anything else. I left the pack, so I'm no good to her."

"But that's crazy."

He shrugged. "That's life in the pack. Maggie serves as second to a guy named Eli. He's running things now."

"I'm sorry."

He pulled me close, tucking his chin on top of my head. "There's nothing anyone can do about it."

"Industrial-grade sedatives for your sister sound like a good place to start."

He snorted. I pressed my face into his throat. I didn't want to look up at him for what I was going to ask next.

"So, on to more recent history. I get why you pretended not to know me when we were introduced at the saloon. I mean, what were you supposed to say, 'Hey, I remember you from bringing down an elk right outside your door'? But after the . . . after I was attacked, why did you act like you didn't know what happened? You were there. You saw. And you still acted like . . ."

"A complete ass," he said, cupping my face so I met his gaze. "The first time I saw you, I thought I'd dreamed you up. I couldn't tell whether it was a real dream or something I'd seen as a wolf. I used to do sweeps by your house at night. At first, I think it was just because you had all those animals tromping through your yard and the hunting was good. I remembered little things, like picking up your scent near the house and feeling warm, calm. I wanted to flop down on the porch and sleep. I couldn't seem to stop myself from coming back over and over. I'm used to the compulsive, instinctual side of my nature, but it was still confusing, that primal part of my brain leading me here every night, just to be near you. It was stronger even than my instinct to return home to my pack. It was such a relief to have one trump the other, like my ears had been ringing for years and suddenly stopped. I was able to sleep, really sleep, for the first time since I left home. As I saw you more and more in my wolf form, I realized I always remembered you the next morning. Your face, your scent, the sound of your voice—they follow me back into my human form. You're my constant. You don't fade away."

"But why were you so horrible to me, even after the alley?"

"Because I hadn't figured it out yet. I couldn't tell the difference between real dreams and wolf dreams yet. And when you . . . when you were attacked, the look on your face, the pain and the fear, that stuck with me. Every time I closed my eyes, your face was hovering there. It was torture. I resented you for it and for the pull you had over me."

"That's it? That's the reason you've been a jerk ever since I moved up here? Because I confused your wolf brain?"

"No. For the last couple of years, I've been a

miserable bastard to everybody, except for Evie and Buzz. It made things easier for me, not having friends, not having connections that could drag me down, make me responsible to anyone. You're just the first person to call me on it. Repeatedly."

"So, you're saying that if Walt or Leonard called you an asshole to your face, you'd be eating post-coital pasta with one of them right now?"

"Let's not even joke about that," he said, shuddering. "The funny thing was, even after I wanted to stop being so rude to you all the time, I couldn't. I would want to be friendly, but then I'd open my mouth, and all hell would break loose."

"And the fact that Alan happened to be talking to me during those moments—provoking your territorial, alpha-male tendencies—would have nothing to do with your inability to be civil?"

"I thought you were sleepy," he grumbled.

"I have my lucid moments."

13

The Ties That Are Binding

I DREAMED OF HOME, OF the hammock in my parents' yard, strung between two peach trees. I felt the warm sun saturating my skin, heard the droning of the bees. My father strung little bits of "sculpture" in the branches when I was a kid—mirrors, little metal bits that Dad seemed to think would help the birds nest. In reality, it just confused the heck out of the birds, but the shiny pieces were pretty to look at when you were stretched out under that fragrant green canopy.

I closed my eyes, and the scene changed. I was with Kara on the beach. It must have been on one of the many spring-break vacations in which her family had included me. The turquoise waters of the Gulf of Mexico lapped at our toes as we read Christopher Pike paperbacks and watched for cute boys.

"He's good for you, you know," Kara said in her

old-sage voice. When we were kids, she'd considered the six months she had on me to be a lifetime
of experience. As this dream seemed to be set in late
high school or early college, she could have been
talking about any number of "he's." And I found I
didn't really care, I just wanted this warm, familiar
moment to last.

"You've said that about all of my boyfriends," I
reminded her, scrunching my toes into the cool,
damp sand as I tipped my head back into the sun-
shine.

"He's going to be the love of your life."

"You've said that about all of my boyfriends, too,
Kare," I said. I reached out to pat her arm as I adjusted my Ray-Bans.

"You know, you're home now, right?" she
asked. "No matter what happens, that's your home."

I opened my eyes to find us in the parking lot
of the Tast-E-Grill, sitting in my old Chevy, which
we lovingly called the Rust Bucket. We were eating
chili dogs and Tater Tots, with our bare feet propped
on the cracked faux-leather dashboard.

This was such a weird dream.

"You're home now," Kara repeated.

"I'm confused."

"You've been a girl without a home for a long
time, Mo. It's time to stop looking. You know where
you're supposed to be. When trouble comes, you're
going to stick. You always have, you always will,"
she said, eyeing my Tots. "Are you going to finish
those?"

I blinked awake, and I swear I could still smell the

car exhaust and the chili dogs. Cooper stirred beside me, his arm tightening instinctually around me as he felt me sit up. I pressed a kiss to his shoulder and flopped my head back onto my pillow.

It didn't surprise me, as it had on occasion, to wake up with a large, naked werewolf curled around my body. These days, we were together morning, noon, and night. Naked Cooper Time was like a drug. No matter how much I got, I ended up jonesing for more. Winter was passing, and I hardly noticed. Don't get me wrong, it was cold, so cold that I occasionally feared losing outlying areas of my body just from walking to and from my truck. There were days when the roads were impassable, even with four-wheel drive, as drifts of snow reaching over my head piled in some lanes. Buzz would have to come pick me up for work on his snowmobile, and I would make minuscule batches of food for the handful of people willing to brave the roads so they could gather around the big iron stove in the dining room and avoid their own cooking.

There were afternoons when the darkness closed in on me like a smothering blanket and the wind howled like some horrible, rabid thing. The light, or absence thereof, controlled what I did, where I went, when I ate. But the claustrophobia and depression I'd expected never really set in. It's not difficult to spend days at a time trapped inside when you've got a warm fire, good food, and generally nude company. It was like a prolonged snow day. The one time I'd gotten a snow day in my brief tango with public school was when we had a freak ice storm my junior year. Hail isn't that much fun to sled on.

Christmas came and went. I counted my blessings that my parents didn't care enough about Christian holidays centered on meat consumption to call and guilt me into coming home. Abner came to the saloon dressed as Santa and gave everybody bottles of his homemade vodka. Cooper said it made a handy antiseptic, but drinking it was taking your life into your own hands.

Cooper didn't mention going home to see his family, so I prepared a low-key feast for him, Buzz, and Evie. I wasn't sure what a girl should buy her werewolf boyfriend, so I stuck with something safe: a sweater. Mind-numbingly boring, I know. Cooper made me a little carved wooden wolf, which we promptly put on my mantel to watch over me when he wasn't there. It was either endearing or a little creepy.

My favorite werewolf seemed to have moved into my house without my noticing. His T-shirts started showing up in my closet. His toothbrush was next to mine on the sink. He showed up with bags of groceries to replace the mountains of food he consumed. We didn't talk about it. It just was. Normally, this sort of invasion of privacy, the blurring of boundaries, would have me panicking. But I wanted him nearby. I had difficulty remembering what it was like not having him in my home, in my bed, nipping and nuzzling and rolling all over each other until his scent seemed absorbed into my pores.

The exceptions to our constant togetherness

were the guiding jobs he took and the nights he was a wolf. He could choose not to change, but staying human for too long made him antsy. Besides, he said it was good for other predators to sense him prowling around the house. And it made the nights he was home that much sweeter. I knew what I was missing when he was gone. And it wasn't just the sex . . . It was home, what home was supposed to be, someone to eat with, to talk to, to sleep with, always touching, always connected, as if we were afraid that when one of us woke up, the other would disappear like a dream.

We didn't talk about Susie, unless it was in relation to Oscar. And he tended to clam up whenever I asked Alan for updates on the missing hikers, so I stopped talking about them in front of him. While Cooper insisted that it was probably just a sick or injured wolf, the probability that a plain old run-of-the-mill wolf was attacking people seemed to be shrinking.

Few of our neighbors remarked on our sudden couplehood, probably because Cooper growled if they did. Responses were limited to smirks and snickers. And Abner assured me that he would wait for me until I realized I needed someone with more experience. While Nate seemed somewhat surprised by my choice of Cooper, he said he just wanted me to be happy in Grundy, which was the equivalent of his blessing. Then he mentioned something about finding a girl for Alan on the Internet, which just made me feel horrible.

For his part, Alan had trouble keeping up a gracious front. I couldn't say I blamed him. I pulled him aside at the saloon and tried to tell him about Cooper, but he cut me off. He understood, he said, but he couldn't help feeling as if something special had been yanked out from under him.

"I'll settle for being your friend, Mo," he said, his eyes tight and unhappy. "But if Cooper ever drops the ball, all bets are off. I'm gonna sweep you off your feet before you know what hit you."

I could only assume that I was the ball in this scenario.

Alan's manner never changed with me. He was just as open and friendly as ever. But he rarely spoke to or about Cooper, especially if I was around.

I blinked again, hoping to get my eyes to adjust to the darkened bedroom. I patted the nightstand until I found my glasses so I could see the alarm clock. It was only 12:20, but it felt as if it should be morning already. With the sun setting so early, my internal clock was ticking out of balance. I sat up, wondering if baking at this hour would be considered workaholism.

Obviously, this dream of Kara was my subconscious reminding me that I was neglecting the people not currently in my bed. The only contact I'd had with Kara over the last few weeks was with pictures I'd sent her of the first measurable snow. I'd had Cooper photograph me standing in a waist-deep drift, grinning like a fool. She immediately started making plans to visit me at the spring thaw. I think that was based more on the pictures she saw of Cooper than on an overwhelming desire to see me. The subject line of her response e-mail was "Do they all look like that?"

"You all right?" Cooper asked, reaching to stroke a hand down my bare shoulder. He nudged the ridges of my spine with his nose, inhaling deeply and nipping at my neck.

"Yeah," I said, shaking my head. "Weird dream about the beach . . . and chili dogs."

Cooper yawned, drawing me close. "Well, I'm no expert, but that sounds like a Freudian field day."

"Yes, because I'm so sexually deprived," I retorted.

Suddenly, Cooper's ears perked up. He leaped out of bed, landing soundlessly on his feet and dashing to the front window. His eyes scanned the yard, and he grimaced.

"Cooper?"

"Wait here. Lock up behind me," he told me, phasing as he opened the door. "Don't come out until I call for you."

I bolted the door, scrambling back into my bedroom for jeans and a shirt. I could hear deep, staccato barks outside. It sounded like a greeting or a warning or possibly a combination of both. I pulled back the curtain and tried to make out shapes in the dark front yard as I slipped my bare feet into a pair of Cooper's boots. All I could see was the outline of Cooper's wolf form just beyond the porch, at full attention, the fur on his back standing straight up. An answering series of barks sounded from the woods, and Cooper was off the porch in a flash. Just inside the tree line, I could see a huge reddish-brown wolf, almost a head and a half taller than Cooper's own furry form, lumber into view. Cooper lunged at the strange wolf in a sort of canine tackle, latching on to the fur near the red wolf's tail. The red wolf snapped its teeth around Cooper's front leg, sweeping Cooper off his paws and pinning him to the ground. They rolled in the snow, barking and biting. I fumbled through the contents of my purse for the bear mace and ran outside.

"Cooper, get away!" I shouted, flipping the cap off the bear mace and preparing to spray the strange wolf as soon as Cooper was clear. I took a swinging kick at the red wolf's side. "Get the hell off of him, you big, furry motherfu—"

The wolf dodged at the last minute, and the toe of my boot just barely caught its rib cage. The strange wolf yelped. I pressed the trigger, and a long stream of chemical spray came shooting out of the canister, right into the wolf's eyes. I coughed as traces of the burning liquid roiled through the air. Cooper rolled away and phased onto his very human feet. He knocked the mace canister out of my hand.

"What are you doing?"

"He was hurting you!" I cried. "I was trying to help."

"I wasn't hurt," he insisted. "That's just how we say hello."

"What?"

Behind me, a loud, gruff voice boomed. "Ahh! What the hell did you spray me with?"

Cooper ran toward the house. I turned to see a large naked man standing in my yard. You'd think at this point I'd be used to it, but no, not so much. The stranger was built like a professional wrestler, gone slightly soft around the middle. Huge biceps, a broad chest, thigh muscles the size of my head. His dark hair, which had a slight auburn tint to it, fell stick-straight into his eyes. Or it would have, if his eyes hadn't been clenched shut against the burn of bear mace.

Cooper came jogging back with my hose in his hands. Apparently, he'd run into the utility room to grab it and had hooked it up to the heavily insulated outside spigot. "Come on, Sam. It will feel better in a few minutes."

"She fucking maced me, Coop!"

I gasped. "I am so sorry. I thought you were a real wolf, not a werewolf. I thought you were hurting Cooper and—"

"You came running to rescue me from the big, bad wolf," Cooper said sternly as a shivering, cursing Samson held his head under the running hose. "Despite the fact that I told you to stay in the house."

"Oh, yes, because I'm so good at following directions. That should be no surprise to you," I snapped back.

Samson straightened, blinking owlishly. The angry red color seemed to be fading from his skin and eyes. "If I didn't heal so quickly, I'd be wicked pissed about this, cuz."

"Mo, this is my idiot cousin Samson. Samson, this is Mo."

Samson seemed distracted for the moment from

whatever errand had brought him to our door . . . and burning agony. He smirked at me. "I wondered why Coop's scent was so faint at his place but reeks out here. Now I see why. Of course, I could be going blind, so who knows?"

"I'm so sorry." I carefully extended my hand, keeping my eyes trained on Samson's. But some bizarre eye twitch kept leading my line of sight southward. Through the haze of embarrassment, I wondered if the heroic proportions in Cooper's family were a hereditary thing or a wolf thing. "Um, would you like to come inside?"

"I'm sorry, I don't have time. Cooper, your mom sent me for you. It's Pops. They think he's had a heart attack or a stroke or something."

"What?" Cooper sat heavily on the ground, the wind and the color clearly knocked out of him.

"Dr. Moder said he didn't have an 'acute episode.' He just seemed disoriented for a little bit, couldn't remember who we were or where he was. He's stable for right now, but he needs an EKG and a bunch of tests. He won't let us move him from the village clinic. The doc says she'll stay with him the whole time and cover up any questions, but he's afraid people at the hospital will be able to tell he's a wolf. Your mom thinks maybe if you told him to go, he would go. We tried calling, but you didn't pick up at home. And you always ignore our voice mails."

Cooper shook his head. "Me being there, it's just going to stir things up, stress him out, make him worse."

"How could you say that?" Samson demanded. "I

figured all I would have to tell you was 'Pops is sick,' and you'd come running. I never thought I'd have to talk you into going, even if you haven't been back in years. It's bad, Cooper. I've never seen him like this. You need to be there. I don't give a shit what Maggie has to say about it! You're going, even if I have to drag you back myself." Cooper shot him a dark, meaningful look. Samson grinned and looked chastened. "Well, I would try."

I noticed that as Samson got more agitated, Cooper had stepped between me and his gargantuan cousin. I'd been entirely too relaxed around Samson, assuming that because one werewolf was friendly, they all would be. I picked up the can of bear mace and clutched it just a little tighter.

"Are you sure about this?" I asked quietly as Samson gave his face one last thorough rinse. "I don't like the idea of you visiting people who bite off random body parts. I like your parts right where they are."

"I need to see my grandfather, Mo. And I need to talk to Eli, ask him a few questions. I've needed to tell him about what's been happening here, to warn him about the people here wanting to hunt down wolves. I've put it off for too long."

"Fine, I'll drive," I offered.

Cooper's eyes narrowed at me. It seemed that both of us were unsure about whether this was a good plan. I knew I had reason to be nervous, heading into a den of his relatives, when there was a possibility that one of them was stalking my neighborhood like a furry Freddy Krueger. Maybe I would see something helpful while we were there, something that could clear the werewolf pack and defuse my moral quandary . . . or maybe a signed confession I could hand over to Alan. OK, that last thing was unlikely, but there was no way I was letting Cooper go alone, especially with Maggie already stressed by her grandfather's illness. Someone had to drive *him* to the hospital if she took off more of his fingertips.

Samson grimaced and for the first time seemed a little unfriendly. "It's faster if we run."

"But you haven't had a chance to rest from your run here. Besides, I did mace you. It's the least I can do."

"Mo, you seem nice and all, but I don't think that's a good idea—"

Stepping around Cooper, I got as close to eye level with Samson as I could and used Cooper's "brook no opposition" voice. "Samson, I'm going with you. Don't waste time trying to tell me otherwise. Now, get your ass in Cooper's truck, or we leave without you."

Samson peered over my shoulder and grinned weakly at his cousin. "I like her."

"Me, too," Cooper said, his tone a little bleak as we walked back to the house to grab some clothes.

"Samson, can I get you a blanket or something?" Cooper asked, sending a pointed look in my direction as he pulled on a pair of jeans.

"Why cover up perfection?" Samson asked, winking at me. Now that Cooper had agreed to go home, he seemed to be sliding back into his natural persona—which apparently was "flirtatious goof-ball."

I countered, "Well, I don't allow bare ass cheeks on my upholstery, so if you plan on sitting down, I'm afraid I'm going to have to deprive myself of your glory."

"I really like her," Samson told Cooper as he shrugged into sweats and a sweater that were at least two sizes too small.

"Me, too," Cooper said, sighing as if affection for me was some sort of affliction.

The two-hour drive to the Crescent Valley was strained at best. The three of us barely fit into the cab of the truck. Samson was fidgety, insisting that they'd be there already if they'd run. Cooper tried to ask questions about his grandfather but came off sounding like a general asking for a briefing before heading into battle. Samson's answers weren't terribly helpful, since he seemed to have run for Cooper's place on instinct without first concerning himself with details.

"How's Mom doing?" Cooper finally asked.

"Worried. She's been at the clinic with Pops for hours," Samson said. "She'll be glad to see you. She worries about you, you know. She said you were too skinny the last time she visited. I'm surprised she didn't try to strap a ham on my back when I left."

"What about Maggie?" Cooper asked.

Samson rolled his eyes. "You know her. She'll never change. But she's pretty shaken up. I don't think she'll be together enough to go for your knee-caps again."

I gasped. "You said it was your fingertips and an ear."

"And kneecaps," Cooper muttered.

"And the eyelids, both ass cheeks, and that time she got hold of your throat," Samson reminded him cheerfully. "That was the time he tried to tell her that she had to leave the valley and go to college. I believe the edited-for-TV version of her response was something like 'Fudge you, you're not my gosh-darn alpha anymore. You don't tell me to leave the fudging pack. Now, get the fudge away from me before I rip your—' What? It was funny at the time."

"And y'all just stand around watching while she tries to dismember him?" I scowled at Samson.

Samson shrugged. "Coop won't let us help him."

"I thought that the alpha was supposed to be all-powerful. Why can't Cooper command her to stop biting off his body parts?"

"Because he won't," Samson said, glaring at him. Cooper stared at the road. "He just stands there and takes it, which is like giving her permission. If anyone else tried it, instinct would stop them from striking at the alpha, active or not. But Maggie basically has an open invitation."

Cooper glared out the window. Samson seemed to get even more ADD when it was quiet, so I asked him about growing up with Cooper. Every time he started a story, Cooper glared at him, and Samson stopped talking. So he turned the tables and asked where I was from, why I'd moved so far from home. I gave them a brief, none-too-sanitized version of my childhood with Ash and Saffron.

I'm pretty sure Cooper thought I was making it up to make him feel better. Unfortunately, you can't make up your dad getting popped for disorderly conduct at a Raffi concert. Ash believed "Baby Beluga" anesthetized children to the horrors of whaling. And hopped onstage during the encore to say so.

"Suddenly, so much about your personality makes sense," Cooper said, wiping at his eyes as we drove past a sign marking the village limits. Samson was doubled over, gasping for breath.

"You know, I didn't laugh at your painful backstory," I reminded him.

"It's hilarious, and you know it," he said. "That's why you told me, to make me feel better and take my mind off my grandfather. That's part of the reason I love you."

"You love me because I'm willing to humiliate myself to amuse you?" I asked.

"That's sort of twisted." Samson snorted. "I like it."

We pulled up to a little cinder-block building marked "Clinic," and I threw the truck into park. Samson climbed out, but Cooper stayed in his seat.

He cupped my face in his hands, tilting my chin so that I was looking right into his eyes as he spoke. "I. Love. You."

"How bad do you think this is going to be?" I blanched dramatically in an effort to cover the Mothra-sized butterflies taking flight in my belly. He loved me. Cooper Graham, one of the most beautiful, amazing, frustrating people on the planet, loved me. And it didn't scare me. I smiled. "What's next? The St. Crispin's Day speech?"

He grunted, exasperated. "Mo!"

"All right, all right. I love you, too, Cooper."

"Pardon me, I think I'm going to yark," Samson grunted through the open passenger door. "Come on, Cooper."

Grimacing, Cooper followed me as I slid out through the driver's-side door. Gripping my hand, he walked across the icy parking lot and through the clinic door. I was right behind him, with Samson bringing up the rear.

A dozen pairs of eyes were suddenly focused in my direction, and conversation died as Cooper's entire family stared in undisguised shock at us standing in the doorway.

Awkward.

14

Medusa Versus the Wolfman

I'D EXPECTED EVERYONE IN the pack to be tall and sturdy like Cooper and Samson, but there was a wide spectrum of shapes and sizes in the lupine family tree. Some were as dark-skinned and petite as Evie; others were almost fair-skinned, with light brown hair and blue eyes. This must have been what Cooper meant about diluting the bloodlines. There were so many genetic strains here it was a wonder the wolf magic had been passed along at all. But it had produced some beautiful individuals.

Beautiful but distinctly *not human*. Cooper had always stood out to me, compared with our Grundy neighbors, although I assumed it was because he was so spectacularly handsome . . . or that he pissed me off so much more than other Grundy residents. Now that I saw a pack en masse, the difference was obvious, and I was nervous. Even the products of "dead lines" seemed sinuous in their movements, purposeful. Their eyes took in everything around them, processing and cataloguing information that might be used later. And they were plowing through a box of doughnuts as if carbs were about to be declared illegal.

"Pops!" Samson thundered across the crowd, dragging Cooper and me in his wake. "Look who's here to talk some sense into you."

Samson pulled us into a little exam room off the crowded, cheerfully decorated waiting room. Cooper's family tried too hard to seem as if they'd returned to normal conversation. It was as if a director had yelled, "And . . . background noise!" to a bunch of really untalented movie extras.

I was stunned when I saw Cooper's grandfather for the first time. Noah Graham might have been laid up in a hospital bed napping, but strength radiated off him like body heat. His face was tanned and leathery, topped by a full tuft of iron-gray hair. A thin green knit blanket covered a body that still seemed solid, capable.

"He's eighty-two? He looks younger than my dad," I muttered to Cooper as we approached the bed.

"Men in my family tend to age well," Cooper said quietly. I felt the tension ebb from his body as he saw that his grandfather was alive, if not completely well. "It's all part of the wolf thing. Our bodies are resilient because of the constant phasing, lots of collagen. Pops is still considered quite the catch around here."

"I'm old, not deaf, my Cooper," Noah said, his voice a deep baritone that rumbled from his chest.

When he lifted his lids, I could see that Noah shared his grandson's blue-green eyes, which twinkled as he sat up to embrace Cooper. A small, compact blonde in blue scrubs and hiking boots laid a gentle hand on his shoulder to keep him reclined.

"How's he doing?" Cooper asked.

Dr. Moder opened her mouth to answer, but Noah waved her away as politely as possible. "I'm fine," Noah insisted, his hands firm on Cooper's shoulders. "There's been a lot of fuss for nothing. But I'd go through it again, if that's what brought you back to your home. It's been too long, Cooper. The pack, your family, have missed you." Noah cast a glance in my direction and lifted his ruler-straight gray brows. "And who have you brought with you?"

"This is Maureen Duvall-Wenstein, Pops. We call her Mo," Cooper said, a note of pride in his voice as Noah pulled my hands into his.

"Very nice to meet you, young lady," he said.

"It's very nice to meet you, too," I said. "Cooper has told me so much about you."

"Well, he hasn't done the same for me," Noah said, giving Cooper a reproachful look without any heat in it. "You and I will have to sit and talk, Maureen."

"What's this I hear about you not wanting to go to the hospital?" Cooper asked, apparently sensing that introduction time was over.

Noah lowered his voice and offered his grandson a level gaze. "We must protect the secret. That is far more important than prolonging the life of any one of us. "

"Pack members have gone to the hospital before with no problems," Cooper said in a voice that was both loving and stern. I looked over my shoulder to see that several of Cooper's relatives had gathered at the door, listening to him. I didn't understand why Cooper had been so resistant to coming home. While I certainly didn't want to test their fondness for strange humans who knew their family secret, I didn't sense any hostility from the crowd huddling at the door. They were smiling, practically smug in seeing Cooper work on his stubborn grandfather.

I carefully scanned each face in the family. Could any of these people be capable of attacking unarmed humans? They certainly didn't look it at the moment, but they *were* sort of on their best behavior, being indoors, clothed, and in the presence of an outsider. I tried to picture the plump little auntie in the purple Red Hat Society sweatshirt wolfing out and devouring teenage hikers.

It was a stretch.

"Dr. Moder says she'll be able to cover up any discrepancies that might come up while they're treating you," Cooper said. "And when you're done, she can remove all of your records from the system. There's no reason to stay here when you could be at the hospital having all those important tests and flirting with the nurses."

"I do not like hospitals."

Cooper countered, "You've never been to a hospital."

"And it's worked well for me so far."

Sensing that the conversation would continue to circle if I didn't give them some space, I stepped away. The crowd parted for me as I approached the door. I crossed the waiting room to an ancient-looking Mr. Coffee and poured myself a cup. Even with healthy doses of cream and sugar, I gagged a little as it hit my throat. This was not coffee. This was the stuff you'd scrape from under Satan's toenails.

"Someone should have warned you," said the tall, whippet-lean stranger who was suddenly standing at my side. "Aunt Glenda made the coffee. She seems to think that if you can stir it, it's not strong enough. I'm Eli," he said, reaching out to take my hand.

"Mo," I choked out. "I'm a friend of Cooper's."

"Must be more than a friend if you're here," Eli observed, his cool lakewater-green eyes scanning me from head to toe. "I don't think it would be too far off to thank you for bringing Cooper here tonight. None of us could convince Pops to budge, but Cooper will. They've always been close. It doesn't hurt that Cooper's still technically the alpha, though he would never force his will on someone like that— much less Pops."

"Are you a cousin of Cooper's?"

"Second or third, we can't really keep track. I tried making a chart once, but . . ." Eli's smile was congenial as he shrugged. "I sort of handle things in Cooper's absence. But we're all glad to see him again. It's been too long. We've worried about him. We may be upset that he didn't want to be alpha, but we still love him. We want him to be happy."

I asked, "Would you mind telling him that?"

"I don't think he would believe me," he said.

Pops was giving Cooper and Dr. Moder a run for their money in the hospital debate. Noah had crossed his arms over his chest and set his face in defiant lines, which I'm sure at one point in his life would have shut his grandson down without argument. The arguments circled around and around the room until Cooper finally said, "Pops, for my sake, would you go to the hospital?"

Noah stared at Cooper for a long moment and cleared his throat. "If it will make you feel better, I will go."

Dr. Moder winked at Cooper. "I'll call the cardiac department at St. Martin's, let them know we're coming."

"I'll pull my truck around," Eli told them.

"Now, that's settled. Let an old man rest," Noah muttered, closing his eyes. He snapped them back open and smirked at Cooper. "How many nurses will there be, do you think?"

Cooper snorted and patted Noah's hand. "Get some rest, you old hound."

I returned to Cooper's side. He wrapped his arm protectively around me as the relatives converged on us. Cooper's cheeks were kissed, pinched, patted, and thoroughly lipsticked. I was generally ignored, which was fine. I think they were waiting for some sort of signal. At this point, surrounded by the crush of bodies, I was just grateful that everyone seemed to be fully clothed.

"Yeah, we need to talk about that Maureen

thing," I whispered as we made it out the other side of the gauntlet, into the waiting room. "You were out of town when my real name got spread around by Susie Q. And, uh, it isn't Maureen."

He stopped in his tracks, a mixture of guilt and apology flashing across his features. "It's not? I just assumed . . ."

"We'll talk later."

"How bad could it be?" he asked as we approached a round, smiling woman with an unlined face.

"Later," I whispered.

"That bad?"

I stopped and murmured in his ear, "Moonflower Freedom Refreshing Breeze Joplin Duvall-Wenstein. OK?"

Cooper stared at me. "Wow."

"Do you have any idea how long it takes me to fill out income-tax forms?"

Cooper's response was cut short when the clinic door burst open. A slim, short woman stomped through the door, followed by an older woman with a worried expression. The younger one scanned the crowd until her obsidian eyes landed on Cooper. Her lip curled up in disgust.

Wait a minute, I recognized that scowl. That was Cooper's scowl.

That was Cooper's sister.

"What the hell do you think you're doing here?" she demanded.

Maggie Graham was hard, lean, and built for speed. Her black hair was cut in sharp layers around her face. She was beautiful in a fierce, alien way, like the old Greek mythical monsters that consumed heroes the minute their backs were turned.

Eli stepped through the door, an apologetic grimace wreathing his face. "Sorry, Coop, she saw your truck. I couldn't stop her."

"Maggie," Cooper said, carefully examining her face. "You went and grew up on me.'

"That happens when you leave and don't look back," she snapped.

"Just for one day, let's not have any trouble."

"I don't have to listen to you, Cooper. You made sure of that a long time ago. Leave the valley now. You're not welcome here anymore. You don't have a home here."

"Maggie, please don't," the older woman pleaded.

Cooper's voice grew harder, more authoritative. "Maggie, just calm down. "

But Maggie was already crouched, springing toward an attack. My human eyes couldn't track her movements as she shifted into a wolf and lunged. A dark shape blurred past me, barreling into Cooper. As a wolf, Maggie was smaller than Cooper but no less intimidating. She was compact, but you could see the strength in her limbs, the barely controlled power as she leaped at him.

Cooper barely had enough time to phase before hitting the ground with Maggie's teeth clamped around his neck. He shook off the tatters of his clothes as he struggled to throw his little sister off his back. Samson started to jump into the fray as family members scattered out of the way, leaving toppled chairs and spilled coffee in their wake.

"No, the fewer involved, the better," Noah said wearily. "Try to corral them outside if you could. Dr. Moder shouldn't have to clean up after them."

Samson and Eli shooed—for lack of a better word—the grappling wolves out the clinic door, and the rest of the pack poured out into the parking lot after them. Cooper was definitely on the defensive, feinting when Maggie snapped at him and rolling when she pounced. But he didn't fight back. There were plenty of opportunities for him to take advantage of his size, his strength. He could have pinned her a dozen times. Instead, he just tried to keep her from doing any permanent damage, like a resigned parent handling a toddler's temper tantrum.

I searched the crowd for some sign of reason, someone who would step in and stop this. But most of Cooper's relatives seemed proud, happy, as if a sibling death match was some sort of cherished holiday tradition. Half were cheering for Cooper, the other half for Maggie. And if I wasn't mistaken, a couple of them were placing bets.

"This is ridiculous. Aren't you going to do something?" I asked Eli. "I thought you were in charge. Tell Maggie to stop."

"I'm not actually the alpha, so I don't have any real authority over her. Cooper's still the alpha until he dies. I'm just the de facto leader. If I told Maggie to stop, she'd just snap off a chunk of my hide and then go after Cooper again. Besides, this is how we work things out. It might do them some good."

I grunted in frustration and looked up to Cooper's giant cousin. "Samson?"

Samson cast a longing glance at the fight but shook his head. "I told you, Cooper doesn't want help. Besides, I've got scars you wouldn't believe from jumping between the two of them."

"Oh, for goodness sake," I huffed, stalking into the clinic. I saw that while Cooper and Maggie fought it out in the parking lot, Dr. Moder was loading Noah into Eli's shiny red SUV, covering him with blankets. I glanced around the waiting room for the most viable solution. Since they didn't have industrial-grade sedatives in the waiting room, I grabbed the fire extinguisher off the wall, pulled the pin, and made my way outside through the crowd.

Getting as close to the wolves as I dared, I squeezed the trigger and shot a dusty white cloud over both of them. The two wolves yelped, separating. Maggie recovered faster than Cooper, who was slumped on the ground and seemed to be bleeding from his neck and one paw. She lunged for him again, but I let out another puff of white dust. When that didn't deter her, I beaned her with the heavy red canister. The pack let out a collective gasp. Maggie whined and wobbled to the ground.

Even as I did this, I wondered what the great burning hell I was thinking. This was not normal behavior for me. Years with my parents had schooled me in the art of passive resistance—letting them rant and rave about my poor personal choices and then doing whatever I wanted to anyway. I did not shout or make threats. I sure as hell didn't put myself between angry supernatural creatures. What was Cooper doing to me?

"What the hell was that?" Maggie growled, phasing and rolling to her human feet. She pushed her lean, naked form into a crouch, growling at me. She pressed her fingers to the purpling lump growing on her forehead. "Who do you think you are, interfering in pack business?"

"Back off," I warned her. "You've made your point. Now, back off. You're not the reason he came here tonight. Your grandfather's going to the hospital, and Cooper's going with him. He can't do that if he's handling your little hissy fit."

Maggie sneered and advanced on me. Being shot with freezing-cold fire-suppressing chemicals again probably wouldn't improve her mood, but at this point, I'd sort of cornered myself, and the fire extinguisher was my only weapon. I supposed I could always hit her with it again.

"Maggie," Eli grunted, his tone far more authoritative than I would have thought possible. "Don't."

"Nobody wants either one of you here," Maggie snarled, ignoring Eli. "You think you're special because Cooper brought you home to meet the family? What a joke. He doesn't care about his family. And he doesn't care about you. When he's done with you, he'll run. That's what Cooper does."

At the moment, Cooper was on the ground and seemed to be struggling to phase back into a human. Maybe he was more seriously injured than I thought. I tried to keep my voice cool, detached, as I backed toward him, fire extinguisher at the ready. "Look, I'm not going to get into some sort of feminized pissing contest with you. I don't do that.

I don't like being rude or making a scene. Not because I'm not good at it. I learned from my mother, who's made a lifelong hobby of making public officials cry. You're a rank amateur, even if you can turn into an apex predator. Now, step off, you hateful little bitch, or—"

I don't remember much after that, because Maggie punched me so hard that I felt my jaw somewhere in the back of my neck. Behind me, I heard a bellowing roar and barely registered the sound of claws skittering over the frozen ground. The fire extinguisher slipped out of my hand, falling to the concrete with a loud *clang*. I swayed on my feet but stayed upright, managing to swipe an upper cross into Maggie's chin. She let out a snarl and hit me again, right in the eye.

I took some comfort in the fact that it was my head smacking back on the pavement that knocked me out and not the actual punch . . . no, it was pretty lame either way.

15

A Brand-new Sense of
Familiarity . . . with a Stick Shift

I WOKE UP ON A strange couch with a steak on my eye.

"Is meat the answer to everything with you people?" I grumbled, sitting up.

"Slow," a low, musical voice told me. Someone was keeping a restraining hand on my shoulders. "You've been out for a while. We're still not sure whether you have a concussion."

I blinked a few times before opening my good eye. Samson, who I was thankful to see was clothed, was sitting in a nearby easy chair. The room was meticulously clean, decorated with scattered photos of Cooper, Maggie, and Samson in various stages of childhood. The walls were a warm, creamy color. A bright blue throw rug was settled comfortably in front of a large brick fireplace. On the mantel were three carved wooden wolves, just like the one Cooper had given me for Christmas.

"We're glad to see you back in the land of the living," the musical voice said with a chuckle as the steak was pulled away from my face. I'd heard the words "pleasantly plump" used to describe women before, but they never seemed so apt as when they were applied to Gracie Graham. She was soft and round and had a warm smile permanently etched across her face. Heck, I wanted to crawl into her lap and ask for a story.

"I've never seen a human girl take a punch like that," Samson marveled. "You know, if things don't work out with Cooper, I'm going to marry you myself."

"It's tempting, Samson. But I've seen you naked. I'm afraid you'd break me in half."

Samson gave a loud snort. I realized I'd said something incredibly vulgar in front of Cooper's mother and felt blood rush to my cheeks. Gracie managed to ignore the exchange completely. I was mortified. But honestly, hello, head injury? I couldn't be trusted to stay tactful even without being concussed. Then again, I'd also called Gracie's daughter a hateful little bitch right in front of her—before the head injury. But given the way she was taking care of me, it seemed Gracie wasn't holding a grudge.

"Where is everybody?" I asked.

"After you used your face to break Maggie's hand—" Gracie shot a stern look toward Samson. He prattled on, oblivious. "Cooper, Eli, and the doc took Pops to the hospital. Cooper wanted to stay with you, but I told him I'd keep an eye on you. Eli and Dr. Moder were sort of afraid they'd get Pops to the hospital and he'd change his mind unless Cooper was there to nudge him inside."

"Where's Maggie?" I asked.

"Well, I picked you up off the ground and carried you into the house. Cooper phased and tackled Maggie. There was a good bloody brawl that we will be talking about for *years*. Gracie jumped between them and made them both phase back to human. Maggie started yelling that it was Cooper's fault for bringing some human here in the first place, and what the hell did he think he was doing showing up after all this time . . ." Samson seemed to realize that he needed to edit himself. "The end result was that Eli told Maggie she needed to go on a long run to think about her actions. It's like banishing her from the village for three days."

"So the angry face-bruising werewolf is going to blame me for her getting grounded?" I moaned. "Fantastic."

"I am very sorry for my daughter's actions," Gracie said, her lip trembling a little as she dabbed the area around my eye with a thick, yellow, strong-smelling salve. "She hasn't been the same since Cooper left. She's a very angry young woman. I have tried talking to her about controlling herself, but nothing helps. Eli can usually talk some sense into her. But seeing Cooper face-to-face after such a long time . . ."

"It's not a big deal. I probably shouldn't have interfered like that. I've definitely learned my lesson," I said, wincing as she probed the tender spot just under my lashes. "I just couldn't watch her go after Cooper like that."

Gracie offered me a warm, gratified smile.

"Attacking Cooper's mate is a big deal," Samson assured me, suddenly looking fierce. "Maggie should be ashamed of what she did. It was an insult to everyone there. No matter what you said to her, or hit her with, she shouldn't have gone after you like that. You're a human. You didn't stand a chance."

"Thanks," I muttered, not bothering to correct his " mate" assumption. "How's Cooper?"

"Pissed, which is a good sign, I think. He'll take that crap from Maggie, but the minute she laid a hand on you, all bets were off. He's never drawn blood from her before, never pushed back like that, even when we were pups. It knocked her on her ass, in every sense of the word, which is good for her." I nodded, staring down at my hands, which were covered with fire-extinguisher residue. "So, you're handling the whole wolf deal pretty well," he observed. "Most human women would have run for the hills by now."

"I like Cooper, a lot," I said, casting a cautious glance at his mother. "And I didn't exactly have the most 'orthodox' upbringing, so I'm used to the slightly unusual."

"Still," Samson said, that touch of awe returning to his voice.

"You are either very brave or very odd to agree to come here," Gracie said, lifting my chin. She seemed to be inspecting the damage but at the same time pinning me with her wide green eyes.

"It's probably a mix of both," I admitted.

"How do you feel?" she asked.

"Hungry," I said. I checked the clock. It was almost five in the morning. Thank goodness it was Sunday, my day off, so I wouldn't have to call in "concussion" and explain my ass-kicking at Maggie's hands to Evie.

"I'll make you some breakfast," Gracie said, rising from the couch.

"No, actually, do you mind if I cook?" I asked, pushing myself to my feet. "It would probably settle my nerves a little bit. And you're exhausted. Have you had any sleep?"

"No," Gracie admitted.

"You sit, I'll cook," I told her. "The best way to tell if I have a concussion is seeing whether I remember all of the ingredients for a western omelet."

Gracie protested, "I couldn't let you—"

"Not so fast, Mom," Samson said. "Cooper's told me all about her cooking. Maybe we should let her get back on her feet."

"Forgive Samson, he was raised by wolves," she muttered.

I quirked an eyebrow. "Is this some sort of test? If I laugh at that joke, will I be tossed out?"

Samson barked out a laugh as he pulled me into the kitchen. "Didn't I tell you, Mom?"

IF MY COOKING was any indicator of cranial well-being, I was concussion-free. The smell of sautéed onions and peppers, dosed with a little garlic, raised my spirits considerably. Gracie had a clean, orderly kitchen. Everything was just where you'd expect it to be. She made coffee, and she and Samson sat at the kitchen table, watching me cook.

There were more pictures in the kitchen. Cooper, Maggie, and Samson in happier times, sledding, fishing, making hideous faces at the camera. Maggie and Cooper were obviously close as kids. In almost every picture, she was right by his side, his arm slung around her shoulders.

"You'd never seen a sister who loved her brother as much as Maggie," Gracie said, handing me a cup of coffee and nodding at the picture I'd been staring at. "Or a big brother who tolerated his baby sister hanging around as well as Cooper."

"I'm sorry, I just don't get it," I said, stirring eggs into a pan. "If they were so close, why can't she just forgive him? Or at least stop trying to rip his face off every time she sees him? Why is she so angry with him? Cooper told me he *had* to leave, but he's never explained what that meant. I thought maybe it was that he didn't feel welcomed by his family anymore, but I see that's not true. What happened to make him feel like he couldn't stay?"

Samson lifted an eyebrow. "He hasn't told you?"

We heard a truck's engine humming outside the house. I looked out the little kitchen window and saw Eli's SUV pull to a stop in the driveway.

"Cooper should be the one to tell you," Gracie said quietly.

As the front door opened, Samson said loudly,

"And then I convinced Cooper to hold the umbrella and jump off the highest limb he could reach. I didn't tell him to jump feet-first, though I thought that part was pretty obvious."

I stared at Samson, bewildered. But Gracie managed to catch on and pick up the conversational thread easily. She sighed. "Samson and Cooper were never allowed to watch *Mary Poppins* again."

"Which was OK, because we saw *Superman*, and I convinced Cooper to climb up on the roof with a red towel wrapped around his shoulders . . ."

"How many of your stories end this way?" I asked, finally catching on, as Cooper walked into the kitchen.

"They're telling you humiliating stories from my childhood?" Cooper asked wearily as he crossed to the stove and inspected my bruised eye. Samson hopped to his feet and poured coffee for Cooper and for Eli, who trudged into the kitchen looking surprisingly chipper.

"Only good things," Gracie promised.

I made a sour face. "Well, I wouldn't consider prolonged bed wetting a *good* thing . . ."

Cooper's mouth popped open in astonishment, and Gracie gave a long, hooting laugh. I cracked more eggs and stretched the filling for two more omelets as Eli and Cooper gave his mother an update on Noah. The tests showed no evidence of heart attack or stroke, but they were keeping him for observation just in case. Cooper looked down-to-the-bone weary, sagging in his chair against the kitchen table. I slid plates in front of them. Samson moaned in ecstasy as he forked his first bite into his mouth.

I turned back to the stove and heard Samson stage-whisper, "How open is your relationship, exactly?" I smiled to myself when a meaty punching sound was followed by Samson's colorful string of profanities. "I was just asking!"

"Children," Gracie warned, but she sounded pleased.

I leaned against the counter with my plate. Gracie tried to get me to sit, but I was happy to hang back, to watch Cooper with his family. But the longer he sat there, the more tense he became. He kept an eye on the front door at all times, occasionally looking up to me to make sure I was, I don't know, safe? Still there? Eli picked up on his agitation and placed a hand on Cooper's shoulder.

"We've got to go," Cooper said, rising, shrugging off Eli. "I'm exhausted. Mo's hurt. I'll call you this afternoon for an update on Pops."

The hard edge to Cooper's voice made my stomach twist. How had the warm, homey feel of the kitchen disappeared so quickly? I finished my eggs and turned to the sink to start the dishes. It gave me something to do with my hands besides wring them and generally behave like a ninny.

"Why don't you stay for the afternoon?" Gracie suggested, managing to keep the note of pleading from her voice. "Take a nap, get a shower, before you get back on the road."

He shook his head and gently nudged his forehead against his mother's cheek. "Time to go."

I cleared my throat. Cooper shot me a long, uncomfortable glance. I tilted my head toward Eli and mouthed, "Grundy."

Cooper grimaced and turned back to Eli. "You've got to keep the pack from running anywhere near Grundy for a while. There have been attacks, incidents in town. People are being hurt. Hell, two kids are missing, and there were wolf prints all over their campsite. People in town are getting more and more riled up. They're talking about organized hunts. If they see a wolf anywhere in the vicinity, you could have a dead pack member on your hands."

Eli nodded slowly, for some reason keeping his gaze steady on me. "We're aware of the situation. I've seen a few things on the news. I've told the pack to cut Grundy a wide berth."

"We usually do anyway," Samson added. "We know you don't like to be crowded."

"But you sent Samson to us last night," I said. "He could have been spotted. He could have been hurt. There are traps everywhere in the woods."

Eli looked supremely annoyed with me for speaking. He gave Cooper a sharp look. "Is this a conversation we should be having now?"

"She's my mate," Cooper said. "She has a stake in this, too."

Samson's eyebrows shot up, and he gave me a speculative sort of grin. Gracie's lips quirked into a subdued smile. What the hell had just happened? With Samson's comment earlier, the declaration felt important somehow. What exactly did being Cooper's "mate" entail?

"We sent Samson running to you because it was an emergency," Eli said.

"And have there been any other emergencies I should know about?" Cooper asked quietly. "Have you noticed anyone going on solo runs?"

Eli's grip on his ever-present grin faltered a bit, and for a moment, he looked truly pissed. "Are you asking whether someone from this pack is making a habit of attacking humans in your territory?"

Cooper's expression hardened. "I just like to know who's running through my backyard."

"No one in this pack runs on his own," Eli ground out. "No one runs without me knowing about it."

"You're sure about that?" Cooper asked in that tone of voice I now recognized as his alpha mode. Official leadership status or no, I didn't think Eli had much choice in answering truthfully.

"Positive," Eli said dismissively. "Look, Cooper, if you're worried about being discovered or being hurt, maybe now would be a good time to think about moving home. You're protected here. You're safe. And it would only help the situation with Maggie. She can't stay mad at you when you're around all the time."

"What are you talking about?" Cooper asked.

Eli shrugged. "This is what's best for everybody, Coop. The pack needs its alpha back, someone with real authority. They follow me, but they *love* you. You saw how everyone responded to seeing you last night. Just seeing you there was enough to set them at ease. I'm a solid logistics guy, but I'm not you.

They need you, Cooper. Sure, you got lost for a little while, but every good leader struggles—"

"Eli, I'm not coming home. I have a life to get back to. Just keep the pack as far away from me and Mo as possible, got it?" He took my hand in his. "We're going."

Knowing better than to argue at this point, I slipped into my boots and coat and got a mildly inappropriate kiss from Samson and a long, hard squeeze from Gracie. "Come back anytime," she told me.

Eli kept his distance, giving me a resigned little wave. This suited me just fine. Cooper took my elbow and wrapped his arm around my shoulders to lead me across the treacherously slick pavement. I tried to convince him that I should drive. Between the two of us, I'd at least had a little sleep, even if it was technically being knocked out. But he just shook his head and lifted me into the passenger seat. He tilted my chin up, taking a long look at my shiner. He gritted his teeth, tucked my legs into the truck, and shut the door.

Cooper was silent on the drive home. I used the time to stew. Had I made a mistake in insisting that I go to the valley? Would he be angry with me? What if he just dropped me off at home and disappeared for a few days . . . oh, my God, what if he didn't come back? What if he decided he didn't want me for his mate anymore? Whatever that meant.

I wasn't used to this sort of anxiety in a relationship. If Tim got mad at me and went back to his place for the night, all that meant was that I got control over the TV. Every once in a while, I would start a fight if I wanted to watch a particularly interesting episode of *Bones*. Tim couldn't stand crime procedurals.

This left me unprepared for the growing dread settling in my belly as the miles slipped by. He pulled to a stop in my driveway and cut the engine. I unclipped my seatbelt and waited.

Cooper kept his fingers curled around the steering wheel and stared straight ahead. I slumped back against the seat. What if he really was pissed at me for getting into it with Maggie? Or for getting so damned cozy with his mother that morning? Why wasn't he saying anything? Should I say something? What if he was waiting for me to talk? *Oh, hell.*

"Cooper, I'm—*mmph*!" My apology was cut off as his mouth clamped over mine, pulling the breath from my lungs with the force of his kiss.

Sliding across the seat, Cooper scooped me up and pulled me into his lap. With some effort, he managed to shimmy my jeans over my hips, shoved my panties aside, and plunged his fingers between my warm folds. I wasn't quite ready for him, and I hissed as a hot sizzle of pleasure-pain barreled through me. He curled his fingers upward, sending an electric shock straight up my spine. He teased my mouth, edging his tongue along my bottom lip, mimicking the movements of his wrist. The heel of his palm ground against my clit with every stroke. I reached back, bracing my hands against the dashboard as Cooper's other hand snaked up to cup my neck, anchoring me to him. My inner muscles fluttered against his fingers as I wailed in release.

Nearly boneless, I slid onto Cooper's lap. The denim of his jeans raked deliciously against my oversensitized flesh . . . which was good, because my shaking hands couldn't seem to master his belt buckle. Through the postorgasm fog, it struck me as funny that this was the first time *Cooper's* clothing was an obstacle. But I didn't laugh, I didn't have time to get past the initial thought. Cooper was moving too fast.

I heard the faint slide of a zipper as my head lolled on his shoulder. I gasped as he pulled me close. By now, I was so wet, so ready for him, that I slid onto him easily, right to the hilt, until I was fully seated on him. His hands stayed on my hips, guiding me up and down, setting a furious pace. And when that wasn't enough, he edged forward on the seat, arching up and wedging me against the steering wheel as he slammed his hips into mine.

There was no tenderness, no gentle touches, nothing to make the moment last. He was pouring all of his grief and heartache into my body, and I absorbed it. He ran his lips down the line of my neck, stopping to graze my throat with his teeth.

He reached between us, his fingers tracing the lines of our joined flesh. His thumb circled my clit, bringing me with him as he growled and bucked under me. I threw my head back again, whacking my head against the windshield. He took my chin in his hands and turned my head away. His teeth brushed along my neck to my shoulder and struck deep. I yelped as his canines broke the skin, marking me.

When Cooper stilled, I leaned my forehead

against his, breathing heavily. He seemed to come back to himself, taking in the flush in my cheeks, the disheveled clothes. He pressed his ear to my chest, breathed in my scent, and listened to the beat of my heart.

When I leaned back, he traced the bite mark with his fingertips. His eyes focused, and his lip trembled.

"I should run."

I cocked my head, sure that I'd heard him wrong. "I'm sorry?"

He gently pulled me out of his lap and fastened my jeans. "I need to run. Clear my head a little. There are some things I need to work through, and I don't want to be around you when I do it." He helped me out of the truck, carrying me to the front door, as I seemed to have lost my boots in the cab somewhere.

"You don't have to go," I told him as he shrugged out of his shirt.

He kissed my cheek. "I'll be home soon."

I heard his clothes fall to the porch and the soft *thump* of his paws hitting the ground after he leaped off the porch. I rolled my eyes at the ceiling.

Werewolves could be so melodramatic.

I WALKED INTO the bedroom and peeled off my clothes, which were now suspiciously stained and smelled of raw steak and sautéed onions. The house seemed so empty, even with the turtlenecked Oscar yipping and yapping at my heels. I'd become accustomed all too quickly to midnight snacks, communal showering (for water conservation, of course), and going to bed together. As tired as I was, the idea of crawling under cold sheets alone was depressing.

I slipped into one of Cooper's T-shirts, pulled Oscar into my lap, and fired up my computer. I'd been dealing with this werewolf issue from the wrong angle, trying to apply stuff I'd learned from movies and myths or Mutual of Omaha specials. I was dealing with real people. Cooper said there were packs all over the world. There had to be other bewildered were-girlfriends out there. I just had to find them.

Unfortunately, you get a lot of weird results when you Google "werewolf girlfriend."

Gingerly touching my spanking-new bite mark, I waded through pages of results before finding a Web site for some occult book shop in Kentucky called Specialty Books. It was the only online store I could find that carried relationship-advice books for people dating were-creatures. It's not as if they carry this stuff on Amazon.com. I bought four hundred dollars' worth of books and agreed to the outrageous shipping prices.

I continued to surf, trying to distinguish the "could be factual" from the "total crap." A lot of stuff I already knew from experience. For instance, according to WerewolvesDebunked.com, werewolves were far more in touch with their natural instincts than most humanoid supernatural creatures, which also made them impulsive, temperamental, fiercely territorial, and intensely physical. Sound like anyone I know?

And I learned why Cooper ate so much and never

gained a damn ounce. Shifting from human to wolf requires huge amounts of energy. Younger were-wolves have to scarf down calories all day to keep their bodies fueled and ready to change. There's also a bit of instinctual hard-wiring to keep fed, because real wolves never really know when their next meal will be.

I didn't know, however, that there was no "magic bullet" solution—silver or otherwise—to kill a were-wolf. While they do have increased healing abili-ties to cope with their rough-and-tumble lifestyle, wolves are as vulnerable as any creature. So if it will kill a real person or wolf, it will kill a werewolf. I couldn't explain why, but that made me feel both more and less safe.

I was surprised to find that there were many kinds of were-creatures. Bears, horses, lions, skunks, cats, dogs. Name any animal, and there is likely a person out there who can change into it.

At this point, I eyed Oscar suspiciously. "If you turn out to be a potbellied, middle-aged accountant, I will be supremely annoyed."

Oscar huffed, as if the very idea offended him.

16

Moroseville, Population: Me

FOR THE NEXT FEW days, my face felt as if I'd been head-butted by a cement truck and didn't look much better. I spent most of the next day in the kitchen to avoid questioning looks from customers. The last thing I needed was domestic-abuse rumors running rampant in Grundy. Alan might clamp a bear trap on Cooper intentionally.

Cooper was reverting to his previous "grumpy bastard" persona to everyone but me. He seemed to want to pretend we'd never gone to the valley. Other than giving me updates on Pops and occasionally inspecting my injured eye, he didn't comment on his family. He was, however, snapping at the general population and being overprotective to the point of annoying me.

It didn't help that he was leaving town for the next few days to escort a group of Tennessee lawyers

interested in hunting caribou about seventy miles
south of Grundy. I wasn't anxious. I knew he had to
work. He'd taken fewer guide jobs since we'd "taken
up together," as Abner called it. But he seemed
afraid to leave me alone, unwilling to be away from
me. It was sweet, but knowing I had that sort of pull
over someone was strangely uncomfortable. I was
used to my parents' overbearing attention, but it
was something I'd worked to avoid. The emotional
growing pains were starting to freak me out.

"I want you to promise me that you won't take
Oscar out at night by yourself," he said in a voice
that sounded so dangerously close to a command I
considered threatening several of his orifices with a
spatula. He was keeping pace with me as I crossed
from the stove to the pass, back and forth, more like
a caged animal than I'd ever seen him. I didn't think
provoking him with kitchen utensils was a great idea
at this juncture. "Don't get out of sight of the cabin.
Lock up tight at night."

"OK, but you're ruining my plans. Evie and I
were going to order pizza, raid the liquor cabinet,
and invite some boys over to play Spin the Bottle."

"I'm not kidding, Mo," he said, shooting a snarling glare toward where Alan sat devouring pancakes.

"I lived alone for years before you came along,"
I told him, taking his chin in my hands and giving
him a stern look.

He countered, "Within six months of moving
here, you were robbed at knifepoint and stumbled
into the path of an angry bear."

I shrugged. "So if the laws of probability hold,

the chance of anything else happening to me is pretty low."

He growled, a low rumble that started deep in his chest. "Mo."

"Honey, I know this is all part of that instinctual protective alpha-male thing, but you're pissing me off. You're the one who's going to be stuck in the woods with a bunch of drunk, armed attorneys. Frankly, I'm more concerned for your safety." I snickered, kissing his chin where I'd swiped flour across his skin. "But I promise, I will not go out alone, tell unknown callers I'm home by myself, or accept candy from men driving unmarked vans."

"That's all I ask," he said, his lips quirking.

IT TOOK ME practically dragging Cooper to his truck to get him to leave, but I managed to get through the afternoon relatively unscathed. Lynette gave me the wrong orders, called me by the wrong name, or just slung dirty dishes at me through the pass. It was kind of nice to return to that normalcy.

Evie had agreed to come over to my place for a Sandra Bullock chick-flick marathon. She was going to make something she called "Melt Your Face" margaritas, which had my stomach lining quivering in fear. I'd just popped *While You Were Sleeping* into the DVD player when Evie was called away from whatever the hell she was pouring into my blender by an obnoxious pop tune from her cell phone.

"Aren't you a little old for Britney Spears?" I asked dryly.

"Buzz?" she snickered into the phone. "I told you,

we're getting drunk and watching people being ob-
noxiously likable. Serious girly business— What?
What's going on?"

I sat down on the couch with a heavy thud. *Oh,
God, who is missing now?* Which one of my friends
was missing or hurt or worse? I thought of Alan,
who had been able to venture out into the woods
more often as the weather warmed up. What if he'd
been attacked? Abner had been going on his pros-
pecting trips into the preserve lately. Walt had been
fishing. Hell, Gertie had been planning to dig a garden in her backyard. None of them was safe. I buried my face in my hands and waited for Evie to get
off the phone and give me the bad news.

She snapped her cell phone shut and returned to
the blender, measuring and pouring with a chemist's
precision. I stared at her, dumbfounded.

"Well?" I asked.

"Alan found the hikers, what was left of them,"
she said, sounding oddly resigned. "Buzz wanted to
let me know that Alan asked him to contact the state
medical examiner's office to handle the remains.
Buzz is heading up the mountain now."

I took the tequila and poured us each a shot.
"Where were they?"

She tossed back the liquor and winced. "A mile or
so from their campsite. They were just . . . bones,
scattered around a ravine. Alan was finally able to
see them now that the snow has cleared. Buzz said
they'd been gnawed on . . . by a lot of different animals. Alan doesn't want to leave the scene until they
can get them somewhere decent."

I didn't know why this news was such a blow, when I'd known there was little chance of those boys being alive, that it was only a matter of time until their bodies were found. Knowing that they'd been found made the situation seem so final but at the same time opened up the same old questions. What happened to them? Who had attacked them? Would there be more attacks? Thinking of Alan, sitting on the dark mountain, keeping watch over bones, made my stomach hurt.

"How about we put this off until another night?" I suggested, reaching for my Tums. "Buzz is probably going to want to see you."

"Buzz is going to help Alan," she said. "And you and I have a date with too-good-to-be-true romantic comedy."

"Evie."

"Moonflower," Evie shot back. "What else can we do? They're up on the mountain, and we're here. It will be hours before they're home. Do you think there's anything you could do to help Alan?"

I shrugged. "What if I told Alan, 'Hey, I know where you can find a huge population of wolves. How about we go make some dental impressions and compare bite marks?'"

"Then you'd betray Cooper and the pack after they trusted you with their secret," she said, slamming the bottle down on the counter. "This isn't something we're meant to interfere with, Mo. If I've learned anything from living with the pack, it's to let them sort out their own problems, figure this out on their own."

"It's not exactly a squabble over the last Moon Pie. The problem is, they may or may not have someone in their pack who's killing people!" I cried. "Your husband is up on that mountain. Alan is up on that mountain. What if whatever is out there comes back to that ravine looking for its trophies?"

"Is that honestly what you think is happening?" Evie demanded, the color draining from her cheeks. "You think someone in the pack is doing this?"

"You're telling me that you haven't thought of it?"

"No!" she exclaimed. "Those people are my family. They might hurt someone in a fight, but none of them is capable of random killing. I meant that this is probably just some rogue werewolf, a loner who enjoys any kill. If that's the case, the pack will hunt him down. Honestly, Mo, sometimes I don't know what goes on in your head."

"Well, then, tell me what to think. You're so sure of yourself, sure of the pack. Tell me what to think so I don't feel so damn guilty all the time. How can you watch Alan beat himself up over not being able to find the wolf *every day*, when you know you could help him?"

"How will handing my family's secret to a representative of the U.S. government help anything?" she asked quietly. "And I can watch Alan struggle because I've had years of practice keeping secrets. Dead-liners aren't able to phase. The one service we can offer the pack is our silence. I didn't grow up in a hippie love commune where you made a collage every time you had a thought or a feeling!"

"Hey, that's not fair!" I shouted. "I don't run

around expressing every thought in my head. I just think we have some responsibility in this situation."

"We don't even know what this situation is."

"Fine," I growled. "But don't use what I've told you about my parents against me, Evie. I don't throw your family's meat consumption and distracting random nudity up in your face."

I clapped my hand over my mouth. Evie's eyes bugged open, and she doubled over laughing. I shook my head. This was not the way I'd wanted the evening to go.

"That was a really impressive growl, Mo. Cooper would be so proud," she said, grinning. "I'm sorry, hon. Sometimes I forget how new you are to all this, how shocking this life has to be for you. I take it for granted sometimes. And if I thought I could stop more people getting hurt, I would find a way to help. But I don't think this is something you or I will be able to stop."

"I didn't mean to yell," I told her. "I hate feeling so . . . helpless. I don't want this to cause problems between the two of us. You're one of the few people I can talk to about this stuff."

"Agreed. We will not allow werewolves to cause problems in our friendship," she conceded, hitting "frappe" on the blender. She asked loudly, "How many girlfriends can say that?"

THE DRINKS AND Sandra Bullock–based confections were consumed, a bonding experience that repaired the minor damage to my friendship with Evie. The next morning, Lynette troubled herself to bring an order to the pass and grumbled, "Mo, you've got a customer who's asking for you. He's cute." Lynette looked supremely annoyed, which was her general expression when it came to me. I didn't know if she was upset by the loss of a potential tip or a potential date.

As I crossed the dining room, Buzz came through the door, stomping mud off his boots. Evie flung her arms around him and squeezed until I thought he'd turn purple. He chuckled. "I missed you, too, babe."

"How's Alan?" I asked when Evie let him come up for air.

"Glad to give the boys' families some closure, but otherwise, he's sick and tired of this shit," he said. "He's still up at the site, helping the coroner, well, gather everything up."

"Did he see any tracks in the ravine, anything to help track the wolf?" I asked, even as Evie arched her brow at me.

"Washed away by the snowmelt," he said, lowering his voice. "Besides, in the winter, food gets scarce. A dead body is going to attract every scavenger for ten miles. There's no guarantee you'd get the right wolf if you could follow tracks."

"What about setting traps in case it comes back?"

"No more scavenger talk," Evie said, shuddering and giving me a pointed look. "People are eating."

Apparently, Evie had given more thought to my "pack member" theory since last night. And she obviously didn't appreciate me telling Buzz to try to capture one of his in-laws. I put my hands up in a defensive "subject dropped" gesture.

"I'd better get to my table," I said, smacking Buzz's shoulder affectionately with my order pad. "I'm glad you're home safe."

When I approached the booth in question, Eli looked up from the menu, flashing his perfect white teeth. "Mo, it's nice to see you again!"

I looked back at Evie, who was so absorbed in her husband that she hadn't noticed the werewolf politician. "Eli, to what do we owe the honor? I've never seen you in here before."

He tapped the table, indicating that I should sit. There was something imperious about the gesture. This was a man used to giving orders and having them followed. Eyeing the string of tickets lining up at the pass, I stayed on my feet. A flicker of annoyance, of doubt, sparked in Eli's eyes, but he covered it well. "Well, I wanted to touch base with Cooper. I figured he made the effort to come to the valley, I can do the same. Maybe if we'd reached out a little more before, we wouldn't have come to this point. But I guess I missed him."

"Have you heard about the hikers?" I asked quietly. He nodded. "Evie says that a rogue, uh, hunter could be responsible. She said that the . . . NRA could track the responsible party down and keep them from hurting anyone else." Eli nodded again, his face grave. "Do you think the organization could do that sooner rather than later? I don't think this is going to stop. I think it's just going to get worse. The warm season's coming up.

We're going to have more people going into the woods—"

"So, what do you do while Cooper's out of town?" he asked, interrupting me with a blithe expression.

Caught off-guard by his abruptness, I shook my head. Was I talking too loudly? Was my gun-control analogy not clever enough? "This," I told him, my eyes narrowing. "I work. I live my life. The world doesn't stop because Cooper's not right here."

"Trust me, I know that," he said, giving me a thin smile. "And that's where I think we could help each other out, Mo."

"I know there are parts of the pack that he misses, Eli. But I also know that there are . . . relationships that he feels are beyond repair. I wouldn't put a lot of pressure on him to come back. At least, not right away."

Eli leveled his gaze at me and used what I can only call a tone of subdued authority. "You need to understand that we are going to get him to come back, one way or the other. Just having him visit the other night did a lot for my pack. Made them feel like things were back to normal for the first time in years. I want that for them. The stability. And I want Cooper to have his family back. It would be nice if we could all get what we want."

I leaned across the table and whispered, "So, you're saying that you'll search for the rogue if I encourage him to move back to the valley? I would think you would want to do that for your own good, for your family's safety."

His lip curled as he peered up at me with those guileless brown eyes. "Well, you're in a position to help nudge him back home, aren't you? I'd hate for you to nudge him in the wrong direction, especially when this situation could work out so well for us. Work with me, Mo. It's what's best for you."

I wasn't quite accustomed to werewolf social interactions, but I knew when I was being threatened. I smiled blandly, refusing to rise to the bait. "Excuse me for a minute."

I went back to the kitchen and returned a short time later with a rare steak, sausage, bacon, four scrambled eggs, and a little sliver of toast. I slid it in front of him with little fanfare. His eyebrows rose. "What's this?"

"Breakfast. I thought I should serve you something; otherwise, people in here might think we were having an unpleasant conversation. I would just hate that."

"Think about what I said, Mo."

I turned on my heel, then whirled back toward Eli. "You're right, you know. What you told Cooper the other night? You're not him. You're not the man he is."

Eli had the sense to look chagrined as I stalked away. I told Lynnette that Eli and his tip were all hers. It was the first time she smiled at me. I was pretty sure it would be the last.

17

Scary Stories by the Campfire

By April, Mississippi would have been green and unbearably muggy. Daffodils would have sprung up in random splashes of yellow in the tiny patch of grass I called a yard. I would be wearing shorts and sandals and getting ready for the Reynoldses' annual Easter weekend barbecue.

Here, late winter bled into what passed for spring. One morning, I noticed an icicle dripping on my front porch. It was as if the earth had woken up and flexed, releasing all of this energy in the form of rushing water. Tree limbs, no longer burdened by a season's worth of ice, snapped up and sprang into power lines. There were a few short outages but none lasting so long that people bothered to turn on their generators.

The people of Grundy became exuberant in the "heat wave." My neighbors flooded back into town.

The grocery shelves at the Glacier were swept clean of everything. It was as if people had survived for weeks on gruel all winter and suddenly couldn't wait to glut themselves on Cap'n Crunch and Cheez-Its.

Everything seemed to burst into bloom at once, which was familiar. Back home, it seemed the foggy, chilled days of February had barely set in before dogwoods and redbuds exploded to life among barely greened trees. Here, there were more exotic colors and textures. Delicate yellow poppies and flamboyant purple irises grew wild by the side of the road.

Nate's worries about a flagging tourism base were for naught. Somehow the story about the missing hikers being dragged into the woods, never to be found, had granted Grundy a touch of mystery and danger for morbid curiosity seekers. Alan spent more time protecting people from themselves than searching for the wolf. Outsiders went into the woods with illegal, powerful weapons, hoping to bring back the trophy of a lifetime. Hikers came into the saloon, demanding stories about the "monster wolf" and directions to the attack site.

I finally understood the locals' hostility toward tourists.

With the influx of strange, gun-toting people in the woods, Cooper couldn't run long distances anymore. He had to limit himself to the area around the house, patrolling the edge of the property for errant rabbits and driving Oscar crazy with his speed. Our poor little wiener dog's legs couldn't keep pace, so he resorted to flinging himself at Cooper's haunches to slow him down. The only person he interacted with at all was me, and lately, that was becoming sort of one-sided. I would talk. He would listen.

And then, one afternoon, Cooper walked into the saloon's kitchen and put his hand over my eyes. Unfortunately, he did this as I was sliding a meat loaf out of the oven and ended up having to catch the scalding-hot pan when I bobbled it.

Thank goodness for werewolf healing abilities.

"What are you doing here?" I asked.

"I have a surprise for you," he said, tugging at my arm and pulling my apron over my head. When I wouldn't budge, Cooper slung me over his shoulder and hauled me out the employee exit. "Come on."

"Cooper, what are you doing?"

"I've already made the arrangements with Evie. The lunch crowd is thinning out. You've got the next few days off. Oscar's going to be bunking at their place. We are footloose and fancy-free."

"Oh, God, they're going to let Buzz cook again." I winced as he loaded me into the truck, foreseeing pots crusted with Buzz's "chili surprise." The surprise was pulverized spaghetti noodles, which was practically a crime against humanity. And chili. "It will take me a week to undo the damage . . ."

"Mo."

"Letting it go," I said, snapping my seatbelt and settling into pleasant fantasies of bed-and-breakfasts and spas equipped with double massage tables.

Unfortunately, Cooper's idea of a surprise was whisking me away to . . . a nature preserve.

"Camping?" I said, incredulous as we pulled

into the parking lot of the Bardwell Camping Area. "Your surprise is camping?"

He gave me a halfhearted smile and reached behind the seat of the truck to hold up a heavy green canvas trail pack. I made a noise embarrassingly close to a whine. I wasn't much of a camper. For one thing, I'd had enough of roughing it as a kid the summer my parents decided to follow the Dead and live out of the family's aforementioned VW van. For another, I enjoyed creature comforts, such as not being eaten alive by mosquitoes the size of pigeons.

He jostled my arm as he dragged gear out of the back of the truck. "Come on, you're always talking about how much you love living so close to nature."

"Yes, close to nature. Not actually out in it. I mean, is this really a good idea considering everything that's going on? The attacks, the crazy gun-toting 'birdwatchers,' the camera crews? You haven't strayed so much as a mile away from the house in weeks, and all of a sudden, it's time for a Super-Fun Death March through the woods?"

His face relaxed under the tension of all that forced energy. It sagged, seeming craggy and drawn. "There's some stuff I need to tell you. And I can't do it at home. I want to do this in a place where we can just pick up and leave it behind."

My eyes narrowed. Was he finally going to talk about his past? His family? Why the stories about the hikers bothered him so much? Or was he just going to give me some sort of talk about how we shouldn't see each other anymore and Samson was currently moving his stuff out of the house? Either way, we couldn't keep going the way we were. I held out my hand. "Give me the damn backpack."

He kissed the top of my head and strapped it onto my back. I couldn't see a tent or a cooler on Cooper's back and prayed that meant we were staying in some secret hunting cabin he had hidden out in the woods. I was proven wrong when Cooper led me on a hike along a barely beaten trail, away from a sign marking the entrance to Bardwell.

"Aren't the campgrounds this way?" I asked, pointing toward the nice, clean, civilized-looking RV park. "With, you know, the electrical hookups and nice, clean picnic area . . . and the grills . . . the showers . . . and the . . . showers."

"Well, I'm more of a roughing-it guy. You'll love it. You know, sleeping under the stars. And I did bring a sleeping bag. Just for you . . . because I'm so considerate." He took in my scowl. "I'm a dead man.'

"Yep." I said, pronouncing the last letter with a distinct *pop* as we pushed through the brush.

I had to admit, it was a scenic death march. Everything was so clear, as if even the limited filters of life in town had been lifted. The light passed down through the trees, green and gold. Cooper, who seemed nervous that he'd overstepped the "Mo patience line," kept up a steady stream of chatter. Funny stories about camping with his grandfather when he was just a pup. Stories about running with Samson in their early days of werewolfdom, most of which ended with Samson waking up naked on the front porch of a ranger station. Old local legends.

The weather. When he started giving me the scientific names of the trees, I let him off the hook and chattered back.

We hiked longer than I'd ever chosen to walk in my entire life. We finally reached a small clearing, flanked by even more trees. The ground was hard-packed and smooth. There was a small stone circle in the middle filled with the black remains of burnt branches.

"This campsite seems pretty well used for being so 'out of the way.' Do you bring all of your girl-friends here?" I narrowed my eyes in mock suspicion as I shrugged out of the backpack.

"Only the ones who know about the werewolf thing," he said as he stacked firewood into the stone circle. "Which would be you and you only."

I dropped the bag. "You've never told any of your girlfriends about the wolf thing?"

He blinked a few times, as if I'd just posed an incredibly stupid question. "I haven't really had that many girlfriends, and none I've stayed with long enough to tell about the wolf thing."

"That's sort of huge. How has this not come up before?"

"You never asked."

I thought back to all of the conversations we'd had. "Oh, my . . . you're right. As a girlfriend, I suck."

"Well, you get bonus points for prying a bear trap off my leg. That can't be discounted."

"Ah, thank God, a retroactive points system. It's really the only way I'll win."

It took surprisingly little time to set up camp. Apparently, experiences with my parents, which included hours spent searching outdoor concert venues for campsites that had good feng shui, had colored my perception of camping. With the thick double sleeping bag, a tent wasn't necessary. As I unfurled it a safe distance from the fire, Cooper set out the rapidly disintegrating toilet paper and a little spade without comment. I chose not to think about that until it was absolutely necessary.

"What now?" I asked, with the fire blazing comfortably near my bare feet.

"Now I'm going to hunt," he said.

My jaw dropped, but I felt immediately stupid for not realizing that Cooper would have to run down our dinner. What else were we going to eat? He grinned and rooted around in his backpack, producing packages of hot dogs and buns.

"Funny," I grunted, slapping at his shoulder. Even though I knew something was brewing, it was sort of nice to have glimpses of the old Cooper back. It was as if he struggled with the decision to have this big "talk" more than the dread of my reaction. Now that he'd made his decision, he could relax.

"Keep up that attitude, and there will be no s'mores for you," he said as I wandered to the edge of the clearing to find some long, thin sticks fit for roasting. I wiped them down as best I could and held my hand out imperiously for a hot dog. "I can do the cooking," Cooper said, somewhat indignant now.

"Men always think they should be in charge of outdoor cooking." I took the hot-dog package from him and skewered a few. "But the Y chromosome has been programmed with the 'the blacker my food is, the more manly I am' gene. I like my processed meats to be somewhere in the unnatural-nitrate-red range. Ergo I will handle the cooking, thank you."

Cooper was quiet for a long moment.

"You're trying to come up with some sort of 'processed meats' double entendre, aren't you?" I accused him as I held the sticks over the fire.

"Yeah, you didn't leave me a lot to work with," he grumbled.

We ate an indecent number of hot dogs and s'mores, careful to hang our leftovers and trash in a tree several yards away from our sleeping bag. As the temperatures dropped into the cool range, I changed into thermals and thick wool socks, something Cooper didn't have to bother with.

"So, what do you think?" Cooper asked, pulling me against his knees and kissing my neck.

"Camping is just like being at home, only much, much more work."

He grumped, "Well, it's not easy for me, either, you know. I'm used to sitting around a campfire with a bunch of overdressed, out-of-shape outsiders, swilling imported beer and pretending to laugh at their jokes."

"The adjustment must be so difficult for you," I said, wiping pretend tears of pity from my cheeks. Cooper got quiet, playing with my hands, lacing our fingers together. "You wanted to talk. Let's talk."

Cooper cleared his throat and dropped my hands. I obstinately grabbed his and lifted his chin so he had to look me in the eye. He took a deep breath and said, "About a year after I became alpha, this other pack showed up one night. They dragged Maggie out of our house, and their alpha threatened to snap Maggie's neck in front of me if I didn't relinquish control of the valley to them. The pack had come up from outside Vancouver. They'd bled their own packlands dry. Their alpha, Jonas, had no choice but to move on to better hunting grounds. He heard that the valley was a pretty good range. They'd done a pretty good job of scouting us out, because they knew about the vulnerabilities of the packlands, the layout of the village, how many able fighters were in the pack, and that I wasn't all that strong of an alpha."

He sighed, plucking at my sleeves with nervous fingers. "I'm standing there in the woods surrounded by my whole family. All I could think to do was offer them a place in the valley. To share it with them. He declined. This fucker has my baby sister by the neck, shaking her so hard I can still hear her teeth rattle, and everybody's looking at me like I'm supposed to know what to do. And the worst part was Maggie—she wasn't even scared. Because she knew her big brother was going to fix it. I was scared out of my fucking mind, and Maggie was sort of smirking at me, like, 'Come on, Cooper, just kick this guy's ass, already.' "

"What did you do?"

"Nothing. I just froze. And the look on Maggie's face when she realized that I had no clue what to do . . . I still have nightmares about that look."

He shuddered. "You want to know how we got out of it? My baby sister sank her teeth into Jonas's arm, kicked all six foot four inches of him in the balls, and called him a jerkoff."

"Wow. That sounds nothing like her."

He gave a little smile. "She always was tougher than me. But I was faster. And when Jonas went for her throat, I was able to change before Maggie. I held him off, but both packs phased, and nothing could prevent blood from being shed. Maggie just wouldn't stay away from Jonas. She kept lunging at him, no matter what I did to keep her away. I got distracted when another male jumped on my back. Jonas got Maggie down on the ground. His teeth were at her neck, and I just lost it. It's one of those rare clear memories I have as a wolf, killing that male without a second thought, knocking Jonas off Maggie, holding him to the ground, and ripping his throat out."

Cooper looked a little green just remembering it. I squeezed his hands, trying to bring him back to the present. "What about the rest of their pack?"

"Maggie took down one. But I killed the rest, one by one. Some of my own pack members tried to help me, and I snapped at them. There were twelve wolves in the other pack, and when I phased back to human, they were all dead." Cooper buried his face in his hands, as if he couldn't look up to see my face.

I was at a loss to understand why. I shook his shoulder. "But isn't that a good thing?"

"No, it's not a good thing!" he yelled.

"You saved your sister. You defended your home and your pack. I'm failing to see the bad here."

"I killed people, Mo! Yeah, they had fangs and fur at the time, but they were people, just like every member of my own pack is a person. Men and women alike. I killed them all. *Something* in me was able to do that. I couldn't stomach what I'd done. Everybody tried to tell me how proud my father would have been, how I'd shown myself to be a great leader. And every night, I woke up screaming from the nightmares. Nothing helped. I couldn't be around my family anymore. I couldn't trust myself with them. I didn't deserve them."

Cooper stared into the fire, his lips barely moving as he spoke. "Maggie could forgive my hesitation. She could forget that I'd killed people in front of her. But when I couldn't just go back to being her goofy big brother, she started to hate me. She hated me for not being able to accept a position that she was obviously more suited for, for betraying the pack. When I left, it was like she was relieved, because she had a reason."

I crawled into his lap, part of me expecting him to shy away from me, to shove me away. "What do you want me to do? Yell at you? Hit you? Scream 'Get away from me, you monster'? Because if that's what you're looking for, you're going to be disappointed."

Cooper sighed deeply, the tension easing out of his body. He nuzzled his face into my neck. "You're not angry with me?"

"I haven't processed it all yet. Mostly, I'm really irritated that you didn't think I would understand. You hurt someone to help me," I said. "Do you think I hold that against you? That I love you any less for it? How could I judge you for doing the same for your family?"

I tilted his head up and gave him my best stern expression. He sighed, pressed his ear to my chest, and listened to my heartbeat, rubbing his cheek against my shirt and inhaling deeply.

"Besides, this still doesn't make you the scariest guy I've ever dated," I said, my mouth twisted into a pert moue.

He frowned. "Mo, I killed eleven people. How many does it take to be the scariest guy you've ever dated?"

"Twelve," I said, shrugging. "That's my boyfriend body-count threshold. I have to have some standards."

"You're a little sick."

"I'm living with a werewolf. I have to be a little sick."

18

On the Next *Dr. Phil*

UNBURDENED, COOPER FELL ASLEEP long before I did.

I drifted off, staring at the stars, mulling over Cooper's tale. Was it disturbing, knowing that my werewolf lover was capable of killing? Definitely. Had I glossed over that a little to help him feel better about telling me? Damn skippy. And while I knew I hadn't quite processed my feelings about it, it's not as if he was murdering fluffy bunnies or even—really—human beings. He'd killed fully grown, capable werewolves who were staging a hostile takeover and would have murdered his family to accomplish it. I'm not sure I wouldn't have helped him, given the chance.

The more I thought about it, the angrier I became with Maggie. Yes, she was young, but how could she come down so hard on Cooper for having what were likely normal posttraumatic reactions to a mass killing? How dare she make her hurt feelings his problem? Who knew how Cooper might have adjusted and accepted what happened if she'd just kept her mouth shut?

Cooper's sister needed to know how much she'd hurt him. She needed to grow the hell up. But short of pinning her with a Howitzer and having a forced intervention with Dr. Phil, I didn't think I would emerge from such an encounter with all of my digits.

However, the image of Dr. Phil yelling Texasisms at Maggie was relaxing enough to put me to sleep.

When I woke the next morning, I could tell something was bothering Cooper. He sniffed the cold, smoke-smeared air, worry furrowing his forehead. He tried to play it off, tried to pretend that he wasn't rushing us off the campsite, that he wanted to get me back to our bed so he could love me properly. He claimed this was the advantage of camping without a fancy RV or tent. "At the end of the weekend, all you want to do is get home, not spend an hour packing up your gear."

"You're just trying to get out of bringing a tent next time." He once again lifted his face to inhale the breeze. "Cooper, what's wrong? You keep doing that. You're not having regrets about talking to me last night, are you?"

"No. Definitely not," he assured me. "Something smells funny. Has since I woke up this morning."

"I told you not to eat all that jerky," I muttered.

"Let's just get going," he said, wrapping an arm around me as we headed through the trees.

We hiked for more than a mile, Cooper growing more tense by the step. We hopped over a dip in the trail, and he suddenly stopped, sniffed, and bolted into the trees.

"Cooper?"

"Stay there!" he yelled.

"Oh, yeah, that's likely," I huffed, following him as closely as I could. I found a trail of clothes in his wake, so it didn't surprise me to find him wolfed out when I hit the clearing. He was hunched over something. As I got closer, I saw the thin legs encased in worn hiking boots. Cooper whined and nudged the fallen form with his nose. "What the . . ."

I gently pushed him out of the way and cried out, "Cooper, it's Abner!"

Abner was flat on his back, his pack still strapped around his chest. His rifle was loaded and unused at his side. There were deep gashes clawed across his chest, dangerously close to his neck. There were dark, slashing stains on his trousers, which I realized were wounds, caked over with blackened, dried blood.

The hair on Cooper's neck was bristled high as he scanned the trees. His back was turned to me as he paced a circle around us.

"Abner?" I whispered, my voice shaking as I gently pressed my fingers to his neck. His skin was cool and dry. His pulse was weak and erratic. I sucked breath through my teeth to fight back the hot tears that threatened to fall. My numbed fingers reached

for the hem of Abner's work shirt, but I couldn't
bring myself to look at the damage underneath. I
was almost knocked over by the wave of shame at
my own squeamishness. *I can do this. I have to hold it
together,* I told myself. *One task at a time. One step at
a time.* I rummaged through my bag for the first-aid
kit and my water bottle.

Cooper turned toward me and whined again, a
hollow, defeated sound. He seemed to be trying to
tell me something as he stared at the first-aid kit.

"Too late?" I asked him, wiping my eyes.
"Bullshit. He's not dead. That's bullshit."

Ignoring Cooper's canine murmurings, I took the
bottle and ever so carefully propped Abner's head in
my lap. I poured just a little bit of water between his
dry, cracked lips. His papery eyelids fluttered open.
A rattling breath wheezed out from his throat.

"Shh," I told him, giving him a weak smile as I
offered him more water. "Don't try to talk. It's going
to be OK. We're going to get some help for you,
Abner." Abner stared at me with the empty delir-
ium of someone who couldn't tell if he was awake. I
smiled at him, pretending that my nose wasn't running, that the effort wasn't making my face hurt.
"You can't go anywhere, Abner. I was about to take
you up on your offer. What kind of girl could resist
warm feet and cable TV?"

Abner smiled, and the effort split his lip. He
raised a feeble hand and patted my arm. A low
whimper sounded from Cooper's throat, even as he
kept an eye on the woods around us. Abner's attention followed the sound. His whole body twitched

as his eyes fell on the black wolf. I could hear the scream building from the bottom of Abner's abused lungs long before it came out, a plaintive, panic-stricken wail. His eyes were wide, unfocused in raw terror. His fingers clutched at my arms as his legs frantically pushed away from the wolf.

"Abner, it's OK, calm down!" I cried. "Please!"

Abner let loose one last bleating gasp and fell still against my legs. I felt warm trails of tears streaming down my face to land on Abner's forehead. I pushed his frazzled gray hair back from his battered face. I kept my fingers cupped around his throat, waiting for some sign of a heartbeat, but his body was completely still. No breath. No pulse. No Abner.

Cooper huffed at me and started toward the trees. When I didn't move, he gave a sharp bark.

"We're not leaving him here."

He growled and jerked his head toward the trail.

"We can't just leave him." Cooper carefully grabbed my sleeve between his teeth and dragged me through the tree line. "Damn it, Cooper, cut it out."

I snagged his clothes as we threaded through the low-hanging branches. We reached the trail, where we'd left Cooper's pack. He phased, grabbing his clothes from my hands and struggling into his boots. "We've got to get out of here, right now."

"We have to take Abner back to town with us."

"We can't do anything for him now, Mo. We'll bring Alan and Buzz out here as soon as we can, but we have to get moving. I've got to get you some-where safe."

"You think whatever attacked Abner is still out here?"

Cooper's expression was bleak as he took my hand and pulled me toward civilization. "Yes."

We all but ran the rest of the way to the trailhead, where my cell phone had enough of a signal to call Alan. Cooper dragged me to the truck. My hands were still shaking, and I was in no condition to drive. Evie came to pick me up while Cooper led Alan and Buzz to Abner's body. I rode home with a nervous, unsettled tension in my belly. I felt like a robot as I walked Oscar around the yard and led him back inside for kibble. I crawled into bed with my camping clothes on and waited, but I woke up alone.

A FLOOD OF curious faces rushed into the saloon the next day, but I didn't see the one I was looking for. To avoid the awful, overbright stares of diners who wanted all of the gory details of Abner's death, I hid behind the grill. I didn't need Alan to tell me that there were two sets of wolf prints at the clearing where we'd found Abner, one of which obviously belonged to Cooper. I didn't need to be told that Abner had sustained massive internal injuries brought on by crushing force on his ribs and sternum, that he'd bled heavily from his wounds while he lay in the clearing overnight, that he'd ultimately died of shock.

Alan was increasingly frustrated with his inability to track the wolf. He called in experts from the universities and the wildlife department, but they always emerged from the woods without anything close to a clue. Alan blamed himself for Abner's death, for the hikers, and even for Susie Q, despite the fact that every expert told him this wolf didn't follow any typical patterns of behavior, that he couldn't possibly predict where or when it could strike. I wanted Cooper to talk to him, to explain about the werewolves, but I knew that wouldn't happen. And I couldn't betray the pack's secrets, even if it would make Alan stop beating himself into an emotional pulp. All I could do was listen when Alan vented and remind him to eat.

We didn't bury Abner in Grundy. His last wishes had been that he be returned to his native Oklahoma, to be buried with his family. We held a memorial at the saloon, where we drank his favorite beer, sang his favorite songs, and told stories about him until our sides hurt from laughing. It was a fitting tribute to a good friend. And Cooper missed all of it.

I hadn't seen him since that afternoon on the trail. He didn't return my calls. Checking on his house became part of my evening routine. Clock out at work, check Cooper's house, walk Oscar, eat, go to bed. I tried to tell myself that he'd been called out of town or had been helping the rangers track the monster that had killed Abner and just hadn't had time to call me back. Then, one night, I saw his kitchen light on. I saw his silhouette against the window as he stood at his sink. From his vantage point, he had to see my truck. He couldn't miss it. I waited, wanting him to come running out of the house or even amble leisurely, armed with a good reason for dropping off the freaking planet. But he moved away from the window and turned off the light.

About a week later, I saw him loading camping gear into his truck in front of Hannigan's Grocery. He looked haggard and miserable, as if he hadn't slept in days. Although my first instinct was to soothe, to brush kisses over those tired eyes and wrap my arms around him, the stronger instinct to smack him won out.

"What the hell is wrong with you?" I demanded, slapping the back of his head.

Cooper seemed to have missed the fact that his girlfriend had just bitch-slapped him on a public sidewalk. He wouldn't even look at me as he raised the tailgate of his truck. "Not now."

"Oh, you're right, we have spent so much time together over the last couple of days, you must be getting sick of me." I followed him to the driver's side.

He opened the door to his truck and stepped in, putting it between us. "I can't be around you right now."

I skidded to a stop. "What?"

"You need to stay away from me," he said, his voice low and hoarse. "You know why. Susie Q, those hikers, Abner. I can't be near you. I can't take the chance that I could hurt you, too. I couldn't stand it."

My jaw fell slack, the indignant anger draining away. "You weren't a wolf on the night Abner was attacked," I whispered, well aware of the crowds gathering in shop windows to watch what promised to be the public lovers' quarrel of the decade.

"We don't know that!" He slammed his truck door, grabbed my elbow, and dragged me around the corner, behind the buildings of Main Street, until we'd reached the trees that surrounded Grundy. No one would hear us there. No one would see.

Cooper let go of my arm, and the momentum of my body carried me a half-dozen steps from where he stopped. "I can't remember anything from that night, no dreams, not waking up to check on you, nothing," he said. "I could have crawled out of the sleeping bag and phased without waking you up. How else could Abner get mauled by a wolf so close to our campsite?"

I protested, "You've never done that at home—"

"But I could have! How many wolves do you think were running in that area? When Abner saw me, he was terrified of me. Like he recognized me as the thing that hurt him."

"You are not a thing, do you hear me?" I insisted. He gave me a long, piteous stare. "You don't bully Oscar when you're in wolf form. Every time I've been around you while you're a wolf, your concern has been for my safety. You've never snapped at me, even when you were wounded. And you were no-where near here when those boys went missing."

Cooper looked at the ground and muttered, "Yeah, I was."

"What?"

"I was worried about you. I couldn't take being so far away from you so long, so I waited until the hunters went to sleep, changed, and ran home to check on you. I changed back, ran through the preserve, and got back to the camp before anybody woke up. Then I got back to town and heard that two kids went missing from the preserve, near your house, on the night I was running. I tried to ignore the signs, Mo, but it all keeps adding up."

"Why didn't you tell me about this?"

"It doesn't matter. As long as there are people being hurt, I can't see you." He turned on his heel and walked away. I managed to skirt around him and put my hand against his chest, stopping him—for the most part.

"So, you love me too much to leave me and too much to let me be anywhere near you? Well, pardon me, but that's the biggest load of crap I've ever heard."

"You can honestly tell me that it's never even crossed your mind that I could be the one doing this?" he demanded. "There's not some little voice in your head telling you that you need to get as far away from me as possible? You know what I can do, Mo. You know I've killed before. You're not stupid."

I looked down, and I felt the tears coursing down my cheeks before I realized I was crying. "Yes, OK? Yes. Every once in a while, I think it's possible that you could do this without being aware of it. But then I look at you, and I have to believe that it's not in you."

He let out a bitter laugh. "Well, that's one of us."

"What do you want from me, Cooper, permission? My blessing to run off and leave me? Or do you want *me* to give up, to leave you because you *might* be hurting people? You want me to give you an out? Well, you're not going to get it. Let's just call this what it is. Instead of facing a problem, you're running again. You talk this big talk about how hard it was to leave your pack, but the truth is that when things get difficult, that's when you run. Running is easy."

Cooper recoiled as if I'd punched him. And damned if I could find it in me to apologize for it. With one last look at me, Cooper took a few steps, his clothes landing with a subtle *thwump* as he shifted midair. After landing deftly on his paws, he disappeared into the woods, his long ululate howl echoing behind him as he ran away from me.

19

Scrambled and Fertilized

IN MY HEAD, I'D understood that Cooper wouldn't want to spend a lot of time with me. But somehow I expected to see him in town. I thought we would be carrying on the pretense of "parting as friends." But he kept his promise to stay away. He told our neighbors stories about hunting trips, backpacking expeditions, fishing. Evie seemed to understand that something had happened, but she was too wise to ask me direct questions.

When I stormed back into town alone, our public spar became the topic of choice for gossiping saloon patrons, until Denny Greene sustained second-degree electrocution burns trying to rig up a TV/VCR on the lip of his bathtub and gave them something better to chew on.

Alan was the only one whose focus remained on me, even in the face of Denny's oddly placed bandages. He took to squeezing my fingers in his while I took down his lunch order. He asked me to movies, to dinner at a new Chinese buffet that had opened in Burnee, to his place to play board games with Buzz and Evie. I appreciated it, but I just couldn't muster the energy to be social after I left the saloon.

It was as if I'd scheduled my day in terms of "8:00 A.M. to 5:00 P.M., generally pleasant person; 5:05 P.M. to 6:00 A.M., total basket case."

I put on a brave face. I smiled, I served, I earned my living. I hurt. Either I couldn't sleep, or I crashed and slept for fourteen hours. I couldn't seem to eat anything, and the smells of the food I was cooking turned my stomach.

I was reminded of my parents' more tragic friends, the ones who hadn't quite gotten past the "if it feels good, smoke it" portion of the free-love era. They'd show up at the commune all jittery and stay long enough to get a decent meal and then amble away. When I looked into the mirror, I saw the same hollow-eyed stare, the unhappy twist to the mouth. Cooper had turned me into a strung-out love junkie.

Convinced I could still smell him in my bed, I bleached my sheets to bone white. I immediately regretted the loss, but it didn't matter. Cooper's scent was everywhere, in the mattress, the pillows, stubbornly resisting my efforts to drive it off.

I skipped over several stages of grief and got stuck at anger. In my more vindictive moments, I hoped Cooper was somehow worse off than I was, that he was somewhere curled up in a fetal position, twitching in misery, and I was just feeling an echo of it.

I don't want him back, I told myself. *I don't need this shit. Even if he came crawling back on all fours, I wouldn't take him.* And an hour later, I knew that if he walked through the door, I'd fling myself at him and forgive him for everything. Back and forth I teetered until I worried that I'd finally cracked, that the depression Cooper's presence had somehow delayed was flooding in. Maybe this was the life I would have had in Grundy if I'd never learned his secret, if I'd never loved him.

I know, even I wanted to slap myself a little bit.

Irony of ironies, my books on werewolf relationships arrived, having been delayed for weeks by some quirk of the postal system. I don't know if it was morbid curiosity or a masochistic streak that had me thumbing through guides to successful relationships with were-creatures. But it proved to be a fascinating way to torture myself. For instance, I learned that the Grundy habit of offering a lady meat as a courting gesture was very much in line with werewolf sensibilities. Werewolves marked nearly every important gesture with food—dating, proposals, apologies. If Cooper came back and offered me a ham, I wasn't sure I could keep from expressing my feelings with a cast-iron skillet against his head.

One night, while perusing *Rituals and Love Customs of the Were*, I found that most breeds of wolves mate for life. And if one wolf in a breeding pair dies, it can send the other into a depression. The

mourning wolf wouldn't hunt, wouldn't do anything to take care of himself, until the pack had no
choice but to let him die. This made no sense. I
wasn't a werewolf. And I certainly wasn't part of a
breeding pair.

Wait a minute. Breeding pair. Not eating, constant fatigue, nausea, mood swings . . . Mentally, I
counted back to the last month.

Shit.

I was late, several *weeks* late, and I hadn't even
noticed. This didn't make any sense. I was the con-
traception queen. To keep up with Cooper, I'd taken
to storing condoms in every room of our house.
Clearly, Cooper's swimmers could not be contained
by mere modern prophylactics.

Stupid werewolf ninja sperm.

"Oh . . ." My hand dropped to my stomach. I put
my head in my hands and gave in to the urge to cry.
What could I do? How could I be sure? I couldn't
run into town to buy a pregnancy test. The entire
town would know before I checked out at Hannigan's. Could I even go to the doctor? Would they be
able to tell that the baby had a few extra furry DNA
strands? Would I have a normal pregnancy? Could I
have my baby in a hospital?

When exactly had it become "my baby"?

I wanted to call Evie. I wanted her to tell me
that this was all a silly misunderstanding and I'd
just skipped a period because of stress. Instead, I
scoured the books for everything I could find on
human women carrying werewolf babies. There
were discouragingly few entries, most of them

concerning shortened gestation periods and over-whelming food cravings. Apparently, wolves carry their babies for only three months, so women carrying werewolf babies split the difference at about six months. That sounded really fast. But it couldn't be all that dangerous or rare, right? Cooper said the wolf magic was carrying on in fewer families because of mingling the bloodlines. Obviously, there were a lot of human women out there having werewolf babies. But somehow I didn't see myself finding a chat room for them. There was no BearingWerewolfSpawn.com.

I checked.

Shaking, I went to the kitchen and forced myself to drink a glass of water. I hadn't been taking care of myself for weeks. I couldn't keep living like this. If things with Cooper didn't change, I could end up raising this baby alone. Was I ready for that? Was I even remotely prepared? Given my parenting role models, I was going to guess not.

I had to make the conscious choice, right then, whether that would continue or whether I would keep this baby. Whether I would start eating or sleeping again, even if I didn't feel like it.

I reached into my cabinet for my daily multivitamins, which I hadn't touched in I couldn't remember how long. They weren't prenatal vitamins, but they'd have to do until I could pick some up. I shook one out into my palm and stared at the little yellow tablet. I put it into my mouth, wincing at the stale, mineral taste, and threw back some water to help me swallow it.

Suddenly exhausted, I leaned my forehead against the counter and sighed. "We're not off to a great start, kiddo."

THE NEXT MORNING, I drove to the Crescent Valley to visit Gracie and Samson. I thought it would help to see their faces. But the moment Gracie opened her front door, the idea of discussing this mess with someone who really knew what was happening pierced me with a misery so acute I stumbled back.

"I shouldn't be here." I stepped back off the porch. "I'm sorry. I should go."

"Don't be silly," she said, pulling me inside. "I'm making some herbal tea. It's a little strong, but it will make you feel better."

She pushed me into a kitchen chair and put a mug of dark, teak-colored brew in front of me. "It's strong," she cautioned again.

"I'm the child of hippies. Your tea doesn't scare me," I told her, taking a small sip. The bitter flavors flooded my mouth, puckering my lips. "Gah!" I blew out a breath. "What's in this?"

"You don't want to know," she said, topping off my mug. "Just drink. You'll feel better."

I winced as I brought the cup to my lips. Thinking better of it, I set it back down on the counter. "Cooper's gone."

"I thought as much," she said, putting her arm around my shoulders. "It takes a strong woman to wait, Mo."

"I can't really leave. I mean, where could I go?" I said, pressing my fingertips against my cheekbones, as if the pressure would somehow keep my face from crumpling. "I'm going to— Oh, God, Gracie, I'm pregnant."

"Oh, little girl." She sighed, leaning my head against her shoulder when I started to cry.

"I don't know what to do. We didn't even talk about kids. And I don't know anything about babies, much less werewolf babies."

"You sound as if you're going to go through this alone."

"Do you see anyone else around?" I asked, waving my arm toward the empty kitchen.

"There's me. And Samson, and the rest of the pack, for now, until Cooper returns, which he will."

The image of Samson trying to strap on a Baby-Björn carrier was enough to make me chuckle. "I don't want to leave. I don't think I could if I tried. But the idea of the baby growing up without a father, it's just too sad. Oh, crap, Gracie, I didn't mean that. I'm sorry, I'm just not thinking straight right now."

"Don't you be sorry," Gracie told me sternly, lifting my chin so I had to meet her level green gaze. "Pregnant women are entitled to be a little weepy and blunt every once in a while. Raising my children without a father was sad and hard. And I wouldn't do it that way again if I could help it, but I couldn't.

"My husband died a strange, heroic death, but that didn't make it any easier on Cooper. Sometimes I think it made it harder. I think he saw his dad as invincible, which I suppose all little boys do. My husband thought he had all the time in the world to show him what it meant to be a man, to be a wolf. Then my son had to become the man of the house, quickly. His grandfather tried to be there for the boys. But when Cooper became the alpha, he had to be his own man, far before he was ready, I think. And he had to deal with problems that no alpha had ever handled before—predator-control programs, aerial hunting. . . . We'd only heard stories about packs encroaching on other hunting grounds before the valley was attacked. We'd never considered it could happen here. And Cooper had to handle it all. He put on such a good front. I didn't realize until later how much pressure he was putting on himself. He moves at his own pace, honey. You just have to outstubborn him. He's trying to make you give up on him."

"Well, you can't really make me do anything. Just ask my mother."

Gracie gave my hand a squeeze. "Good girl," she said. "Have you been feeling all right? Is that grandbaby of mine mistreating you?"

"Well, I just kind of figured everything out recently. I thought I was just depressed over . . . well, you know. I haven't been drinking and bungee-jumping or anything, but I haven't exactly been Miss Conscientious Prenatal Care, either."

"Why don't I take you by the village clinic?" Gracie suggested. "Dr. Moder works with our pregnant women, helps the births look normal and human for the government paperwork. She'd be happy to take a look at you, get you started on the right track."

"I don't want anyone to know just yet. I know

how small-town news travels. Someone will see me at the clinic, a few phone calls are made, and before you know it, everybody's chewing this over with their dinner. I don't want the whole pack knowing before I can tell Cooper."

Gracie just smiled at me. It turned out Dr. Moder made house calls, Lord bless her. She was efficient, no-nonsense, and eager to get out of the clinic for an hour if it meant getting a piece of Gracie's rum cake. She didn't even mind when I burst into tears when the pregnancy test showed a blazing pink positive result. She just patted my shoulder and explained that shortened gestation meant my hormone levels were nearly double what a normal pregnant woman had to deal with. She drew my blood for tests, gave me a bottle of extra-strength prenatal vitamins and a hand-typed pamphlet titled "What to Expect When You're Expecting a Werewolf." She said I should consider it a sort of appendix or special reference section for the actual book, which she also gave me. (And if anyone saw it, I was supposed to pretend it was a joke.)

I was due in just four months. Four months to prepare for another little person, who most likely would be able to turn into a four-legged creature. There's a reason elephants gestate for two years.

I was just shrugging into my coat when Maggie came crashing through the front door with Eli at her heels.

"What is she doing here?" Maggie demanded, flinging her arm toward me and missing my face by a scant few inches.

"Mo is a friend and more than welcome to come for a visit whenever she pleases," Gracie informed her coolly.

Maggie turned on me. "You don't belong here any more than he ever did. Did he make promises to you? Did he tell you he loved you? Did he disappoint you? Join the club."

I shot to my feet, advancing on Maggie. For a moment, shock rippled across her face, but she stood her ground. That, at least, I respected. "That's it, Scrappy Doo. Do you know what you've done to your brother, someone you supposedly loved? Cooper won't come home because he can't face you. He's cut himself off from everybody on the planet. He's convinced he can't be trusted to love anybody. Because you're a spoiled, selfish little bitch who needs a good kick in the ass. You're pissed off. Your brother disappointed you. Well, put your big-girl panties on and get the hell over it."

"You have no idea what you're talking about. You're not part of a pack. You don't know what he did to us." Maggie's lip curled back from her canines. My fists balled up as she stepped close enough to bump her forehead against mine. Gracie pulled my arms, trying to drag me away from Maggie, and yelled at her daughter to sit down.

Eli slid between us. "Look, everybody, let's just calm down."

Maggie sneered as Eli pushed her shoulder away. "Don't you tell me when to—"

"Step down, Maggie," Eli told her, the quiet ring of command edging his voice.

His hands steered her away from me toward the door. She fought him, leaning toward me and taking a decisive swipe. I ducked back and was grateful for good reflexes.

Eli barked, "Maggie, I lead this pack. You will step down."

After straining toward me for another second, Maggie snarled and stomped out of the door, slamming it behind her.

With Maggie gone, the tension eased slowly out of the room. I sagged against the wall, wondering what good I'd thought would come of this visit. I would never regret spending time with Gracie or telling her about the baby. But some part of me had to have known that my presence would provoke Maggie. And then to take a verbal jab at Maggie was complete madness. Had I finally crossed into suicidal territory? This visit was an unqualified disaster, worse than the time my parents arranged for Kara to spend a week at the commune with us while their "naturist" friends happened by for a visit.

"I'm sorry, Gracie." I kissed the top of her head. "I should get going before Maggie blows up my truck or something."

She let out a shaky breath. "I'm going to have a talk with her, a long-overdue talk. Come back soon, Mo. Call me anytime. Take care of yourself. And *be stubborn*."

I managed a laugh.

"Could I talk to you for a minute, Mo?" Eli asked. "Outside?"

I nodded, slipping into my jacket. Apparently still

smarting from my comments at the saloon, Eli was now treating me with careful deference. He swept a dignified hand toward the aluminum lawn chairs Gracie had set out for nice weather. I accepted another mug of tea, which Grace had assured me was perfectly safe for me and my . . . pup.

I was contemplating how weird it was to think of my baby in animal terms when Eli cleared his throat. "We're becoming concerned, Mo."

"Regarding?" I asked, though I knew the answer.

"Cooper. It's unnatural for any wolf to be away from his home for so long. Most of the time, it means the wolf is hurt or dead. But since he abandoned the packlands years ago, we're not sure how strong his tie is to the area anymore. Hell, he may not be able to have strong ties to anything anymore," he said, sipping his tea. "We all thought he was attached to you, and look—" The expression on my face made Eli look instantly aghast. "I'm sorry. I'm not good at this sort of thing, Mo. Especially with women outside our pack. It's different. I don't mean to hurt you. I feel responsible for what's happened. I put an unfair amount of pressure on you to push Cooper back home, and he ran."

"That's not what happened, Eli." I ran my thumb over the mug handle, trying to concentrate on the warmth of the ceramic against my fingertips. "It had nothing to do with you. Susie, the hikers, Abner— Cooper thinks he might have hurt them while he was in wolf form."

"Well, that's not possible," Eli said, his brow creasing. "Cooper doesn't have that in him."

"I know that. But he's convinced. He's staying away from me because he's afraid he's going to hurt me."

Eli squeezed my shoulder and gave me a pitying look. "One thing I know about Cooper, once his mind's made up, that's it. As much as I would hate to see you leave, I wouldn't wait for him. If you have somewhere you'd rather be, someone else you'd rather be with . . . I'm sorry, Mo."

Eli handed me a slip of paper with his cell-phone number on it and told me to call if I ever needed help from him or the pack. He moved back toward the door, leaving me there, absently rubbing a hand over my aching breastbone.

As I DROVE home, the odd conflict between Eli's and Gracie's advice played out in my head. Gracie knew Cooper better, but Eli saw the problem from a male point of view. Wouldn't another man be able to see the signs of a wolf gone for good? Maybe Cooper could come back to Grundy if he knew I was gone. Maybe by staying I was keeping Cooper from the only home he'd really known. But what if Gracie was right? What if Cooper finally came home and found that I'd left, that another person who was supposed to love him had abandoned him?

More confused than when I'd set off that morning, I saw my cell phone flashing, indicating a voice mail. "Hi, sweetheart, it's your mother. We haven't talked in a while, and your father and I would like to see how you're doing. If you have time, could you call us?"

I arched my eyebrow. That sounded almost . . . normal. It was neither passive nor aggressive. The sort of message that Kara's mother left her on a regular basis. And the paranoid part of my brain wondered if it was a trick, if the past few months of peace were a trap. When I needed help or advice, my instinctual reaction was to turn away from my parents, to head off the inevitable lecture on personal responsibility, global awareness, or vital importance of ear-candling. Now some combination of morbid curiosity and desperation had me dialing my parents' number. It actually rang a few times, and I found myself worried that I'd missed them. That was a new sensation.

"Spirit Wind Bed-and-Breakfast. How can I help you?"

I pulled the phone from my ear and checked the display to make sure I'd dialed home. "I'm sorry, I must have the wrong number."

"Mo?" I heard my mom's familiar squeal.

"Mom?"

"Baby!" she cried. "Oh, my baby, how are you? I'm so glad you called. Ash, she's on the phone!"

I heard the clatter of the extension as my father did his usual juggling of the phone before actually putting it to his ear.

"Oh, honey, we miss you," Ash said. "How are you doing?"

"I—what was with that bed-and-breakfast thing?"

"Oh, honey, you'll never believe it," Mom said. "We've turned the commune into a spiritual retreat.

It was your father's idea. We've been booked solid for two months."

"People sleep there? And they pay you?"

"Well, not necessarily. We accept in-kind payments or 'sweat equity' on the farm, but sometimes, yeah, we take cash."

Dad interjected, "We're the only totally organic, vegan ecotourism destination in southwestern Mississippi."

"But—but where did this come from? You've never even talked about wanting to run an ecotourism project before. And you hate it when outsiders come tromping around in your garden."

Dad chuckled. "Well, when you left, I thought about my little girl being out in the world, in a strange place, and I wondered how much of what we've taught you was going to stay with you as you traveled down that road. And how many people out there don't have the benefit of growing up the way you did, being taught the values that we gave you."

I tried to contain the snort, I really did. Dad did a masterful job of ignoring it, continuing, "I realized that as much as we love our little community, it would benefit so many more if we opened it up to travelers, people who need to have their eyes opened up to what's really happening in their minds, their bodies. It didn't take much time to convert the place. A little paint, a little elbow grease. We had a couple of cabins that were empty anyway. We all work. Sven prepares all the meals and teaches cooking classes. Sundrop teaches yoga.

Your mother leads meditation seminars and nature walks. We've had great reviews in a couple of the trade magazines, and now we're practically turning guests away."

"Oh, we would never turn anyone away," Mom corrected him. "When we have overflow, we just put the guests in your old room."

"You turned my room into a guest suite?" I was shocked to find I was a little hurt by the idea of complete strangers sleeping in my childhood nook. I'd practically expected my parents to enclose it as a shrine. As much as I griped about home, I'd always known I could go back if I needed to. And now it seemed that space was filled. With neo-hippies who craved an uncomfortable twin bed, sunrise yoga sessions, and organic carrot lasagna. I didn't have a fall-back position.

Automatically, I reached for the Tums, determined to forestall the worst of the heartburn. But the acidic ache in my throat never came. I took a deep breath and kept my tone pleasant. "Are the guests bothered by the fact that there aren't any walls?"

"Oh, everyone has loved it; they say it's very cozy. They feel just like part of the family." Something was different in my mom's voice. There was a temperance of mood, a restraint she'd never shown before. I realized that this was the most time my parents had ever spent telling me about what they'd been doing. Normally, they were either preaching at me or peppering me with questions about my life, my work, my dates, my recycling habits. And it occurred to me that I usually didn't ask what they were up to. I was too focused on getting off the phone as soon as possible. The ache I'd expected came in the form of twisting guilt, genuine and deserved.

"It sounds great," I told them. "I'm glad it's working out for you. Can you send me some pictures?"

"Sure, sure." Dad chuckled. "Or you can just look up our Web site."

"You guys have a Web site?" I cried. "Who are you people, and what have you done with my parents?"

They laughed on the other end of the line. Dad cleared his throat, which was apparently a cue to Mom. She took a deep breath and said, "You know, Mo, sweetheart, we've been talking, and we realized that you were right."

I waited for the punchline, but nothing came. "I'm sorry?"

Mom sighed. "Your moving away was the right thing to do. We did need a break from each other. And we did put a lot of pressure on you."

I demanded, "Are you trying to be funny?"

"We were scared, honey," she said. "We spent so much time fighting against becoming some boring old married couple. When you came along, it was like we'd created this miracle. And how could we be boring if we were tending to a miracle? So we were unwilling to let that feeling go."

"What your mother's trying to say is that we were

scared to death that when you left, we were going to be staring at each other, wondering what the hell to say." Dad snorted.

"And now we don't have to worry. You've been gone for almost a year, do you realize that? A year. And we're just fine—better than ever, really, because we can focus on each other," Mom said. "We've rediscovered our passion, our primal urges—"

"Mom, you're on the verge of ruining a beautiful moment with too much information," I warned her.

"Sorry, baby."

"So, what you're saying is that I was right," I said tentatively. "That when I said I needed my own space and my own life, I was right. And that I was right to leave and move all the way across the country for it."

"Yes," they chorused.

"And you were wrong," I said. "Wrong, wrong, totally wrong."

"Yes," they chorused again.

"OK, seriously, are you two about to jump out from behind my couch and yell 'Surprise'?"

Dad chuckled again. "We haven't heard anything about the Great North Woods. What's it like up there? Do you have friends? How's the job?"

"It's good." I sighed. "I love my little house. I have a lot of friends, and I love my job. I'm making some changes with the owner, Evie, to the menu, and they've gone over really well. My chocolate chess squares are a big hit."

I waited a beat for my mother to lecture me on pushing poisonous sugars to the masses, but she was simply listening.

"Are you happy, baby?" Mom asked.

Well, until recently, I'd been peachy-freaking-keen. I murmured a noncommittal "Mm-hmm."

"That's what's important," Dad told me. "That's all we want for you. We can work out the rest."

How many times had I wanted him to say that? How much anger and anxiety could have been prevented if we'd had this conversation when I was a teenager, instead of a thirty-year-old? I sighed, feeling a little weight wiggle loose from my chest. There was still pressure there, from Cooper, from past hurts, but it was eased enough to let me breathe.

"I've got to go," I told them, my voice thick. "I love you guys, I really do. I'll try to come home for a visit soon, OK? Iloveyoubye."

A few minutes after I hung up, the cell phone rang again. It was such a relief to see the caller ID and not feel that dread. I smiled. "Did you forget something, Mom?"

"What's bothering you, baby?"

I opened my mouth to protest. "Nothing's bothering—"

"I know this is probably a strain on the delicate peace we've just built, but honey, I know when something's wrong with you. Is it a man?"

I hung my head. "How did you know?"

"Well, I've never heard that kind of hurt in your voice before. And you've never been in the kind of relationship where you could be hurt like that," she said. "So it stands to reason that this is something new for you."

"It sucks, Mom. It really, really sucks."

"Can you tell me about it?"

This was new, too—Mom asking for information instead of demanding answers, which was good, because I was going to have to edit heavily anything I told her. I was not ready to tell my parents about the baby yet. For one thing, they might insist on coming up to visit, and I couldn't have them traipsing through the complicated werewolf soap opera that had become my life. And second—well, really, the possibility that they might come to visit was reason enough. One good phone call isn't going to make me *that* optimistic.

"I can't talk about it right now, Mom. There's too much going on. But I will, soon. I'll call in a few days, OK?"

"I love you, Mo. I just want—I want you to be happy. You say that you needed to figure out who you were without us. But you've always known what you wanted, honey. And sometimes I made it hard for you to have that because I thought I knew better. And I'm sorry. I never wanted you to doubt yourself. You know what you want. You wouldn't have traveled so far without knowing what you want. You've gone the distance. Now, maybe it's time to sit back and let what you want come to you."

"Thanks, Mom." My forehead creased as I stared at the phone and wondered what exactly my mother had been smoking to bring out her logical side. "That's oddly appropriate and well-timed advice."

"Oh, honey, don't be sarcastic. I'm trying here."

"I'm not!" I exclaimed. "Seriously, that's very helpful."

"Really?" Mom sighed. "I'm so glad. Though, honestly, I don't know why you sound so surprised. I've been giving you good advice for years."

"Don't push it."

20

The Hormones Speak

I WAS BAKING A THIRD batch of what Evie was starting to call my triple-chocolate "misery brownies"
—a new bestseller for the saloon—when Oscar set
up a howl and ran for the door. I jumped at the soft,
insistent knock. I tried to control the pounding in
my chest as I raced to the door, oven mitt still on my
hand.

I yanked the knob (somewhat clumsily, given the
oven mitt) and found my local forest ranger on my
doorstep with a bottle of red wine and a pizza from
Mama Rosario's, the only decent place for a pie in a
fifty-mile radius.

"Alan." I sighed, instantly ashamed at the disappointment coloring my voice. "Funny, I didn't order
a pizza. Someone must have prank-called the ranger
station."

Alan laughed. "I hope you like pepperoni and

sausage. And I hope you don't mind me just stopping by. Mo, you—you just looked so sad at work this afternoon. I wanted to come by and cheer you up."

It was galling how quickly that made me tear up. I smiled, opening the door and taking the wine, a nice table red, from him. "I love pepperoni and sausage."

We sat on the couch, chowed down on the best pizza available in northwestern Alaska, and talked. But I couldn't seem to get comfortable. I sat with my back against the armrest, my legs folded against my chest like a shield, as I sipped grape juice. Alan gradually slid closer across the couch, until he pulled my feet into his lap. He traced the bones of my ankle lazily with his fingertips. I pulled my feet under my butt and sat on them.

"I'm glad we did this," he said. "We haven't been able to spend a lot of time together lately, but now that you and Cooper—"

"I don't want to talk about Cooper."

Alan's smile seemed to brighten. "Me, neither."

Quicker than I could blink, Alan leaned in and brushed his lips across mine. I froze as his hands skimmed gently along my ribs, brushing the sides of my breasts before resting on my shoulders.

It would be so easy just to let him kiss me, to let him make everything all right for just a moment. I was tired of the constant, nagging loneliness. I was scared of being alone, of raising the baby by myself. Alan could take some of that away, even for just a little while. But it was so wrong. It was beyond betrayal to be kissing one man and knowing I was pregnant with another man's baby. I was dizzy with nausea . . . and not because of the pepperoni and sausage. I whimpered and pushed him away gently.

"Are you OK?" he asked, his brows drawing together when he saw my pale, clammy cheeks.

"I'm sorry, I really can't," I told him. "With things the way they are right now with Cooper so unsettled, I just can't. I couldn't do that to him. I'm sorry, Alan. You're such a—"

"Please," he said, leaning his forehead against mine. "Please don't give me the 'you're such a nice guy' speech."

"But you are." I smiled and was relieved when he grinned back at me, kissing my forehead.

"Fat lot of good it does when I can't find a nice girl who will have me."

"It's not you, it really is me. Look, I haven't told anyone here in town yet, but I just want you to understand why I can't— Oh, hell, Alan, I'm pregnant."

All of the color drained out of Alan's face, then it turned a sort of eggplant color and then back to bone white. "Oh," he whispered quietly, gathering me close to him and giving me a squeeze. He rested his chin on my head. "What are you going to do?"

I shrugged. "I'm going to have the baby. And I think I need to stay here to do it."

"Have you told Cooper?"

I shook my head.

"When was the last time you saw him?"

"That afternoon I slapped him in front of the

grocery store." I smiled despite myself. "Oddly enough, the slapping was not pregnancy-related."

"Don't you want to tell him?"

I laughed, pressing my hands to my eyes. "I know he deserves to know, but I don't want him to feel like he *has* to be with me, like he's obligated to stay because of the baby."

"If you'd let me, I would take care of you, both of you. I would make you happy, Mo." Alan pulled my hands away from my face and laced my fingers through his.

Somehow I knew he would offer. Alan was just that kind of guy. And he *would* take care of me and the baby. He'd be the kind of dad who would tell bedtime stories, coach hockey, spend hours on Christmas Eve putting together bicycles and dollhouses. But I couldn't do that to him. I couldn't take away his chance to have children of his own with a woman who loved him, really loved him, as more than just a good friend.

"That is the best offer I could ever ask for," I told him. "But it wouldn't be fair, to any of us."

He nodded, disappointment hardening the line of his jaw. "I understand." He stood up and then awkwardly plopped right back next to me. "You know what? No. I don't understand. Cooper is gone. He hasn't been back in weeks, Mo. And he's either too selfish or too lazy to come back and end things with you permanently. Why would you want to wait around for him to *decide* to come back and *decide* whether he wants this baby? Why are you letting him do this to you?"

"That's none of your business, Alan. Don't bad-mouth Cooper because you're angry with me. You're a better friend than that."

The expression on his face was thunderous as he stood again, squaring off against where I sat. "Fine, then, as your *friend*, I'm telling you you're wasting your time on someone who isn't good for you. I hate seeing you like this, all pale and miserable. You were so bright and alive when you got here. I want you to have that spark again, the one that made me fall for you the minute I laid eyes on you."

"Alan, don't. I can't. I can't feel that way about you. My feelings are . . . they're my problem. I'm sorry if it's hard on you to see me like this, but I'm working through it. Please don't be angry with me or with Cooper. You're one of my best friends here, and I couldn't stand it if I lost you. But I can't let you talk about him that way, either. I'm sorry."

"No, I get it," he said, his mouth set in a grim line. "It's like you said, my feelings are my problem." He slapped his ball cap onto his head and grabbed for his keys. His face softened when he saw my own tight, distressed expression. He kissed my cheek.

I whispered, "I'm sorry."

"If you need anything, anything at all, you call me. I've seen my sisters pregnant enough times to know the drill. Even if you just need Saltines at two in the morning, you call me, got it?"

I nodded. Alan gave me a brief hug and let himself out.

At the sound of the door shutting, I sighed, scrubbing my hand over my face. "That went well."

I gathered the dirty plates and dumped the wine into the sink. I turned on the shower and let it beat over my neck and shoulders, which seemed to have been clenched since Alan first kissed me. How could that have gone so wrong so quickly? I wasn't exactly caught off-guard by Alan's interest, but I thought I'd sent clear signals that I wasn't available. I found myself analyzing every little detail of the night, everything I said, everything I did, to try to find something that Alan might have interpreted as a "go sign." Maybe I shouldn't have let him into the house in the first place. Maybe I should have started ignoring him the moment Cooper left, to prevent this sort of thing.

When the hot water ran out, I pulled one of Cooper's shirts from my closet, wrapping myself in his scent, and I caught a glimpse of myself in the dresser mirror. My eyes were red and puffy from crying. My face was paper-white. I looked like one of those vengeful ghost characters from an Asian horror film.

"Pathetic," I grumbled. I dragged a quilt from the bed and padded out to the front porch. I settled into one of the Adirondack chairs Cooper and I had picked out and stared up at the sky. It was a full moon, watery silver light washing over the yard, the trees. The air was soft and as warm as it could get at night in Alaska. Oscar settled at my feet, standing guard against feral squirrels. I tried to think of something calming. I closed my eyes, listened to the trees rustle, and thought about sleeping out under the stars on that horrible camping trip. The more details I tried to recall, the more real the picture became. I focused on the smell of singed marshmallow and woodsmoke. I felt strong arms wound around me and the warmth of the fire against my face. I heard a branch crackle under pressure from the flames.

And then another.

My eyes popped open. That wasn't my imagination. I'd really heard that. I sprang to my feet, quilt puddling around my ankles.

"Cooper?" I called.

For a moment, I thought I'd miscalculated, that his presence was only imagination, a pretty story I told myself to ease my hurt feelings. I feared that there was something else in my woods, the thing that Cooper was afraid of. And I was standing defenseless on my front porch in a T-shirt and my underwear.

In the distance, I heard paws beating against the ground, underbrush whipping against whatever was running toward me. I saw the glint of moonlight reflecting off blue-green eyes before I saw his face. The blurring transition of wolf to man no longer shocked me. It was as much a part of him as his smile or the smooth golden skin that was so clearly defined in the pale light as he stepped out of the edge of the trees.

I sprinted toward him. I'm not sure what Cooper was expecting, but I doubt he foresaw my right hook landing against his jaw. Several things happened at once. I shouted "Ow!" and shook out my smarting fist. Cooper yelped and cupped his hand around his face. I used my good hand to continue Cooper's well-deserved whoopin'.

"You asshole!" I spat. "I can't believe you did that to me! How could you?"

I smacked his shoulders and chest over and over, growling, "Stupid! Thoughtless! Arrogant! Moron! Werewolf!" with each blow. He let me rage against him until my arms were weak and my head was resting against his neck. He picked me up and carried me toward the house, murmuring apologies and pressing kisses on my jaw, my chin, my mouth.

Cooper opened the door and slammed it behind us. He carried me to the spot in front of the fireplace where we'd made love for the first time. There were no flames in the hearth, but I didn't miss the gesture: time to start over. My shirt had been discarded somewhere near the door, and my panties were an unmourned casualty.

Cooper grabbed my hips and pulled me toward him, wrapping my legs around his waist while he ran the tip of his nose from my temple to my navel, kissing and licking my overheated skin at every step. He smelled of man and woods and animal. His hair seemed shaggier, falling over my eyes as he kissed my eyelids, the bridge of my nose, the curve of my jaw. He buried his hands in my hair, pressing his face into the wild, dark strands. "Missed you," he growled. "Missed you so damned much. Love you."

His mouth traveled from my neck to my ankles, stopped to nip and lick at my collarbone, my belly button, my hip bones. He blew a teasing hot breath between my legs before darting away and pressing kisses on my thighs.

His lips skimmed back to my breasts, lavishing attention over one tight, oversensitized nipple and then other with his tongue. He pinched them gently between his teeth as I writhed under him, slipping his mouth over the curve of my breast as I wrapped my fingers around his warm, hard length. I guided him toward me, but he pitched his hips forward and slid inside me, strong and sure. My body welcomed him back, pulling him deeper with warm, steady strokes. I felt moisture seeping down my thighs as we rocked our hips together. Cooper's hands kneaded my ass, my hips, keeping me moving in time when I was too lost to keep up.

"Mine," he told me, making me convulse around him like a velvet-covered fist.

Just as he reached his climax, Cooper's irises seemed to darken and expand, closing out all of the white. Teeth bared, he threw his head back with the final thrust and clamped down on my shoulder, just where it met my neck. I shrieked at the intrusion of teeth against my flesh, but Cooper held me fast against him. My hands batted ineffectively at his shoulders as my skin tore like paper under his mouth. This painful, alien sensation sent me toppling over the edge of sanity. My pulse jumped, my breath caught, and all of my muscles seemed to contract at once, shuddering through the most powerful orgasm I'd ever had. As I shook and screamed, Cooper gathered my fluttering wrists with one hand and used the other to slip soothing brushes along my brow. I felt a trickle of blood down my back as Cooper's head fell to rest against mine.

Our breathing slowed and he rolled off me, gathering me to his side. Once I'd regained use of my arms, I reached out and smacked the side of his head.

"Ow!" he cried.

"You bit me!" I groused, pressing my hand to the wound. "Again!"

He flushed with guilt but kept a defensive note in his voice. "It's a good thing! It means you're mine. The scar is a public declaration. It means you're my mate. It means no other wolf can claim you. It means you're under my protection and the protection of my pack . . . if I had one."

"Like a pimp."

He made a sour face. "It's no different from me peeing on your doorstep."

"You peed on my doorstep?"

He winced. I don't think he realized how gross that sounded until he said it aloud. "Right before I told you I couldn't see you anymore." His expression was alternately sheepish and defensive. "I was marking the territory. It keeps other predators away. I had to keep you safe somehow. You stumble into the path of pissed-off grizzlies, for God's sake."

Suddenly, my hand snaked out, and I hit him again.

He winced. "Ow! What was that for?"

"Apparently, I'm still a little mad at you."

"Mo, I'm sorry if it hurt—"

"Yes, Cooper, that's why I'm mad, because you bit me." I snorted.

"—but marking you is best for the baby," he insisted.

My shirt slithered out of my hand. "How did you find out?" I whispered.

"Well, my mom sort of tracked me down and proceeded to beat the ever-loving hell out of me until I admitted you were the best thing that's ever happened to me. And that I would have to be an idiot not to run back to you and beg for forgiveness. With the understanding that she plans on beating me at regular intervals just to keep me on my toes. She's had some sort of violent epiphany, I think."

I lay back, feeling as if all of the air in my lungs had been pulled out. He knew. He knew, and he didn't say anything? Shouldn't that have been maybe the second or third thing he'd said? Maybe right after "Missed you so damned much," he could have mentioned "Love you, and I'm so sorry I ran off and left you to suffer through your first trimester alone." How would I know now? How would I know whether he wanted me for me or because he felt he had no other choice?

"Is that the only reason you came back? Because your *mom* implied that you were being less than a man?"

"No, it's not the *only* reason."

I hopped to my feet. "Because I don't need you to raise this baby. I don't need you or any other sperm carrier just to be a good parent."

Cooper's jaw dropped, and somehow he found the gall to look offended. "Sperm carrier?"

I glared down at him. "Am I supposed to be

happy that you came running back because you heard you knocked me up? I don't want you here out of some sense of obligation."

"But you do need me. You're going to need me to help you. I want to be with you, Mo. I want to be a family."

"You know, I find myself not really giving a crap what you want," I said, nudging him with my feet until he was forced to get up. I threw a blanket at him, which he wrapped around his waist.

"You told my mother. You had to know that she would get word to me eventually."

"Yes, but now that I realize that's the only reason you're here, I find that I'm really annoyed about it!" I cried. "And actually, no, I didn't know she'd get word to you eventually, Cooper, because I didn't know where you were. Your mother didn't know where you were. Hell, as far as I knew, I was never going to see you again. You didn't see fit to let me know whether you were ever coming back. How am I supposed to feel about that? You know what? Get out. Get the hell out of here. Until I tell you to come back, you just stay the hell away from me."

I shoved him toward the door, blanket and all. He tried to stand his ground, but it was hard for him to push back when he knew I was pregnant. He tried to lay his hands on my shoulders but loosened his grip to almost nothing. I was not so kind, stomping on his bare toes, forcing him to move his feet toward the door. "Mo, you're not making any sense! We just got back together, and you're already kicking me out?"

"Well, suddenly, I'm not really making rational decisions anymore. It must be all the hormones!" I yelled, slamming the door and locking it behind me.

"I'll just stay out here, then!" he called through the door. I could practically hear the smirk coming through in his voice, which made me want to throw a birdfeeder at him. "Love you!"

I snapped the curtain over the window. I cleaned up, carefully bandaging the bite mark on my neck as I got dressed for bed. It was already healing into a wide crescent scar. I wondered if that was because of Cooper's magic or the baby's. Before I turned out the lights, I marched to the front door and pulled back the curtain to see if he was still there. He'd changed and was curled up in a ball on the welcome mat, sleeping. I felt a little flare of guilt. It wasn't especially cold outside, and he'd probably slept through worse, but not on my account. I could open the door and at least let him sleep in the living room. After all, wasn't this what I wanted? Wasn't this what I'd made myself miserable for, having Cooper back? How contrary and prideful was it to turn him away now?

The truth was, I wasn't ready to let him back in yet. He'd hurt me. I couldn't trust that the next time things got hard or he started feeling guilty, he wouldn't just run off again. I wandered back into my bedroom and crawled under the covers. Oscar, who had been hiding under the bed, hopped up near my feet and nestled beside me. I sat up and scratched between his ears. "Oscar, you are the only trustworthy male in this house, canine or otherwise."

When I woke up in the morning, Cooper was still in wolf form, still on the porch. He huffed at me and scratched at the door, but I went about my business, getting ready for work. He walked me to the truck and sat in the driveway while I pulled out, his paw raised in a sort of wave. I didn't speak a word to him, not that morning or that night when I got home. Or the night after that or the one after that. For a week, Cooper stayed in wolf form, watching over the house, walking me back and forth from my truck whenever I left. I stayed silent. Even Oscar gave him the cold shoulder when he went out to play. But neither rain nor sleet nor Arctic blasts from a wiener dog could keep my werewolf boyfriend from his self-appointed rounds.

One night, I came home to find a pile of flowers, pulled up by the roots, scattered over the front stoop. Cooper sat on his haunches, surrounded by wildflowers, and huffed.

"What's next, a dead squirrel?" I asked.

Cooper barked.

I sat down on the steps and stroked his fur. "Look, I get it, you're sorry. Would you please change back into a man so we can talk about this like grown-ups? I promise I won't hit you again."

Cooper shifted and wrapped his arm around me. "I'm sorry. I should have said that first. I'm so sorry I left you. I thought I could handle it. I knew that biting you that first time, marking you, meant that I could never mate with anyone else—"

"What?" I demanded.

He shrugged. "That's how it works with us. Once

we mark our partners, that's it. It's more magic than science, but after we mark the one we choose, our DNA won't mix with anyone else's. Wolves mate for life."

"You walked away from me, knowing you might never have kids? That you'd never find someone else?"

"I wouldn't want anyone else."

I slapped at his shoulder. "Jackass."

He pulled me close. "I love you. I can't stay away from you. I don't care if that makes me selfish. You make me happy. You're the only spot in my life that makes sense right now. Even without the baby, I would still feel that way. And until I know for sure what's happening, until I find out whether I'm the one hurting people—"

"You're not," I told him sternly, holding his chin to make him meet my gaze.

He nodded, but I could tell he was just placating me. "Until I know for sure, one way or the other, you're stuck with me."

I conceded, "I know you were just doing what you thought was right. Your heart was in the right place, even if your head was up your ass."

"I hope the baby has your special way with words." He sighed.

"Good." I wrapped my arms around him, as if I could make him keep his promise by just holding him there. I nuzzled his neck. "So, um, when was the last time you had a shower? Ballpark guess?"

"I don't know. I rolled around in a creek about a week ago." He shrugged. When I wrinkled my nose, he was indignant. "I was running around in wolf form, beating the hell out of myself, and wallowing in misery. I wasn't at a damned spa."

"I'm sorry," I told him. "I love you in spite of your pungent manliness."

"Well, now you're just patronizing me," he grumbled. I laughed. His stomach growled loudly.

I rolled my eyes, chuckling as I stepped over the flowers into the house. "How about I fix pancakes and you take a shower?"

"It depends. Is this a trick to make me lower my guard so you can punch me again?"

"I slapped you, I didn't punch!"

"I'm sorry if my bruised skull can't tell the difference."

COOPER STEPPED OUT of the shower looking far more chipper than I'd ever seen him. And the mammoth pile of pancakes waiting for him only improved his mood. I sat beside him at the counter while he chewed thoughtfully, obviously trying to choose the right words. "I know I don't have the right to ask, but why did I smell Alan here?"

"You're right," I told him softly. "You don't have the right to ask that."

"Mo."

"Alan was here. Nothing happened," I told him, knowing that a heavily edited version of my evening with Alan would be best for everyone. Cooper might not get angry with me, but he probably wouldn't grant the same courtesy to Alan. The last thing I needed was for Cooper to be arrested for tearing the head off a federal official in the middle of Main Street. "He made it pretty clear how he felt, but I told him that he was just a friend to me. I'm not going to say I didn't consider being with him, just to get you out of my system. To hurt you back. But when it came down to it, I just couldn't. There's no getting you out of my system, Cooper. You're there to stay."

A relieved, grateful smile broke over Cooper's face. "I bet Alan didn't take that well."

"Actually, other than insulting you, he was a gentleman about it. Unlike a certain smug werewolf who gave me a permanent hickey to mark his territory. And peed on my doorstep—which you will be hosing off, by the way."

Around a mouthful of pancake, he muttered, "Yes, yes, I am Alan's emotional inferior. I'm sure that will keep him warm at night."

"Now, that's plain mean."

21

Stasis

IF ANYONE COMMENTED ON Cooper's sudden return to Grundy, they didn't do it in front of me. It was obvious that we'd reconciled. He was back in the saloon every morning, keeping a quiet, careful watch over me and his impending pup. He'd swoop in and pick up any object heavier than ten pounds if I tried to lift it. He made me take regular breaks to get off my feet and growled at anyone who spoke to me in anything but the sweetest of tones. When he tried to talk Evie into cutting my hours at work, we both told him to mind his own business. Seriously, there are limits.

I was back in the kitchen, cheerful, productive, talkative. It was as if my friends stopped holding their breath around me. Conversation was normal. The banter was back. I think they were so glad to see the old Mo that they didn't have it in their hearts to rib me about it. Lynette, however, was even more sour than usual.

Nate Gogan drew up the papers for me to purchase the house. It was the first place I'd really considered my own home. I couldn't imagine raising the baby anywhere else. I thought he was going to cry when I signed them. When I called to inform Kara that I was a homeowner, she was a little sad but started making plans for a visit within the next month, while it was still warm. I think she'd been holding out for me to come home, but it felt good to have made a decision, to know that I was a permanent resident of Grundy, Alaska.

Cooper and I were slowly moving to a more permanent arrangement. He gave up the lease on his place and moved his stuff into my cabin. He put a picture of Gracie, Samson, and Pops on the mantel. He made a little nursery by screening in a corner of our room, although we knew we would eventually have to add on another bedroom. The house was a little crowded and more than a little "sporty," but it was nice feeling that he had a stake in the place.

And miracle of miracles, he actually asked me out on a date, having realized that we'd known each other for almost a year and were expecting a baby in a few months but had never actually left the house for a meal. So there I was, one glorious Thursday morning, standing in front of my side of the closet, trying to find something to wear to dinner that Friday. And Cooper came out of the bathroom, pulling up his camouflage overalls.

"That doesn't look like fine-dining attire," I

said, arching my eyebrow as I sipped my ginger tea. "Your outfit definitely won't go with this dress."

I held up a little blue number that he'd admired on several occasions, even though I knew it would be a miracle if I fit into it anymore. My jeans were feeling pretty tight these days. I would be bidding my precious La Perla a fond farewell soon. Eventually, we were going to have to tell everybody we were pregnant. I had only so many forgiving sweatshirts I could wear to work.

Cooper groaned at the sight of the dress. "You're killing me, woman. I just got a last-minute call from one of my regulars," he said.

"Which makes you sound like a hooker."

Cooper rolled his eyes. "This guy wants to take some clients fishing down at the Snake River. It's some stupid spontaneous bonding thing he thinks can prevent economic disaster. He's one of my steady clients, and he's a grudge holder. If I turn him down once, he'll blab to all his buddies that I'm an asshole and they should take their business elsewhere. With the season coming up . . ."

"Cooper, it's just a one-day trip. No big deal. Don't worry."

"I'll be back in the morning, to take you and that blue dress out on the town, I swear."

"Actually, maybe we should put it off until another night," I told him. "I'm not really feeling all that great, hence the tea. Your child seems intent on making me throw up until I turn inside out."

He kissed the top of my head. "Ugh. Now I really don't want to leave you. And we *are* going out tomorrow night. There's some stuff we need to talk about."

"OK." I poked him in the chest. "But if you take me camping again, I'm going to kick your ass."

He smiled, nuzzled my neck, and kissed me long and hard before slipping his cap onto his head. "I believe it."

I sat on the porch, drinking my tea and waving as he pulled the truck out of the driveway. Would this be what our future would be like? Me waving as my big, strong man went a-hunting, leaving me behind to tend the home fires? How positively medieval.

"I've got to go to work," I told myself, shuddering, setting the cup aside and pushing to my feet. "Bring home some bacon, fry it up in a pan, something, before they take my feminist membership card away."

WORK WAS QUIET that day. I managed to get through a breakfast shift with minimal nausea and was grateful for it. People ordered their usuals and appreciated the little touches I remembered, such as the fact that Walt didn't like his toast to touch his eggs or that Gertie was allergic to garlic. I'd almost gotten through the workday unscathed when Maggie appeared at the lunch counter. My grip on the butcher knife I was holding got a little bit tighter.

"Maggie," Evie warned. "Your mom and the rest of the family may put up with your bullshit, but if you start a fight in here, you will pay for every single thing you break."

"I'm not here to start a fight," Maggie snapped back. She looked up at me, her expression unreadable. "I need to talk to you. Can we take a walk?"

"I am not dumb enough to walk to a secluded area with you alone," I told her. "That's how women end up on CNN specials."

"I'm not going to hurt you." She sighed. "I've been thinking about what you said to me the other day at my mom's. And there are some things I need to say to you. Outside."

"Don't go any farther than that bench across the street," Evie told me. "I'll be watching."

"Jesus, Evie," Maggie exclaimed. "I said I wasn't going to hurt her!"

"See that you don't," Evie retorted. "She's carrying your little niece or nephew."

Maggie's jaw dropped, and so did mine. "How did you know?" I asked.

Evie patted my head. "Oh, honey, we've all known for weeks. You've been throwing up every time you look cross-eyed at food. Didn't you think we'd notice?"

Everybody at the lunch counter nodded.

"We're having a shower for you next month," Gertie said, grinning at me. "There will be a theme, a cake, and embarrassing games. And you will love it."

"Well, shit." I sighed. "I wore all those baggy shirts for nothing."

We walked across the street, with Maggie eyeing me carefully. "Is this going to be OK for you?" she asked gruffly as we sat on the rough plank bench.

"I've been feeling fine," I told her. "But thanks for asking."

"Mom should have told me," Maggie huffed. "But it explains why she's been knitting nonstop."

"Well, we didn't know how you'd respond, Maggie. Honestly, what would you expect?"

She stared at her hands and plucked at a hangnail. "Hunting and fighting have always come easy to me. I'm not good at talking about things that bother me. It's just so much easier to, you know, hit something."

I scooted a little bit farther down the bench. She snorted but smiled a little.

"When Cooper left, it wasn't just that I was pissed," she said. "I was hurt. It wasn't that I was ashamed of him. It wasn't even that he was scared when the other pack attacked. Hell, I was scared, too. When he left, it felt like he was ashamed of what I'd done that night. Like I should be ashamed of being able to fight, to kill, to defend what I love. He was always the one who told me to be proud of what I was, that I was just as tough as anybody in the pack. And all of a sudden, it was wrong? It was like everything he'd ever told me was a lie. Our whole relationship was a lie. I'd depended on him to be everything—a brother, a father. And to have him take that away . . . I was beyond hurt. I went a little crazy. And for years, I kept expecting the hurt to go away, even just a little bit, but instead it got worse."

"What about Samson?"

"Samson's great," she said, shrugging and suddenly looking very young. "But he's always been sort of . . . cuddly? He loves to hunt, but he hates to fight. Eli really stepped in when he took over the pack. He's been a sort of kindred spirit. He's always said he's just holding Cooper's place until Cooper comes back. And if I was honest with myself, maybe I didn't want Cooper to come back.

"Why shouldn't I be alpha?" she demanded. "I'm one of the strongest in the pack. I'm the fastest. Except for Eli, I'm probably the smartest. I'm the one who stood up for the pack when we were attacked. Why shouldn't I take over where Cooper left off? He didn't want it, so why shouldn't I have it? Why should he be able to just throw it away like it's nothing?"

I tentatively patted her hand. "Obviously, there's a little bit more going on than the standard sibling abandonment issues."

"Yeah, for years, I've been . . ."

"I can think of a few adjectives if you need some help."

She glared at me. "I've been a spoiled, selfish little bitch who needs a good kick in the ass. I've been a shit to him for years. Because I didn't think he was hurting enough. Eli always said that he seemed fine. And somehow that made it worse. I figured I was hurt, so he should hurt more, you know? When I saw that you made him happy, it was like he was getting out of his punishment. I didn't know how badly he was hurting. I didn't know that he missed me, too. I was so angry at him for so long. I don't know how to come back from that."

"What do you want from me, Maggie? Advice? Absolution? Go forth and be a bitch no more."

"No. I wanted to know, do you think Cooper can forgive me?" She looked up at me, and suddenly, she seemed very young.

I put my arm around her. Well, I put my arm on the bench behind her without actually touching her, but my intent was clear. "I think you and Cooper need to talk. He misses you—a lot. But there are some things you need to talk about."

"Thanks." She mumbled before straightening, "This doesn't mean I like you."

"Oh, no, I still think you're a horribly spoiled little snot. And the minute I'm not pregnant anymore, I plan on kicking your ass. Scrappy Doo."

She smirked at me, then got up and walked into the woods at the end of the street. I couldn't see her phase, but I heard the long howl that followed. I shook my head. This is something you'd never see on *Dr. Phil*.

WHEN MORNING CAME, Cooper hadn't returned. He hadn't even called. I went to work, thinking he might go straight there from his hunting trip, but by lunchtime, he hadn't shown up or answered calls to his cell phone. I was cooking and covering for Evie, who was at home recovering from a fairly hideous dental appointment. And although I wanted to run home and check to see if Cooper was there, I couldn't leave.

I wondered if Maggie had taken my advice literally and tracked Cooper down the minute she left the saloon. Maybe they'd made up and were enjoying some wolf-sibling bonding time? It seemed more likely that they'd had a knock-down, drag-out fight and Cooper was curled up in the woods somewhere, recuperating from a severe testicle injury.

I grew more and more fidgety. I tried to distract myself, keep my head down, and throw myself into getting plates out the pass. I tried to tell myself I was being silly, overreacting. There was no reason to think Cooper was in trouble. For all I knew, his hunting party was doing well and he was being paid overtime. But I couldn't get rid of nagging little flares of worry in back of my head as I rounded the counter, preparing to take Alan's lunch order.

"Hey, Mo," he said. "How are you feeling?"

"I'm OK. I've stopped throwing up every time I crack an egg, which is an occupational plus."

He started to laugh and looked down at his belt when his cell phone rang. "Sorry. Give me a minute. Hey, Walt, what can I— Slow down, Walt. Tell them to stop yelling, I can't hear you."

I tilted my head, sending him a questioning look. He rolled his eyes and shrugged.

"You shot what, now?" he exclaimed, standing, knocking his stool to the floor behind him. "No, don't bring it here! Take it to my barn. Yeah, I'll be right there."

Alan snapped his phone shut. "Walt and a couple of his friends shot a wolf outside of town. They said it's a big sonofabitch and want me to come see if it could be the wolf that attacked Susie and Abner."

I stopped in my tracks, blood roaring through my ears. The pad slipped from my hands, clattering to the floor.

Alan looked up and grimaced. "You OK? You look pretty pale. Why don't you sit down?"

"What about the wolf?" I heard myself ask.

"They're driving it out to my place now, so I can take a look at it. I need to take some measurements, some pictures, call a vet to do a necropsy . . ."

My head spun as my stomach did an unpleasant slide. I turned on my heel, pulling my keys out of my apron as Alan called, "Mo? You OK?"

Lynette strolled through the door, preparing to flirt with Alan. I caught her arm and pulled her with me as I headed for the door. "Lynette, I need you to take over bar duty. The lunch rush is over. Pete's taking care of the dishes. I just need you to keep an eye on things for a little bit."

"It's my day off." Lynette scowled, jerking her arm out of my hand.

I snarled, backing her into the wall. "Now, you listen to me. I've put up with your bullshit for almost a year. Your lousy attitude, your piss-poor work ethic, and the fact that you take more than your fair share of the tip jar on more nights than I can count. And despite the fact that I've had to cover for you, I've never said anything. But so help me God, if you don't step up to the plate this once, I am going to tell Buzz about those butt prints I found on the shelf in the walk-in freezer."

Lynette blanched. "You can't know that was me."

"Well, I didn't, but I do now," I said, throwing an apron at her. "Take drink orders, collect on tabs, do your damn job."

Lynette nodded, mute, as I stalked out the door.

Just because Walt shot a wolf didn't mean it was Cooper, right? There were dozens of wolves in the area. Walt could have killed any one of them. That's what I kept telling myself as I pulled away from the saloon.

In the rearview mirror, I caught sight of my neighbors through the saloon window—normal people, eating burgers and living normal lives. I used to be one of them, totally unaware of the world beyond ours. And for a split second, I felt sorry enough for myself to want that ignorance back.

On the drive to our house, I prayed to Jesus, Buddha, Gaia, the Great Spirit, and every other deity I could think of to let me drive home and find Cooper climbing out of his truck, with some story about a flat tire and a dead cell-phone battery. When I got home and found the driveway empty, I realized how asinine that hope was. I climbed out of the truck and dialed Cooper's cell phone again while I opened the front door. I was sent to voice mail as I did a cursory sweep of the house. "Cooper, if you get this, please, please call me so I know you're all right." I snapped the phone shut.

I paced on the porch and tried to work through all of the scenarios in my head. I could rush over to Alan's, throw myself into the group of triumphant hunters, and . . . what? What would I do if it was Cooper in wolf form? I would collapse, possibly start screaming and beating the men in the hunting party, and get hauled away to jail. It would be awfully tough to raise my baby in a prison mental ward. And what if the wolf wasn't Cooper? I swiped at the tears flowing steadily down my cheeks now. What if it was one of Cooper's relatives? How would I handle that? What if it was just a plain, everyday wolf? How would I explain my sudden overwhelming desire to see a carcass?

I was way over my head here. I pulled out my cell phone and called the only number I could think of.

"Eli?"

22

We're Going to Need
a Bigger Tranq Gun

Where was Jennifer Garner when you needed her?

Alias superspy Sydney Bristow could sneak through the woods outside Alan's cabin, do a reconnaissance mission, and seek out her possibly dead werewolf boyfriend, then escape without any problem. If Sydney Bristow had a werewolf boyfriend. It would probably involve a *Supernatural* crossover.

I, on the other hand, had to call Eli and ask him to sneak me over to Alan's and help me get through this. I'd left Cooper ten or so increasingly desperate voice mails demanding that he call me back. In my final message, I told him where I was meeting Eli and begged him to keep me from seeing my first dead wolf close. So far, he hadn't responded.

I was crying full-tilt by the time I pulled my truck

into a little clearing off Alan's drive. Eli was waiting there for me so we could trudge through the woods behind Alan's house and sneak into the barn. I hadn't thought much beyond that.

Eli's expression was sympathetic when I climbed out of the truck. He opened his arms as if he planned to hug me. When he realized I wasn't stepping closer, he smoothly lowered them and placed his hands on my shoulders.

"Thanks for coming," I told him. "I didn't think I could do this alone, and I didn't know who else to call. And if it is Cooper, I didn't want Samson or Gracie to see him this way."

"If you're not up to it, I can do this alone," he said.

"No, I think it won't be real for me unless I see it myself," I said, shaking my head.

"This is one of the worst parts of my job." He sighed, leading me into the trees. "Being the one to take on the bad news."

"We don't know that it's bad news," I said, my tone just a little petulant.

He smiled, but I could tell it was just to humor me. "Of course not. Sorry, Mo."

I shrugged. Eli was moving quickly and quietly through the trees, leaving me in the dust. I had to half-run to keep up. About a mile from Alan's house, I had to double over to catch my breath.

"Hold up," I called. "I'm sorry. I can't keep going at this pace."

Eli made a sour face and moved back toward me. "Are you hurt?"

"No, pregnant." I drew deep, lung-stretching breaths.

"What? Why didn't anyone tell me?" he demanded, the color draining from his face.

"I asked Gracie not to say anything until Cooper and I got everything worked out."

Eli seemed livid at having been left out of the loop. I couldn't tell if the injury was personal or professional. Clearly, as de facto alpha, he expected to know everything going on in his pack members' lives.

"Aw, damn it, Mo." He pushed through the trees at a slower pace. He seemed to have recovered his usual bland demeanor. "I wish I'd known. I wouldn't have let you come. You shouldn't see this. This shouldn't be the way you remember Cooper."

"It might not be Cooper," I insisted again, getting annoyed that Eli seemed hell-bent on the worst-case scenario. He took my elbow and assisted me a bit more gallantly during the last mile. We finally reached the edge of the trees, just in time to see the hunting party walking toward their trucks, slapping one another's back in that "manly men together" manner. I heard several voices call, "Meet you at the Glacier. You're buying!" Alan was the last to drive away after locking the barn up tight. He pocketed the key.

Eli and I ran for the barn. Eli grabbed a rusty pipe wrench lying near the concrete pad and bashed the padlock off the door. I blinked into the dim light of the barn, assailed by dust and the faint smell of motor oil. Eli tossed the wrench onto a workbench.

I squinted, my eyes adjusting enough to take in the blanket-covered form on the wooden trestle table. I stumbled toward it. Eli pulled back the blanket, and I cried out, wanting to shield my eyes but unable to look away.

I covered my face with my hands, muttering something like "Thank you, thank you, thank you." The fur was too light, the body too lean. It wasn't Cooper.

I was flooded with simultaneous waves of relief, confusion, and embarrassment at dragging Eli all this way. I wiped at my eyes, wondering again where Cooper was and whether he was OK.

Eli stared down at the body, his pupils tight little pinpricks in eyes that were growing increasingly golden. His mouth was set in a grim, unhappy line.

"Is it anyone you know?" I asked, instantly ashamed of my insensitive reaction. "Is it a werewolf?"

"No, it's just your normal, run-of-the-mill wolf," Eli said, his voice flat and unaffected.

"Eli?"

"Sonofabitch!" he screamed, tossing the trestle table over. The wolf's carcass fell to the ground with a soft thud.

"Eli, what are you—"

"If you want something done, you can't trust anyone to do it for you!" he raged, his face flushing purple. "Do you have any idea how long it's taken me to set this up? And these dumb fucking roughnecks kill a real wolf?"

Eli's eyes were now completely yellow, his cheekbones protruding sharply. He was starting to change, a shadow creeping over his skin instead of the light of transformation I was used to from Cooper. This was something primal and scary. And as I finally processed what Eli was saying, I realized I was in deep, deep shit.

Eli drew back and slapped me with an increasingly pawlike hand, sending me flying across the room and into a tool chest.

Jennifer Garner totally would have seen that coming.

I sat up carefully, my hand curving protectively around my belly. "Why, Eli? Why are you doing this?"

Eli rolled his neck, stretching his body in a long, lean line, willing the change to withdraw as he shrugged out of his clothes—which was, I will admit, disturbing. He was fully human again, his eyes a bitter chocolate color. He smirked. "Would you believe . . . I just enjoy screwing around with short-order cooks?"

He sat down in front of me. My only comfort at this point was that the concrete had to be extremely rough on his bare ass cheeks.

"Do you know how long I've been waiting for this?" he demanded. I tried to look away, because of the nudity issue, but he grabbed my jaw and forced me to keep eye contact. "I've worked for years to get where I am today. Cooper was weak. He was too worried about being fair and equal when what we needed was strength. I'm a leader, Mo. I was born to lead my pack. And they're too damn stubborn, too stuck in the Dark Ages to realize it. Do you know what it's like to know your potential and have no one else recognize it? Because of Cooper. As long as Cooper was around, I would only be the second best, the substitute."

Just over Eli's shoulder, on the opposite wall, I spotted a tranquilizer gun. There was no way to make a direct grab for it. My only hope was that Eli would keep talking, allowing me to shift positions and get to it.

"That rival pack was strong, though, as it turned out, not especially subtle," he said, looking annoyed. "They bungled the whole thing, after I'd been sending them information for months! I mean, really, if you can't trust the people you're staging a coup with, who can you trust? That turned into a total fiasco, and I had to act just as surprised and shocked as everybody else.

"But it did get rid of Cooper, which was the point. I stepped in. I comforted my people. I was the reluctant hero. I was a brother to that little pain in the ass Maggie. I fed her everything she wanted to hear about what a horrible person Cooper was, how I'd always be there for her, never abandon her like Cooper. God, it was so freaking tedious listening to her all the damn time! Her stupid, petty little teenage problems, on and on and on."

He sighed. "I thought, with him gone, I would finally receive the respect I deserve, but the pack just keeps waiting for him to come back. I'm strong enough to lead, Mo. I've shown that over and over again, but what do I get from them? Prayers for

Cooper's return. So, I had to come up with a more permanent means of getting rid of him. I tried to get Maggie riled up enough to take him out for me, but she turned out to be almost as sappy and sentimental as he is. The whole damn family is a waste of good genes. I thought I could get one of your neighbors to gun him down. So I *may* have created the impression that wolves were gobbling up the locals. I've always had more control in my wolf state, a better recall of my wolf memories, than Cooper, who has always been so damned whiny and conflicted about our nature.

"Targeting a few humans wasn't a problem. A hiker here, an old woman there. Hell, I followed you on your little camping trip, thinking maybe I could make a grab for you, but he never leaves your side, does he? Stumbling across that old man so close to you was just plain good luck. Your friend Abner put up a good fight for an old man, but he was only human, after all. You're all so damned fragile. I was afraid Cooper might smell me that time, but he was so quick to blame himself. It didn't matter what his instincts told him."

My lip trembled. I swiped at the tear that threatened to spill down my cheek. Eli had hurt Susie Q. He'd torn those poor hikers away from their campsite and scattered their bones like discarded toys. My head snapped up. He'd killed Abner.

"You sonofabitch!" I snarled. Without thinking, I flew at him, my fingers curled into talons and aimed at his eyes. He caught me by my throat, holding me off the ground, my feet scraping against the dirt floor. Coughing and gasping, I clawed at his hands, finally managing to kick him in the gut. I don't think it hurt him much, but it annoyed him enough to make him drop me on my ass. I kicked at his feet, hoping to trip him up. He growled and backhanded me, banging my head into a cabinet. The impact knocked the wrench off the utility bench and had bright red stars dancing behind my eyes.

Note to self: Stop picking fights with werewolves. It couldn't be good for the baby.

I cupped my throbbing head in my hands. "Why not just attack Cooper directly?"

"I can't hurt the alpha myself. It's a biological imperative." He sneered. "Cooper's never stopped Samson or Maggie from going after him, but I can't touch him unless he attacks me first.

"But I can make things extremely difficult for Cooper; there's no rule against that. I didn't count on your local game warden being such a damned bleeding-heart incompetent. Or your neighbors being such pitiful shots. Honestly, what does it take to get an effective angry wolf-hunting mob going in this town? I hoped maybe he would love you enough to want to protect you from the big bad monster that he is." Eli rolled his eyes. "But he just can't seem to stay away, can he? And now he'll never leave you, especially now that you're having his pup. You've forced my hand, Mo."

He grinned at me suddenly, his eyes glassy and bright. He trailed a finger along my cheek, swiping through a trail of blood streaming from my temple. He brought the blood to his lips and inhaled, as if he were enjoying the bouquet of old wine. "You know, it's actually pretty nice to be able to talk to you about this. I mean, I've never told a soul. Cooper's right, there's something about you, Mo, something that just makes a wolf want to . . . mmmm." He licked at his bloodied fingertips. I shrank back from him as he leaned closer and sniffed at my neck. "If you weren't already knocked up, who knows? Maybe I'd take you for my own mate." He smiled at me, showing long, white teeth. I stealthily curled my fingers around the fallen wrench.

"Ah-ah-ah!" he exclaimed, slapping the wrench out of my hands, catching the tips of my fingers, and grinding them against the concrete floor.

I hissed, pulling them close to my chest. "Asshole."

"Language, Mo, language. I thought you Southern girls were supposed to have better manners than to try to brain a family friend with a wrench."

"Obviously, you haven't met many Southern women," I retorted.

Eli smirked. But I grabbed the wrench and brought it crashing down on the crown of his head. Eli howled with rage and punched me in the jaw. I staggered back, sure that my entire face would shatter. A coppery swell of my own blood pooled in my mouth. Between the smell and the taste, my stomach pitched into my throat, and I couldn't hold it in. I leaned against Alan's work table and vomited.

Eli looked at me, distaste curling his lip. "You know, this might work out better than I'd hoped. Killing you is probably going to push Cooper right

over the edge. He won't want to live without you
and the baby, after all."

Eli's features stretched obscenely as the transformation began. His body shifted to all fours, blocking
me from the exit. I clutched the wrench in front of
me and prayed that it would be enough. Eli pulled
his lips back, revealing his fangs, and lunged for me.

I heard a howl from over my shoulder, the most
beautiful music ever to reach my ears. Cooper barreled into the barn on all fours, shouldering Eli out
of the way and crouching in front of me in a defensive stance. Maggie, speedy and savage, was hot on
his heels, leaping onto Eli's back and sinking her
teeth into his neck. The sound of ripping flesh made
my stomach flip-flop again. Eli shook violently,
throwing Maggie off, sending her crashing into a
wall. She yelped but struggled to her paws, taking a
place at Cooper's side.

"Cooper. You have the worst timing," Eli said,
sighing, shifting back into human form as he rolled
to his feet.

Cooper phased to human while Maggie stayed a
wolf. The fur on her back bristled as she stepped between Cooper and Eli.

Cooper was a little calmer; pushing me behind
him, he raised his hands in a gesture of surrender.
"Don't touch her, Eli. Your problem is with me,
not her."

Eli snarled. "Oh, it's one and the same. As long
as you're around, they won't follow me. You had the
lead position, and you just wasted it. Well, no one
handed anything to me. I took it."

Eli smirked, circling dangerously close to me. Maggie followed him step for step. Cooper growled and feinted, angling him away. This rotation brought me closer to my goal, the tranq gun. With no one looking at me, I grabbed the gun, aimed at the back of Eli's neck, and squeezed the trigger. *Hiss-pop.* Nothing.

The damn canister was empty. I waved it like a club and smacked Eli over the head with it. Or I would have, if he hadn't turned on me and phased on the fly, lunging at me. Cooper snarled, phasing mid-leap as he jumped between me and Eli.

"Damn it," I grumbled as Maggie butt-checked me into a safe corner.

She stood there, fur on end, fangs exposed, watching as the two other wolves circled. Eli and Cooper scanned each other, alert for openings, weaknesses. Losing patience, Cooper snarled and charged. Eli lunged for Cooper's leg. Cooper dodged out of the way, turning to claw at Eli's back. Eli snapped, catching Cooper's left rear haunch and dragging him across the floor. Cooper yowled, jerked out of Eli's grasp, and butted his head into Eli's stomach.

Cooper was shoving him farther and farther out of the barn, away from me. He fought with deadly concentration, until Eli made a move toward me or Maggie. Eli picked up on that, used it to distract and disorient Cooper. Maggie apparently didn't like being used this way. Huffing impatiently, she leaped over Cooper's back and pounced on Eli, digging teeth and claws into places Eli would definitely feel later. He yowled, reached over his shoulder, and clamped his jaws over the back of her neck, throwing her off. Cooper barked, a warning to his little sister to back off, but Maggie just kept rushing Eli until he threw all of his weight on her. Eli looked up at Cooper, speculation evident in his golden animal eyes, and lunged at Maggie's pinned form. Cooper crouched low and sprang, knocking Eli away from his sister and forcing him to the ground. Cooper's jaws closed over Eli's neck, ripping into the flesh viciously.

Eli's last whine was cut short, and a large red pool spread onto the grass. Seeing that the struggle was over, Cooper detached and circled, putting himself between me and the dying creature. Maggie whimpered and ducked her head into Cooper's side. Cooper licked the top of her head.

As Eli wheezed his last breath, Cooper sank to the ground, resting his chin on his paws. With a deep breath, he phased back to his human form, blood spattered across his face and neck. Maggie followed, rising unsteadily to her feet and offering me an awkward little wave.

Cooper stumbled toward me. He wrapped his arms around my waist and pressed his face against my stomach. I stroked his back and murmured, "I know this is a bad time for 'I told you so' . . ."

"Yeah, yeah," he grumbled. "You were right. I wasn't homicidal. I was wrong."

"Let us hope that all of our arguments end this way," I said, rubbing soothing hands down his still-tense muscles.

Maggie snickered, cradling her arm to keep the weight off her injured shoulder. Still, I could see the bite mark fading. Her skin was reknitting itself before my eyes.

"I'm glad to see you," I told her. I took off my jacket and wrapped it around her shoulders.

"Never thought you'd say that, huh?" she asked, grinning cheekily.

I shook my head. "No."

"Maggie tracked my hunting party down. And after she made it clear that she wasn't planning on doing me any long-term damage, we had a long—"

"Incredibly long," Maggie muttered.

"—talk," Cooper finished dryly. "And we straightened some things out."

Maggie said, "I wanted to believe the worst about Cooper, because it was a lot easier than seeing how I might have hurt him. And Eli saw it, fed right into it. I let Eli blow so much smoke up my skirt I'm surprised I don't have ass cancer."

"Eloquent." I snorted.

"And I didn't exactly man up and stick around to explain myself," Cooper admitted. "I used Maggie as an excuse to stay away."

"And you didn't answer your phone during this long heart-to-heart. Why?" I asked.

Cooper winced. "I left my cell phone at the camp. I didn't get any of your calls."

"We started putting the pieces together, all the times Eli played me like a cheap violin," Maggie said, blushing slightly. "And we wondered why. If he was as reluctant to lead as he said he was, why was he finding ways to keep Cooper away? We started talking about you, Pops's heart attack, the attacks in Grundy, and it all just started clicking. Eli taking little trips into Dearly, the timing of the attacks—it all matched up. Cooper went back to the camp to let his clients know he was leaving. And he heard your messages. When Cooper realized you were here alone with Eli, he just about lost it. It's the first time he's ever outrun me."

"I'm glad you finally beat her at something," I told him.

Maggie sighed dramatically. "He's going to be impossible from now on, you watch."

"What do we do about this?" I asked, nodding toward the prone gray form. "How do we explain?"

"He'll stay in his wolf skin," Cooper said. "I'll take him back to the pack, tell them what he's done. They'll give him a proper burial. I'll be as kind as possible. They don't need to know every detail, just what he tried to do to you, to the baby. For that alone, I had a right to kill him."

"What about his family?" I asked.

"Eli's sort of the last of his line," Maggie said. "His dad died when we were in high school. He takes care of his mom, our Aunt Billie. She's been really sick lately. Alzheimer's. The pack will take over for him there. We take care of our own."

"No regrets," I told Cooper when I found him staring at the ground. "No torturing yourself. No guilt."

"None," he agreed, wrapping his arms around me. "I guess I'm going to have to marry you now," he muttered, his chin tucked over my shoulder.

"My parents aren't even married," I scoffed.

His warm hand closed over mine, skimming it over the belly that would be full and round in just a few weeks. He sighed, snuffling at my neck. "Please marry me, Mo. Raise our baby with me."

I leaned into him, nuzzling his neck. "I have one condition."

He sighed again, much more content this time. "Shoot."

"We pick a normal, traditional name for this kid. The baby is going to have enough to deal with, what with the whole half-werewolf deal. So, no flower names, no tree names, no gemstones, no names of musicians who asphyxiated on their own vomit, no intellectual ideals as middle names—"

"How about Noah for a boy and Eva for a girl?" he suggested, his hands up in a surrendering gesture.

"I agree," I said, thinking of how happy Evie would be.

"What, we're not naming the baby after a favorite aunt?" Maggie demanded testily. When I arched a brow at her, she rolled her eyes. "All right, too soon. You could at least put me in the running for the middle name."

"We are not naming my son Noah Margaret," Cooper told her.

"Why are we making up again?" she asked grumpily.

"No idea," he replied, wrapping an arm around each of us.

I made a sudden conversational lane change. "How do you have the big bad evil confrontation moment with a naked guy and keep a straight face? I didn't know where to look."

Maggie shrugged. "It's a matter of eye contact."

"Blech."

23

Smothering at 20,000 Feet

"Take it easy, sweetheart," Cooper said as my parents' little puddle jumper of a plane landed at the Dearly Airport. We were waiting at the airport's single gate, watching through the glass doors as the plane taxied down the tarmac. I found myself wanting to rush out toward the plane, eager to set eyes on the very people who'd driven me to Alaska, to Cooper.

"I'm fine," I promised as he buttoned my light jacket, skimming his fingers protectively over the ever-growing bump of my belly. It was hard to believe I was only four months along. If this were a human pregnancy, people would have guessed at least seven or eight. Other than the accelerated timeline, I seemed to be having a normal, healthy pregnancy. Well, almost normal. Dr. Moder had sworn that the baby wouldn't be born with a tail, though a full set of teeth was a distinct possibility. This had me seriously reconsidering breastfeeding.

My stomach was quite the topic of conversation when Cooper and I had married a month before in a small civil ceremony in my front yard, overseen by a beaming Nate Gogan. People ribbed us good-naturedly about shotgun weddings and pretended to be highly offended by my fallen state. But there were worse reasons to get married, and most people forgot the "scandal" of an expectant bride by the end of the reception. Heck, some of the guests had forgotten their own names by the end of the reception.

I'd wanted our wedding to be traditional, as traditional as the union between a werewolf and his pregnant bride could be. I wore a white dress and flowers in my hair. Kara had made what she called a "once in a lifetime" trip from Mississippi as planned and served as my maid of honor. She hadn't left yet. She and Alan started making goo-goo eyes at each other during the ceremony and hadn't stopped since. Having learned his lesson from taking his time with me, Alan was more overt in his attentions to Kara. He asked her to stick around for the Big Freeze party, which was still months away. They were currently shacked up at the ranger station, only emerging for occasional trips to Bulk Wonderland for mega-packs of condoms. I was ecstatic for both of them.

As a wedding present, Evie and Buzz had offered me a twenty-percent share in the saloon, since I'd increased the receipts by at least that much since my arrival. They'd already set up a little nursery in the office at the Glacier, so I could keep working after my maternity leave. As wrong as it seemed to have a baby in a bar, I knew there would always be a patron there to cuddle or coo . . . assuming that his or her father wasn't already there, in Cooper's words, "showing off his son." I asked him what he would do if the baby was a girl. Cooper turned a little green and started muttering about setting traps around the house when she turned thirteen.

Cooper still had no interest in being the pack's alpha, but in the wake of Eli's loss, he did visit the packlands more often. After an all-night meeting, the pack finally decided on a more democratic process of selecting an alpha: secret ballot. Maggie won by a landslide.

Samson had been nominated, but none of the wolves believed he would take the job seriously. Maggie stepped into the job and was handling it all beautifully. Even without the genetic conditioning required, she had the authority of a true alpha. Because most of the pack was terrified of her. Her judgment was surprisingly fair, swift, and, generally, in the best interests of her people. And she was finally happy. She'd actually smiled at me during my last visit to the valley.

Well, it was more of a lip twitch, but it was devoid of face-melting hatred, so I'm counting it.

My parents hadn't been able to make it up for the wedding, but I didn't resent that the way I thought I would. They did things in their own time. I sent pictures, and they sent a long, heartfelt letter filled with good wishes. This visit was to be the first step toward a happier balance.

Cooper and I waited patiently while my parents' plane slowed to a stop. After a few minutes, the door opened with almost frantic *pop*. The two pilots and a handful of passengers scrambled over one another to get down the little staircase and onto safe ground. They cast frantic glances over their shoulders as they rushed to the gate's entrance.

"I see my mother is being her charming self." I sighed, keeping a determined smile on my face.

"She's not going to talk about my colon, is she?" Cooper asked, grimacing.

"I can't make any guarantees," I said. "But I am not responsible for her or to her."

Cooper pursed his lips, keeping a careful eye on the plane. "Meaning?"

"If you two have a problem, you're going to have to work it out between yourselves."

"Coward," he snorted as my parents made their way down the stairs and onto the blacktop. Mom had some poor tourist by the arm. I could only imagine that she was regaling the poor woman with a sermon about the mood-enhancing benefits of a daily Saint John's wort regimen.

"It's a process," I whispered as Dad waved from across the tarmac. My parents had on winter clothes that would have been fashionable in 1984. It had been that long since they'd needed anything heavier than T-shirts and shorts. My dad, however, was wearing sneakers instead of his usual flip-flops, so I appreciated their efforts at sensibility. They burst through the door and stared at me, as if they were trying to memorize every detail before I bolted.

"Hi!" I exclaimed as my father put his arms around me, awkwardly reaching around my swollen middle to hold me close.

"Oh, my little Moonflower." He sighed into my hair. He leaned back and took in the sight of my swollen belly. His eyes swam with tears. "Look at you. I guess you're not my little girl anymore, huh?"

"Daddy, this is Cooper, my husband," I told him as Mom bid good-bye to her poor, harried Saint John's wort convert.

"So, you're the young man who had the nerve to steal my daughter's heart *and* make me a grandfather without even talking to me first?" Dad asked, his voice suddenly stern. Cooper looked stricken. I gaped between the two of them, stumbling for a response. Dad guffawed, wiped at his eyes, and pulled Cooper in for a hug. "Just kidding, man. Welcome to the family."

Cooper gave a nervous laugh and shot me a nervous glance, which only grew more panicked as my mother's attention focused on me.

"Oh, baby, look at your hair!" my mother exclaimed, clutching my face in her hands. "It's so pretty, grown out like that. It's just the perfect length."

I shook my head. Never once had my mother complimented my hairstyle. She'd never even mentioned it. I was the only person alive who'd never had to worry about her mother criticizing her appearance.

"And look at you!" she said, taking my hands in

hers so she could get a better view of my stomach. "You look so healthy and happy! How have you been feeling?"

"I'm fine, Mom. The doctor says I'm the picture of health," I promised as the four of us made our way to the luggage claim.

"Well, you know, you have to keep a constant vigil while you're pregnant. Have you been eating organic? Getting enough vegetables? You've cut back on your processed-meat consumption, haven't you? I brought you some special tea for nausea; it's in my suitcase. Oh, and the most wonderful book on putting together an eco-friendly nursery. You'd be amazed at how easy it is to use cloth diapers now!"

Sensing a tangent coming on, I squeezed my mom's hands and said softly, "Mom, we have it covered."

And while I could see the struggle rippling across her face, instead of taking offense, miraculously, she smiled and kissed my cheek. "Of course you do. You've always been my sensible girl. A complete pain in my ass, of course, but sensible."

"Oh, yes." I snorted. "I was the pain in *your* ass."

"You were always hassling us to pay our taxes, take you to the dentist, sign permission slips. You were more of an adult at twelve than we ever were. It made me feel guilty. And if I was . . . controlling or manipulative, maybe it was because I was trying to prove that you still needed me."

I wrapped my fingers around hers. "It's not important now. And by that, I don't mean you're invited to continue. Let's just not worry about it."

I watched as Dad and Cooper gathered not one, not two, but three huge secondhand suitcases and several boxes marked "Perishable Foods—Organic." My heart started to hammer a bit. "Mom, isn't that an awful lot of bags and supplies for a one-week visit?"

"Oh, well." Mom gave a tinkling laugh. "Your father and I have talked about it, and we've decided that it would be best for us to stay until the baby's born. You should be surrounded by family right now, Mo. And the bed-and-breakfast practically runs itself with all the help we have. There's no sense in us staying home. We're here for you, honey, for as long as you need us. Oh, wait. Ash, that's the box with the wheat germ in it. I'm afraid some of it might have spilled during the flight. I thought I heard something crack."

I stood speechless as my mom dashed over to direct my dad on the proper handling of spilled wheat germ. Cooper ambled over to me, a suitcase in each hand. He hadn't looked this gray since I'd pried the bear trap off him. "Did she say they were staying until the baby is born?"

I nodded, my expression frozen in horror. "That's two months."

He dropped the suitcases and jostled me gently. "Breathe, Mo. Breathe. It will be OK. I love you."

"It's a damn good thing, because I love you, too." I looked up at him. "How quickly do you think we could move to Australia?"